How far would you go to find where you belong?

Would you cross a continent?
An ocean?
A universe?

"If you like epic fantasy that sweeps you to amazing, immersive worlds and while following intriguing characters, be sure to add this series to your to-read list." —Once Upon a YA Book

"It's a great medieval tale, and would be equally as interesting for men as women. (It's no wispy piece of fluff fiction!) ... plenty of mystery and twists and turns." —Beth Hobson

"I adore the world building of the novel. It just felt like a thin mist crawling in ... rearranging the landscape. Everything was so detailed and full of imagery." —Fire Star Books

"Wonderfully written. I was hooked right away and loved that I couldn't predict what was to come next. 5 out of 5 stars! Highly recommend to young adults and older." —Memories Overtaking Me

"A new mystical world ... the characters and setting most definitely will leave you wanting more." —Let's Get Booked!

"Deborah J. Lightfoot just really has this way of bringing the reader into her world." —My Reading Addiction

"This author has woven such a spell ... I can't seem to get enough of this series." —Once Upon a Book

"Lightfoot does a wonderful job at creating a story. She has created an environment that is easy to understand yet complex enough to keep the reader thinking through her story. Her writing style is engaging and she has great pacing." —Bookworm Lisa

"The story just keeps getting bigger and bigger." —Book Briefs

Waterspell Book 4:
The Witch

Waterspell

Waterspell Book 4:
The Witch

Deborah J. Lightfoot

Seven Rivers
Publishing

Seven Rivers Publishing
P.O. Box 682
Crowley, Texas 76036
www.waterspell.net

Cover design by Tatiana Vila, Vila Design
www.viladesign.net

First Paperback Edition: February 2022
First Electronic Edition: February 2022

Waterspell Book 4: The Witch
A Fantasy by Deborah J. Lightfoot

Summary: In the House of Verek, it's five years later. The waters are
troubled. Memories are darkening. If the story is to end "happily ever after"
for Carin and Verek, old demons must be laid to rest.
Readers of the Waterspell fantasy series will welcome this long-awaited
fourth book for the answers it provides to questions raised in volumes 1
through 3: Does the *wysard* Verek regain his powers, and will Carin make
her way back to him? Have Carin's parents survived the plague that
devastated their world, and will she ever see them again? Did Lanse survive
the attack by Carin's defender? Is Lord Legary really dead? And not least:
Did the necromancer die in the jaws of Carin's conjured dragon?
Remember: there was no blood in the water. These questions and more
are answered in *Waterspell Book 4: The Witch*, which picks up the story
of the lovers, Carin and Verek, half a decade after readers saw the pair
separated in the closing chapters of the original trilogy.
By the blood of Abraxas, it's about time we learned what happened next.

ISBN 978-0-9728768-9-6 (Paperback); ISBN 978-1-7377173-0-0 (Ebook)
ISBN 978-1-7377173-1-7 (Audiobook: The Complete Series—Books 1–4)

For Crystal,
who taught me the meaning
of persistence and what it is
to show grace under pressure.

CONTENTS

"There is another shore, you know,
upon the other side."

"The Lobster-Quadrille"
Charles Lutwidge Dodgson
(Lewis Carroll)

Prologue

Vengeance

"She's still out there," Verek murmured. "As I feared."

Carin slipped within the reassuring circle of his arms and for a moment said nothing, too shaken by his words to reply.

She had been reading in the manor's library when the pool of the *wysards* exploded with such violent agitation that the noise like a foundation-shattering flood reached her at the big desk under the windows. Verek had been in his ground-floor workroom. Both of them raced to the stairs that plunged downward through bedrock to the enchanted wellspring, Verek a few steps in the lead. Bursting into the cavern, together they witnessed a maelstrom.

Waves billowed above the pool, their crests halfway to the ceiling of the enormous cave. As each wave collapsed, frothing and roiling, it sent the waters of the wizards' well fountaining up to crash against the cave's walls. Carin and Verek were forced back to shelter within the stairwell, their hands clapped over their ears, the thunder of the waves beating at them and ringing from the cavern's walls with a note like a deep bass bell.

The maelstrom died within seconds. Silence returned. The waters of the enchanted pool flowed back into the perfectly circular basin and grew still, the pool's surface regaining its flawless mirror sheen.

For minutes, neither Carin nor Verek spoke. Her head throbbed from the deafening noise, and the assault on her ears had left them feeling stuffed with cotton wool.

Verek stood a little in front of Carin, his hands still at his ears as if he had forgotten them. Then he flung out his right arm and held up his hand in a gesture of warding, his fingers stiff and pointing at the ceiling. His gaze remained locked on the waters of the wizards' well.

"What do you see?" Carin questioned him in a whisper.

He did not immediately reply. Quietly, to avoid breaking his concentration, Carin stepped nearer, standing close at Verek's side and peering at the surface of the enchanted pool. It showed her nothing except a red-tinged reflection of the cave's rough ceiling, high above them. But her husband had always seen more deeply than she into the pool's depths. He was following something there, something that held his gaze for long enough that the ringing in Carin's ears had largely subsided by the time he turned to her and took her into his arms.

"She's out there," he said quietly. "And she's attempting to recross the void."

Carin had no need to ask who "she" was. Only one woman of Ladrehdin could possibly be "out there," beyond the void, now that Carin had returned from that mind-bending place after destroying the crystals which had complicated her own world-spanning travels. Only one woman of Ladrehdin could possibly work the magic required to cross the void and return here, to exact her revenge on the pair who had exiled her.

"You don't think she died in the jaws of the dragon?" Carin asked the *wysard* who held her close.

Verek shook his head. "I saw no blood in the water that day. The lack has troubled me." He paused, then added, "Would that your dragon had ripped her open and devoured her entrails as we watched. Then would my soul be eased."

Chapter 1

Remembrance

Master Welwyn returned to Ruain in the early summer of the year in which the daughter of Carin and Verek turned five, and the couple's son reached his fourth birthday. As the brown-robed "monk" observed the youngsters at their roughhousing in the courtyard of the manor house, Carin only had to cast the spell of stone once — to stop Galen from setting fire to a garden planter-box.

Both children had been delightful until the age of two. Then, each had turned into a barely manageable hellion. Impulsive, stubborn, and possessing intuitive gifts for magic, both could work it before learning the first thing about controlling it. Red-headed Galen would have made a firedrake proud, the way the boy sparked flames with scarcely a thought. His raven-haired sister Nina had her own untamed talents, hers lying in the opposite element: water. The nymph raised small but mighty floods that toppled statuary and cut muddy channels through Weyrrock's flowerbeds.

In near-desperation to control the children, Carin had thought of the 'scrying stone that Verek had once employed to trap the woodsprite in his library. She'd also remembered, with distaste, the shackle of sorcery she had worn — the *chalse* Verek had clamped on her ankle to keep her from deserting their quest into the mountains to face a necromancer. Reading about both devices now, however, when she had a few rare moments in which to read, convinced her that the things were borderline black magic. *Wysards* who followed the teachings of Archamon frowned on their use.

It was evidence of Verek's own desperation that year, that he had been driven to such extremities in his early dealings with the mistrustful "accidental conjurer" who held the key to summoning an otherworldly dragon. So urgently had Verek desired Carin's help in overpowering the sorceress Morann, he had resorted to behaviors he would condemn in any other circumstance.

As she reshelved the books that described those questionable devices, Carin also put away any thought of using them to monitor or restrain her children. Slightly ashamed of herself for even considering such methods, she heaved a sigh of resignation and thought, *I'll just never sleep again or have a moment to myself, until the hellions grow up and leave home.*

Oh, she shouldn't say she never slept. When exhaustion drove her to it, Carin dosed the children with Aunt Megella's sleep-for-now powder. The wisewoman kept her supplied with that concoction, which had proved to be a sanity-saver. Carin used it liberally to keep the children in their beds at night and out of mischief.

She also had the spell of stone at her command, but she employed it sparingly. Petrification was the first spell learned by any novice magician, and it was as easily broken as cast. Carin used it on the children as little as possible, to maintain its effectiveness for as long as possible. No doubt both Nina and Galen would soon figure out how to free themselves from the spell's control, discovering the trick on their own, needing no word of instruction from their parents.

This afternoon, after Verek had picked up Galen's small, rock-hard body and swung the boy away from the planter he'd started to burn, Carin lifted the spell and listened as her husband explained to his now-fidgety son why burning garden decor was unacceptable. Verek redirected the boy's attention to a wood-filled fire-pit, well away from Nina's muddy floods, where Galen could practice his flame-throwing.

Master Welwyn, standing in his monkish robes at Carin's side, watched all of this, and chuckled. When Verek rejoined Carin, Welwyn turned to them both and declared:

"My lady, m'lord, you make handsome children, the pair of them as gifted as they are beautiful. But these offshoots of yours need taking in hand, don't you know. Leave them to me. From this moment, I am their governor and tutor."

Carin tried to pretend she was insulted by Welwyn's seeming to cast aspersions on her parenting abilities. She rounded on the monk, spluttering a little, and managed to assert in a tone that was faintly indignant, "They're happy and healthy!"

Verek, however, made no effort whatsoever to feign any response except relief. "Good," he snapped, and turned to his housekeeper, who sat beside the kitchen doorway enjoying the sun as she snapped beans into a pot.

"If I recall aright, Myra," he addressed her, standing with his hands on his hips, "in the main wing of the house there is a suite of rooms spacious enough to house Welwyn comfortably, and alongside him our two hellions … securely. We will move the children into a nursery there, where their new governor may exercise his oversight of them as they merit."

The relocation was swiftly accomplished, as neither child had ever shown an inclination to stay much indoors or to accumulate possessions. Karenina—she they called Nina—wanted only her favorite toy, the pincushion that Carin had transformed into a huggable sea urchin bristling with soft "spines." Galen happily left behind his box of playthings, demanding only his wooden rocking horse, a miniature likeness of Brogar that Verek had made for the boy, complete with a tooled leather saddle and bridle.

As Welwyn picked up his saddlebags and started to follow the children to their newly assigned apartments, the monk paused and laid his fingers on Carin's arm. The round little man gazed up at her with a sympathetic eye, then raised himself on his boot-toes to kiss Carin's cheek.

"Give them into my hands," he murmured, "and go pour yourself a stiff drink, my dear. You've earned it."

Carin did exactly that. Joined by Verek, she downed a glass of *dhera* in the library, almost gulping the tart liquor. As she and Verek sat together drinking, not talking, Carin tried to feel guilty about the heady sense of liberation she was experiencing at having Welwyn arrive, just as she neared a breaking point, only one more fire or flood away from screaming insanely at her potentially destructive offspring. She could summon no guilt, however, only intense gratitude.

After drinks came supper, and after that, bedtime. When all three—Welwyn and his charges—were comfortably settled in their suite of rooms, no sound but their laughter drifted down the long upper-story hallway of the house's master wing. For a time that evening, Carin and Verek stood listening in the doorway of their own nearby apartment. Not once was Welwyn's voice raised loudly enough to reach their ears. Shrieks aplenty came from the children, but these were sounds of glee, not alarm or protest. As the night darkened, all noises ceased.

Even so, Carin and Verek left their hall door open when they went to bed. Both had learned to sleep lightly, alert to any patter of bare feet that might be passing by on the way to burning down the house.

Very soon after Galen was walking, on a night when all the household slept, the child had paid a stealthy visit to Myra's kitchen. On the cooking hearth he had sparked a conflagration so enormous that flames were shooting up the chimney—and out into the room, threatening the trestle table—before Myra could awaken and sound the alarm.

Carin and Verek had found the boy sitting so close to the inferno, his bright-red hair was in danger of catching fire. But Galen only giggled and clapped his hands in delight at what he had made—his gestures sending the flames higher and hotter with each clap.

Nina was there too, at the sink basin, working the hand-pump so vigorously that she'd flooded the kitchen floor three inches deep—but not, evidently, with any thought of dousing the fire. As her parents rushed in, slipping on the wet floor, barely avoiding broken necks—Carin sidestepping a drowned mouse—Nina came sloshing to them, laughing, stomping her bare feet. With a summoning gesture the girl sent the water up the walls, to drip from the ceiling and steam in the fire. Which only made Galen giggle harder.

After that episode, Verek went around the house placing spells of suppression on every unused fireplace in all the then-vacant rooms in the manor's main wing. And he secured the kitchen hearth with a spell of confinement so restrictive, Myra complained that her cooking fires would hardly boil an egg.

Maybe that will keep Galen from burning us all alive, but it still leaves us the Nina problem, Carin thought, mulling her daughter's love of water and what might happen—the uncontainable magic that might flow forth—if the budding *wysard* got into the blue bedroom and conjured with the potently pristine springwater pool adjoining it. Unsettled by the prospect, Carin suggested unbreakable locks on that bedroom's door. Verek, alive at once to the danger, his face a study in fatherly pride mixed with alarm, rushed off to secure the chamber with both spellwork and metalwork. Laboring late that night in his downstairs work-room, he forged iron door-locks that neither a tidal wave nor dragon-fire could have breached.

So it was that both parents listened closely and slept lightly for several nights after Welwyn took the children under his tutelage.

On one of those evenings, Carin sat gazing into the fire in the bedchamber she and Verek had taken in the master wing, a few doors down from the sprawling apartments where Welwyn lodged with his pupils. Carin was remembering her first meeting with the monkish *wysard* — or trying to remember it. Her memories seemed to be everywhere and nowhere. Images and episodes flashed through her thoughts, vivid but oddly random. Many of them, Carin couldn't assign to specific places or times.

She looked up and smiled as Verek came in through the open bedroom door. He left it ajar behind him, the better to hear any uproar that might arise from the hellions down the hall.

With a contented sigh, Theil settled beside her on the thickly cushioned couch.

"By the Powers," he said, "it is a fine thing to apprentice those two adepts to the only *wysard* of Ladrehdin fit to take them under his wing. Welwyn is a matchless teacher, and we are fortunate that he is willing to accept the task."

"'Willing'?" Carin laughed. "Master Welwyn didn't need his arm twisted. The man was barely off his horse before he was laying claim to his new apprentices."

"No marvel, that. He sees in them what you and I see. Perhaps more. Welwyn can assess those two — and train them — unencumbered by parental affections. Certainly he will be a stricter taskmaster than I have been." Verek's expression was rueful. "I fear I am too fond to demand what I should of them."

Carin took Theil's hand, interlacing her fingers with his. "You're much better at parenting them than I am. You take the time to explain why walls should be left standing — not burned down or toppled by a flood." With her free hand, she rubbed her forehead. "It seems all I can do is shout 'Stop that!' and turn them to stone when shouting fails. I'm sure Welwyn will manage them better than I have. He is a good teacher — he had me shuffling along on snowshoes in less than a day, and those *Briga* bearpaws of his were not easy to walk on."

"No part of that journey was easy," Verek muttered. With a small motion of his head, a slight dip of his chin, the *wysard* caused the flames in their fireplace to burn a little dimmer. The softer light made the huge, echoing bedchamber feel cozier, more intimate. This oversized apartment in the master wing was not their favorite bedroom. They both preferred the plainer room which had been Verek's alone during that eventful month when Carin slept in the blue bedchamber just down from it, in the minor wing of the house.

Verek put his arms around Carin and pulled her to him, where they sat together on the couch. She settled into the hollow of his shoulder and breathed the spiciness of the herbs that clung to his clothes. The smell of him wrapped her in memories, all of which fell sharply into line. But casting her thoughts back to the winter's journey that had introduced her to Welwyn, Carin found disordered, broken images, seemingly adrift in the flow of time. From many of these fragments she could derive no meaning, since she could not tell what had led up to those episodes or what events had proceeded from them.

Focusing her mind's eye beyond Welwyn, widening her gaze to encompass other past encounters and incidents, revealed other gaps in her memory. Except they weren't gaps: Slivers of imagery and splinters of impressions filled the holes that memory should occupy. The harder Carin stared at the shards and scraps, the farther apart they flew and the more stubbornly they eluded her grasp. But would the pieces not form a coherent whole, if she could somehow force them to join together into their proper places?

Her perplexities only deepened as Carin sought for a means of telling Verek about them. How to convey, in words, a disarray that she couldn't clearly identify within her own thoughts? After a time, as they gazed together into the bespelled and shadowy fire, she decided to start by reminiscing about Welwyn. It was, after all, her effort to recall her first meeting with the monk that had made her realize she couldn't catch hold of some of her memories.

"Welwyn being with us," Carin began, "he has me thinking about his cabin, his deer herd, and those snowshoes … But it's the strangest thing, Theil. I can't quite remember how I got to his cabin, or exactly when or how I left that glen where it sits." She tilted her head, her finger rubbing at her lower lip. "I have impressions, but things seem … broken up, split apart … and not in order. Events before and after don't line up in sensible ways."

Verek's embrace of her tightened. "*Fìleen,*" he murmured, "I remember every step of that wretched journey, for I did not believe we would survive it. If you find yourself at a loss for the particulars, ask me and I will tell you what I recall."

Carin smiled. Theil wouldn't see her expression in the low light, with her face turned to the fire. But he would hear the smile in her voice. "My lord, your memories are apt to be very different from mine. I remember enough to know that we experienced that journey in quite different ways, from two opposing points of view."

At this, Verek's arms tightened further, and he made a noncommittal sort of grunt, deep in his throat.

He might prefer that I not *remember certain parts of our trek into the mountains,* Carin thought—such as that damned *chalse* on her ankle.

To spare him coming up with a reply, she went on speaking.

"With my mind on Master Welwyn, and wizards' apprentices, and teaching adepts to control themselves, I've also been thinking about the *Book of Archamon*. When Lord Legary's spell of concealment was on it, I couldn't read its pages because the words broke apart into letters that scattered themselves across the paper. Worse, even the letters fell apart. They were nothing but tiny lines, dots, and curls that swirled over the pages. It was like trying to read a stirred-up anthill."

Carin spread her fingers and moved her hand in a circle, mimicking as best she could the dizzying gyrations of the characters in the once-ensorcelled book.

"Some of my memories are like that," she continued. "I recall bits and pieces—and I think the bits and pieces are all there, inside my head, same as every letter and word remained within the *Book of Archamon*. But like the letters of the *Book*, the bits of my memories are broken up. I can't read meaning in the fragments. Some of the things I remember, I can't pin down long enough to understand where they go. Trying to arrange the pieces so they make sense is giving me a headache."

Carin turned in Verek's embrace to meet his gaze. "Can you help me put my memories back together? I don't want to forget a moment of our lives together."

In the flickering light, she couldn't be certain, but she seemed to see a small grimace flit across Theil's expression. What settled on his countenance, however, was a look of puzzlement.

"I am confounded by what you tell me," he said. "Were you merely mortal, I would surmise that the magic of Ruain has taken your memories, so that you know nothing of any world beyond. Ancient wizardry safeguards this province against discovery by those who do not belong here."

Carin shook her head. "I'm not under the spell of omission. Welwyn explained how it keeps Ruain secret from the rest of Ladrehdin. And Megella has told me how the magic tried to steal her memories of the south country when she first returned to this northland." Carin paused, then added, "I'm fully aware that there are worlds beyond Ruain. And I'm *wysard* enough to be sure this place isn't magicking away anything that gives me strength—or makes me who I am. I need my memories, and I'm fairly certain I still have them.

"But they're in a jumble, some of them—a mixed heap of bits and splinters." Carin tipped her head again. "It's odd, but until Welwyn came here and started me reminiscing, I hadn't noticed that parts of my memory needed sorting. I haven't had time to think about the past, my love, because I've been too busy raising those hellions you beset me with."

11

Verek laughed. He fingered a lock of Carin's hair.

"Children are a blessing and a curse, are they not? They run mothers and fathers ragged." With his fingers still twined in Carin's hair, he stroked her cheekbone, then touched her lips.

"My lady," he murmured, "I will do all in my power to put your memories to rights. Perhaps it will aid our task, if we may know the reason for their ... dislocation." He studied her, his dark eyes catching the firelight as he raised a quizzical eyebrow. "Could it be a consequence of your final journey through the void? You returned to Weyrrock, that last time, with your body overtaxed, heavy with our first child and exhausted in your flesh from all that you had endured. Was your mind affected as well?"

"Probably," Carin admitted. "Time behaves so strangely in the void. It can speed away, stretching to forever, but then seem to turn back on itself and slow to a crawl. When time is meaningless, I suppose memories could have a hard time locking into their proper places. They might just fall to bits."

She paused, then added, "I'm not convinced, though, that traveling the void is completely to blame, or ultimately at the root of my broken-up memories. This feels different. It's a jumble, not an absence. My recollection of getting to Welwyn's glen isn't *gone*, not in the way my earliest memories were lost, that first time I crossed the void, in my childhood. I do recall riding to Welwyn's cabin, but it comes to me in pieces—enough pieces, I think, to make a complete picture, if only they'd stick themselves together. It's a difficult thing to explain. In my mind, where my early impressions of growing up on Earth should be, I have only a blank—no fragments, not even splinters. That picture is truly lost. But these more recent memories that I'm trying to pin down aren't gone, they're ... jumbled. That's the best word I can find for the mess they're making in my brain. I've got pieces, and the pieces refuse to fall into place."

"Hmm." Verek looked thoughtful. "Though I am far less familiar than you with the oblivion between the worlds, I have experienced something of the distortions it engenders. My exposure was trifling, however, compared to the over-many journeys that you have made within that realm." Theil settled against the cushions at his back, as though preparing for a long session of memory-sorting. "Whether the void begat your 'jumble,' or we must seek a culprit elsewhere, I can say only this: My recollections are intact, *fileen*, and at your disposal. Ask what you would."

Gifted with such an open-ended invitation, Carin considered only briefly before choosing a matter that she knew had been satisfactorily resolved, though she could not piece together the when or where of it.

"All right, then. Put me straight about this: I remember you lost your powers for a time. When exactly did you get them back?"

Verek dropped his fingers from her hair to grip Carin's hand. "Power returned to me when you returned to this world," he murmured, looking into her eyes with an intensity that revealed the feeling behind his words.

Carin needed no time at all to sift through her recollections. Reuniting with Verek stood apart from the splintered heap: of that event, her memory was perfect, having no breaks in it. But still she could not shake out of the jumble the precise time or place of Theil's full wizardly restoration.

"At the sea cliffs?" she asked. "Where the cedar forests meet the ocean on Ruain's east coast?"

Verek looked pleased that Carin remembered those details about the far reaches of his lands. But he shook his head. "You had healed me before then, my lady. Throughout all the months of your absence from this world, I remained powerless. But when you reappeared to me, rising in mist above the *wysards'* waters, in that blessed moment I felt the Power flow in my sinews with a heat like molten metal."

He raised Carin's hand to his heart and pinned it there, his fingers gripping hers as though he'd never let her go. For a moment, Verek seemed unable to continue. When he did, his voice was husky, conveying a depth of emotion barely implied by his words.

"It transpired that you had arrived on the shores of Ladreh-din well south of my borders. You were not so far down as East-haven, but still you faced a lengthy journey alone, wending your way up the coast toward Ruain. You told me you would meet me at the sea cliffs … though as I hastened to saddle my horse and head east with all speed, I was prepared to ride as far as Granger, if need be, to reclaim you."

Granger, Carin remembered in every particular. But *East-haven?* That name rang no bell … challenging her previous assumption that all her memories remained in her head, only broken, in a disconcerting number of instances, into pieces too small and scattered to read.

She refocused on Verek as he continued, his manner absorbed, his head atilt.

"I found it unnecessary, however, to ride so far. I'd barely begun leading my horse down the steepness of Ruain's coastal edge when I spied you racing up the trail toward me. We had arrived at the sea cliffs at the same moment in time."

That part, Carin certainly remembered. The horse had been left on its own to scramble back up to the grassy tops of those cliffs, there to graze in solitude for quite a while. Verek and Carin had come together under wind-twisted trees high on the cliff face where the precipitous, zigzagging trail leveled off. They'd dispensed with words: actions spoke louder. Carin had not been heavy with child then, and her body had been neither overtaxed nor exhausted. All of that would come later, as together they recrossed the length of Ruain to return to the old stone mansion called Weyrrock. By the time they reached the house, Carin would be shockingly wrung out and mere days away from giving birth to Nina.

But at the moment of her reunion with Verek on the nearly vertical face of the cliffs that looked out seaward, Carin was slim and fit, and needing her lover in ways heightened by a time of separation that had seemed infinite. Indeed, their separation had missed becoming permanent by only the space of a single grain of sand.

The pair were a long time satisfying themselves, that day, that both were back where they belonged: in the magical land of Ruain and in each other's arms, with liquid fire coursing through their veins.

"I remember," was all Carin could whisper now, as they sat safe at home in a firelit room, and she looked into Verek's darkly brilliant eyes.

Her gaze had been locked with Theil's during all the moments of her remembering, and whatever other questions Carin might have framed for him had flown out the window. Thought itself had flown. They were again in a state that required no words, and again they had their privacy. Or would have it, as soon as Verek stood, shut the hall door, and took his wife to a bed blissfully remote from the hellions a few doors down—those formerly shrieking children whom Welwyn had miraculously quieted.

Thank the Powers for old wysards who show up on the doorstep just when you need them.

Chapter 2

Restoration

As it became clear that the venerable Welwyn was more than capable of mastering two headstrong apprentices, Carin and Verek shared sighs of relief and moved back into their old bedchamber, Verek's former bachelor quarters just down the hall from what had been Carin's bedroom. Though the apartment was smaller and simpler than the almost palatial quarters they had been occupying in the manor's master wing, both favored the more cloistered space. In Verek's canopied bed, under its simple blue blanket, Galen had been conceived in due season after Carin's return to the world called Ladrehdin.

Nina, of course, was the offshoot of those months when Carin and Verek had worked their way north from Granger, over the plains on their journey-of-many-detours back to Ruain. Upon their eventual return to the manor house, and in its cavern of power, Carin had suspected she was with child when she threw herself into the void. That couldn't be helped. She had done what she must to end the hemorrhaging of the world's lifeblood.

Afterward, in questing through the void to finish the task it had been given her to do, Carin had become thoroughly unanchored in time. Given the strange effects upon her body of the void's time-twisting, she could not count backward from the month of Nina's birth to establish the moment of conception. Reckoning from the child's birth-day put Carin somewhere in the void — or on the world called Earth — when Theil Verek's seed begot their first child within her. That, clearly, could not be so, for he had not been with her. Carin had made that journey alone.

Therefore, Nina must have sprung from their "trips behind the wagon," as Megella put it, that summer they traveled the plains in company with the wisewoman. On that journey, Carin and Verek had finally felt free to give, each to the other, what each had longed for.

Nipping back to the more secluded bedchamber in the lesser part of the house freed husband and wife for the delights of love-making in complete privacy. They could be as noisy as they pleased. They'd originally moved to larger quarters in the master wing to gain space for Galen's crib and Nina's cot. But merely keeping the children with them in the same apartment had proved insufficient for managing two resourceful escape-artists and mischief-makers. The imps had found ways of slipping out even when their parents were wide awake. The one seemed capable of turning into a liquid and flowing soundlessly under the door. The other, Carin suspected, could transform into a smoky will-o'-the-wisp and drift out through the keyhole.

"Your imagination is running away with you," Verek said when Carin voiced her thoughts about their offspring. "No *wysard* of Ladrehdin has been capable of shape-shifting in five thousand years."

"Maybe not," she replied. "But you and I are living in the present, not the past, and I'm telling you these two can do it."

In the end, during the weeks before Welwyn's return, the pair had found their only recourse for a disaster-less night was to bring the children into bed with them and sleep—or try to sleep—with the youngsters squeezed in between. Verek disliked using his great-aunt Megella's sleep-for-now powder, though Carin freely dosed the devilkins with it when Verek was away overnight—as he was at times, seeing to his lands and holdings. She also wouldn't hesitate to fling Meg's forget-for-now powder into the face of a child who persisted in some misbehavior that imperiled life or limb. By the time the powder's effects wore off, the mischief-maker had generally turned from the first fixation and found his or her way into new trouble—leaving the spell of stone as Carin's last resort.

But children could not spend the night bespelled to stony immobility. Hence, in the face of Verek's opposition to sleeping powder, the hellions were squashed into bed with their parents.

From all this had sprung Verek's unhesitating "Good!" when Welwyn laid claim to the younglings. Carin, though feeling it must reflect poorly on her, could not help the sense of relief that acted on her taut nerves as the release of an arrow relieves the tension on an overdrawn bowstave.

Now the children were thriving under Master Welwyn's tutelage, learning self-discipline while learning the craft of their forebears, losing none of their high spirits, gaining daily in knowledge, understanding, and control. Verek became their weapons master, teaching them swordsmanship and tutoring them in archery.

With considerably more patience, Carin observed, pleased by what she saw, *than Theil could muster with me when he was trying so hard to guard his heart.*

Carin herself taught the children — and Welwyn — how to make and use a sling. The old *wysard* had read of simple stone-throwing devices but he'd never seen one used. He watched intrigued as Carin showed her pupils how to make the strap from leather, affix cords, arm the weapon with a stone, whirl it, and discharge the missile at exactly the right moment.

"Most excellent, Lady Carin!" the monk exclaimed as she demonstrated with a string of bull's-eye hits that, despite years with little practice, she had lost none of her mastery. "Had you carried such a weapon when first you met his tetchy lordship Verek, he might never had got the better of you, don't you know."

"Oh, I had a sling then," Carin replied. "But Lord Verek took it away from me before I could let fly and spill his brains in the dirt."

"Fortuitous indeed!" Welwyn's laughter rumbled up from his jiggling belly. "Had you managed to kill him, I would not now have these two vessels of raw power to shape into something we can all live with!"

Turning to the children who had been slinging stones at the archery targets, the monk disarmed them before they knew what he was about—that being the secret of his success, Carin surmised from watching him assert his jolly, easy authority over Nina and Galen. Welwyn stayed ahead of the imps, acting before they knew it, moving before they saw him move.

It's sorcery, Carin supposed, *and exactly what my hellions need.*

Adding to her satisfaction with the new arrangement, in no way did Welwyn usurp Verek's place as the children's father. The monk was their teacher, governor, wise friend and trusted counselor. The lord of the manor was unquestionably their father and sovereign. And their hero and champion. From infancy the children had the confidence that comes from knowing with their whole selves that their father would keep them safe from any harm. Being themselves "vessels of raw power," as Welwyn put it, they sensed and responded to Verek's overarching power—

—Power that Carin had restored to him, after Verek's confrontation with the necromancer in the mountains had so drained him that he could not spark even a campfire during their later journey across the plains. Here, in his own realm, in the presence of his deep wellspring of magic, Verek was strong again.

He's stronger, now, Carin thought, watching him help Nina brace her little bow, *than he was when I first entered his world.*

It was she who had strengthened him, and not only as his wife and lover and the mother of his children, though certainly she had healed Verek's heart from the torment of losing his first wife and son to demonic murder.

Alesia and Aidan were not forgotten, would never be forgotten. Their bodies rested in the family tomb in a remote part of the grounds within the manor's encircling wall. Unbeknown to Verek, Carin had gone there when Galen was born, compelled by a half-formed impulse to share the event with Alesia and receive the dead woman's blessing. She had come away feeling that her predecessor was indeed pleased with her, pleased that Carin had brought Verek out of his soul-crushing grief and restored him to fully lived life.

But in a much larger sense, Carin had restored the fullness of life to the whole of Ladrehdin. By removing the parasitic crystals from this world, she had ended the ruinous drain on the realm's primordial energies.

Now this world burst with life. The trees grew green-leafed and strong in Verek's formerly blighted woodland. Ferns and flowers thrived in the understory. Even the pond had returned, the lake of the lilies in which the necromancer had drowned Alesia and Aidan. Verek never went there, but Myra visited it often. Carin sometimes accompanied her and helped the woman cast bread upon the waters. What Myra meant by the ritual, she never said and Carin did not ask, but she understood the housekeeper's impulse to make a memorial offering. Myra, the queen of the kitchen, the cook who had elevated the task of feeding her household into the highest of callings, was as bound to offer food to the dead as Carin had been to seek Alesia's blessing on her newborn son.

At the root of all the robust newness in the world lay, unquestionably, the restored life-force of Ladrehdin's heart. By ridding the world of the energy-draining crystals, Carin had made possible a core deep and globe-spanning healing.

In the cave of the magic wellspring, she watched the healing progress over time. At first, it was noticeable only as an easing of tension in the cavern. As Carin sat on the bench of the fish and gazed into the mirror pool, she felt a kind of relaxation spread through the chamber. At times, she fancied that a breath stirred in the cavern, like a sigh, and it seemed a sigh of contentment.

Gradually the signs of restoration became more evident. The light from the cave's glowing walls lost its reddish tinge and brightened until it shone clear like the strong yellow-white of the walls around the undamaged pool upstairs. The surface of the enchanted wellspring lost its mirror sheen as a current began to stir, ever so gently in its depths. The flow increased weekly, until the current became a visible stream that bubbled up in the center of the enormous pool, then bathed the stone steps below the pool's rim as the current circled back, down into the depths.

As it streamed up, around, and out again, the current began to carry hints of the outside world. Carin caught the fragrances of mosses, sweet-flag and marsh marigold, and other plants that grew on the edges of quiet streams and ponds.

Also wafting into the air was the smell of wet rocks and the earthy odor of subterranean passages. That odor suggested light-less caves far beneath the cavern of the *wysards'* well. Into those hidden places the current flowed unseen, spilling from the pool's nethermost reaches, down into the bones of the world. There, the waters of the *wysards* joined the wider realm of Ladrehdin, mix-ing with underground rivers that surged in the depths for thou-sands of leagues before bursting to the surface or emptying into the oceans. In her mind's eye, Carin traced the hidden flow: the seaward current, then rain clouds forming offshore, moving inland, flooding rivers, storm-waters filling secret passages and sunken, pitch-black caves … an endless cycle.

After millennia of near-total separation from that cycle, the pool of enchantment was rushing to return to full participation. In the waters that came circling back, in the ever-stronger current that welled up in the pool's center, Carin caught whiffs of the faraway ocean: the tangy smell of salt air, salt water, seaweed.

The day came when a pronounced tang in the air brought Carin to her feet. From the bench where she often sat to meditate, she walked to the pool's rim, crouched, and put her hand in the water. Her every fiber tensed, expecting to feel the mind-dead-ening, bone-shattering, heart-stopping cold that, in the past, had nearly killed both her and Verek.

But no! The water was warm. On Carin's skin, it felt like heated velvet.

She slipped out of her clothes and leapt down the steps into the pool. Many times she had bathed and dove in the spring-water pool upstairs, and had thought it the most glorious, luxurious experience that any body of water could offer a swimmer. But this! This warm velvet was a sensual, carnal delight beyond anything her body had known in this world or any other.

Three times Carin swam the width of the pool. Then she dived as deeply as her held breath allowed, but she could not see the bottom. This pool was immeasurably deep. Its waters, however, testified to the pool's hidden recoupling with the wider world and all that it held. Carin smelled rain and sun and fertile soil. She felt life overflowing, within and without. She tasted salt — *like the seawater that runs in my veins*, she thought.

Carin swam to the rim and bounded out of the water. Sprinting naked across the cavern's smooth floor, she spiraled up the stairs to the landing that opened on both the library and Verek's workroom. Bursting through the latter door, she found Theil at his labors, shaping a longer bowstave for Nina, who had outgrown the first bow Verek had made her.

"Come quickly!" Carin exclaimed. "It's happened! You must come."

"What?" Startled, Verek dropped the stave on his workbench and stared at Carin. His dark eyes flashed with the flaring of desire at the sight of her naked body standing, dripping, in his doorway. "My beautiful lady, I will go with you anywhere. But tell me *what* has happened."

"You'll see! Follow me."

Carin turned and ran back down the stairs. She hurtled across the cavern and sprang high from the pool's rim, to execute a clean dive into the bubbling, upwelling current at its center.

When she surfaced, she discovered Verek standing at the pool's edge, gaping at her. "Come in with me!" she cried. "The water is warm. Beyond *'warm'*. You can't imagine how good it feels."

Verek hesitated—*and for sound reason*, Carin thought. This pool had nearly frozen the life from him more than once. But she swam near the rim and with the flat of her hand sent a spray of water into his face. At its touch he cried out, not in pain, but astonishment.

Hurrying backward several steps, Verek sat on the bench of the crescent moon and tugged off his boots. He lunged to his feet, shed his clothes, and strode to the rim. Very deliberately, as if still not sure that what he had felt on his face could be true, he lowered one bare foot to the pool's uppermost step.

"By the Powers!" he swore. With a kind of awestruck slowness, he brought his other foot down beside the first. As the gloriously soft, sultry, sensual water of the *wysards'* well swirled around his ankles, Verek stared first at his feet, then at Carin.

"I know," she whispered, treading water. "It's … beyond words. We're the first in five thousand years to feel this. Come in with me."

He did, but still moving as if entranced, foot by foot descending the steps that dropped from the rim toward the pool's depths. Watching the water rise gradually up his naked form, devouring with her eyes the lean, graceful body that she knew so well, with its erect stance and the proud set of his head, Carin wanted him with an urgency that wouldn't wait.

A kick of her feet sent her arrowing at Verek. She knocked him backward forcefully enough to get a deep-throated grunt from him. She pushed him down until he sprawled on the steps with only his head above water. The ends of his long hair swayed like seaweed, awash in the waves thrown up by Carin's onslaught. Tasting salt in her mouth like sweat now, she grabbed Verek's shoulders, digging her fingers into his muscles, kneeling on the steps astraddle him, open to him.

Half off-balance but jolted out of his trance, Verek caught her hips and moved hard to her, pulling Carin to him. The water that bathed their joined bodies was soft as velvet and intoxicating like liquor, and powerful as the elements unleashed — quaking rock, tidal wave, storm-wind, fire — for it was the raw power of the world itself, the living essence of the world.

Around them the cavern rang with their cries of a pleasure exceeding anything they had yet known together. Again they coupled, and again, sometimes buoyed up by the current that rose in the pool's center, sometimes supported by the wide stone steps that did not feel stony under them, but cushioned them — *soft as featherbeds*, Carin thought, only dimly conscious of any touch but Verek's and the water's.

They stayed in the pool for hours. If Welwyn had not been there to supervise the children, up above in the nearly forgotten daylight world far over their heads, no doubt the imps would have burned down the house while Carin and Verek remained lost in each other, transcendent, their senses heightened almost beyond what flesh and blood could bear.

At last, spent, they climbed from the pool and fell exhausted on the cavern's floor. As her wet body began to dry, Carin felt no chill. The polished stone under her was warm. She stretched, luxuriating in a warmth like that of a sun-heated boulder on the shores of a summer pond.

She rolled over and studied her husband where he lay asleep beside her. With no feeling of surprise — how could it be otherwise? — Carin saw that the hair at Verek's temples was no longer streaked with gray. Every hair on his head and in his close-trimmed beard was a glossy crow-black. Verek's face, unlined, bore an expression of such inner peace that Carin struggled to recall the looks of angry exasperation he had directed at her in their earliest days together.

She drew a strand of damp hair off his face, and lightly rubbed her thumb across his lower lip. Verek stirred. Though not wholly roused to awareness, he pulled Carin to him and kissed her, gently exploring her mouth with his. He opened his eyes then, awake, and gave her a look of glittering intensity.

"My lady," he murmured, "I've always known you could be the death of me. But I would die a thousand deaths, and suffer each twice over, and gladly, to have you take me like *that* again."

Chapter 3

Message In a Bottle

With his knack for getting his way before anyone knew what he was about, Welwyn had the entire family horsed and on the road before they realized they were departing.

"How long has it been?" he asked Verek. "I think you have not shown yourself across the breadth of this land since the day you rode seaward to collect your wayfaring lady. It is past time, don't you know, that you went among the common folk and exhibited your handsome children, and let the people see again the exotic creature who stole your heart." The monk added, with an admiring glance at Carin, "I've no doubt that many a song has been written and many a ballad sung, the length of Ruain, about the green-eyed lady who came to you from afar. Let us go and hear the music."

Welwyn was correct that Verek had not ventured any great distance from the manor house since he'd fetched Carin back from his country's easternmost cliffs. The new life Theil had seeded in her womb, before Carin left Ladrehdin, had quickened with uncanny—indeed, unnatural—speed upon her return to this world: another reason to believe that time had behaved inscrutably during Carin's travels in the beyond. Verek had brought her back to the manor heavily pregnant, and she'd given birth to his daughter barely a week after their return.

Thanks be to Drisha for Megella and Myra, Carin thought whenever she recalled that experience. Too much had happened too quickly. She had been deliriously happy to be in Verek's arms again, with him body and soul under the brow of the sea cliffs, then riding at his side once again, back to their home. From the clifftops westward, however, Carin could remember little of their journey, so absorbed had she been in Verek, and in his child that burgeoned within her.

Theil had not voiced amazement at the speed with which Carin's belly swelled, but she'd read it in his face and in his tender care of her. Each time they came to a village, he would ask whether Carin might not be more comfortable riding in a wagon or carriage. She always declined, unwilling to delay their return journey even long enough for Verek to buy a wheeled conveyance and a cart-horse to pull it. In any event, that mode of travel would have slowed them more than Carin could accept. On horseback, even in her condition, they would cross the length of Ruain far more quickly than they could by wagon.

And the farther they progressed, the more urgently Carin felt the need for speed. She wanted this child born in Verek's house, and she wanted Megella with her when it came. An experienced healer Verek might be, but Carin wasn't convinced the man could keep a level head when it was his young wife—well, young lover at that point, as they hadn't yet had the benefit of a ceremony—but when it was his lady love giving birth to a child he had seeded within her before losing her in the void. Carin wanted Megella's calm competence midwifing this birth ... particularly since she had no way of knowing what her travels through oblivion might have done to the child.

Carin suppressed the thought whenever it forced its way to the surface. But the worry of it lurked beneath her conscious consideration during the whole of that increasingly feverish journey back to the familiar rooms of Verek's manor. For all she knew, she carried a monster in her womb.

Upon Carin's arrival at Myra's kitchen doorstep, the housekeeper had half crushed her in a weepy embrace, and then tried to feed her. Megella the wisewoman, however, took one look at Carin and hustled her up the stairs to the blue room, there to put her to bed.

Where Carin stayed for a week, sleeping a great deal, rousing only to eat and to reassure a constantly hovering Verek that she would be fine. His furrowed brow and worried eyes spoke mutely of his doubts. Toward the end of that week, Carin was too far gone in a shadow world of twilit dreams to even know he was there.

But then she went into labor. The pain roused her to acute consciousness. She opened her eyes to see Megella at the foot of her bed, ready with mountains of linen and basins of hot water. The wisewoman barked instructions at her, which Carin followed as best she could between contractions that seemed to rip her open.

From his place at the head of the bed, Verek took a step as if intending to join Megella at the business end of this blessed event. The wisewoman stopped him with a snapped: "You! Hold her hand!"

Verek spun around, reaching for Carin as frantically as she clutched for him as the pain bore down, filling every inch of her. He grabbed her hands and locked them in something like a death grip for what seemed hours, until—gasping, screaming, and cursing—Carin was delivered of their daughter.

With practiced hands, Megella slapped breath into the newborn, who let out a lusty howl at such treatment. The wisewoman checked the infant from head to toe, then swaddled the child and laid it at Carin's breast.

"Perfect," Meg announced. "You have a beautiful daughter. I congratulate you both. Though clearly, Carin's is the greater achievement." Megella looked at her great-nephew Verek. "You, sir, did naught but take your pleasure. This remarkable voyager, however, carried your seed through every danger, to far shores, through the abyss and back. And here at the end of her ordeal, she presents you with a fine, strong daughter who will grow to look exactly like you. May Drisha and the Powers have your life, liver, and lights if you do not cherish this young woman."

"I do," Verek whispered. "I cherish her more than any but the Powers themselves can know." He gazed at Carin with a kind of hunger, then glanced back at the wisewoman. "Leave us now, Aunt," he ordered with his habitual stern authority. "I would be alone with my lady."

Megella laughed. As she gathered up bloody towels and drew a coverlet over Carin's naked legs, she said: "Not alone, m'lord. You were two; now you are three. And by the light I see in your eyes, nephew, you will soon be four."

The wisewoman prophesied correctly. Carin got pregnant again when Nina was but three months old. With Megella and Verek plying her with magic-infused herbs and elixirs, Carin recovered rapidly from childbed. More lingering were the effects of otherworldly travel, the fracturing of time and memory, the near-delirium of the final days of her first pregnancy. Yet all of that, too, had seemed to pass away from her, in good time. Meg had said that Nina's birth was the end of Carin's ordeal. And whether the wisewoman had meant it as a true prophecy or merely a casual remark, Meg's words appeared to be largely accurate.

Carin found herself quite comfortable suckling Nina while pregnant with Galen. She informed Verek that she wanted him to seed their next two children even closer together than he'd sired this pair. "It's efficient," she said. "I can't do much else while I'm nursing a baby, so I might as well be bred with the next one at the same time."

He bent to give her a long, deep kiss. As he straightened and looked upon her newly swelling body, Verek murmured, "As fertile as you are, my lady, I think I must bring herb-lore into our marriage bed, to spread out these children more rationally. Else, we shall be overrun with them."

He did as he said. And by the time Nina and Galen were walking, Carin was fervently glad that Verek's herb-use had forestalled the conception of more hellions.

Don't call them that, Carin chided herself. *They're headstrong, but no one could ask for children happier, or more good-natured, than these two.*

The fact remained, however, that her offspring were born of a long line of wizards on Verek's side … and their mother was a creature unnatural to the world of Ladrehdin. Verek had once called her "more than mortal." Carin had never presumed to think of herself as truly magian, but the facts were indisputable: She had traveled the void using magic of her own making.

Welwyn's return relieved Carin of most of her worries over the children. If anyone could raise up two devilkins in the way they should go, it was the monk who had trained generations of Ladrehdin's adepts. Sometimes as she watched Welwyn teaching her children, Carin wondered how old the monk really was. But she put the question aside as both unanswerable and irrelevant. Ordinary concepts of age did not apply to *wysards*.

In fact, the sorcerer she'd married seemed to get younger with time. Their passionate afternoon in the reborn well of enchantment had removed all trace of silver from Verek's hair. The fine lines at the corners of his eyes, never more than barely noticeable, were also gone now. His hands, though hard and calloused from years of swordplay, had lost their scars.

It's the same for him as it is for his world, Carin realized. *Those evil crystals were taking his strength as they slowly drained this world of power …*

Carin mused on all of this, and more, as she rode forth with Verek, Welwyn, and the children to begin the journey across Ruain that Welwyn insisted they make.

Verek expressed no great enthusiasm for the trip, but neither did he forbid it. He only demanded that their first stop be Fintan, there to collect Megella and send her back to the manor.

The wisewoman had called it a waste to have two skilled healers dwelling in the same domicile. "Nephew," she'd said, soon after Carin was back on her feet after Nina's birth, "you have no need of me here. You were physician to all your household before I came, and fully capable you are of tending to the new addition." Meg was holding the newborn as she said this, and tickling the baby, eliciting a happy gurgle from Nina. "I wish to live near you but not with you. I'll wager there is some village close by, where a wisewoman of my abilities might be wanted."

There was. Fintan, the market town well known to Myra, was delighted to welcome a close relation of their lord and master. Meg was given a neat cottage with a kitchen garden and henhouse, and soon felt more at home in Fintan than ever she had in the narrow confines of the southern village, Granger.

"Theil, why do you want Megella at Weyrrock while we are away?" Carin asked him in a whisper as they rode up the lane to Meg's cottage.

"Because Myra cannot enter into the great wellspring's presence," he whispered back. "And we must have a watcher posted at that pool, in the event the *daēva* attempts again to recross the void."

In hardly more words than that, Verek explained his need to Megella. The wisewoman nodded, then kissed Carin's cheek and ruffled each child's hair as she spoke a polite "Master Welwyn" to the monk and received his respectful "Mistress Megella" in return. Briskly, she set off down the lane behind them. She would not walk all the way to the manor. Verek had a man in the village who was ready, any hour of the day or night, to drive Meg in a comfortable carriage. The wisewoman need not even pack a bag—Myra kept a room ready for her, with such clothes and trappings as Meg might require. Even the wisewoman's hens and milk cow would be looked after. The driver of the carriage would see to that.

"Now," Verek said as he watched his shawl-draped great-aunt stride away down the lane, "we may begin this journey in earnest. If our purpose, as Master Welwyn contends, is to parade the children before the populace of Ruain, let us commence the parade."

It took weeks to visit every major town and many a minor hamlet. But they did it, with far fewer "exhibitions" from their children than Carin had anticipated.

Galen started a dozen fires, all but one suppressed in an instant by Verek's spellcraft. The blaze that Verek allowed to burn was upon the cooking hearth of an elderly man whose stiff joints made firewood-gathering a painful chore. For the old man, Galen conjured a hot little flame that rose, undying, from a single small log. Lest the magic attract undue attention over time, from the elder's more regular visitors, Verek unobtrusively refined the conjuration so that the fire's "fuel" seemed to gradually burn away, to be replenished in the wee hours each night by fresh wood.

Watching her man and his son work their good deed, Carin recalled what Welwyn had said about the spell of omission that hung over the province of Ruain. Its people both knew, and did not know, that their lord was a wizard. Verek, when abroad in his lands, did not display his powers overtly. But neither did he forbear to work magic, inconspicuously, when the situation called for it.

Nina, like her brother, showed a generous spirit in her wizardly impulses. Giggling the whole time, as though she viewed her water-magic as a great game, the girl brought forth a gushing spring to water the communal gardens of one small village. The people, exclaiming over the sudden rush of clear water from a crack in a boundary-stone, gave thanks to Drisha and the mercies, and rushed to fetch their spades and buckets. As the housewives filled their pails with the cold, fresh water, the farmers dug trenches to channel the flow to every corner of the gardens. Nina jumped in to help, squealing with delight, scooping up mud with both her tiny hands, ending the day mud-caked from head to toe. And still giggling.

At last the travelers reached the eastern limits of Ruain, coming to the seacoast at a point far north of the vertical cliffs that had been Carin's only previous view of the country's shoreline. As they rode down from these more gentle headlands and walked their horses along a white-sand beach, her urge to swim in the ocean overpowered her. Carin had not glimpsed the sea, with other than her mind's eye, in nearly six years, since arriving back on these shores from her journeys beyond the void. The sea-water that flowed in her veins, though Earthly in its origins, had found its resonance in the oceans of Ladrehdin. This sea called to Carin, and every drop of her blood responded.

She swung off her horse and raced for the low breakers, pausing only to remove her riding boots. The sun shone in a clear sky, the winds were calm and the waves gentle, lapping at the shore. Carin stood hip-deep in the water, eyes closed, inhaling the fresh salt tang, feeling the cool brine wash away the sweat of this day's riding.

She was starting to push out deeper when Verek called to her.

"*Fileen!*" he shouted. "Attend to our water-nymph. She's escaped me."

Carin turned to see Nina splashing into the water behind her. The girl, too, was fully clothed.

"Wait, child!" she called, and waded back to scoop Nina up and carry her onto the beach. "Your mother has set you a poor example. Most people undress before swimming in the sea. Let's get your clothes off."

Carin stripped the child, and peeled away her own garments down to her smallclothes. Looking around for the monk and seeing him nowhere, she called a question to Verek, who was sitting with Galen halfway up the beach. The two of them, fire-masters both, already had a campfire blazing in a ring of stones on the sand.

"Where has Welwyn got to?" Carin asked, loudly enough to be heard over the murmur of the ocean behind her and the crackling of the fast-burning fire.

"Gone up the coast a ways," Verek called back. "He absents himself for you. Swim naked as the fish that you are."

Grinning, Carin shed every stitch and splashed back into the waves, as gleeful as Nina. This was the child's first time in the ocean, and the girl took to it like a porpoise. With no coaching, Nina swam and dived with a gracefulness that the girl had yet to develop on dry land. Soon she was playing tag with a school of fish.

Was I swimming with such skill at her age? Carin wondered as she watched the nymph. She could not remember her own early years, when she'd lived with now-forgotten parents on an island far from Ladrehdin, across the void. But in a letter from that world, left for her there—and which, improbably, Theil had found—Carin's mother had described her lost daughter as a little fish. Clearly, the trait had passed to the new generation: Nina was as at home in the sea as any creature born to it.

The two of them had swum out far enough that Verek was getting concerned—Carin's glance back at the beach found him standing at the water's edge, shading his eyes against the sun, watching them. He was himself a strong swimmer, as Carin fully appreciated from their times together in the wizards' well of Ruain. But he did not love ocean-swimming the way she did—or as ecstatically as their daughter now did.

Verek wouldn't need to rescue either of them this day. Carin waved to signal their imminent return, and swam over to collect her porpoising child. But Nina had ceased her leaping, and was now staring out to sea.

"Mama," she piped in her little-girl's voice. "What is that? What's it doing?"

Carin followed the child's gaze and saw a dolphin leap, not far from them. Her hitherto landlocked daughter had never before seen such a creature. Carin gave Nina both of the names that she knew for it, carefully pronouncing the Ladrehdinian word as well as the name this species bore in her own native tongue of Earth. Treading water, Carin held Nina in the crook of one arm, and remained watching the dolphin's antics, a little puzzled by what she saw.

"I'm not sure what it's doing, child," Carin said at last. "Is that a ball it's playing with?"

"No, Mama. Not round like a ball." The girl watched a little longer, then said, "It's got one of Papa's medicine bottles."

The dolphin made a great leap then, and as it reentered the water, it swept round toward them. The object of its play bobbed in the swells ahead of it. With such speed that Carin had no time to think, only to react, the creature caught the thing on its snout and flung it at her.

Carin threw up one hand and snatched the object out of the air. The speed of its flight spun her around and half under. By the time she'd got her head above water again and could look for it, the dolphin was gone.

Nina—whom she still held tightly—was staring at her wide-eyed. Carin, though a bit unnerved herself, tried to smile reassurance.

"It's all right," she said. "The dolphin was only playing. See how friendly? It gave us its toy."

At this, the child beamed and reached for the object in Carin's hand—which was indeed a small bottle similar to those that Verek filled with his herbal compounds. Except this one was wrapped in a thin veneer of wood.

Carin shook her head and held the bottle away from the girl. "Let's take it to your father. He's waiting for us."

She released the child, and together they swam to shore, Carin executing a sidestroke so as to not let Nina out of her sight.

They covered the distance quickly, untroubled by any further meetings with playful dolphins. Splashing through the shallows, they joined Verek at the water's edge.

As Nina spilled out the story of their adventure, her words tumbling over each other, Carin silently handed the bottle to Verek. He examined it, his brow furrowed, then thrust the object into his pocket and crouched on the wet sand to give his full attention to the tale his daughter was delivering with great animation.

When Nina finished her reenactment of the dolphin encounter, Verek praised her bravery, her swimming, and her mastery of the fine new word, *dolphyn*. Then he sent the girl up the beach to join her brother at the fire. Galen was toasting bread — burning it mostly, but turning out a few pieces that were edible when smeared with jam.

"That bottle looks like one of yours," Carin said when they were alone. "Except I don't think I've ever seen one wrapped in wood like that. And it's the wrong color."

"Entirely the wrong color." Verek stood for a moment studying her, then added, "I do not think that this object comes from any apothecary of Ladrehdin." He bent to pick up Carin's discarded chemise, and handed it to her with a distracted smile. "Seeing you rise naked from the deeps would ordinarily compel me to take you 'behind the wagon'," he murmured, watching as she pulled on her clothes. "But now I believe we must find Master Welwyn and hold counsel together."

Carin took Nina's clothes up the beach and got the girl dressed. They wolfed down the edible bits of Galen's culinary efforts, then caught up their horses and rode farther north along the seacoast, following the hoofprints of Welwyn's sturdy mount until they found him, deep in conversation, with a group of fisherfolk who were mending nets on the shore.

The fishers directed Verek's party up and over the headland to a bustling coastal community, where they found lodgings for the night. After bathing the sea-salt and the campfire smoke from themselves and their offspring, eating an excellent supper of fish and crab legs, and putting the happily worn-out children to bed, Carin and Verek gathered with Welwyn at the dining table. The proprietress of their lodging-house brought glasses of a local wine that was surprisingly drinkable. The vintage earned even Verek's praise. Flushed with pleasure, the woman dropped a curtsy, gave them the flagon, and left them to their counsels.

"I like this not," Verek said without further preliminaries as he pulled the wood-wrapped bottle from his pocket and handed it to Welwyn. "It feels ... wrong." Turning to Carin, he added, "My lady, if you please, tell Master Welwyn how you came by this object."

Carin complied tersely, and far less theatrically than Nina as she described the incident with the dolphin and how the creature had seemed deliberately to fling the bottle at her.

As she spoke, Welwyn held the object in front of a candle flame and peered into it, turning it this way and that, seeking an angle that would give him a clearer view of the interior, which was almost entirely obscured by the close-wrapped veneer. Only a neck of ruby-red glass appeared above the wooden wrapper.

When Carin finished telling of the bottle's strange arrival, Welwyn looked up and said, "There is something inside. Shall we open this gift from the sea and discover what Lady Carin has been given?"

For a long moment, Welwyn's companions made no reply. With a sigh of reluctance then, Verek muttered, "First, a spell of containment." He raised his right hand in a grasping gesture, as though to hold fast whatever forces might flow forth. Then he nodded at Welwyn.

Taking pains to not damage the veneer, the monk used the corkscrew from their table wine to ease out the bottle's stopper. As it came clear with a *pop*, Carin half raised her hands, an involuntary defensive reflex.

But nothing emerged. Welwyn peered into the bottle's open neck, then turned the object upside down and shook it.

What fell out was paper, tightly rolled.

Setting the bottle down—near Verek's hand, Carin noticed, as if the monk wanted the object well within the containment the wizard had raised—Welwyn picked up the paper and unrolled it. After a moment's study, he shook his head. "I do not know this language." He passed the paper to Verek.

The wizard looked long at the writing on the topmost page—Carin could now see that there was more than one sheet in the roll. Slowly, Verek raised his eyes to hers.

"Nor can I read it, Master Welwyn," Verek said while looking only at Carin. "But I'll wager that my lady can."

Theil handed Carin the paper. It rolled itself up again, taking the shape it had had inside the bottle. But the paper was not brittle, and Carin easily pulled it flat, pinching it between the thumb and forefinger of each hand.

She held it to the light of the nearest candle ... and caught her breath.

The writing was perfectly clear. She knew these words: they came from the language of her birth.

And they'd been penned by a hand that she also knew, for Carin had once before read a letter written by ... her mother. By that woman of Earth whom Carin couldn't remember.

Chapter 4

Blood Ties

Carin forgot the two men who sat at the table with her, watching her. She had eyes and thoughts for nothing except the words that spoke to her in her mother's handwriting.

My darling Karen, the letter began, then continued in the same flowing script:

> The strangest thing has happened. Your father and I have met a friend of yours. It calls itself a woodsprite, and it takes the form of a talking tree. Preposterous, I know. But your parents are not yet senile, and as far as we can tell we are not insane.
>
> In any case, what the sprite has told us about you has been a great comfort, so we choose to believe it. We've become such believers, in fact, that we've done as it suggested and written you this letter, a message in a bottle, to be cast into the great wide ocean and probably never reach you. But it eases my heart to think that you might—just might—read these words some-day.
>
> If you do, you'll be a grown woman reading them. It's hard for me to picture you that way. I know only the child we lost to the sea.
>
> Lost in a hurricane, so the sprite says. I'm not sure about that. I think I would remember a hurricane, but the only disas-ter I've lived through since you disappeared is the bleeding disease that killed most of humanity.
>
> I don't want to write much about that. If you get this letter, you are not to be anxious about us. Your father and I, along with a few hundred other survivors—possibly a few thousand, worldwide—seem to have a natural immunity.

The woodsprite tells us stories about the life you've led since we lost you. If even half of the creature's tales are true, I shudder for you, Karen! But the sprite says I shouldn't worry, that you can take care of yourself.

I'm trusting that you can, that you have, that you're alive and happy out there somewhere.

We love you, daughter. Reply if you can. The woodsprite seems to think it's possible, but won't say how or when. But if you can't send us a message, then know this: We will never forget you.

The letter closed with hand-drawn hearts beside two scribbled signatures. Carin supposed that the second scrawl was her father's. She could read neither name clearly.

She read the message twice before finally looking up and discovering Verek and Welwyn staring at her. Carin reached for her glass of wine, drained it in one gulp, and held it out to Verek. He refilled it without a word.

After another swallow that seemed to do nothing to steady her, she returned to the letter's first page and read the message aloud. She still found it easy to translate from her native tongue into the common speech of Ladrehdin. Since Nina's birth, Carin had made an effort to recall the words of her earliest language and teach the child a few of them.

Now, for the first time, she wondered if she'd perhaps been unwise to speak those alien words to the water-nymph.

When she'd finished her translation, Welwyn said only, "By the Powers!" and reached for the flagon of wine.

Verek took the papers from Carin's hand, rerolled them, and slipped them back inside the bottle. Almost absentmindedly, staring into the distance and not looking at what his fingers were doing, he worked the stopper free from the corkscrew and pressed it into the bottle's ruby-red neck.

As he set the bottle back on the table and turned to Carin, she found his gaze was now sharply focused. On her.

"Do you wish to attempt a reply?" he muttered.

Carin met his gaze. "No. When I set out years ago to break the bridges between the worlds, it was to protect *all* of them. Not Ladrehdin alone, but every world that could be threatened by strangleweed or pestilence or anything else that might cross over those bridges." She paused, then added, "I think we've learned that what the void divides is best left separated."

She reached for the alien bottle and fingered its wooden wrapping. With a sigh, Carin murmured, "Woodsprite," and fell silent.

Verek had lost none of his talent, however, for reading Carin's thoughts. "You believe the wood-goblin made this covering?"

She nodded. "By the time we'd reached Deroucey on our way to Master Welwyn's cabin, the sprite was able to shape wood."

Carin had long ago told Verek about the slim wooden blade the sprite had made to help her lift the latch of a closed shutter, so she could slip back inside a room that the *wysard* had not known she'd left. Now, for the monk's benefit, Carin recounted the story and pointed out the similarities between that slim tool of wood and the thin veneer which wrapped the bottle.

"Is this the way of it, then?" Welwyn responded with slow thoughtfulness. "The creature persuaded your mother to write her 'message in a bottle'" — the monk nodded at the container Carin still held — "and then the sprite took pains to wrap the bottle in its own handiwork. Why? For what purpose? To send you a message of its own?"

Carin shrugged. "Maybe. Or maybe it thought the wrapper would help the bottle find me."

She dropped the object and pushed back her chair. "I had hoped the woodsprite would be content in its earthly home among the trees. I wanted the creature to forget me." Getting to her feet, Carin added, "Clearly, it hasn't. Now if you will excuse me, gentlemen, I'm going to bed."

* * *

They were halfway along their return journey to the manor, by a different route than they'd followed to the coast, when Nina came running to Verek, piping in her girlish voice, "Come quickly, Papa! Aunt Meg wishes to speak with you."

The travelers had spent the night in a tiny hamlet, in one of the most secluded lodgings they'd enjoyed during their weeks on the road. The guesthouse was small but neat, the beds comfortable, and the meals flavorful with sun-ripened vegetables from the house's garden. A wishing-well stood in the midst of the garden, separating the vegetable patch from the flowerbeds under the house's windows. Fresh-cut flowers brightened the dining table, the bedchambers, even the immaculately clean outdoor privy.

Carin found the place enchanting. And their host and hostess, the house's owners, seemed rapturous with the pleasure of welcoming Lord Verek, his exotic wife, and Verek's young heirs.

The proprietors were perhaps less thrilled to house the odd fellow who wore a monk's robes but had nothing of a monk's demeanor about him. Carin could almost see the thought form in the mind of their hostess: "That old reprobate is no more a man of Drisha than I am the queen of a castle."

Madam, you'd be surprised, Carin thought, knowing of Welwyn's fondness for his former monastery and his genuine embrace of its teachings. But she said nothing to the woman.

After a night's rest, the travelers were up early but in no great hurry to be on their way. Carin and Verek lingered over a breakfast of cheese, bread, and sweet slices of muskmelon. Welwyn, whose moist eyes missed little, took his brown-robed self to the garden to chuckle over the questions he'd clearly raised in his hosts' minds. The children were with him in the garden, romping in the morning sun.

Sated with cheese and fruit, Carin walked with Verek to the stableyard to begin saddling their horses and securing their packs. They hadn't quite finished their preparations to leave, when Nina came skipping up with her message for Verek.

"Aunt Meg wants you, Papa," the child said, taking her father's hand and tugging at him. "She's in the wishing-well."

Startled by this assertion, the *wysard* went where his daughter led. Carin followed. Welwyn joined her as she stepped past the flowerbeds, and together they arrived on Verek's heels at the stone-rimmed well that was set amid blooms and fruiting vines. Carin, Verek, and the monk peered over the well-curb … and Megella's face peered back.

"Speak nothing," the wisewoman ordered. "Time is short and my message urgent. *I saw her.* In the blue room's springwater pool. Her face appeared for an instant only, but it was *her.* Come home. There is danger."

The final word was barely said when Megella's face winked out. Carin stood frozen alongside Verek and Welwyn, each of them leaning over the well's rim, staring into the featureless depths. Only a glint of reflected sun now showed on the surface of the water down in the well.

Nina—too short to join her elders in peering over the well-curb—had seen nothing. But the girl heard every word of Megella's message. Now she burst with questions: "Aunt Meg has a blue room? I've never seen it. Where is it? What's a sing-water pool? Who did she see? Can I look? Are we going home?"

The child's tumbling words roused Carin from immobility. She stepped back from the well and scooped Nina into her arms.

"Yes, darling one," she murmured. "We're going home now."

From that morning, Verek gave up parading his offspring on an easy, meandering course through the countryside. He set the fastest pace that could be sustained by two young children on ponies and a portly monk who rode a sturdy but not swift horse. Carin brought up the rear, ever ready to shout "Wait!" when Verek pulled too far ahead of his family cavalcade.

All were exhausted when, several evenings later, they reached the gates of home and clattered into the courtyard. Verek sprang from the saddle, tossed his horse's reins to the stableboy who had replaced the ill-fated Lanse, and rushed into the house to consult Megella.

Carin tarried in the yard to supervise the unloading of their packs and satchels. It was swiftly done; they had traveled light, knowing they would find lodgings and good meals along their route. Ruain was a prosperous realm where people did not go hungry. In every corner of the land, Verek was welcomed, for he treated his people with consideration and respect, and in return he had the respect and loyalty of his subjects.

Indeed, from what Carin had seen on her journeys across Ruain at his side, Verek had his people's love. Certainly his children did. On their best behavior *almost* everywhere—*More a credit to Welwyn than to their mother*, Carin thought, with nothing but gratitude in her heart for the monk's influence—Nina and Galen had charmed everyone they'd met.

Now the children were asleep on their feet. Carin scooped up Galen; Welwyn lifted Nina in his arms. They carried the pair up to the youngsters' beds in the master wing. Carin kissed the brow of each sleeping child, then left Welwyn to unpack his bags and the children's satchels.

Descending to the kitchen, Carin took a moment to greet Myra.

"Oh my, dearie!" the housekeeper exclaimed. "So glad I am to have you home. I'll not say a word against she who claims me for her sister. Proud I am, to call her my kin. But she's not one for chatting 'round the kitchen table, and these last few days she's been positively *fierce*. I am half afraid of her when she falls into a mood of such grimness as has seized her this week."

Carin made soothing noises but was too preoccupied to attend to Myra's chatter. Getting the housekeeper's confirmation that Verek and Megella were in the library, Carin slipped down the hallway and pushed open its heavy door.

She entered the half-lit room to hear Megella speaking:

"You felt nothing, nephew? No rumor of trouble reached you?"

Carin crossed to the high-backed benches that were paired before the fireplace. She bent to kiss Megella's cheek, then skirted the low table between the benches and sat down beside Verek. Arching her back tiredly, Carin leaned against the cushions and studied her husband's profile, with its straight nose and firm jaw.

He was shaking his head in weary negation.

"Nothing. Tell me: was the greater wellspring disturbed?"

Meg flicked a corner of her shawl, a gesture of uncertainty. "Not that I saw. After *she* vanished from the pool upstairs, I hurried to the cavern—shaking like a leaf, I am not ashamed to say—but I could see no sign that the greater of the pools had been disquieted."

Carin interjected a question. "How did you come to be in the bathing room upstairs? I thought those doors were locked."

Verek, turning to her, answered for his aunt. "I removed the locks and spells shortly before we left home that morning. It was my wish that Megella sleep in the blue room, where she might take note of turmoil in either of the pools. As I remember, *fileen*," Theil added, smiling at Carin a bit crookedly, "when you occupied the blue bedchamber you could clearly sense upheaval deep in the vault of wizardry."

Carin nodded, recalling the times she had been drawn down the upper-story hallway and down the paneled staircase to witness tumults in the enchanted pool belowground.

Turning back to Meg, Carin asked, "What did *she* look like? I've only seen her the one time, and to me she seemed strangely young. That was an illusion, I believe."

Megella grimaced. "Aye, widgeon. She was a vain enchantress when I knew her — or knew of her. I can well imagine, that however much she had aged over time, there in her mountain fastness, she would assume a young face ... for as long as she could sustain the trickery."

Meg looked from Carin to Verek. "But in the springwater pool, nephew, I saw a hag. Oh, it was *her* — I've no doubt of that. Same eyes, same brow as yourself. And her hair, though dull and tangled as a cap of thorns, was as crow-black as yours. I recognized her straightaway, despite the ruin of her face."

"I count that a hopeful sign," Verek said, sitting up straighter and staring at Megella. "If she no longer has the power of glamour, and may cast only her true guise — and *that*, only as an image without substance in the dormant pool upstairs, without disturbing the well of wizardry in the rock below us — then perhaps she lacks the power to return. Perhaps Welwyn and I together may secure the upstairs pool with spells enough to stop even her spectral castings. Then we need no longer trouble ourselves about her."

Carin listened, skeptical, watching Verek as he spoke.

It won't be that easy, she thought. *And I expect he knows it.*

Even so, Carin would have him make an immediate start on his impregnable spellwork, for quite a different reason.

"Theil, I know you must be tired," she murmured. "We've had a long, exhausting journey. But for Nina's sake, please restore the locks on the blue room — and do it tonight, before you sleep."

Carin turned to Megella. "Aunt, you must never mention the blue bedroom or its springwater pool to Nina. Theil and I have been at pains to keep the pool's existence secret from the child, for fear of the havoc a budding magician might wreak with the virgin power in that pool." Carin shot Meg a meaningful look, and saw understanding in the wisewoman's eyes — understanding tinged with a touch of terror.

"Unhappily for all of us," Carin continued, "Nina heard every word of your message to Theil in the wishing-well. The girl has plied me with questions about it, and I've answered her with lies. I've told her, that in your cottage at Fintan, you have a room done up in every shade of blue. I've explained away the pool as nothing but the bucket in which you fetch water. I've said the face that you saw is your own face, your reflection in the bucket."

Beside her, Verek snorted. "And our daughter believes no word of it, I'll wager. The child is quick to know pretense."

With a tired sigh, Carin nodded and said no more, only looked at him with sympathy.

"Yes, I see the need, my wife," Verek muttered, and got to his feet. Looking across at Megella, he added, "I fear I must turn you out of the blue bedchamber, Aunt, and at once. Will you come and collect your belongings?"

With a small, soft grunt, Megella hoisted herself up. The wisewoman had gained weight, Carin noted, during these weeks when she had been eating every meal at Myra's table. The woman patted Carin's shoulder as she passed, and followed Verek out of the library.

Voices reached Carin from the hallway beyond the door, the sounds of greetings exchanged in passing. Then Welwyn entered the room.

"Good evening, my lady," the monk rumbled as he approached the fireplace and took the seat Megella had vacated a moment before. "I am surprised to see you awake. It has been a long day."

Carin shrugged. "I would say the same to you, Master Welwyn. I think your day has been longer than mine, shepherding those hellions who give you no peace."

He chuckled. "Wonder of wonders, we may finally have discovered a way to wear them out: Take them across Ruain, then bring them back at the breakneck pace your husband set for our return." Welwyn rubbed his neck muscles and winced. "The children are sound asleep, and I shall soon be seeking my pillow as well. But first, I would hear what news you may have of the uproar which occasioned our hasty homecoming."

Carin nodded. Briefly she repeated Megella's account of the face in the water, and she gave the monk Verek's assessment of the threat the manifestation might, or might not, pose.

"I'm sure he doesn't think that demon is harmless," Carin added, "even if she appears unable—at present—to do more than project her face. Theil and I have seen her raise magic far stronger than that. Long before Meg glimpsed her in the upstairs pool, the witch drove the *wysards'* waters below us into a frenzy."

Welwyn tipped his head, his look thoughtful. "Certainly we must not underestimate the necromancer. But in some regards, I am as sanguine as Theil. Remember: You and he drove her from her mountain stronghold. She no longer stands in her own corrupted pool of power. Your dragon forced her to flee."

"To where?" Carin muttered. "I'd give much to know."

"Would we all," Welwyn said. "But one thing we may safely surmise, based on what knowledge we have: She was much diminished by her encounter with your dragon. Perhaps injured."

Carin shrugged again. "There was no blood in the water."

"Ah. But a worker of wizardry may sustain injuries far worse than any physical wound. I think her panicked flight from your dragon drained her of strength. Wherever she washed up, she was vastly degraded in power. It has taken all these years for her to recover enough to cast her shadow, once again, over the life and the loves of Theil Verek."

"Damn her," Carin snapped. "How I wish the Jabberwock had torn out that fiend's heart."

Welwyn stretched wearily. "This world—and every other—would be the better for it, had she not escaped your dragon's jaws." He smiled and added, "But if wishes were horses, paupers would ride. We must face the situation as it is, not as we would wish it."

"That's exactly why we cannot lower our guards," Carin flamed. "By all means, shut the springwater pool behind every spell that you and Theil can weave. But in my heart I believe more will be needed to safeguard the children of House Verek from that monster."

The next time I meet the witch, Carin added silently, *I will kill her. As Drisha and the Powers are my witnesses, I will cross the cosmos if I must, and pursue her in the fires of farsinchia, to keep her from taking my babies as she took Aidan.*

Behind Carin, in the library's shadowed recesses, the room's spell-shrouded second door creaked open, admitting Verek and interrupting her thoughts.

"The blue bedchamber and its pool are secured, at least for this night," he said to Carin, nodding at Welwyn as he reseated himself beside her. "Mistress Megella has moved to a room near the children. As she passed by their doors, she looked in on them, for your talk of Nina's curiosity about the pool made her uneasy."

"How did she find them?" Carin asked.

"Oblivious, seemingly. Galen was in the land of dreams." Verek arched one eyebrow. "But Megella could not swear that our Nina slumbered. She half suspected the child was feigning sleep."

"That is worrisome," Welwyn exclaimed, leaning forward, claiming their attention. "Now that I have you both together, I will tell you of your daughter's new and profound — nay, *obsessive* — love for the sea. On our way eastward many weeks ago, both Nina and Galen attended to all that I taught them about the terrain through which we passed. Fascinated they were, by their first glimpses of Ruain's snow-fed rivers and vast forests, its farms and rolling fields."

The monk leaned back again, and with a shake of his head, he continued. "On our return journey, however, Nina would talk to me of nothing but the ocean. She refused my every attempt to redirect her thoughts. Her questions poured forth, about waves and *dolphyns* and the strange, small creatures she had glimpsed in a tidal pool."

Carin looked at him, uncomprehending. "Why is that worrisome, Master Welwyn? Isn't it natural that a child would be captivated by her first experience of the ocean? Water is Nina's element, after all."

"Indeed it is," Welwyn rejoined. "Just as it is yours, my lady. But riding ahead with your husband — as was your wont before you fell back to harry us stragglers when our return became a race — you did not see the longing glances Nina threw over her shoulder as we turned westward and left the seacoast behind us. You did not hear how the girl dwelled ceaselessly upon maritime themes as I took the children aside for their lessons. And you did not hear the promise the girl made to herself — under her breath, as she thought — that she would run away from home and return to the ocean, the first chance she got."

"Beggar it," Carin swore.

"Drisha's teeth!" Verek erupted. "Am I to get no rest tonight?"

He turned to Carin with a look almost despairing. "Do not wait up for me. I will be late to bed. Every spell I have cast upon the blue room's threshold, I must now repeat at the main gates and the postern door." He shook his head. "We may be obliged, at some point, to chain that child to her bed."

With a groan, Verek banged his half-empty *dhera* glass down on the table. He gave Carin a quick, distracted kiss, stood, and strode from the room.

For a few minutes then, silence reigned in the library except for the crackling of the fire. Carin and Welwyn sat in tired but companionable stillness, each thinking their own thoughts ... Carin reflecting on her friendship with the woodsprite, which had made up in intensity for what it lacked in duration. She'd thought of the sprite often since receiving its wood-wrapped bottle.

She stirred, and turned to the monk.

"Master Welwyn, I have wondered ... What became of Lanse? I cannot imagine that he survived such a wound as the woodsprite dealt him—speared through the gut with a tree branch. But these past few years, Theil has never so much as mentioned the boy's name to me."

And I've never asked him, Carin silently reproached herself, before adding aloud: "I don't even know where Lanse is buried."

"Oho!" the monk exclaimed, and lowered his *dhera* glass to peer at her. "I thought you lovebirds told each other everything." Welwyn took a quick sip of his drink, then cradled his glass in both hands. "Though it may astonish you to hear it, the boy did indeed survive. Remember, my dear, that Lanse had three super-lative healers attending him—Mistress Megella and myself, aided by your lord to the extent Verek was able, distracted as the man was by your absconding. We took it in turns to tend Lanse night and day. The boy's recovery was long and painful ... and ultimately incomplete."

Welwyn sighed, then added, "The blood loss had proved too great. Lanse's heart and brain were starved. When finally the boy could leave his bed, he had little of his former strength. And his mind ... near lost. Half-witted he'd become, where once he had been, perhaps, overly imaginative."

The monk shot Carin a glance, and she knew to what Welwyn alluded. In Lanse's mind and heart, boyish resentment had darkened to such a twisted hatred of Carin that the boy had tried, at least twice, to murder her. And twice the woodsprite had saved Carin from him, using tree branches as weapons.

You owe that creature your life, and how did you repay the debt? she asked herself, hiding her thoughts behind her *dhera* glass from the monk's keen eyes. *You marooned it beyond the void.*

But the sprite had seemed happy enough to be left on that deserted island of Earth, Carin reminded herself, recalling the creature's excitement upon discovering the sentience of the island's trees and seeking to converse with them.

Throwing off her musings, Carin looked back at Welwyn. "Then where *is* Lanse? What have you done with him?"

"I've given him a home of safety and comfort," the monk said a little sharply, as if he'd heard a note of accusation in Carin's question.

"I'm glad," she said, and smiled to mollify him. "If I may ask ... where?"

Welwyn reached for the decanter on the low table between them and refilled his glass. Leaning back, relaxed once more, he replied. "I took the boy to my old monastery at Cardan. It was long before Lanse's flesh knit together enough that he could travel, and I myself was content to remain here as the boy recovered ... and while your man watched, half-demented, for your return."

This reminder of the pain she had inflicted on Theil made Carin flinch. But in truth she could feel no real guilt about hurting him, because she had done what she must. *"Take it away!"* the voice of Power had commanded her. Without hesitation, Carin had obeyed, leaping into the void to save this world that had become her home.

"I was disappointed, Master Welwyn," Carin said, smiling at him again, "that you weren't here when I eventually got back. I'd wanted you to administer our marriage vows."

"That, my dear, is among the great regrets of my life, don't you know," Welwyn exclaimed. For a moment he looked sad, then shot her a mischievous grin. "Are you, indeed, a lawfully married woman? Or only Theil's favored mistress still."

She laughed. "I went to my wedding nursing his baby daughter and ripening with his new son. But yes, Master Welwyn, we satisfied the civil authorities. Theil got the chief magistrate down from Fintan to marry us. Meg and Myra were witnesses for me, and our nearest neighbor, Cian Ronnat, and Ronnat's eldest son stood up with Theil. Theirs is the place with all the horses, you may remember."

Welwyn beamed. "It is good and right that magian folk should observe the customs of the lands in which they dwell. You both signed the magistrate's marriage record, I take it?" When Carin replied that they had done so, the monk went on: "However unlikely a challenge might be in future, to have had your nuptials solemnized will establish your children as Verek's entitled heirs. Theil may live for centuries, my dear, now that you have renewed the wellspring of his strength, but even a wizard cannot live forever. And successions are sometimes contested, don't you know."

Carin frowned at the monk, disturbed by nearly every word of this speech. Could there ever be any question that *her* children would inherit Verek's lands and sovereignties? Was Welwyn suggesting that the foreignness of their mother might make her children unacceptable, in time, to the people of Ruain?

Or was the monk hinting that Verek had other progeny scattered about, by-blows that he'd fathered in the years after Alesia died and before Carin came to him? If Theil had such offspring, he'd never mentioned them to her or acknowledged them publicly. Would any unadmitted bastard offshoot dare to call himself Verek's heir?

Welwyn noticed the effect his words had on her. Indeed, he could hardly miss Carin's sharply indrawn breath, her suddenly clenched fists, and the scowl that tightened her brow.

"Apologies, my dear!" the monk exclaimed. "Pay no attention to the ramblings of an aging *wysard*. I live too much in the past, recalling a time when magic nearly died in this realm … when the gifted ones, outcast, fled to mountain hideaways and lived in obscurity. I remember what it was to be ostracized, and I would not wish any such rejection on any child of this House, or indeed on any youngling of this reborn world."

Welwyn smiled at Carin, then hoisted himself to his feet and raised his glass to her.

"I drink to you, my lady — you who removed the cancer that had withered this world since far-off times. With the resurgence of the Power, even the most aged of the gifted ones are venturing forth again. Apprentices are appearing, eager for instruction in the craft. The masters again have students to whom we may impart the collective knowledge of our kind. You, my lady, have done this old *wysard* the great honor of entrusting to my care the two most powerful apprentices in Ladrehdin. I thank you and esteem you for it."

Welwyn drained his glass and bent to set it on the table. "Now, my dear, I will bid you good-night and look in on those hellions. Both are glad enough, I think, to be back in their own beds, for now at least. But as Megella would remind me, he who aspires to govern those scamps must be ever watchful."

The *wysard* surprised Carin then by bowing to her — a formal courtesy Welwyn had never extended to her before. Turning, he stepped to the library door and was gone.

Carin lingered awhile, alone with her thoughts, watching the fire dwindle on the hearth. When she went up to bed, she found the room empty, but Verek came in only minutes after she'd slipped between the sheets.

She listened to him bathe, as she had done, in the waterfall that streamed down the stonework at the room's far end, beyond the arched opening which separated the bathing alcove from the bedchamber. When Verek slid into bed beside her, Carin flung her arms around him, feeling his hair damp against her face and his naked body radiating warmth from the cascade of the hot spring.

"You're awake," he whispered. "Good."

"We're alone," she whispered back. "Even better."

She pressed against him, fire rippling along her nerves. As tired as they both were from riding the length of Ruain and back, here in the privacy of their bedchamber — separated from the rest of the household — they were free in a way they had not been for weeks of travel alongside Welwyn and the children.

Verek's hands traced Carin's contours, his caresses losing their gentleness and betraying the iron in his grip as she kissed him, hungry for him. Sensations built to a deep, searing pleasure that was carried beyond the carnal by the wizardry of them both. In the marriage bed of two servants of the Power, passions eclipsed what mortal flesh could know.

It was long before they drew apart, spent, each gasping for breath. They lay side by side, silent for a time.

When eventually Carin could speak again, she raised on one elbow and asked him bluntly but in a whisper: "Theil, do you have other children? I'm sure you didn't sleep in an empty bed every night of those years when you were alone. But did your seed bear fruit?"

Carin felt him reach for her in the dark beneath the canopy of the four-poster bed. Verek pulled her head against the hard muscles of his chest and muttered, "What a question, *fileen!* Surely you can't be jealous? You know I love you more than life." He stroked her hair, and fell silent. The beat of his heart pulsed strongly in her ear, evoking in her memory the times of risk and pain he'd endured in his love for her.

After a moment he stirred again, and answered her. "Following Alesia's death, I did take comfort where I could. In that, you guess aright.

"But I think, my lady," he added, "that you have forgotten what manner of man you married. Have you not ample proof that I possess a mastery of herb-lore? It is a simple matter, to one who has such knowledge as I, to ensure that I cannot seed your womb when I do not wish to do so — no matter how vigorous our strivings in that regard." Carin heard the satisfied smile in Theil's voice, and felt his arms tighten around her. "You may be certain — as I am — that in the years after Alesia, and before *you* came to bewitch me, I got no woman with child. Karenina is my only daughter, and Galen my only living son."

Carin could think of nothing more to say, other than a soft, "Thank you, my love." She raised her lips to his and kissed him. They fell asleep in each other's arms.

Chapter 5

Forbidden Sorcery

In the latter days of summer after their return home, life for all the household went on much as before, but with newly instituted precautions against renegade children. Megella returned to Fintan to do up her cottage in every shade of blue, so as to be ready to intercept a runaway child, at need. "Fintan lies on the girl's most likely route between Weyrrock and the coast," Meg pointed out. "If Nina gets past you, she shall not elude me."

Even so, every adult in Nina's life was enlisted to keep watch over the girl, including the scullery and chamber maids who had been retained to help Myra with the work of an expanded household. The stableman was warned to never let Nina take out a horse unaccompanied. The gardener was instructed to trail her around the grounds—unobtrusively, if he could—whenever the child was out-of-doors without her tutor.

That seldom happened, for Welwyn preferred an open-air setting for leading his pupils through their daily lessons. He kept both children occupied from sunrise to dusk, but attended especially to Nina, letting the would-be truant know that his eye was on her.

While her hellions learned at Welwyn's knee, Carin bent to her own studies in Verek's library. She had read scores of books by now, but hungered for greater knowledge still. In the years of her marriage she had learned the history of Ruain and its ruling family. She had vastly increased her mastery of the common tongue of Ladrehdin. And she had learned much about the customs of her adopted world, including its established system of fosterage.

In this, Carin found a ready explanation for Verek's embrace of Welwyn's offer to tutor their children. In ages past, both Nina and Galen would have been sent away as apprentices to master magicians, with Verek and Carin expected, in their turn, to train other promising young adepts.

But master magicians—and gifted apprentices—were far less numerous in Ladrehdin now. And though Carin hated the circumstances—the parasitism—that had reduced the *wysards'* numbers, she was relieved beyond measure that her children would not be sent away. Instead, Welwyn had come to them. She loved him for it.

And she valued Welwyn's guidance of her own studies. Verek had been Carin's first teacher, when she was an awkward, ill-at-ease, but resolute "little wretch," as he had called her then ... not without cause.

Time and experience, however—and repeated trips through the void—had remade her. In every important way, Carin was now Verek's equal. From time to time, Theil would offer her his counsel still, but he just as readily accepted her advice to him. He willingly answered Carin's questions, and directed her to the books from which she could learn more.

But on no account would Verek lecture her, as he might once have done. Theil had seen Carin cast aside his own powerful magic as if it were cobwebs. He had watched her conjure a dragon, then leap into nothingness, and against all odds make her way back to him ... having saved his world while she was wandering somewhere "out there"—as all of Ladrehdin's surviving *wysards* now knew.

No, Lord Verek would not presume to treat his otherworldly wife as anything less than coequal. They left the tutoring to Welwyn, an arrangement that suited them all.

Verek's days were full enough, in any event, that he need not add the mantle of teacher to his duties. On a morning weeks after their return from the coast, the sun had barely risen when Carin entered the library to find Verek at the desk under the windows. Before him on the age-darkened wood of the desktop was a stack of letters and messages, sent by the stewards and magistrates who managed the day-to-day affairs of his realm.

As Carin entered, Verek pushed back his chair and swung around to greet her.

"Good morning, my lady. Would you have the desk?" He gestured at the papers. "This is dull reading. I will gladly abandon it if you desire to work here."

Carin smiled, and shook her head. "Thank you, sir, but no. I have something else to ask of you." For a moment she gazed out the windows at the neatly kept but unimaginative gardens beyond.

This groundsman is no Jerold, Carin thought with a little pang of grief. She missed the old gardener-*wysard*'s scowling face and gruff voice.

Turning back to her husband, Carin posed her question. "Did you destroy the bottle with the message from my parents?"

"Certainly not," Verek answered almost sharply. "What right would I have to do that?"

"Every right," Carin murmured. She added more audibly, "If it's here, may I see it?"

"Of course." Verek rose and walked to the small cabinet that was set among the bookshelves. From it he removed a flagon of *dhera* and four crystal goblets and set them aside. Reaching deep, Verek gave a sharp tug and pulled free the narrow slat that sealed the hiding place behind the cabinet. From down inside that cavity, he brought out the wood-bound bottle which the *dolphyn* had flung to Carin in the sea of easternmost Ruain.

She took it from Verek's hand, and stepping to the window held it to the morning light, studying the thin, pliable veneer that wrapped the bottle. The wood was lightly scratched, bearing such scars as might well mark an object that had traveled as it had—across the void, to become a dolphin's plaything. But the veneer bore no marks suggestive of writing.

Resourceful though the woodsprite had proved itself to be, it evidently had not yet learned to inscribe words. *Or,* Carin thought, *it had no more to say to me than is conveyed in this wrapper alone.*

Shifting her examination from the wooden layer to the glass of the bottle itself, Carin angled it to catch sunlight in the bottle's neck. In color, the glass was a rich red. Light glowed within it as in a precious ruby gemstone.

Carin's breath caught. She turned to Verek, feeling her eyes widen as she looked at him.

He'd moved to join her at the window. For a moment Verek's gaze was on the bottle in Carin's hand. Then he looked into her eyes.

"Do you remember?"

Carin returned his steady gaze, getting a bit lost in Verek's darkly brilliant eyes, as she always did when he looked at her with such intensity. But somewhere in the far recesses of her mind, a memory was struggling to surface. For moments, it eluded her. It remained just out of sight, clouded by time, distance, and the odd jumbling that plagued too many moments of Carin's recollections.

But then she glimpsed it.

"Those things the necromancer had on her dreadful little altar ... the black orb, the brooch like a green-leafed vine, that little shred of bark ..." Carin paused. She had handled all those things, had endured the peril of them all. Standing now with Verek in the safety of his library, Carin felt again in her hands the textures of those alien artifacts. Not one of them had been natural to this world.

The necromancer's collection, however, had included a single amulet that did belong here: the water-lily pin with its delicate white flower ... such a beautiful thing to have been so deadly. For the pin was the means by which the necromancer had murdered Verek's Alesia and Aidan.

Pushing those thoughts aside, Carin refocused her inner gaze, struggling to remember every object the necromancer had displayed. The altar had risen in rows or tiers … the hideous black orb topmost, in pride of place … the next level holding brooch, pin, strip of bark, and a silver neck-chain bearing two crystal pendants …

Below that was a third level on which rested a miscellany of objects, none of them memorable save for one small, bright, bejeweled—

"Ruby bottle!"

Carin nearly shouted the words as a sliver of memory moved sharply within her. "Oh sweet Drisha. Theil, she had a ruby-red bottle in her hand. Am I remembering this right? This color?" Carin held up the wood-wrapped vessel.

Verek closed his eyes, breaking the gaze by which he had held Carin almost spellbound. He nodded.

"Yes. I was not certain you would recall it, for you stood somewhat apart that day, mercifully dismissed by that proud enchantress." Verek opened his eyes, and with the back of one finger, he stroked Carin's cheek. "Thank the Powers she ignored you, *fileen*. But watching her sidelong, you could have had no such immediate view, as I did, of her talismans."

Verek all but shuddered, and Carin knew he was reliving the pain and horror of his confrontation with the sorceress who had attempted to destroy him.

"Did … ," Carin began, then paused anew, searching her broken memories for the moment when the Jabberwock answered her summons and slashed at the necromancer with its scimitar claws. In that instant, however, Carin had been trying to see everything at once: her dragon, its intended prey … and Verek, who then lay injured on the flagstones out away from the witch's pool, his face twisted in pain.

Try as she might, Carin could not clearly picture the dragon's talons sweeping the necromancer out of the pool. In her mind, it was a fragmented blur. Her most vivid memory was of Verek, hurt, but laughing almost maniacally as he watched Carin's dragon fall upon the demoness who had killed his family. In that moment, Carin had at last known her own heart: She loved him.

And she had avenged him. Or so they'd both thought.

But time had proved them wrong: the necromancer lived.

Carin shook her head. "I can't remember all of it, Theil. The dragon had her … then she was gone. No blood in the water meant she'd been swallowed whole, or so I thought at the time." Carin frowned. "Did she … are you sure … did she still have the ruby bottle in her hand when she disappeared?"

Verek also frowned, wearing an uncharacteristic look of uncertainty on his face. "I did not see. But consider: Was the bottle anywhere on that high pavilion after the witch vanished? In color, the thing would have dazzled against those sickly flagstones. Was it there?"

Carin tipped her head, invoking another shard of memory. "No, it wasn't. I walked across that strange floor, packing up the amulets I had to take and the ones you would carry, and then getting you safely away and collecting the woodsprite. I would have seen it on the flagstones or on her altar.

"But," Carin added with a shrug, "the witch could have dropped it in the pool. In that bubbling vat of acid, the bottle would have disappeared. And probably been destroyed."

Verek rubbed his jaw with his thumb. "True." He paused, then said: "But there remains the possibility that the witch held it locked in her fingers as the dragon attacked. Indeed, I count it a *probability*, given what you and I and Megella have witnessed. The amulet was the means by which she made her escape."

Crossing the void to my homeworld, Carin concluded silently. *That's what you're getting at. That's where your thoughts have gone, and sent mine.*

Then: "Drisha!" she exclaimed. "Is it *this* bottle?" Carin hooked her fingernail under an edge of the veneer and started to peel it off.

Verek stopped her. "No. This bottle is of a different shape. I recall the witch's amulet was smaller, more delicate, more rounded in form. And were you to strip the shell from the bottle you hold, my lady, you would find no gemstones encrusting the glass. Press your fingers to the wood. Feel how thin and supple it is. Feel the smoothness of the glass beneath it." As Carin did what he suggested, Verek continued: "I distinctly remember the witch's amulet was bejeweled. This object has borne no such ornamentation."

The wrapper was almost paper-thin. Carin's fingertips told her Verek was right. Even if the jewels had been pried from the glass before the sprite veneered the bottle, traces of their settings would remain. She would have felt some roughness, but under her fingers there was only glassy evenness.

Carin gave a sigh of relief. "I couldn't think how the witch's bottle might have held a letter from my parents—with the sprite's message wrapped around it—unless they'd all three fallen under the demon's spell. Thank the Powers this isn't the same bottle." She paused, her head atilt as she held the object to the window for another look at the only part of the glass that could be clearly seen, the neck. The morning sun turned its red to rubies.

"But, Theil," Carin asked, "can you remember *this* color so exactly, that you will say *her* bottle and this one must share a common origin?"

"I can." Verek answered without hesitation. "The witch waved her trinket in my face as she tried to tempt me into her perversions." He grimaced at the memory. "Even then, absorbed as I was in the perils of the moment, I could not help but note the bottle's striking hue. To my knowledge—and Welwyn agrees with me—no glassmaker in the whole of Ladrehdin has ever known the secret of such a brilliant red."

Carin had held the bottle in the sun for so long, it was feeling hot in her hand. She lowered it and said, "Then when you saw the color again, in the dolphin's 'toy,' you knew it at once."

"I did."

Carin turned from the window to study Verek as her thoughts moved back to that day on Ruain's coast, when the dolphin had flung the object to her. "Why didn't you say something at the time?"

Verek took the bottle from her and held it back to the light. He met her gaze.

"Because I did not want to influence your memories. I wished to see what the color might mean to you ... what it might call to your mind." He paused, then added, "I have never been certain what you saw that day, or how much you remember of the necromancer's attempts to seduce me."

"I'm not certain, either," Carin admitted. "Thinking back— or trying to, when so much of it just jumbles up in my brain—I can picture the place ... poison bubbling in the pool, and a yellowish pallor in the flagstones, like ... like death approaching."

She caught a sudden snippet of memory: Long ago in Granger, she had watched with Megella at the deathbed of an old woman. As the end neared, the crone's skin had turned a pallid yellow ... exactly the shade of the paving stones on the necromancer's pavilion.

With a shudder, Carin took her mind's eye off the images of death and refocused on the murderess who had escaped justice. "I can still see the gown she wore, and the throne she conjured for herself." Carin reached for Verek's free hand. "But what I most clearly remember is what I *felt* in that woman's presence." Sensations welled up in her, and she hunted for the words to describe them. "The witch seemed to send out waves that beat at me … a surge of cold and darkness … a flood of brutality and malice."

She shivered. Still holding Verek's hand, Carin pulled him away from the windows and to the benches at the fireplace. As they seated themselves, she added:

"I've been meaning to ask, and this seems like a good time: Exactly what kind of 'necromancy' does that witch practice? I've been reading about communing with the dead, but what I've read doesn't match what I saw—or felt—that day. She's doing something much worse than ritual necromancy, isn't she?"

Verek looked almost ill. Slowly, he nodded.

"Merely conjuring spirits to seek knowledge of the future— as if the dead could know aught of what awaits the living!—even that dark art would be benign compared to the particular species of malefic sorcery the demoness practices." Verek shook his head. "I call her a necromancer and a *daēva,* only because I have no right word for the evil that she does. You will get no clear explanation from me, my lady. No book in this library delves deeply into the foul arts of death … her singular way of empowering herself."

Verek swept his arm up and around, indicating the vast collection that surrounded them.

"You know that my forebears built this library over many long ages. It contains books that are now found nowhere else in this world … writings dating to ancient times before *wysards* arose and learned the craft of magic. But never in all those thousands of years did any of my ancestors allow the practice of such poisoned magic as *she* works."

Oh, Theil, Carin thought, looking at him with sympathy for what he knew but never spoke aloud, or perhaps found too painful to even acknowledge privately. *How it must tear at your soul, my love, to know that witch is indisputably one of your ancestors.* But if Verek chose to deny it, who was Carin to contradict him?

Keeping her thoughts to herself, she said instead, "But if any books in this room even *touch* on forbidden sorcery that is similar to that woman's demon-craft, I would like to read them. Do you have any?"

Verek sighed. He set the wood-wrapped bottle on the table before him and got to his feet. A heaviness in his movements communicated his reluctance as he trudged to the farthest reaches of the library, to seek among the hidden shelves that lay perpetually in shadow. Carin's former efforts to reorganize the library had ended well before she'd ventured into those gloomy depths. Even now, she seldom went in there.

Presently, Verek returned to the sunlit side of the room, bearing in his arms six large volumes. Four, bound in chalky brown or faded black leather, looked sullen, as if resentful of being woken and desiring only to return to their long sleep. But another, wrapped in a venomous shade of green, and the last, its binding the red of heart's blood, seemed to demand attention, and to scream warnings. Verek stacked the six on the table between the benches, then retook his seat.

"During the years of my apprenticeship," he said, staring at the books with distaste, "he who was both my grandfather and my master let me nowhere near those volumes. After Lord Legary was gone and I sought out the books for myself, I found I had no stomach for the tales they tell."

Verek raised his eyes and sought Carin's. She felt riveted in place by the force of his gaze.

"Be warned," Verek murmured. "Many have said that knowledge is power. And I know you, *fileen*. I know you are seeking for any knowledge that may give you power over *her*. But to learn of the matters which are treated in these volumes is to risk your soul's tranquility." He pointed at the books. "If what you read in those pages is too unsettling, then I urge you to set the books aside and seek Welwyn's counsel. I believe he can tell you as much as you need to know … while sparing you the ghastly particulars."

Verek held Carin's gaze a moment longer, then stood.

"By your leave, my lady," he said, smiling at her a bit crookedly. "I must now depart and tend to the business of horses. The stableman says I'd be fool if I don't buy the warmblood he spied in Fintan."

Carin laughed. "That man most certainly did *not* call you a fool. Unless he himself is one! I think, however, that Hollis knows as well as I do what would happen if he spoke to you in that manner."

Verek gave a half nod of acknowledgment. "Perhaps I do not convey the man's words precisely. But behind his words, Hollis made his meaning clear. If he feels so strongly about the beast, then I must go and look. In his time here, the fellow has proved himself to be a good judge of horseflesh."

Theil took his leave of Carin with a kiss.

When the library door had closed behind him, Carin picked up the thinnest, and least musty, of the six age-brittle books. She settled with it at the desk. With some trepidation—she seemed to hear the voice of a long-forgotten Drishannic priest whispering in her ear: *"They are undone, who meddle with witchery"*—Carin opened the book and began skimming.

Three hours later, she slapped closed the sixth volume—the bloody red one—and pushed it away as if it were a rotted human head crawling with maggots.

Such *filth*. Perversions beyond anything Carin could have imagined. Grotesque acts of violence and defilement, in the service—supposedly—of gaining knowledge. But in reality, she thought, those who could inflict *this* level of degradation on any being were only greedy for power, not knowledge.

She stood, and though hesitating to touch the books again, Carin spread all six on the desktop so the noontime sun would shine on their covers. Their tooled leather bindings were ancient, flaking and cracked; exposure to sunlight would only damage them further.

Good, she thought. *Let the putrid things fall to pieces.*

Each of the moldy volumes had been more obscene than the last, but for sheer depravity the red one topped them all. Carin could picture a demonic figure propping the book open on his — or her — altar of evil for easy reference while committing the horrors described therein. The book's pages were stained dark with long-dried blood. A smear of tissue that she took to be brain matter half-covered the instructions for extracting the contents of a freshly cleaved skull — with the skull then to be used as a cookpot for boiling the brains with maggot-worms, rooster's entrails, and dead men's fingernails. When cooked with foul incantations over a fire of oak logs, this witches' brew — to be drunk while still hot — would unlock for its maker the secrets of command over dark forces, so the recipe claimed.

Nina and Galen must never see these, Carin thought as she stood back and wrinkled her nose at the stench rising from the sun-baking books. Their bindings, as they warmed, gave off nauseating odors. *If Theil can't bring himself to burn these things, then he must bury them under the farthest of Weyrrock's walls.*

She locked the library's hall door before leaving by the hidden portal that opened to Verek's ground-floor workroom. The library was normally left open for Welwyn's use, and as needed by the young scholars he tutored. But while those loathsome books lay on the desk in full view, Carin would not risk the children coming upon them.

She made her way through the far more aromatic spaces of Verek's workroom and herbarium, and up that room's spiral staircase to their bedchamber. For many minutes she stood under the falling water in the room's bathing alcove, scrubbing so hard, her skin reddened. She held her eyes half open in the warm, fast-flowing stream, wishing she could remove the orbs from their sockets and lather away everything she had seen in those books of foulest sorcery.

Still feeling dirty—and knowing she would feel polluted until she could force her thoughts away from what she had learned—Carin dressed in a crisp white blouse and her favorite trousers, and went down to the kitchen. The children were there with Welwyn and Myra, the youngsters begging the house-keeper for sweet treats, and Myra indulging them.

"Good afternoon, Lady Carin," the monk greeted her. "How goes your day?"

She considered before answering him, and opted for blunt-ness. "It's been a horrible day so far, Master Welwyn. My memories are dark, and my reading repulsive."

The monk eyed her, concerned. "What may I do to help you, my dear?"

"You may meet me in the library this evening, if you will, as soon as the children are settled for the night. I must speak with you."

"I shall be honored, my lady."

Taking the children in hand before Myra spoiled their sup-pers, Welwyn started out the kitchen door with his pupils, but paused on the threshold.

"When my mind is troubled, my dear young woman, I've always found a spot of exercise to be a useful palliative," he said. "Will you join us for an hour of practice with the sling? You are far and away the best of us with that weapon."

Carin seized on his suggestion. To be out in the fresh air was just the thing to oust from her nostrils the lingering reek of those books.

"I'll come at once." Turning, Carin ran back up the stairs to the bedroom. From the chest at the foot of the bed, she took the sling she had made for herself in the days of her south-country servitude. It was the weapon with which she had killed enough rabbits and birds to avoid starvation on her long walk up from the southern plains — only to have it confiscated by an angry *wysard* of the northern woods.

Carin smiled as she recalled the look Verek's face had worn when he'd dug the weapon out of what was then his clothing chest. Almost hesitantly, he'd offered it to her. The occasion had been the day she'd moved into his bedroom, after recovering sufficiently from the birth of their daughter Nina. Carin had not thought the *wysard* was capable of displaying real apprehension, but his expression that day came close. Verek looked like he thought Carin might scratch out his eyes, or worse.

But as he stood braced for the furious reaction he clearly expected, Carin only welcomed the sling as she would an old friend. Then she threw her arms around Verek and kissed him.

"Am I forgiven, *fileen?*" he murmured as he held her close. "I'd no right to take that from you."

"Perhaps you had no right, but you were wise to do so. If you had not, I think I might have killed you with it."

"Precisely my reasoning. I am pleased we agree."

Recalling that moment now, as she rushed downstairs and out the kitchen door, Carin was in much better spirits when she joined Welwyn and the children for their practice.

They stayed at it all afternoon and were still in the courtyard when Verek, accompanied by Hollis, rode in toward dinnertime. The stableman led a muscular gray steed that even Carin's less-practiced eye for horseflesh could see was a breed apart from the saddle mounts housed in Verek's stables. This long-legged gray had a deep girth and powerful hindquarters — it could have been a warhorse. But despite its hefty build, the animal's head was refined, its eyes large and mild, and its neck elegantly arched.

Carin liked the beast immediately. But that was nothing to the children's reactions. Nina and Galen dropped their slings and raced to the newcomer, shrieking like banshees. The horse Hollis rode took fright at their sudden noise and shied. Even Verek's mount jigged sideways before he regained control.

The haltered gray, however, merely swung his head toward the children, watching them run at him with no alarm, only curiosity. He stood foursquare, a large and solid presence with his hooves planted like foundation stones on the ground under him. The horse didn't startle a hairsbreadth when Galen wrapped himself around one pillar-like foreleg, hugging with all his might, or when Nina flung up her hand to pet the animal's muzzle. The horse only blew gently through its nostrils, and regarded the girl with a quiet eye.

"Hallo!" Nina greeted the beast. "What's your name?"

"Ghost," Galen declared from where he stood clinging to a chiseled, silver-gray leg.

"Yes!" Nina agreed. "Like in those stories Master Welwyn is telling us."

Eyebrows raised, Carin rounded on the monk, who had followed from the practice field at a more leisurely pace than the children had left it. As the monk reached her side, she shot him a question. "Ghost stories, Master Welwyn? Give them nightmares, and it's you who will lose sleep. Not me."

The monk chuckled. "Nothing bloodcurdling, my dear. Merely old legends. The western mountains hide many an ancient ruin that is said to be haunted. I may have mentioned a ghost or two in giving your children the history of those places. Some say the mountains speak with the voices of the dead, don't you know."

Carin was mulling a reply when Verek joined them. He'd dismounted, and at Nina's urging he'd lifted both children onto the gray's broad back, Galen behind his big sister.

Standing now with Carin, Verek watched as their daughter directed the horse across the stableyard with nothing but giggled commands and soft pats on the animal's neck. "Remarkably sensible fellow," Verek muttered. "Mild enough for an infant. In

Fintan I wondered, as soon as I bought the creature, what purpose it could possibly serve here. Nina has shown me: it's *her* horse."

Carin bit off a little scream of laughter. "She looks like a minnow on a whale! Oughtn't she to ride something nearer her own size? Her pony, perhaps?"

Verek shook his head.

"Look at them together," he said, lifting his chin toward the riders. "That horse is alert to Nina's every movement, every shifting of her weight, slight as it is. Galen is an absent-minded rider, craning his neck, interested only in seeing familiar places made unfamiliar by viewing them from such a great height. But Nina's every thought is for the animal under her, and for its close attention to her wishes. Rarely have I seen horse and rider bond as immediately as these two have. Mark my words: We'll not keep the girl and that horse apart. He'll carry her farther than we'd like, I'll wager."

The group of onlookers broke up then, Welwyn going to reclaim his charges, and Verek crossing the yard to speak with Hollis about stabling the new beast. Carin drifted back toward the kitchen, musing on the prospect of headstrong Nina mounted on a horse that looked strong enough to carry her halfway across Ruain in a single night.

But then another thought flitted through Carin's ruminations, an unfinished bit of her conversation with Welwyn. *The mountains speak with the voices of the dead,* he had commented.

Before she reached the kitchen's side door, Carin stopped in the twilight, turned, and gazed westward, toward the far-distant mountains, unseeable from Ruain, where Morann's stronghold had been. A fleck of memory, almost as distant, was fighting to come clear. Hadn't Carin herself once heard a dead man's voice echo sternly down from those mountainsides?

Touch him not, Morann.

Yes, that was it. That's what Carin had heard: the voice of a ghost … Lord Legary's ghost.

As Carin recaptured the memory and tucked it away, she thought with a small inward twinge: *Now I'll never be able to hear Nina call her big gray horse 'Ghost' without thinking of the time that I – like a necromancer? – summoned the spirit of a long-dead wizard I never knew.*

Chapter 6

The Arts of Death

"Perishing oaths!" Welwyn exclaimed. "Who's been reading these obscenities?"

With dinner finished and his apprentices asleep, the monk had come to the library to join Verek and Carin for evening drinks. But Welwyn was brought up short by the volumes displayed on the room's desk, their very presence unwholesome as they gave off fumes from their afternoon under the sun.

In answer to Welwyn's question, Verek pointed wordlessly at Carin. She, equally silent, acknowledged her guilt with a short nod.

The monk gaped at her, his mouth working but no sounds issuing. Carin took advantage of Welwyn's momentary speechlessness to find her own voice and turn to Verek.

"Now I would like it if those vile things were forever removed from this house." Verek started to protest, and Carin held up her hand. "I know, husband—they're ancient and rare, probably the only copies left in the world. I merely said I'd *like* to have them removed. I don't actually expect it of you. But I *do* expect you to never allow Nina or Galen near them.

"You'll outlive me, Theil," she rushed to add, making herself ignore the stricken look Verek gave her—his thoughts flying ahead to the day he would be widowed a second time, Carin imagined. "Upon your oath," she continued, relentless, "I want your promise that you'll never let our children see those books."

"I vow it," Verek murmured, gazing at her bleakly.

"Enlighten me," Welwyn broke in, recovering his voice and sounding displeased. "Theil, why have you allowed Lady Carin to see these things?"

"Why? Because she asked," Verek snapped, raising his voice and biting off his words. He turned to glare at the monk, clearly irked by the older man's tone.

"And are you, sir, incapable of saying no?" Welwyn shot back.

Verek crossed his arms and stood with his feet apart and planted, eyeing the monk.

"I have found it unavailing to refuse Carin anything," he grated, speaking through clenched teeth. "She generally does as she pleases, regardless of my wishes."

"That's unfair!" Carin exclaimed, feeling the need to remind these men who were discussing her that she stood in the room with them. "I always listen to you, Theil."

"But you do not always hear me," he growled.

Carin didn't want to argue with him in front of Welwyn, but she couldn't help replying, tartly: "In this case, sir, I wish you *had* refused me. I'll have night-terrors over those revolting books. At least one of them is splattered with the blood and brains of some long-dead sacrifice to sinister magic."

"Is it really?" Welwyn interjected, with interest. "That's history worth seeing, don't you know."

But as the monk turned back toward the volumes on the desk, Verek charged past him and gathered up all six.

"You've seen blood and brains aplenty in your time," he growled at Welwyn. "Ancient stains belong to ancient sins and need no gawkers peering back at them through the ages."

"I wasn't gawking," Carin protested, feeling peevish about this whole "conversation," if such it could be called. And in the look with which Verek answered her grumbled remark—he glowered at her with rising exasperation—Carin saw the danger in letting this "discussion" continue undiverted.

"Please, my lord," she said, softening her voice. She tossed her hair back and almost—not quite—batted her eyelashes at him. "Put them away now." Carin gestured toward the library's shadowed depths. "Return them to the darkness where they belong, before the ugly things have us at each other's throats."

By the time Verek had shelved the books and reappeared in the firelight, Carin had poured glasses of *dhera* for each of them. As Theil sat down beside her, she handed him his drink. He drained half of it in a gulp. Then he took her hand and held it, signaling without words that he had mastered his temper.

Welwyn watched them from the opposite bench, cradling his goblet in his beefy, thick-fingered hands. Both men waited now for Carin to speak. Verek would anticipate a report on her reading, and Welwyn would want to know what had driven her to the folly of perusing those volumes.

Carin swallowed a little *dhera*, then turned to the monk.

"Master Welwyn, I wish to know what kind of sorcery the necromancer practices, and how to defeat it—and her. We will never be free of her while she lives. I believe there's no question that she is attempting to return to Ladrehdin, or perhaps strike at Theil from whatever world she now occupies." Carin shot Verek a glance, knowing her thought must echo his: *The witch dwells in the world of ruby-red glass.*

"I learned little of value in those books of malignant magic," Carin admitted with another quick look Verek's way—this one contrite. "Nothing in them told me how she uses ... or abuses ... the dead. I have seen her vassals, and they are *very* dead."

Welwyn made a strangling noise, and Carin paused to be certain he wasn't choking on his drink. But the monk had set his goblet down and was taking deep breaths, as though to steady himself. After a moment, he focused on Carin, and his look was intense.

"Her vassals, Lady Carin?" Welwyn murmured. "Pray tell me of them. What did you see?"

She shrugged. "Eyes, mainly. That day in her city of ruins, twilight had fallen by the time Theil was safely gone, and I was trying to make the first relic—the wand—take me wherever it would. Anywhere would be better than that sick place of acids and rot." Carin paused, seeming to smell again the odors of decay.

I remember more than I thought I could, she realized as she continued. "The wand didn't work immediately. It left me standing on the rim of the witch's pool long enough that some of the dead things crawling up from below almost grabbed me. As I jumped into the void, I felt something touch my heel." Carin shuddered at the memory.

"I got only a glimpse of those crawling horrors," she added, looking straight at Welwyn. "But what I saw was putrid and maggot-eaten. Those things had not dwelled in the land of the living for a very long time."

A lengthy silence followed Carin's account, broken only by the crackling of the fire. Carin continued to lock gazes with Welwyn, for the old monk seemed as much dazed as appalled. She watched to be sure he wasn't about to pass out.

Welwyn shook himself and dropped his gaze to the flagon of *dhera* that Carin had left on the table. He poured himself another goblet full and drank deeply, grimacing as he swallowed the last of it, seeming to choke it down. Carin had long suspected that the monk had no taste for Verek's tart, slightly sweet liquor, but drank it out of politeness, or when his nerves needed steadying, as now. Setting his goblet down again, Welwyn leaned back. He swore softly at her.

"By the Powers, Lady Carin! That was a close shave." He rubbed his face. "I have known of no other who felt the cold touch of the *daēva*'s servants—and lived to tell of it."

The monk looked at Verek with mingled horror and admiration. "Your lady is made of stern stuff, my friend. Few would have escaped."

Verek had sat silent, holding Carin's hand as she spoke. Now he raised her hand to his lips and kissed it. "You tell me only what I know," Verek muttered, answering Welwyn but looking at Carin. "Without this woman's nerves of steel, as she took charge of me that day and flung me through the void, I would now be as dead and forever lost as the vassals of the necromancer."

Carin returned Verek's look, inflamed by a desire to strip off his clothes and push him down to the cushions, then and there on the bench in front of the fire. Only Welwyn's presence stopped her.

Not now! she ordered herself.

By a wrenching effort of will, she bridled her lust, tore her gaze from Verek's, and turned back to the monk.

"My husband has reminded me, with his mention of that ambiguous word, 'necromancer,' that our foe isn't truly one of that breed," Carin said, speaking briskly, if a little breathlessly, and determined to redirect the discussion to her original question. "Theil advised me to avoid those books on the forbidden arts and ask you instead, Master Welwyn." Carin squeezed Verek's hand. "I'm taking his advice, as I should have done all along, and I'm asking: Can you tell me what the witch is doing with—and to—all that dead and rotted flesh?"

Welwyn looked green. Absently he picked up and sipped his drink, and just as unaware, grimaced at the taste. For a time the monk seemed away in the clouds … working out how to say what he knew of Verek's mother, Carin supposed—with a minimum, she hoped, of the "ghastly particulars" that would sicken her and torture Verek.

Finally the monk put down his goblet and spoke.

"I have only oblique knowledge of her practices, you must understand. Morann comes from a line of sorcerers with whom Ladrehdin's true *wysards* never dealt more than we must. I believe her forebears took great pains, for long ages, to hide their dark inclinations from the larger society of *wysards* who followed the teachings of Archamon.

"But occasionally," Welwyn continued, "whispers would be heard of terrible acts, of atrocities committed on the bodies — living and dead — of innocent villagers. Few witnesses came forward to describe what they had seen. I believe that most who espied the dark deeds did not live to tell of it, or were too terrified to speak, or too unbalanced in their minds by what they had witnessed. Even so, rumors reached me."

Here, the monk paused, gazing at Verek. *Choosing his words carefully,* Carin thought. *I would, in Welwyn's place.*

Seeming to decide on his phrasing, the monk nodded to the *wysard* and spoke directly to him. "Theil, I do not believe your grandfather could have heard the same vague, unsettling rumors that came to my ears. For much of my long life, I have dwelled in the foothills of the western mountains. Morann and her forebears secluded themselves even farther west, choosing high, cold, inaccessible places for their strongholds. It is no marvel that Legary would fail to hear the worst that was said of the witch. I barely heard it, and I was considerably nearer the places where the evil was said to be happening."

Speaking now to both Carin and Verek, the monk went on. "Ruain, as you well know, is peculiar in its isolation from the wider world. News does not travel freely into this place." Welwyn brought his hands together and steepled his fingers. "I cannot believe, Theil, that Legary would have given his son to Morann if he had heard the whispers or known the depths of her corruption."

Verek snorted. "Legary knew enough. Do not try to defend him, Welwyn. I gave up the effort long ago. My grandfather craved the power the necromancer had, and he did not trouble himself overly much to learn where she got it." Theil jerked his hand dismissively, a gesture of annoyed impatience. In clipped and angry tones, he said, "You have strayed from the purpose, sir. Kindly leave off these mawkish attempts to spare my 'feelings,' and answer Carin's question. How does the *daēva* profit from dead flesh?"

Welwyn gave Verek another brief nod, acknowledging Theil's implied permission to speak frankly of his mother, the depraved witch.

The monk turned back to Carin and continued his attempts at explanation.

"As I say, my lady, much of what I ever heard about Morann and her sorcery was merely rumor. And rumor, don't you know, is not the most reliable guide to the truth. Obscuring matters further, those who spread the rumors came largely from the ranks of the ungifted. Mostly the talkers were the family and friends of the ignorant, powerless villagers whom Morann savaged. They hardly had the words to describe what they saw.

"But," Welwyn continued, "from various sources, including a handful of extremely fortunate eyewitnesses—and also, oddly enough you may think, from the scholarly monks of the monastery where I spent some years—I know the basis of Morann's practices ... how she feeds upon the pain of death, drawing power from bodily torment, and from the force that is released with the expiring of life ... the vitality exhaled at the moment of death."

As Welwyn paused, Carin, aghast but intrigued, made a beckoning gesture.

"You'd have more, my lady?" Welwyn held up his hand to stay her. "Then give me a moment, pray, to shape my phrasing. It is not a subject that comes easily to a monk's tongue, don't you know."

He picked up his goblet and swallowed a little warm *dhera*, then fell silent again, staring into the middle distance, seeking words, or perhaps memories. When Welwyn found what he wanted, he refocused on Carin and smiled at her.

"Do you remember, my dear, that time you visited me in my little cabin, there in the glen 'neath the mountains? I believe I mentioned then that I had absconded from my erstwhile monastery with twenty temple scrolls. One of them became a much-read and deeply studied companion during those long winters when snow locked me within four walls."

Welwyn shifted on his bench and stretched his boots toward the fire, as if his feet again felt the chill of those winters. "In that favorite scroll," the monk continued, "an ancient philosopher wrote of death as a part of life—the other side of the coin. He described the circle of life, how it begins with the wonder of birth and ends in the mystery of death. He reasoned that, for the circle to become complete, the forces of life must eventually round back to a new birth.

"However, it is not the notion of re-embodiment that most concerns us here—though I think it has some bearing on the matter, and is not to be dismissed out of hand. But rather, I am thinking more of what my ancient philosopher friend wrote of *pain*. He said the flaming arc of life must end in the pain of death-throes, as it begins with the pangs of child-birth."

Carin gave a little gasp. Welwyn studied her, then nodded.

"Yes, my lady. I expect you vividly recall the pain you endured in giving birth to Nina. Theil has told me of your agonizing labor, and how he feared for you. He trembled at the thought of losing both you and your daughter." The monk sighed. "It is a fate which befalls many a woman in childbed, even those who are expertly midwifed as you were."

Carin raised her goblet and rubbed it against her forehead to ease a sudden twinge. "Without Megella—and Theil—I don't know that I could have stood it. My body felt torn apart."

She paused, remembering, then lowered her glass and tipped her head to the side. "I believe I'm beginning to understand, Master Welwyn. When I was in labor with Nina, I was sweating and shaking, screaming, straining, pushing. Afterward, when Meg laid the baby in my arms, I barely had the strength to hold the child. I felt drained of life. If sorcery could have been worked with the energy I expended that day, I think it would have had the power to move mountains."

"Yes!" the monk exclaimed, pulling in his feet and sitting forward on his bench. "You have it. You've caught my meaning. That's the source the witch and her forebears learned to tap: the hot-blooded, screaming, flaming arc of *life* at its most intense, in the tortures of childbearing and the torments of death. Morann has locked women in weeks-long labor to feed upon the power of their pain—I've no doubt of it, from what the eyewitnesses recounted.

"But primarily," Welwyn added, "the witch draws strength from the agonies of death. Her methods include throat-cutting, disemboweling, the gouging out of eyes, and the slow extraction of vital organs—all while her victims descend slowly, agonizingly, toward their deaths, toward the final exhalation of their life's breath. What is left of their carcasses—after she has wrung from them all the pain she can—is too corrupted to ever reenter philosophy's 'circle of life.' Those ruined shells become the crawling horrors that you and Theil barely escaped on her altar of despair."

"I thought you were meant to spare me the ghastly particulars," Carin muttered, so far under her breath that Welwyn didn't hear. But Verek did, and pulled her close.

"That is sufficient explanation," he growled at the monk. "I believe we now understand what manner of evil we face." Verek ground his teeth. "And to think that I once believed that woman possessed a great mastery of magic. I was in awe of her powers." He scoffed. "All that she and her forebears built in those mountain wastes, that city in the heights: It lies now in ruins, for it was built on blood, not bedrock. In the end, her power cannot and will not prevail, for it is a perversion."

As Verek fell silent, Carin recalled that she, too, had once harbored a deeply mistaken view of the witch.

For the love of mercy, she thought. *I had it in my mind that Hugh's death left behind a 'young widow.' Drisha! That hag may be nearly as old as the mountains.* Did Hugh ever know that Legary had forced him to marry a ghoul? Did Morann reveal her true self to her nineteen-year-old husband at the instant she murdered him?

Verek leaned to refill his goblet. He took a sip, then resettled close to Carin on their bench.

"Let us turn away from the story of how we reached this juncture," he said. "We must address our present situation. The question facing us is this: How much strength can the witch draw from a world where most of the inhabitants — reportedly — are dead or dying?"

Carin turned to look at Verek. "A world where my parents are among the few still living," she muttered. "And the woodsprite is there, too, with them … telling them all about me."

Verek returned her gaze, one eyebrow arched. There was worry in the depths of his dark eyes.

Presently, he looked back at Welwyn.

"If it's death the witch craves," he said, "then her new realm would seem tailor-made to feed her depravities. Weak though the necromancer may have been when she fled Carin's dragon, I fear she gains strength hourly where she now dwells."

Welwyn tipped his head and seemed poised to speak. But then he stretched, lifting his shoulders, and hoisted himself to his feet.

"However the case may lie with her, my friends, I see little that we can do to thwart her … and nothing at all that may be accomplished tonight. With your kind permission, my lord and lady" — he nodded to them both — "I'm for bed now."

The monk stepped to the hall door, but paused on its threshold and looked back at Carin.

"By the way, my dear young woman. As likely as your husband is to enjoy a very long life, you are even more likely to outlive him. If I may judge from your words earlier this evening, you seem to still regard yourself as a nearly ordinary mortal, when in truth you are anything but. Have you forgotten that the whole strength of this living world has flowed through you? That strength will continue to be yours for the asking, I daresay, for centuries to come."

Welwyn leveled his gaze at Carin and added, "It will be you, my lady, not Theil, who keeps your children eternally safe from poisonous books and forbidden sorcery."

* * *

Welwyn's words came often to Carin's mind in the days following their evening of drinks and "ghastly particulars." She had not given much thought, lately, to the events of her second journey from Granger north to Ruain—the events to which Welwyn had alluded. Much of that journey seemed distant now, not even half-remembered. It came to her indistinctly, a kind of dreamy prelude to the life she'd been leading since her return to Verek's domain—a life devoted to her husband and her children. Carin couldn't deny, that with motherhood her world had narrowed. And with it, her mind? The inside of her head did have a slenderness to it, which might indicate a sharp focus—or merely suggest that it held less than it once had. For nearly six years, Carin had been giving little thought to anything at all beyond her babies and their passionate wizardly father.

But now, increasingly, she found Welwyn's presence stirring up memories of earlier experiences—or stirring the mishmash of fragments, splinters, and impressions that passed for so many of Carin's recollections. Reaching deep, she pulled up a broken and hazy remembrance of serving as Welwyn had said, as a conduit for a great strength that had flowed through her—a healing power that had combined into one all-embracing force the elemental water, air, stone, and fire of this world.

Early on a morning when Verek was off on his rounds, visiting their horse-breeding neighbor Cian Ronnat, and while Welwyn had the children engaged in their lessons, Carin slipped down the spiraling stairs to the chamber of *wysards*. The cavern was her favorite place for sitting and thinking. It no longer overawed her, but always she showed proper respect to the forces that flowed in its rock and water.

Well, Carin thought, *except for that time in the pool when Theil and I sort of went off the deep end together.* But would the forces in that cavern have regarded their lovemaking as disrespectful, when it was the potency of that place that had heightened their elemental passions? Carin reconsidered, and thought not.

Now as she entered the cave, she paused behind the bench of the crescent moon and bowed to the pool. She advanced quietly, to stand on the pool's rim with her favorite seat—the bench of the fish—behind her. Once again she bowed, and posed her question.

"Amangêda," Carin whispered, feeling the name strange in her mouth—she had not spoken it for years. "If I cross the void to my homeworld, to challenge the sorceress who threatens everyone I love, will you lend me your strength to destroy her?"

The pool's only reaction was to slosh a little warm water over the rim and over Carin's bare feet.

Taking this for a sign that she should submerge herself, Carin shed her clothes and descended the steps into the wizards' well. When she was deep enough, she pushed off and swam to the far rim, then back, and then to the absolute center of the pool, where water welled up from far below … seemingly from the core of the world.

As she floated in the upwelling current, Carin waited for an answer, but none came. Softly she repeated, "Will you help me do what I must, Amangêda?"

At first there was no discernible change in the waters that bathed and supported her. But then a small wave formed at the edge of the pool nearest the bench of the key. Carin watched it travel toward her. As the wave reached her, it buoyed her up and carried her to the side of the pool nearest the bench of the fish, where she had left her clothing.

Interpreting the wave as an order to withdraw, Carin climbed from the pool. She dressed quickly, bowed again to the unseen Power of the cavern, and saying no more, left as she had come, up the winding stairs.

Alone in the library, drying her hair at the fire, Carin pondered the meaning of the pool's "answer," if such it had been. In sweeping her on its gentle wave toward the bench of the fish—the seat Carin had occupied when she first learned of her otherworldly origins—had the Power of that place said yes? Did Carin have Amangêda's blessing to travel to that other world, with the promise of virtually unlimited strength aiding her against Morann?

Or was the Power merely telling me to get out of the pool? Carin wondered. Perhaps it had found her question presumptuous and would not deign to answer such audacity, coming as it did from a creature of flesh and blood who could be nothing to the Power of the Elements except its servant.

Carin left the fireside unsatisfied. All that day, as she went about her work among the books, then went for a ride and practiced an arrowpoint-sharpening spell that Welwyn taught her, Carin's thoughts drifted to the little splash of water on her feet that had drawn her into the pool, and the small wave that had carried her out of it. But no amount of puzzling over the pool's meaning would bring her to any definite conclusion.

Maybe, she thought at sundown, giving up the effort to pierce the veil of mystery, *Amangêda just needs to think about it awhile.*

Chapter 7

Dead Things

An urgent pounding on their bedchamber door woke Carin and Theil long before dawn.

"*Where is Nina?*" came Welwyn's booming cry through the thick oak. "Is she with you?"

Brought instantly awake, both sprang from bed and grabbed whatever clothes were at hand, Carin snatching Theil's shirt off the floor and pulling it over her head while he tugged on his trousers. Verek reached the door a step ahead of Carin and yanked it open.

"Welwyn!" he bellowed. "What do you mean, '*Where is Nina?*' Where in the name of mischief would she be at this hour, but in her bed?"

"Therein lies the trouble *and* the mischief!" Welwyn bellowed back. "The child is *not* in her bed, and I can find her nowhere in this house."

"Beggar it all," Carin swore. "Has she run off to the ocean?"

Or worse, Carin thought but wouldn't say aloud until she had checked the locks. *Has Nina discovered the springwater pool and made it take her Drisha knows where? Into the void, even?*

"I'll meet you at the stable, Theil," Carin called over her shoulder as she pushed past the men who stood in the doorway.

Covering the short distance along the hall in two seconds, she knelt to examine the iron shackle with which Verek had secured the door to the blue bedroom. The moonlight that seeped into the hallway through its high windows was too dim to see by, but her searching fingers found the physical lock intact, and her magian senses detected the wizardry: Verek's spells of forbiddance were unbroken. Nina had not passed through this door.

Carin stood and raced back down the hallway. As she passed by their bedchamber, she met Verek emerging from it. He was now fully clothed, and dressed for riding.

"I'll check the wizards' well!" she called as she flew on, not slowing from her dead run.

At the corridor's end Carin leapt down the three long flights of stairs that led to the cavern's hidden portal. Verek had long ago reworked the magic which guarded that door. It would no longer burn an uninvited hand to cinders, but would simply refuse to open to any living being other than Verek or Carin, or by special dispensation, Welwyn and Megella. Carin lifted the concealed latch, shoved the door open, and sprang into the cavern with none of her usual subdued reverence.

"Amangêda!" she cried. "Has my daughter been in this chamber?"

A wave arose on the far side of the pool and rushed toward Carin, to break upon the pool's rim with the sound of the surf battering coastal cliffs.

"Never," replied the shimmering, seashell voice of the *wysards'* well.

It was the first time Amangêda had spoken to Carin in years. Despite her anxiety over Nina's whereabouts, she took a moment to bow to the well and utter a soft, "Thank you."

Then Carin was running from the cavern, leaping back up the flights of stairs, sprinting down the hallway, and dashing into her bedroom. Pausing only long enough to don riding breeches and slip a heavier tunic over the shirt of Verek's that she wore, Carin pulled on her boots and clattered downstairs to the kitchen.

Myra was there, rousted from bed by the commotion. A fire blazed on the hearth, and the woman was frying bacon and making porridge.

"Oh my, dearie!" she exclaimed as Carin burst in. "What has that child done now?"

"Gone east, I suspect," Carin said. "Myra, if you're still able to send a message in a bucket, then alert Megella that Nina may have taken the road to Fintan."

"Why, dearie!" the housekeeper exclaimed. "I haven't tried that trick in years." But even as she spoke, Myra was grabbing an oaken bucket to fill at the kitchen's hand-pump.

Carin left her to it. Yanking open the side door, she crossed the moonlit yard at a run. At the stable she found Verek already mounted and her own horse saddled and waiting. He tossed her the reins, and they left the courtyard at a gallop, riding side by side.

The last light of the moon saw them far along the northeastward road, nearly to the outskirts of Fintan. They spoke little other than to exchange terse reports: Carin affirmed the security of both pools of power, and Verek pithily described Welwyn's state of wretchedness.

"He's cursing himself with curses I have never heard, and that's saying something," Verek muttered. "He holds himself to blame, though I do not doubt that a *wysard* of Welwyn's years and experience worked all the spellcraft that might *be* worked to keep that child from straying. After raising the alarm this night, he returned to the nursery to glare at Galen. That boy is in for it, I'll wager."

Carin sighed. "When we get Nina back—we *will* get her back, Theil—Welwyn will want to put her in fetters and lock her in the dungeon. And Galen with her. It's hardly likely the child knew nothing of his sister's leaving."

Verek grunted, grimly. They rode on in silence, reaching Fintan by owl-light as the village mostly slept. Only a few craftsmen and tradespeople were stirring. The riders spoke to no one, unwilling to reveal themselves or their errand if it could be avoided. Calling his people to join the search for Nina might become necessary, but Theil made it clear by his posture that he preferred to keep his family business out of the public eye. He rode almost hunched, with his hood drawn over his face.

They took the lane to Megella's cottage and found the wise-woman standing in her yard, awaiting them.

"Myra reached you?" Carin greeted her without preliminaries.

Meg flicked a corner of her shawl. "Woke me. Shouted at me from the water bucket. Said Nina was missing?"

"Yes. We think she's trying to get to the coast."

"On foot?"

Verek shook his head. "The horse I bought this summer in Fintan is gone from its stall. Nina took too great a liking to that beast the moment I brought it home." Verek growled a curse from his own impressive store of them. "But thank the Powers the animal is calm and sensible. It won't deliberately hurt her, but she could break her neck falling from the back of a horse as tall as that fellow stands."

Megella scowled. "Wheesht. I have been watching since Myra broke in on my dreams, but I've seen neither a great horse nor a wayward child. Shall I help you raise the town to look for her?"

"Wait a bit. Carin and I will ride on a ways eastward first. We may yet find her on the road, though Nina has a few hours' head start on us."

"Tah! What was Welwyn doing, that he allowed the child to escape his custody?"

Carin, feeling the need to defend the monk, interjected: "Welwyn never relaxes his guard where those children are concerned. But there is no doubt in my mind that both Nina and Galen are already capable of working magic of their own devising. Welwyn says they are extraordinarily gifted, beyond any apprentices he has ever undertaken to train. The wonder, to me, is that Master Welwyn has managed to hold them in check for as long and as well as he has."

For a moment, Megella was silent. Then she muttered, "Drisha help us all."

Verek snorted, and in his wordless commentary Carin read the thought: *This matter is beyond Drisha, and possibly beyond every living wysard of Ladrehdin.*

They turned to go. But barely had they started toward the lane when an in-breaking thought had Carin reining around to speak again to Megella.

"Have you finished draping your cottage in blue?" she asked the wisewoman. "When we find Nina—wherever she is on her way to the ocean—I would like to bring her to you here. It would ease my mind regarding *one* of the child's obsessions, at least, to convince her that yours is the only 'blue room' she's ever heard mentioned." Carin shot the woman a meaningful look.

"By all means," Megella replied. "When you recover the runaway, haul her here by her ear and I will show the girl my bedchamber decked with the bluest of trimmings and trappings. *After*," Meg added, "I skin the child alive."

But there was to be no skinning that day, nor even much in the way of tongue-lashing. Barely had Carin and Verek regained the main road that cut through Fintan when they saw the ghost-gray horse standing half asleep outside the stable from which Verek had purchased the animal weeks previous.

Sitting on its broad back like an imp was Nina. The child kicked for all she was worth, and pulled the horse's mane—doing her utmost to command her steed without the aid of either bridle or saddle. The horse merely swished its tail and shook its mane in mild protest at Nina's determined pulling. It stood with its long legs planted like posts, lifting nary a hoof to obey its gnat-like rider. Except, as Carin stared at the mismatched pair and felt the laughter rise within her—laughter she fought to suppress lest it burst out in a kind of hysterical relief—she saw the animal shift its weight, a change in its stance clearly meant to keep its tiny rider settled on its wide, bare back.

Verek saw it, too. "Extra oats for that fellow tonight," he muttered as he lifted his own horse's reins and rode toward the pair, Carin at his side.

Nina spotted them and exclaimed, "Make him mind, Papa! Ghost has been standing here for *ages*. Make him move! I want to go to the beach."

Not a glimmer of guilt in that face or that voice, Carin thought, still laughing but only inwardly. *She's not a bit sorry for giving Welwyn the slip, only angry that her horse is better behaved than she is.*

As they joined the child, Carin saw that Verek was not smiling. Indeed, the scowl he directed at his daughter would have frozen the heart of many a mortal man. His lips were clamped together as if he held back fury.

"Theil," she whispered, hoping to stave off an eruption.

Verek barely glanced her way. He slid quick looks up and down Fintan's main thoroughfare, where more townsfolk were now abroad in the early light. None, however, seemed to pay attention to the little family group that was clustered in front of the still-closed stable.

Assured that they were not watched, Verek raised his right hand and pointed two fingers at Nina's horse. At once, the animal swung its head toward him, alert and questioning, and as Verek reined his own horse around, the big gray turned and followed.

Carin brought her horse beside the smooth-gaited gray. The animal was so tall that Nina's face was nearly level with Carin's as she rode alongside the child.

"That's better!" Nina said. "Now we're moving, we can go to the beach."

Stifling a sigh at the child's single-mindedness, Carin said in her most diplomatic tones, "But right now we're riding to Aunt Megella's cottage. Won't you be glad to see her?"

"Yes!" Nina exclaimed. "Aunt Meg didn't get to go to the beach before. She can come with us this time."

"Well," Carin replied, "you may ask her. I'm sure she'd like to be asked."

In an effort to change the subject and extract useful information from the urchin, Carin commented, "Ghost is very tall, isn't he. How did you manage to get on him by yourself?"

"Easy!" Nina said. "He stands by the boards of his stall and I climb up."

"What a good horse," Carin remarked drily.

"He is!" the child exclaimed. "Ghost is the best horse ever."

An assessment with which I tend to agree, Carin thought, *provided he never carry her farther than his old stable in Fintan.*

From in front of her came sudden, loud guffawing. They were now far along Megella's lane, away from Fintan's busier streets. And Verek, Carin realized, was letting out everything he'd been holding in. A blistering medley of swearwords mixed freely with his roaring mirth as Verek pushed back his hood and put his hand to his face to wipe away the tears of his half-manic laughter.

He was terrified, Carin thought. *Not angry with Nina. He wouldn't show it, but that man was scared beyond words that he might lose another child.*

Beside her, Nina fell briefly silent, peering ahead at her father's back. Then the girl turned to Carin, and with her brow charmingly furrowed, she asked, "Is Papa all right?"

Carin laughed. "Yes, darling one. Your papa is just happy to have you back with us. We were a little worried about you, is all, when we woke up this morning and couldn't find you at home. You know you shouldn't go off without telling us. It's not safe."

"Oh, Mama," Nina said, exasperation in her voice. "Ghost and me can take care of ourselves."

Megella's greeting saved Carin the necessity of replying. They had reached the wisewoman's cottage, and Meg stood on tiptoe, stretching to pull the child off of Ghost's back and into a smothering embrace. Only when a muffled "I need air!" was heard from somewhere under the wisewoman's enveloping, multicolor shawls did Megella loosen her hold.

Meg did not entirely release the child, however, but hustled Nina indoors with many exclamations of "Tah! You foolish girl," and "*Never* do that again," with answering cries from Nina of "What is *wrong* with you all?" and "Let's go to the beach *now.*"

Carin did not move to join them in the cottage. She walked instead to where Verek was tethering their horses, in a lush, well-watered pasture just beyond Megella's vegetable garden. The summer was now far advanced, and timely rains had greened the land. Verek's stewards would have no trouble this year seeing that every mouth in Ruain was fed, and every larder richly stocked for the winter.

"I hope Megella doesn't actually skin the child," Carin remarked as she joined Verek, "but I'll be grateful if she pins Nina's ears back. Somehow I cannot find it in myself to properly discipline that girl."

"Humph," Verek grunted. "Nor can I, more's the pity. She has me wrapped around her little finger … and I fear she knows it."

"Well," Carin said as she patted the big gray's shoulder—Ghost had his head down, tearing up mouthfuls of grass, relishing his breakfast—"we have Welwyn for that, thank the Powers. When we get her home, Nina may see a side of her governor that she has not seen before."

With a final pat, Carin left the horse to enjoy his reward. Taking Verek's hand, she said, "Let's go see how Meg is dealing with our hellion."

They entered the wisewoman's cottage to find her and Nina just leaving Meg's bedchamber.

"You have so many pretty things!" the girl exclaimed. "Will you do my room to look like yours?"

"Certainly, if you like," Meg replied. "Then we'll both have blue rooms."

Nina nodded vigorously, and asked, "But where's your sing-water pool?"

Beggar it, thought Carin with a small sinking feeling. *That child remembers everything and misses nothing.*

But Megella proved herself equal to the girl's probing.

"It's a 'spring,' child … but indeed I *have* heard it sing," she replied without hesitation. "It's down below the pasture. Let's walk there and eat our breakfast beside it." Nodding to a covered basket that was set on the table, Meg added, "I've bread and cheese enough for an army. And if your mother knows how to milk a cow, we'll have fresh milk with it."

Carin opened her mouth, ready to protest that if she'd ever known how to milk a cow, she'd long since forgotten. But Verek put his hand on Carin's shoulder and shook his head almost imperceptibly.

"Nina," he said, gazing down at his daughter, "help Aunt Megella carry the basket to the spring. Your mother and I will join you shortly."

"Yes, Papa."

As soon as the two were out of earshot, walking across the pasture with Meg holding the basket by its handle, and Nina clutching the wickerwork's thick rim, Verek steered Carin toward the cowshed.

"Watch and learn, *fileen*," Verek said, almost grinning at her. "Watch and learn."

To Carin's astonishment, Theil grabbed the milking stool and seated himself beside the flank of Megella's large, brindled cow. Its udder was swollen and full.

"Hand me that pail, if you please," he directed, pointing to a clean wooden bucket that hung from a peg inside the shed's door.

When she had done so, Carin squatted beside her many-talented *wysard*, marveling as Verek squeezed a little milk from each teat and then set to work with both of his strong, long-fingered hands, in a rhythm that pacified the cow.

"How in the world did *you* learn that?" Carin asked. "I can't imagine that milking is a skill commonly possessed by members of the nobility."

Verek laughed. "You forget, my lady, that Ruain is an out-of-the-way, country province. Those who would rule it must understand the ways and the daily arts of its people. Myra taught me to milk when I was a boy growing up in the fields and woods of this land."

"Then she must also teach Nina and Galen," Carin declared. "It's a wonderful thing to know."

Verek stood and picked up the pail that brimmed with fresh, warm milk. Carin returned the stool to its place, and together they walked down to the foot of the pasture ... where a spring bubbled musically into a clear, rock-lined pool, and Megella and Nina sat on a blanket at the water's edge, eating bread and cheese.

"We've left you a little," Meg commented as Verek set the bucket on the grass beside his aunt, and settled himself with Carin on the blanket. The two had left more than a little, it turned out. When the wisewoman opened her basket to remove four cups and a ladle, a feast was revealed inside.

For a while then, the three adults ate much and spoke little. Carin had not realized how hungry she was. Leaving home so early and in such nervous haste, she'd neither eaten a morsel nor drunk a drop all this long morning. Verek, too, dug in eagerly, washing down his breakfast with long drafts of the fresh milk that Meg ladled into cups for each of them.

But Nina had finished her meal almost before her parents began. The girl was on her feet, exploring. She circled the pool, squatting to study the small creatures inhabiting it. Nina caught a frog, stroked its head, held it up to peer into its eyes, then released it back into the pool. The girl accorded this same careful examination to various insects, a crayfish, and a legless creature that was either a freshwater eel or a water snake—from where Carin sat, she couldn't tell.

"Theil," she murmured, nodding toward the child.

"I'm watching," he muttered back. "It's not venomous. Even if it were, I'm inclined to let her learn from her own mistakes."

Spoken as only a master healer could speak, Carin thought. She glanced from him to Megella, and relaxed a little with the realization that, between the two of them, Meg and Verek could remedy almost anything short of decapitation.

Presently, Nina left off studying the spring-fed pool. Jumping to her feet, the child bounded past her still-breakfasting elders and headed up the slope toward the top of the pasture.

"I'm going to visit Ghost!" she called as she darted past.

"Stay where I can see you!" Verek shouted at her.

Nina waved to signal that she had heard, but the child did not slow her ascent until she stood with the big horse under the trees atop the rise.

"I hope you've still got that horse bespelled," Carin said, watching the girl who was now—to her mind, at least—uncomfortably far from them. "Else, Nina will be away again before you can swear by Drisha's teeth to put her in chains."

Verek grunted. "The horse answers to me. Even so, I'm not letting that child out of my sight." He moved over on the blanket to have an unobstructed view of Nina at the ridgetop.

"So, Meg," Carin said, turning to the wisewoman. "Do you think she's convinced? Of your blue room and springwater pool, I mean."

Megella flicked the fringe of her apple-red and pearl-gray shawl. "Who can say? Young and innocent as she seems, that child knows how to safeguard her secrets. I cannot read her. She's well able to keep her thoughts from showing on her face."

And how could Nina have come by that enviable skill, I do wonder? Carin thought, wryly, studying Verek as he watched their daughter explore among the trees at the pasture's upper edge. How many times, in her earliest acquaintance with this magician, had Verek turned upon her the unreadable, noncommittal looks that drove Carin half mad with wondering what he was really thinking?

"Has Nina invited you to the beach yet?" Carin asked, returning her thoughts to the present and her attention to the wisewoman. "I can't say I'm surprised that the girl's obsession with the ocean has us breakfasting in your pasture this morning. She's not only determined to go back to the coast, she told me you're to come with her."

Megella rubbed her nose, and smiled. "Indeed, yes, the child has issued her kind invitation. The moment Nina crossed my threshold today, she was speaking of the sea. Every scrap of blue in my cottage — or, in truth, any object that came to her notice — seemed to remind the girl of some marvel she had seen on the eastern shore. 'That's just the color of the ocean!' Or, 'That's as blue as a starfish!' Or, 'The *dolphyn* that played with Mama and me was a pretty gray, like in the shawl you're wearing, Aunt Meg.'"

Carin sighed. "Perhaps it was a mistake to ever let Nina see the ocean. But no," she immediately rejected her own words. "The child needed to go there, to feel it and begin to know it. That girl has made it perfectly clear — since her infancy — that her gifts arise from water." Carin pictured the times Nina had flooded the kitchen, sent her bathwater streaming down the corridor outside her bedroom, or brought forth a torrent from a crack in a farmer's border-stone.

Verek had been listening without speaking as Meg and Carin chatted and he watched Nina among the trees. Now he interjected a question.

"Honored Aunt, did the child happen to mention, while you were showing her your 'blue room,' how she managed to get past Welwyn's spells of confinement? I have checked them myself, at his invitation, and can attest to their strength and—I believed—their invulnerability. To prevent another midnight expedition, we must learn how Nina got out last night."

I've told you, Carin thought, knowing Verek didn't believe in shapeshifting but half convinced, in her own mind, that it was the only possible explanation. *That girl can slip as easily as water through a crack under a door.*

Megella tapped her chin thoughtfully. "No, nephew. Nina told me nothing of her daring escape." The wisewoman paused, her head back, and added: "Though I'm not at all sure she considers her escape to be 'daring.' The entire enterprise may have come so easily to her that Nina thinks it commonplace to break spellwork laid by a master *wysard* and take horse in the middle of the night and embark cross-country entirely alone."

Verek scowled. "That is what worries me. A limitless gift needs boundaries. The greatest *wysards* to have lived in this world have known where the lines are … and they have stopped themselves from crossing those lines."

As Morann did not, Carin thought. *That witch and her forebears crossed a forbidden line, to grasp for a power beneath wizardry, descending into depravity.*

Verek stood, and in the clipped tones he used when issuing orders, he called to the child who was still poking around under the trees.

"Karenina! Join me. I wish to speak with you."

"Yes, Father," the girl answered at once.

Nina came bounding down the slope to stand before Verek, straight-backed and respectful with her hands clasped behind her back.

Good, Carin thought, watching them. *She knows what she can get away with when it's 'Nina' and 'Papa.' But let him use her full name in that tone of voice, and he's instantly 'Father,' the lord of the manor, and she his dutiful daughter.*

"Tell me," Verek ordered, as forcefully as if he addressed a lawbreaker who had been hauled before him on charges. "Master Welwyn secures your door at night to keep you safe. How did you break his safeguards?"

Nina started to shrug, but then seemed to think better of it in the face of her sire's flinty manner. Instead, the girl rocked up on her toes several times, as if gathering her thoughts before answering.

"Sir, I did it with the ocean," she said, clear-voiced, and her expression more matter-of-fact than defiant. "I washed his spells off the door."

"How?"

This time, the girl did shrug. "Master Welwyn's spells were in my way. I wanted to open the door and get Ghost and go to the ocean. The ocean has waves — I went swimming in them with Mama! So I made a wave. I made it splash the door and wash Master Welwyn's spells away."

Verek was silent for a moment. Then, staring hard at the child, he addressed her in his sternest voice. "I am displeased with you, daughter. You are not permitted to 'wash away' Welwyn's spells. He is a master of magic; you are his apprentice. You *will* abide by whatever restrictions Welwyn chooses to place upon you."

Again, Nina bounced on her toes … possibly from nervousness in the face of her father's ire …

But, Carin thought, watching, *that child looks more impatient than alarmed.*

When Nina offered no other response to his reprimand, Verek crouched, bringing his eyes to the girl's level. Severely, he demanded, "Do you understand me, child?"

"Yes, sir," Nina answered, nodding, and bouncing ever more impatiently.

Verek put his hands on Nina's shoulders to hold her still. He locked gazes with the child, as if trying to read in her large dark eyes—eyes as obsidian black as his own—what Nina was really thinking. After a moment, he grunted, "Humph," and leaned to kiss the girl's cheek.

Releasing Nina then, Verek rose to his feet. "That will be all," he said, gruffly, and waved the child on her way.

Freed from the interrogation—as unmoved by her father's rebuke, Carin suspected, as Ghost had been by Nina's mane-pulling—the girl skipped over to where Carin still sat with Megella. Carin's mind was so occupied with the picture the child had painted, of an ocean wave from the easternmost coastline drenching a door inside a stone-built mansion at Ruain's western edge, she was not immediately aware of what Nina pressed into her hands.

"Look what I found, Mama, up there," the child said, pointing to the trees atop the rise where she had been exploring. "It's dead. I wish it wasn't."

"What is it, Nina?" Gathering her thoughts, Carin looked at her hands, which had cupped themselves without her conscious intent around the object Nina placed in them.

It was the body of a baby bird, naked and gray, and not freshly dead. Worms wriggled in the empty eye sockets.

"Oh!" Carin exclaimed. Her arm jerked, her muscles tensed, ready to cast the thing as far as she could. But a stern maternal voice commanded: *Do not throw away a gift from your daughter.* Heeding the command, Carin found the strength of will to merely stretch her arm beyond the edge of the blanket, open her prickling hand, and drop the wormy body into the grass.

"Nina, child, you shouldn't pick up—" *Nasty things,* Carin started to say. But she'd heard enough of the lessons Welwyn taught the children in the out-of-doors—not forgetting her own profound experiences with elemental forces—that Carin knew nothing in the natural world was dirty or impure. Worms, rot, putrefaction … all had their proper and necessary places in the circle of life. So she amended:

"You shouldn't disturb dead things, Nina. I'm sorry the little bird lost its life. Most likely it fell out of its nest in those trees. It would have been well to leave it where you found it."

"Yes, Mama," the child said, not contritely but with an attitude of attention.

"What's done is done," Carin added. "Since you've brought it here to show me, what shall we do with it? I'll help you bury it, if you like."

Nina considered this proposal, then shook her head.

"No, Mama. I don't want to put the bird in the ground. Let's put it in the water." She pointed to the bubbling, singing spring.

Is there any road this child could take that wouldn't lead to water? Carin wondered, mentally sighing as she rose from the blanket.

"No, Nina, we mustn't put anything dead in the spring. Aunt Megella drinks that water. But see the little stream flowing downhill out of the pool? We can put your bird there, where the water moves fast and will wash the body clean."

Nina assented, and the "funeral" was quickly concluded. Carin took the opportunity to scrub her hands in the spring's swift outflow … careful to wash them upstream from the small dead body.

By the time they rejoined the others, Megella had the breakfast leftovers packed up, the thick blanket folded, and all else in readiness for their departure, which Verek would not further delay.

"I want that child under Welwyn's eye, and under his cane if he sees fit to thrash her," Verek muttered as he walked beside Carin, angling up toward the horses.

Not likely, Carin thought. Welwyn could no more strike the lass than Verek could.

But aloud, she said only, "Yes, we should be getting back. I'm sure he's frantic with worry. And I think the three of us have much to discuss about Nina 'washing away' Master Welwyn's strongest spells of confinement."

Verek grunted something, half inaudible, about "guts and gall."

Carin had no need to ask him to repeat it. She'd heard the oath before.

They were still several steps below the crest of the slope when Carin realized she'd been absentmindedly rubbing her hands on her breeches, still feeling on her skin the naked, worm-eaten body of the baby bird. Why had that pitiful dead thing troubled her so? Drisha knew, Carin had plenty of experience with dead animals. Years ago, struggling to survive as a lone traveler on the grasslands, she had killed, gutted, and eaten every bird and rabbit she could bring down with a stone from her sling.

Musing on Nina's odd determination to show her the body—the girl must have been squeezing it in her hands as she held them behind her back while Verek questioned her—Carin suddenly recalled that day at the seashore, when Nina had been fascinated by a dead jellyfish the child found on the beach as they followed Welwyn up the coast.

And before that, Carin remembered with a growing sense of horror, *Nina drowned the mouse.* That night when Galen started an out-of-control blaze in the kitchen, and Nina's contribution was to flood the floor three inches deep, Carin had floundered up against a floating mouse corpse. When Myra later found the thing wedged and stinking in the corner by her bedroom door, the housekeeper exclaimed, "Never in all my years within these walls have I seen a mouse in my bedchamber. I'll thank young Nina to not wash any more of the vermin my way!"

Dead mouse. Dead bird. Dead jellyfish.

Nina's dead things, Carin thought, in an instant so sick to her stomach that she stopped, doubled-over, on the slope below where the horses grazed. *What's next? Crawling horrors?*

As Verek bent over her, his features sharp with concern, saying something Carin couldn't hear for the sudden buzzing in her ears, a truth exploded in her brain like the flare of a just-lit torch:

Why have I never realized it before? Carin thought, incredulous that the simple fact of lineage had escaped her conscious notice until this moment. *The death-loving ghoul who is my husband's mother is grandmother to our children.*

Chapter 8

Spellwork

Carin explained away her sickness as overeating at breakfast—"Didn't you see how I gorged myself?"—or perhaps the release of tension that came with getting Nina back safe: "I guess I was more frightened for her than I realized," Carin said to Verek and Megella when she recovered enough to speak.

Neither of them seemed wholly convinced. But soon the homeward journey was under way, Verek leading his little family party by a circuitous route which avoided Fintan. Ghost clopped along behind him with an impish, now drowsy rider nodding on the horse's back. Carin, bringing up the rear, alone with her thoughts, watched Nina sag until the child was limp, her face pillowed in Ghost's silver-gray mane, her arms hanging on either side of his neck, as deeply asleep as if curled up in her own bed. Such trust between the two of them, tiny rider and great horse …

If the child must go where she has no business being, Carin mused, *it's good she has this oversized nursemaid to carry her with slow and plodding care.* Though, as Carin eyed the horse's muscular hindquarters, she couldn't doubt that Ghost would be capable of great bursts of speed and long, effortless, obstacle-clearing leaps, should the need arise.

Wending their way down the backroad took hours: The threesome arrived at the manor shortly before sunset. Verek had barely lifted Nina down from her high perch, and the stableman was just reaching for the reins when Welwyn came trundling across the courtyard, straight to the child.

"So you're back." The monk, though not a tall man, towered over Nina, cloaking her in his shadow, the iron in his voice bringing the child fully awake. "And here you shall stay. Missy, you will *not* leave these premises again unless either I, or the lord or lady of Ruain, give you express permission. Do you mark me well?"

"Yes, Master Welwyn." The girl nodded vigorously, and for the first time that day, she looked abashed.

Thank the Powers for Welwyn, Carin thought as the monk hustled Nina toward the house. She had come to heartily approve of the fosterage tradition long practiced by Ladrehdin's nobility, with its counterpart among the *wysards* of apprenticing young adepts to masters of magic who were not their parents. It spared doting mothers and fathers the unpleasantness of disciplining fractious offspring.

And of seeing what Welwyn may actually do to that child, Carin thought. She never inquired too closely into the monk's methods, only watched for the results. Many times Carin had seen both Galen and Nina chastened, bending to their studies with renewed diligence as Welwyn took them through lessons in everything from astronomy and alchemy to history and herblore. But never had she seen either child flinch away from the monk or appear frightened or wary of him, as might be the case if the punishments he doled out really hurt them.

On the contrary, both children seemed genuinely fond of their tutor and governor. These days, Nina held herself to be too old for crawling into Welwyn's lap in the evenings when he read storybooks to them. But the girl curled up at her master's feet, while Galen settled in the crook of the *wysard's* arm, and both listened raptly to Welwyn's readings of folklore, legends, and ancient Ladrehdinian fables.

This evening, as Carin sat silent, a little apart from the trio, hearing the monk's resonant voice and seeing Nina's contented smile as the girl rested her head against Welwyn's knee, she was again reassured.

However he does it, Carin thought, *that old wysard manages to put the fear of farsinchia into them while never cowing or hurting them.*

Once or twice she had considered asking Welwyn if he could teach her his way with children. But she'd decided it was inimitable, a thing like the *gift* itself: one either had it, or one did not. Carin's aptitude for spellcraft had proved itself many times over, but as a disciplinarian she was hopeless.

Indeed, as a *wysard* she was still very much a student. Some spellwork had come easily and intuitively to Carin. But the more she learned, the more she appreciated the difference between being born to magic, and being *awakened* to it. In her children, the ability to work magic was innate, and almost immediate. Their training consisted largely in understanding the spellcraft and developing restraint and skill in controlling it.

Carin, however, had come to the craft much later than most apprentices, for in her the magic had fully awakened only after her arrival—and her coming of age—in Ruain. Even then, the power oftentimes manifested only when she was under stress or in mortal peril—when facing a demoness, for instance. Carin needed to learn better control, certainly. But she also required more specific tutoring in basic spell-casting than any native-born Ruainian *wysard* would find necessary.

Recognizing Carin's need, Verek had directed her to a section of the library, just behind its veil of shadow, where detailed instruction manuals were shelved, rank upon rank of them. Every book had teachings penned in older forms of the common Ladrehdinian script, so that Carin had to combine her learning of spellcraft with her language studies.

A week after thwarting Nina's seaward plans, Carin felt brain-sore from her hours in the library, translating ancient texts while forcing her mind and her fingers into difficult wizardly configurations. The work demanded a single-mindedness that she could not give it, for her thoughts—and suspicions—strayed persistently to Nina's "dead things."

In the early dawn of the seventh day after fetching the girl home, Carin took horse again and rode out, alone, on the northeastward road. Her long auburn hair was tucked into a slouchy, shapeless cap; she wore trousers and a loose jacket. Her body, rounded by time and motherhood into womanly curves at bust and hips, was otherwise as slim as she'd been at seventeen. Much practice with bow, sling, and throwing knife, and almost daily exercise on horseback, had restored Carin's figure after two pregnancies. In her baggy britches and coat, she'd still pass for a boy. A casual glance from any rider Carin met, on the broad main road to Fintan, would perceive only a well-mounted young man who had a better eye — or perhaps more money — for good horseflesh than for tailored clothes.

In the late morning, Carin reached Megella's cottage and found the wisewoman at work in her vegetable patch. As Carin called a greeting, the woman straightened, pressing one hand to her back as she shaded her eyes with the other.

"Widgeon!" Meg exclaimed, using the pet name she typically reserved for times when she and Carin were alone. "You're very welcome, but I did not expect to see you again so soon. Nothing is amiss, I trust? No runaways to collar?"

Carin shook her head. "Nina won't try it again while Welwyn has her on a tight rein. That child earned herself double lessons and triple chores. She's falling into bed after supper too exhausted to even think of another overnight ride."

Megella chuckled. "Yet I suspect she has learned no lesson, for all of Welwyn's efforts, at least as far as 'beaches' and 'oceans' go. I would think the girl was under a spell of compulsion, so unshakeable is she in her longing for the sea."

Like that spell you laid on me, Megella, Carin thought as she dismounted, and with a gentle slap sent her horse to graze under the trees. *The compulsion you seared into my blood and breath that forced me to walk to Ruain would have carried me even farther north — to my death ... If Theil Verek hadn't been fascinated by, and* slightly afraid of, his brazen trespasser with the tangled auburn mane, big green eyes, and blind spot for the dark, destructive magic he had once committed in a madness of grief.

On impulse, Carin wrapped her arms around Megella and hugged her.

"Tah, widgeon," Meg protested mildly as she extricated herself. "Are you quite well?" A frown replaced the woman's fond smile. "You haven't been retching again, have you?" Then Megella brightened and exclaimed: "Oh, duckling! Happy news? Has my nephew got you with child again? That lusty rake."

Carin smiled. "No, Meg, I'm not pregnant and I'm not sick. The only thing wrong with me is my memory." *Well, my memory and half of what I'm guessing or imagining,* Carin amended silently. *But let Meg come to that as she will.*

She gestured at the rickety table on Megella's swept and shady front porch. "Sit with me awhile, Aunt, and help me remember … everything."

"Wheesht! *That* may prove to be hungry work. Let me see what I have."

From her cottage, the wisewoman brought refreshments including ale, and listened without comment as Carin described walking to Ruain from Granger. Megella did not require many details of that first journey—the woman had extracted from Carin the full particulars while the two of them rode together in a wagon on Carin's second northbound trip.

"When I think back on that first time, Meg," Carin said as the wisewoman settled at the table and began slicing cheese, "I can almost smell the haystacks where I slept, and taste the rabbit and redberries that kept me alive. But then when it was you, me, and Theil traveling nearly the same road, just farther east of where I'd walked before, I lose track, somewhere this side of … Plainsboro, I think the town was called." Carin rubbed her fingers across her forehead, trying to dispel the haze.

Meg handed her a plate piled high with fruit and cold meat. Not meeting Carin's gaze, the woman busied herself slicing an apple and filling her own platter.

"Tah, widgeon," the wisewoman said after a stretch of silence, still focused on her ceaselessly moving paring knife. "Can you truly wonder at it? That first time, you were desperately alone and in constant peril, risking life and freedom with every northward step. Is it any marvel that the events of that journey would be burned into your memory? Or that you would forget much of the second trip, which you made in far greater safety, escorted by two experienced healers? Myself, long a southlander, knew the roads and the ways of the village folk. Theil Verek, while sapped of his wizardry for a time, remained wholly capable of handing any highwayman his head, or putting an arrow through the eye of a charging bull at a hundred paces."

At this, Meg raised her eyes. As she held Carin's gaze, the woman added, "It's no surprise to me that you've forgotten most of that second journey, widgeon. You and my nephew were so lost in each other, if I hadn't been there to force you out of one another's arms from time to time, you might yet be wandering the grasslands." Megella clucked her tongue, a little slyly. "With a pack of brats in tow, I don't doubt."

Carin laughed. "Did we make it awkward for you? In truth, that's the only part of the trip that I *do* remember clearly — all those glorious nights with Theil, behind the wagon, on a blanket under the stars."

Megella reached across the table and patted Carin's arm. "I am not unversed in the ways of the world, duckling. I know a bit about relations between hot-blooded men and fiery young women." The wisewoman smiled as she leaned back in her chair. Around a bite of apple, Meg added, "Awkwardness never entered into it, from where I sat. I was vastly entertained by the show you two put on."

"Megella!" Carin exclaimed in mock outrage. "Tell me you didn't watch?"

"How could I not?" the woman shot back. "A wagon wheel hides little, and the pair of you hid nothing at all. You went at it like mad minks."

Carin blinked at Megella until, together, she and the wise-woman erupted in laughter, tittering and giggling like naughty schoolgirls. Megella brought up a corner of her purple paisley shawl to wipe away tears of mirth, while Carin's sides began to hurt from her laughing so hard.

Finally they both quieted, except for a last, lingering, appreciative chuckle from the wisewoman. For a time then, they ate in silence, listening to the drowsy hum of bees in Megella's flowers, and the melodic burbling of the spring at the foot of the wise-woman's pasture.

At last, steeling herself, Carin swallowed some of the woman's stout ale and gathered the courage to ask the first of the questions she had come here to have answered.

"Meg." Carin's voice was so soft, the wisewoman looked sharply at her, alert to her sudden change of mood. "There was someone else on that journey. You, me, Theil … and a man. A stranger." Carin tipped her head, trying to slide her flecks and fragments of memory into some readable pattern. "We picked him up along the way. I don't remember when or why. I only know he was there … and then he wasn't." Carin bit her lip. Hesitantly, she continued. "But I think I didn't like him. And I think, maybe …"

She locked gazes with Megella. In a voice half pleading, half commanding, she said, "Don't lie to me, Meg. I need to know. Did I kill that man?"

The wisewoman heaved a great sigh. For a moment she only looked at Carin, and remained pushed back in her chair. But then Megella leaned across the table and took Carin's slim hands in her own warm, strong ones.

"Tah, widgeon," the woman muttered. "How I hoped you had lost that memory altogether. What good can come of recalling a terrible thing done without conscious intent, without malice, without knowing what you were doing?"

Carin stared at her. "What *did* I do, Meg? Tell me. All of it."

Megella clamped her lips together, and Carin feared a battle lay ahead. A battle she intended to win, however hard the wisewoman might oppose her.

But Meg seemed to read in her face the futility of resistance. The woman squeezed Carin's hands, then said through clenched teeth, "Flynn. That was his name. Insufferable fool. He insulted you. Your temper flashed, and he became sand."

Sand!

Carin yanked her hands from Megella's grip and rocked back in her chair so violently that she would have toppled over rearward, had she not collided, joltingly, with the wall of Meg's cottage.

The spell of sand. That was it. That was what Carin had come for.

She smiled at the wisewoman. "Thank you, Meg. I don't know how I could have forgotten. How does a *wysard* forget a spell they created from the depths of their own mind and being? It was mine. I lost it for a time, lost it in the jumbled wreck of my memories. But now ..."

Carin left the thought unspoken, though Megella was looking a question at her. Clearly the wisewoman had expected some other reaction from her, not a smile and gratitude.

She dropped her chin and murmured, "Later, Aunt. I'm too scattered now to explain. This was sudden. I must think on it."

As she reached for her mug and took another sip of ale, Megella did likewise. In the silence that followed, her thoughts swirled, round and round, until they fastened upon the other matter that had brought her here today to seek the wisewoman's counsel.

"I'll need to leave before long." Carin glanced overhead at the now westering sun. "Theil will worry if I'm out after dark. But something happened when we were here with Nina. Meg, I need you to tell me if it means anything near as bad as I think it may mean."

Quickly, urged to brevity by not only the advancing day, but also her distaste for the subject, Carin distilled for Megella what Master Welwyn had said about Morann's malignant sorcery of blood and pain, how the demoness glutted herself on the agony of the dying. In response to the wisewoman's grimace of disgust, Carin said only, "I'm sorry, Meg, but this may be important." Onward she rushed, describing Nina's fascination with the dead jellyfish on the beach, and with the rotting chick the girl had gripped in her bare hands while Theil reprimanded her.

And before either of those dead things, Nina had drowned a mouse.

"Am I imagining it, Megella?" Carin asked, and she heard the note of pleading in her voice. "'Dead things and crawling horrors' … though I have only scattered memories of what I saw in Morann's realm, I've always remembered what Theil called those monstrosities that came for us when the necromancer fled my dragon." Carin swallowed, her throat dry despite all the ale she was downing. "And now I see my daughter surrounding herself with dead things, and suddenly there's a thought in my head that is so obvious—more glaring than the summer sun—but so obscene that I never let myself think it before. Now I can't escape it: The blood of a demon flows in the veins of both of my children."

Megella narrowed her eyes. The woman made as if to reach again for Carin's hands. Then Meg stiffened in her chair, her spine straight.

"Wheesht!" the wisewoman exclaimed, bolting to her feet and rounding the table. Megella grabbed Carin's arms and hauled her erect, standing her up with a steely strength that had

Carin flashing back to the times, years ago in Granger, when she had seen this dumpy, white-haired woman wrestle a young bull to the ground for doctoring, or subdue a thick-necked townsman who was out of his head and violent with fever.

"You listen to me, widgeon, and you listen hard," Meg snapped into Carin's face. "There is nothing—*nothing*—of that hag in your children. Drisha's mercy, woman! How is it that you could have carried each of them under your heart for months, and now observe those clear-eyed innocents daily, and you could harbor *any* thought of such an evil taint upon them?"

Megella was glaring. In the face of the woman's outrage, Carin felt ashamed of the dark paths her thoughts insisted on following. But insist on it, they would.

"Meg," Carin murmured, "I know you love those children. I've seen how happy all of you are—you, Welwyn, and especially Theil—to have those powerful young adepts grow stronger every day, learning the craft, securing the future of an ancient house." Carin crossed her arms to lay her fingertips on Megella's hands, which still held her tightly. "But consider whether your love and your hopes might not be clouding your sight. The demon—their grandmother—feeds on death," Carin whispered, "and Nina is drawn to dead things. I have seen it."

"Tah!" Megella scoffed, so forcefully that she sprayed spit into Carin's face. "You have seen nothing but a child's curiosity. *Think,* woman! How could any youngling resist the novelty on her first trip to the seashore, seeing a gobbet of jelly heaped on the sand? Did you not tell me the thing was brilliantly red and blue, and tinged with pink? Use your imagination! Drisha knows you have one. See the dead jelly through Nina's eyes. Would it not have looked, to her, like a spilled jar of jam?"

As if realizing she gripped Carin's arms tightly enough to make them tingle, the wisewoman released her visitor with a gentle push that sent Carin collapsing back into the chair behind her. Meg returned to her own seat at the table.

Carin barely noticed as her mind's eye roved back to the scene on the beach. In death the jellyfish had retained its vibrant colors, a bright spot on the otherwise pale sand—bright enough to draw any eye. That day when Carin spotted Nina off her pony and crouched over the thing, poking it with a piece of driftwood, the gelatinous mass had indeed looked like an upended bowl of jelly.

Slowly, Carin nodded. "I take your point, Aunt. Simple curiosity could account for Nina's interest … that time." Not yet wholly convinced but wanting to be, she added, "But that dead bird! Any other child would recoil from touching a body crawling with worms."

"Any other child!" Meg exclaimed, looking at Carin with exasperation. "Are you truly so daft, as to think either Nina or Galen is 'any other child'?" Megella shook her head wearily, as if tiring of explaining the obvious. "A *wysard's* strength is the strength of the primal world, the raw power of the world. From infancy, a gifted child knows without being told that in nature there is magic. You should celebrate your daughter's embrace of all that she finds in field, forest, ocean, and stream—even a flyblown carcass, for it once teemed with life."

From the table, Meg took a slice of apple. It was turning brown, so long had they sat together, picking at Carin's worries more than at the food.

"What does it matter, that Nina's dead chick was feeding a few worms?" Megella demanded. "Has her mother grown so fastidious as to look with disgust, as well, upon a bit of apple which has sat out too long?" The wisewoman popped the brown slice between her teeth and chewed noisily. Speaking around a mouthful of pulp, Meg added, "Had you displayed such delicate sensibilities in your own girlhood, my duckling, you would have starved before you reached Ruain."

That's true, Carin silently conceded with an inward squirm. Skulking over the grasslands, avoiding settled places, raiding the

115

occasional barn or store-shed and taking anything remotely edible that she could catch or steal, Carin had not been choosy. More than once, she'd chased the carrion crows away from some newly dead animal … or not so newly dead, when it was either eat what she found or lose the strength to go on. The latter had not been an option: she would not abandon her quest. And so Carin had survived, any way that she could.

Megella seemed to catch her thoughts. For as the wisewoman finished chewing and washed down the brown apple with a swallow of brown ale, Meg added, "Furthermore, don't talk to me of dead mice as though *they* are anything out of the ordinary." The woman sniffed. "So thick are the field mice on the plains, they would have scattered before you as you walked those grassy places. Widgeon, I do not doubt that in your travels of old you cooked and ate more than a few of the flea-bitten little beasties."

The wisewoman smiled knowingly as Carin hid behind her own ale mug. Eating rodents was nothing she cared to remember, or to admit.

"As for the drowned mouse that seems to have started all this nonsense about 'Nina's dead things'," Megella went on, "I know for a certainty that Myra's kitchen corner is not so free of the vermin as she would have you—or her master—believe. If Nina washed a mouse out of its hole and drowned it by chance in the excitement of working magic with her brother that night, then she did a better job of housekeeping than my chatterbag sister Myra does. Tah!"

The wisewoman reached for the nearly empty jug of ale and sloshed a little into Carin's mug, turning the gesture into a flourish as she had her final say. "Duckling, I advise you to spend less time with your imaginings and more with your children, if you again find yourself doubting their characters. Those kitlings show only their true selves, for they haven't the artifice to do otherwise. You'll soon see — as all others have — that they bear no trace of their foremother's evil."

Carin considered asking Megella to move back into the manor house so that she need not ride half a day to have strong ale and good sense poured into her. But the wisewoman had been asked before, and always declined, saying the house of Verek was too busy for her.

"I've lived on my own too long," Meg would excuse herself. "I want peace and quiet, and my own garden, cowshed, and hen-coop. And none to gainsay me." Always, too, there was Megella's argument that a healer as skilled as herself ought to live near the townsfolk, so that *they* need not ride half a day to seek her.

As Carin relaxed into the feeling of relief she'd gained from this talk with Aunt Meg, a name flicked into her mind like a loose strand of a frayed memory. Surprised by its suddenness, she spoke it aloud, with no expectation of anything except a varia-tion on Megella's arguments for continued singlehood — though with the name came an impression of a gentle, craggy-faced giant who had shown a marked interest in the wisewoman who stopped for a night at his cabin in Ruain's eastern forests.

"Shen!" Carin exclaimed, looking at Megella. "I've no idea why, but just now I thought of Theil's steward who lives a long way east of here in those cedar forests by the sea-cliffs. Remem-ber him, Meg? He was taken with you."

Megella narrowed her eyes again, her head atilt. Slowly, the wisewoman combed her fingers through the scarlet fringes of her purple shawl.

"I believe your memory surpasses mine, widgeon, for I had forgotten that fellow until hearing his name pass your lips. Wheesht! The lapse disturbs me. Not so much for care of Master Shen, for I've no mind to encumber myself with a man at this time in my life. But neither would I choose to lose the memory of him lifting me down from horseback as though I were a

117

feather in his hands." Megella smiled … then frowned, and hoisted herself up.

"Much as I dislike the headache it inflicts and the sorry state it leaves me in, I'd rather suffer a dose of forget-for-now antidote than to forget my life," the wisewoman muttered, half to herself. Tipping the ale-jug, Meg peered into its emptiness, then raised her eyes to Carin's. "Eat more bread, widgeon, to soak up all that beer you guzzled, while I fix myself a strong cup of memory tea."

Carin sat bolt upright, her gaze locked with Meg's. "*Memory* tea, Aunt? By all means, bring me a cup, too. A large cup."

"Surely not!" Megella exclaimed. "The stuff will split your skull open. I'll wager any sum you please that never in your life has your head hurt the way my forget-for-now counter-charm will make it hurt."

Carin rubbed at her lower lip. "I believe you'd lose that bet, Megella. Try cracking your skull on the floor of a warlock's dungeon and knocking yourself out, and tell me then how your head feels in the morning." She raised her mug to the wisewoman and added, "In any case, I'll have a headache from all this ale you've drowned me in. So fix me a cup of your memory tea, and let's see what pain the two together can inflict."

Grumbling her disapproval while tapping her thumbnail against her teeth, Meg disappeared into her cottage.

The woman was gone long enough for Carin to eat every crumb of bread and cheese that still remained on the table. For truly, she *was* feeling the effects of more ale than she had ever before drunk at one sitting. Her eyes were losing focus and she felt lightheaded. If she tried to head homeward any time soon, falling off her horse seemed a distinct possibility.

So Carin ate more than she really wanted, her stomach needing a bulwark against too much alcohol. And when Megella handed her a large cup of steaming tea, she gulped half of it, risking a burned tongue in her eagerness to thin the homebrew that sloshed around inside her.

"*Wheesht!*" the wisewoman exclaimed. "Go easy—that's not mint you're drinking. This tea is powerful. Sip it. If you gag on it, be pleased to get off my porch before you upchuck. I do not wish my cottage filled with the stink of vomit and beer."

In Carin, however, the tea provoked no retching. Quite the contrary: it settled her stomach, dispelled her dizziness, and sharpened her sight. By the time she'd drained her cup—while Megella sat barely tasting hers, sipping as if to stretch the drink through the afternoon—Carin felt wonderfully revived and ready to turn for home.

When she said as much, the wisewoman scoffed. "You're tipsy, duckling. You'll stay here till morning. I'll not let you break your neck, half drunk and riding a benighted road. When your head begins to shatter—as it will—you'll be glad I kept you."

Carin put down her teacup and stood.

"No, Meg, I'll not stay. I have much to think about—so much more than I realized, in fact, thanks to your magical tea. A leisurely ride is exactly what I need." Carin looked down the lane toward Fintan, then turned back to Megella. "I'm inclined to take the long way home—that winding path through the hills. It's much prettier than the main road."

"But far longer!" Megella protested. "You won't be halfway home before the sun sets. It's such an empty byway, widgeon, you'll not likely see another traveler."

"I'm counting on that, Meg. My mind wants solitude this evening." Carin reached for the woman and gave her a parting hug. "Don't worry. I'll be careful."

"You'll be riding alone into darkness. And there was a time when you disliked being alone in the dark," Megella muttered.

Carin shrugged. "I got over it." With a smile, she added, "And anyway, a starlit night just can't compare with the blackness inside the void. That's a deeper dark than I'll ever know in this world."

To Megella's barely audible, "Tah!" Carin responded, whispering in her ear, "Thank you, Aunt. You cannot know how you have eased my heart. I've been so frightened for Nina."

The wisewoman patted Carin's back, then slipped indoors while she went to collect her horse from the grassy slope under the trees.

Remounted, Carin reined to a halt at the porch for a final word as Megella stepped from her cottage to hand up a loaf of bread and cheese.

"Make your breakfast on this, widgeon," Megella said, resignation in her voice. "As surely as the sun will set on your homeward journey, if you're resolved to take that lonely byroad, then you may see the new dawn along it as well. Travelers have been known to get lost in those hills after nightfall. Most especially tipsy travelers with aching heads."

Carin only smiled, took the bread, and waved good-bye.

Down the lane from Meg's cottage, she skirted the edge of Fintan and picked up the tree-lined byway that wound through ranks of low hills. Afternoon daylight still remained to her. Carin would have sufficient sun, at least at the start, to do what she intended on that deserted trail through empty country.

She began small, and waited until she had passed well beyond Fintan's outlying precincts. Watching and listening to her surroundings, assured that she was utterly alone, Carin bespelled a dead twig that jutted into her path from an oak growing close beside the track.

The twig crumbled, and sand sprinkled like rain onto the bare soil of the road in front of her horse's hooves.

Carin halted, dismounted, and crouched in the road to study the residue of her spellwork. Yes, it was as she had known it: the subtle but euphoric thrill of power flowing through her; the gritty texture of the sand she made; and most importantly, the absolute control she exercised over this wizardry of her own devising. It had not left her. Though for a time she'd lost all memory of it, Carin still had the mastery to bespell a single dew-drop or a lone blade of grass … or to destroy an entire hillside thick with trees, if she chose.

Or, to blast to *farsinchia* the demon who had once escaped her justice.

Not this time, Carin thought. *This time, the witch will have no-where to run.*

Chapter 9

Patterns

Carin rose from her crouch in the road and threw her magic upon a towering dead stump that loomed at a distance from where she stood with her horse. The once-proud tree, blasted by lightning, stood forlorn, clothed by not even a climbing vine. The tree seemed to call out to Carin to end its decrepitude, and in a heartbeat she had done so, leaving only a pile of sand to mark where the stump had been. In time, other trees would take root and grow in that fertile residue.

With a small bow, she paid her final respects to the tree's remains, remembering as she straightened how Nina had been determined to give the baby bird an equally proper "funeral"—proper, in Nina's mind, meaning disposal in water.

Carin shook her head at her former misgivings. How could she have suspected sinister magic in anything that child did? Nina was no more "drawn to death" than Carin was. As she continued along the road, not remounting but ambling along, leading her horse, Carin reduced random dead sticks and branches to powdery sand, reveling in the tightly controlled flow of her own spellcraft ... but being minutely careful to take only the dead, touching nothing living.

The rediscovery of this power within her had opened a floodgate, and under the influence of Meg's potent memory tea Carin let the torrent wash over her. Recollections rippled through her, of the horror she had felt at her involuntary killing of the goatherd Flynn, and how terrified she had been that she might do the same to Theil or Megella—her lack of conscious intent being no assurance, in those early days of experiencing her own strength, that she wouldn't kill them as well.

Carin's thoughts roamed wide, seeking and securing the fragments of memory that had long eluded her. She could now recall every circumstance of her first meeting with Master Welwyn: how she had followed Verek through a canyon to reach the monk's cabin in a mountain glen. Carin also remembered bidding Welwyn farewell on the morning of their departure, as they began their climb into the mountains. She could picture the mare Emrys, stabled in Welwyn's deer-shed. Carin had nearly cried that morning as she stole a moment to give the mare's ears a scratch before leaving the animal behind—never to see her again, she had thought at the time.

But Lanse the stableboy had dragged himself back down the mountain after Verek and Carin leapt into nothingness and abandoned the boy. Nearly a year after leaving Ruain, Lanse had returned, riding Verek's once-spirited hunter, Brogar, and leading Emrys.

The boy had left the mare with their horseman neighbor, Cian Ronnat. Gripped by obsession, however, and with shocking disregard for the animal's welfare, Lanse had ridden away again on a worn-out Brogar. When at last Verek returned to Ruain and located the horse, Brogar was beyond saving. With tears in his eyes, and a clean knife-thrust through the horse's brain, the *wysard* had ended his favorite mount's suffering. Carin suspected that Lanse's maltreatment of the horse lay behind Verek's refusal to utter the boy's name. Lanse's attempts to murder Carin might be excused—for Verek himself had once ordered the boy to kill her. But to ride Brogar into the ground was unforgivable. Lanse had forever lost his master's good favor.

In Cian Ronnat's care, however, Emrys thrived. The mare had remained with their neighbor, pampered and petted, the queen of Ronnat's pastures. Her foals were prized. The horse Carin now rode, in fact, was one of Emrys' progeny.

Carin smiled at the memory of visiting Emrys while taking her pick of saddle-horse from Ronnat's stables. The mare had greeted her as eagerly as ever, and displayed the same fondness for the treat of an apple, which Emrys nibbled with delicate manners from her former rider's outstretched hand.

Now as the sun dropped toward the horizon, Carin remounted the horse that had been hers since that day at Ronnat's. In the tree-shadowed byway, it would soon be too dark to safely continue her practice of the sand spell. She would not risk blindly destroying anything that possessed life. She would work her magic in ways as far distant from Morann's sorcery as it was possible for her to be.

Carin rode close under the branches of a tall oak that grew beside the trail. There she paused, and raised her hand to grip one limb.

"Honored elder," she murmured to the tree. "Please ask the *wysard*, Master Welwyn, to tell my Lord Verek where I am."

Carin fancied she felt a slight quivering in the branch under her hand. But it might have been only her imagination.

Welwyn, when she knew him in his tree-shaded glen, had mentioned that he had "little ways" of getting messages to other wizards. Since the old monk had come to live at Weyrrock and tutor the children, Carin had seen him grip a limb of an oak near the manor's main gate, and there bend his head as if in thought. When he'd caught her watching, he'd only winked and laid a finger alongside his nose, looking enigmatic. From this Carin had formed the suspicion that Welwyn's "little ways" involved old oaks.

Now, with a mumbled "Thank you," she released the tree and rode on, giving her horse its head, trusting the animal to find its way home to the manor. In the day's failing light, under a moonless sky and closed in by trees, she could see little.

Briefly, Carin toyed with the idea of summoning a witch-light orb, a ball of flameless fire, bright and cool, such as Verek could call to his hand. But she'd never attempted it—had never even asked Theil to show her how.

As much as she loved and adored her children, the care of them had taken almost all of the five-going-on-six years since Nina's birth. As Carin's thoughts filled the silence of the evening which deepened around her, she reflected that Welwyn's arrival had been not only a boon to the children's education, it had freed her to pursue her own as well. Not merely in the library, with books, but out in the world, with magic.

Carin held her hand in front of her, palm up. Around her, pressing close, she felt the trees, and they seemed to whisper a warning:

Do not make fire. Do not burn us.

She heeded the whispers and dropped her hand. She'd be foolish to attempt potentially dangerous magic that she did not know how to make. Her "witchlight" might blaze forth as blistering fire rather than cool brilliance. And even if Carin managed to produce a proper orb, its sudden glow could spook her horse, sending the beast charging off the path and into the hills, there to lose the way. Then, as Megella had foretold, Carin would be breakfasting on stale bread after a long night of wandering.

So she merely settled herself in the saddle, comfortable on this good horse foaled by her beloved Emrys. Carin rode with a loose rein and let her eyes close, as there was nothing to see.

But so much to remember … going back to the winter of their quest, when Verek had dragged her high into the western mountains. Then, Carin had been his unwilling accomplice, not understanding that she alone could wield the otherworldly magic that would defeat the necromancer, the worker of blood sorcery.

Or seem to defeat her. Morann was proving to be a hard demon to slay.

That hag, however, must die. This time, Carin would not fail.

Her roving thoughts lingered on the image she had seen in the *wysards'* well, of Verek's first wife and their only child, Aidan, who had drowned amid water-lilies in the blue lake outside the manor's walls. Morann had done that. From her altar of evil in the far west, the demon had sprung the trap that killed Verek's young family, and nearly drove him mad with grief.

Unbeknownst to Verek—for he never visited the graves— Carin had directed the new gardener to clear the overgrown thicket around the family tomb at the back of the grounds. A small, neat garden now circled the tomb, bright in springtime with Alesia's favorite blue flowers, and pristine white in the depths of winter, when none but Carin ventured there to offer her predecessor her Mydrismas greetings.

The evil that took Alesia and Aidan must never touch Verek's new family. Morann must come nowhere near Nina or Galen. Carin must see to it. She must remove the threat that hung like an executioner's axe over House Verek.

She was riding now with her head down, eyes tight shut, bending her mind to the task of channeling the flood of memory into linear time instead of the swirling images that seemed to splash up into her consciousness, many of them coming to her without regard for their proper place in the flow. Verek had supposed the disorder that afflicted Carin's memories stemmed entirely from her travels through the void, a place where time stretched and twisted, curved and collapsed, and lost its meaning. During her journeys in that strange place, Carin had come to view the void as existing outside time. Or perhaps it manifested in another time.

All she knew for certain was that she'd gone into the emptiness more than once, and while in that place of seeming nothingness, she had experienced time differently than in the tangible world of daily sunrises and changing seasons. In the void, she had ripened, finding upon her first return to Ruain that her body—and her heart—were no longer girlish, but had matured to womanhood.

And yet, on Carin's later journey through the blankness, time had seemed to go the other way, hanging almost suspended, its passage delayed. Theil's seed in her womb had not grown while Carin was beyond the void. But as if to make up for lost time, she had quickened with distressing rapidity upon her final return to Ruain. The demands on Carin's body, made by that fast-developing imp who would be Nina, had been so heavy in the last week of her pregnancy that Carin, bedridden, had suffered delirium and fever.

Now, riding in the silence of the dusk-darkened hills, at last gaining mastery over her own recall, Carin could weave her thoughts into a coherent history. In her mind's eye she watched her previously fragmented and splintered memories knit themselves together. Methodically she aligned her recollections until she could trace them, almost without a gap, from the time she rode west with Verek, through the confrontation with Morann and Carin's subsequent bridge-breaking, to the days of their journey with Megella across the grasslands, and thence to Ruain and Carin's unexpected return to the world of her birth.

Throughout this meticulous retracing, she had foremost in her thoughts the location and situation, both known and conjectured, of the sorceress Morann. *Could* the demon possibly know that Theil Verek had again fathered children?

Carin thought until her head ached. *You're right, Megella,* she conceded silently. *That tea of yours packs a punch.*

But as full dark fell, enveloping her in a night like velvet, fragrant with the scent of nocturn flowers, she was rewarded by the relief of a conclusion beyond doubt: No, the demoness could have no knowledge of Nina or Galen. Morann had been gone from this world, with the vastness of the void between her and Ladrehdin, before Nina was conceived. The only possible way the witch could know was if the woodsprite had told her. But had the sprite itself known Carin was pregnant?

Carin and the woodsprite had talked together while both lingered near her childhood home on Earth. But she had not been showing during that interlude. Indeed, she'd not been absolutely certain, then, that she was with child. She had definitely never mentioned the possibility to the woodsprite.

Furthermore, the sprite would have had no reason to find the sorceress or breathe a word to that demon. More than anything, the woodsprite feared a return to its own homeworld. There, the creature was only a weed, one strangling vine among a multitude of wiry green creepers that had overrun and choked their world. While the woodsprite might feel gratitude for Morann's original "fishing expedition" which had hooked the creature and brought it through the void to Ladrehdin, its overriding emotion would be terror that the sorceress might retake it and fling it back to the world whence it came.

No, Carin was certain: The sprite would have told Morann nothing, even if the creature had known there was a new story to tell of wizardly heirs for House Verek.

It followed, then, that Morann's purpose in testing the waters of the *wysards*, and more recently showing her face in the springwater pool abovestairs, was *not* to lure Theil's new children to their deaths, as she had lured Aidan. Morann was after something else.

And given that the witch valued nothing in the cosmos except power and dominion, it must be the power of Ruain itself that the demon wanted — the unrivaled potency of the magic that flowed in the very rock and water of this hidden province.

Morann had said as much, hadn't she? Casting back through her recovered, newly reconstructed memories, Carin found the words the enchantress had flung at Verek, the woman's voice contemptuous, that day they faced the demon in the west:

"I will take your stronghold, my son. I shall be mistress of Ruain, and with the power of that place I will summon to my service an army of fiends."

"In your dreams, you witch," Carin muttered.

Though she spoke softly, her voice sounded loud in the long unbroken silence of the hills. Her horse snorted, mildly startled, and jigged a step or two.

Then Carin was herself startled, as a much louder and intimately familiar voice demanded from out of the darkness ahead of her: "Name yourself, rider!"

For an instant Carin played with the idea of teasing him, saying no more, making herself mysterious in the night. Then: *Drisha!* came a thought. *He might bespell first and seek answers later.*

Unwilling to discover what would happen if Verek turned her to stone and she toppled from her horse—snapping off her petrified head as she hit the ground?—Carin exclaimed in semi-earnest alarm: "Spare me, my lord, for I name myself your wife."

Straightaway, a witchlight orb appeared in his hand, illuminating the short stretch of road that lay between them. Verek urged his horse up beside Carin, and flung the orb to rest on his shoulder, so that his freed hand could reach for her and cup the back of her head. Yanking Carin half off her horse, he jerked her face to his and kissed her with ferocious intensity.

"Woman!" Verek barked when he let her go and Carin pulled herself back into her saddle, her every nerve aflame—exquisitely so—from the heat of that kiss. "What in the kingdom of Greatrakes are you doing out here?"

"Thinking," Carin replied, in a tone so flippant that it was obvious—to herself and undoubtedly to Verek also—that she *was* tipsy. Megella's ale boasted nearly the potency of the wise-woman's magical tea. As if to announce how freely she'd drunk of both, Carin gave a little belch, and giggled.

Her husband was not amused. By the light of the orb at his shoulder, Carin saw a deepening fierceness in Verek's scowl, but the reasons for it escaped her. She had expected to meet him somewhere along this road tonight, but she had not foreseen that he would come to her wearing an angry frown on his lean and handsome face. What was troubling him?

Verek growled at her. "I see little evidence of you 'thinking,' my lady. But if you are indeed engaged in the effort, then I invite you to think on your actions today." His voice was brittle. "You leave without a word before daybreak. Through all the sunlit hours you are absent, and at nightfall I look in vain for your return. What would you have *me* think, Carin? That *you'd* left me, too?"

"Oh, Theil!" she exclaimed, instantly sober and dismissing any thought of teasing him. It was all there, in that little word, *"too."* Every reason for Verek's anger, his fierce glare, his accusing tone: Why was she only now seeing it? His beloved Alesia had gone out one morning, strolling to the lake that lay a comfortable walk from the manor. When that young woman did not come home, Verek had ridden out at nightfall to seek her. He'd found her, dead, their only child dead with her.

He's been reliving a nightmare all day, waiting for me, Carin realized, her self-reproach like a fist to her gut. *How cruel and selfish I have been.*

She reached to caress his face. "Leave you, my love?" Carin murmured. "Never think it. Never allow such an idea to come into your head." With her fingertips she traced Verek's frowning lips. "Didn't Welwyn tell you where I was, or Megella speak of my visiting her today, and my notion to take the long way home?"

Verek grunted, a sullen sound, but one that hinted of lessening anger. He caught Carin's hand, held it slightly away from his lips, and demanded, "How would you think that either of them could convey such a message to me? I've sat by a window at home all day, alone, watching for you."

Carin winced at the pain in Theil's voice. Then she sighed. Apparently she had expected too much of Megella's bucket-magic and Welwyn's tree-talking.

"I do beg your pardon, my lord," Carin murmured, her voice soft with contrition. "I thought Meg might use her water pail to send you a message. Besides that, I had an idea—foolish, you may think—that Welwyn talks to oak trees, or them to him. Before sundown, I asked an old oak to entreat Welwyn to tell you what road I was riding." Carin smiled at Verek, and in the witch-light she saw his face relax a little. "I am sorry, my love. I didn't want you to worry. You know I can take care of myself."

"Humph." Verek made no other response, except to press Carin's fingers to his lips. This kiss was forgiving, with little fury remaining in it, but intense with relief.

Verek released Carin's hand then, and reined his horse around so that both their mounts faced the direction of home. They started for it at a walk, riding side by side in a lane that was nearly too narrow. Verek took the witchlight from his shoulder and tossed it ahead of them. It never hit the ground, but hung suspended in midair, lighting their way.

"As it happens, *fileen*"—Theil's use of the endearment as-sured Carin that his temper was rapidly cooling—"Welwyn may have received your tidings, though he shared no word of their source with me. As I rode out at nightfall to search for you, the man said only, 'Among the hills and under the trees you will find what you seek.'"

"Wizards!" Carin exclaimed in exasperation. "Can you lot never speak plainly? I see no reason for Welwyn to have made a mystery of my message to you."

"Perhaps," Verek replied, "your intermediary only repeated the message that he received. Does it not occur to you, my lady, that mystery may have entered into it when you chose an oak to bear your words?"

"Oh." Carin fell silent as she considered the trees that crowded close on either side. Then she nodded. "That could be. The oaks may have understood my intent but not my exact words."

"Yes. In my dealings with messengers who go on two legs, I've known news that travels from one's mouth to another's ear to end its journey with nothing remaining of whatever meaning it might have held at the start. I count it a feat that the trees made clear your whereabouts with so little misdirection. But you must ask Welwyn if you wish to know more. His use of oaks is a wood-craft that I have seldom practiced."

Verek glanced at Carin, and for the first time he seemed to notice her apparel. His eyes raked her from slouchy hat to baggy britches, and on down to her own good boots — the only gear she wore that actually fit her. In a voice half amused, half appalled, he demanded, "What in the name of glory are you wearing, woman?"

Carin laughed. "These are my new riding clothes. Myra got them for me."

Verek sniffed. "From where? A cowherd's hovel?"

She wrinkled her nose. "From the way they smell, I think that's likely." Carin paused, then remarked with studied flippancy, "They're very comfortable."

Verek came close to rolling his eyes, but he said nothing further.

For a time then, they rode without speaking, although Carin could almost hear the questions churning in her husband's mind. Verek would burn to know why she'd ridden alone to visit Megella, why she'd taken this long way home, and what cause she had to lapse into silence with him at her side, offering him no explanations, giving him no satisfaction. But he asked nothing, only waited for Carin to break the lengthening silence.

I can't tell him I've called again upon that deadly spell of sand, she thought. *He'll guess at once what I'm planning to do with it, and where I mean to go.*

Neither would Carin speak of the fears she had laid before Megella, that Verek's children might carry within them the evil of his mother. *Demon's taint upon his gift.* Theil must never know that Carin's thoughts had strayed down so dark a path.

The silence between them was building toward oppressive before Carin marshaled her thoughts sufficiently to interrupt it. When at last she'd arranged in her mind all that she meant to tell him, she began conversationally—as though they hadn't been riding together without speaking for what felt like miles.

"I've had a profitable day," Carin said, and pressed on before Verek could interject a grumble about how he'd spent his, waiting at a window. "I've finally managed to pull my memories together and tack them into place. They make sense to me now, instead of flying apart like the shards of a dropped bowl with tiny pieces scattering everywhere."

"Excellent," Verek murmured, but in a tone more wary than pleased.

Puzzled by this, but too fixed on her train of thought to question it just then, Carin continued. "I'd found it odd that I couldn't remember getting to Welwyn's cabin. Or exactly when we left it, to head up the mountain. But it's all come back to me now, and I think I know why I lost those memories for a time. A little before we rode out of the canyon and into Welwyn's glen, I worked strong magic.

"—Not on purpose," Carin hastened to add. "Not consciously, anyway. But we'd been caught in an ice storm, I was so near frozen I blacked out … and all unawares, I made knives and firebrands fly through the air. Didn't I? I remember you telling me I'd done the magic. You and Welwyn seemed rather impressed by it."

"We were," Verek muttered. "Deeply impressed. And alarmed. Welwyn had caught the inflections of a strangely foreign birth in your way of speaking, and the man heard the implications as clearly as I had done when first you spoke to me …

"Indeed," Verek added after a brief pause, "upon my discovery of you in my woodland that autumn—inside the barrier which should have forbidden you entry into my domain—I first imagined that you were like unto the fabled priestesses of the sacred oak groves, perhaps able to slay with a thought as they were reputed to do. I was soon persuaded, however—as Welwyn would be in his turn—that you must instead be a water spirit *far* strayed from your native realm." Verek gave a low chuckle of remembered amazement as he recalled his first encounter with Carin. "Yes, my lady. Welwyn and I were deeply alarmed by you. You'd come to this world from Drisha knew where, you'd had no training in wizardry that we knew of, and you were exhibiting powers—raw strength, neither tempered nor controlled."

"Too much strength, too soon, I now think," Carin said. "In the hours I've spent tonight pinning down my memories, I've found a pattern. Or two patterns. One lies in the void between the worlds, where time defies expectations and has worked its own kind of magic upon my body ... unpredictable magic, but producing results that have been satisfactory to you and me both, I believe."

"Eminently satisfactory," Verek murmured. He reached to run his fingers down Carin's sleeved arm. His touch, as always, sent the heat to her blood. But taking pleasure in each other tonight would have to wait. Carin had more to say, and Verek respected her need to say it: he pulled back to his side of the narrow lane they traveled.

"Two patterns?" he prompted her. "One in the void, as I've suspected since you told me of your memory 'jumble.' But where lies the other?"

"In magic," Carin replied. "There's a pattern to the ways the working of strong magic can affect a person's mind—especially if the mind is unprepared for it."

"As, perhaps, yours was unprepared for the power that flowed through you, deep in that night of ice and snow?"

Carin nodded, though she doubted Verek would see her do so in a darkness lit only by witchlight.

"Yes, I think so. Now that my memories are holding together instead of flying apart, I'm picturing every league of our journey to the mountains, our 'side trip' to the Granger millpond, and our travels with Megella across the southlands. But in the picture, I see a blank space. Between the time I killed the goatherd—"

Verek's sharply indrawn breath made Carin pause. When he said nothing, however, she merely commented, "Yes, I remember that man. Flynn was his name." Then she continued:

"Between the time I killed Flynn, and that night when I served the Powers as a conduit for the magic that cleansed this world of plague and pestilence, I remember nothing, Theil. In my mind there's only an impression of anguish … a kind of dazed desperation … and abject terror that I would do to you or Megella what I'd done to the goatherd."

Carin paused again, then added, "You once mentioned a town on the coast. Easthaven." She touched her forehead. "Even after dragging into place every fragment of memory from that jumbled heap I carried in my brain, I have no recollection of a place called Easthaven."

She turned to Verek. "Did something happen there? Have you bespelled me to forgetfulness to keep me from knowing it?"

"Never!" Verek exclaimed. "By the oath of my House, Carin: never would I presume to force spellcraft upon you, secretly, without your knowledge or permission. I do freely confess, however, that I have longed to make you forget certain events—chief among them, the death of that louse-ridden goatherd."

Verek sighed, a heavy sound, almost sad. "Much of what you endured in Easthaven is dark to me as well. Only this can I tell you: I took you to the harbor mouth and asked you to clear it of the deadly weed which choked it. Your spellwork that night was … raw power unleashed. I, however, caught barely a glimpse before finding myself being carried into our lodgings, bleeding and bruised. I know not how you came to be in the water, close by the docks.

"Rumors reached my ears that you had attempted to drown yourself. I gave them no credence, but for days afterward you were wretchedly silent, refusing to speak either to me or to Megella." Verek stretched his hand to Carin, a gesture near to imploring. "Had I possessed the means to take from you the malady of spirits that afflicted you, I would have done so. But remember, *fileen:* I was powerless then."

Carin took his outstretched hand and held it for a time as they rode, feeling its strength, its warmth, and its ever-present potential for magic, the power that seemed to crackle just beneath his skin. She said nothing, only closed her eyes and tried to find within her memories a match to what he was saying. Impressions surfaced, nothing definite, but shading by degrees into conformity with what she *did* remember of her experiences, especially as he continued speaking of less-distant events.

"As we resumed our journey up the coast, leaving East-haven and its troubles behind us," Verek said, "we made our camp one evening at the foot of a great waterfall. There, I saw lightning flash from a storm of magic and accept from you the healing you offered it. After that, I rejected all thought of attempting to bespell the one through whom the Powers of this world had worked their will. In that moment of two Powers touching—Amangêda, and yourself—you were one with the goddess. You joined the Elementals. They set you far above me, Lady Carin. As I say, I would not entertain such presumption in myself, as to attempt the erasure of any part of you who are my goddess."

Carin's eyes flew open. She stared at him, speechless. Slowly then, she swiveled her gaze forward and contemplated the orb of witchlight that floated along the path ahead of them. She looked within it for a way to answer him.

"I … don't know what to say, my lord," she murmured at
last, finding no words. "That's, um … rather unexpected." But
why should it startle her to hear Verek speak of her that way?
That he held her in high regard, he'd made clear long before
tonight. But to elevate her to the ranks of the Powers? That per-
turbed her view of herself, and shifted their relationship to what
felt like a different level altogether. A kind of cosmic level.

After a long moment of half-stunned silence, Carin worked
back through everything Verek had just said to find the question
of hers that had brought all of this out of him. She looked over
and said gently, "My love, I never seriously suspected you of
putting me under a spell of forgetfulness. Forgive me for even
asking. I just needed to rule it out, before laying the blame on
Amangêda for pushing me right to my limits, and beyond them."

"What are you saying, *fileen?*" Verek regarded her, frowning
slightly.

She shrugged. "Merely bringing into the open something
you, me, Welwyn, and probably Megella have all thought these
last five or six years: What became of that remarkable young
wysard who showed such promise?—she who broke Lord
Legary's spell of concealment on the *Book of Archamon*, freed this
world from alien exploitation … and aided the Powers in defeat-
ing alien plagues." Carin sniffed. "Now I can barely cast a spell
of stone, unlock a door, or sharpen an arrow-point. There was a
time when I frightened you all with my strength: you, Welwyn,
Megella, maybe Jerold …"

Certainly Lanse, Carin thought, but wouldn't venture to say
aloud. She hurried on:

"Rest assured, my lord, I couldn't have scared any of you
worse than I terrified myself. Every day brought me a new shock:
Within myself I found the power to burn invading vermin and
deadly weed with magian fire. I commanded magical talismans
to carry me where I wished, to other worlds beyond the void. But
now?"

With another sniff, Carin glanced again at Verek. "Now, I'm in your library day after day, struggling to learn magic that a native-born *wysard* knows instinctively. I'm begging Welwyn to teach me a few simple spells. Drisha's teeth, Theil! I can't even conjure Ercil's fire," Carin snapped, using the term that Verek preferred to the vernacular "witchlight."

"I see," Verek replied, thoughtful, rubbing his chin. "You feel you were subjected to too much, too soon."

Hardly aware of doing so, Carin pulled off her cap and shook her hair loose. The act felt freeing. As did Verek's observant presence at her side. She had thought to make an accusation, or at least air a grievance. But her flash of resentment could not be sustained in the velvety darkness of these oakwoods. When Carin spoke again, she could only speak what she knew to be true, and to speak her truth without anger: She had been used, and very nearly used up.

"Amangêda pushed me very far, very fast, preparing me," Carin murmured, "from the first day I set foot in Ruain. A task lay ahead of me: collecting those otherworldly crystals and removing them from Ladrehdin before they drained every last dribble of power from this world. Amangêda needed me ready in a hurry to undertake that task. I was not prepared for the power that flowed through me ... the Power that *used* me to accomplish its ends.

"I understand, now," Carin added, with a feeling of resignation but no bitterness, "that the working of strong magic has consequences. Where once I fell headlong into it, gaining power too quickly, these days I'm almost starting over, learning spellcraft like a dull novice."

She paused as Verek muttered, "No part of you, in brain nor body, may be called 'dull,' my lady."

Carin smiled. "Kind of you to say so, m'lord. When I'm wrestling with your ancient books of spellcraft, though, my wits are barely equal to the task of deciphering them, much less con-juring with them. I am hopeful, however, that my mended memories may lead to better results after tonight. I've got more to work with now. That strong magic Amangêda forced me into, and channeled through me …" Carin heaved a sigh as she con-templated the damage it had done. "In a sense, it took my mind apart. It shattered me in places.

"But at least it left me some pieces that I could put back to-gether. Other parts of my life, though, are gone, and I don't think I'll get them back. I believe I may never recall my childhood on Earth — which is just as well. That's not a loss I grieve. And any-way, that's down to the void, as you told me years ago. The nec-romancer spinning me through the oblivion between the worlds when I was a child — that's what took my earthly memories.

"But the events at Easthaven are also lost to me. Whatever happened there, I'm left with nothing except impressions of light and darkness, desperation and hope … and a feeling that I expe-rienced something both terrifying and sublime."

"Perhaps you were not meant to retain the memory of all that happened in that place," Verek murmured. "Some knowledge is forbidden, even to *wysards*."

Carin nodded, again forgetting the darkness of the night around them, for so much had come clear in her mind this even-ing. "I'm just glad, and deeply grateful, that I've been allowed to remember everything else — every moment of my life with you, anyway."

"Hunh," Verek grunted. "*Every* moment, *fileen?* Not omit-ting the stormy days of our earliest acquaintance?"

Carin's laugh was light, playful. As she grinned at him from the shadows where the witchlight barely reached, she felt like teasing him again. "You may be certain, my lord, that every hour of *those* days is permanently engraved in the book of my life."

The stretch of road they now traveled was not hard-packed, but powdery soft under their horses' hooves. The animals' steps made hardly a sound. So deep was the silence that lay on the hills that Carin heard the long breath Verek drew in through his nostrils. He exhaled as slowly, and then spoke, his tone subdued, nothing of playfulness in it.

"I fear, my lady, that you have been ill-used by both the Powers of this world and by the *wysard* who rides at your side. I contend that the Powers may be excused their conduct, for their need was great and you were the vessel best suited to fill it.

"For my own treatment of you, however, when first we met, I can offer no justification so noble—no excuse that is in any way acceptable. I can say only this:

"By the third week of our acquaintance, I had seen enough in you—and in the chamber of *wysards*—to know my fate: I must kill the enchantress who had borne me. Matricide is a hard thing for any man to contemplate ... even for a son born of a demoness. But I was resolved to make the attempt—knowing I would almost certainly fail unless you, Carin, summoned your other-worldly dragon to my aid. And if you helped me against the necromancer and I survived the encounter, then I would be obliged to kill you, to protect this world from the damage that I believed such a powerful worker of alien wizardry might do in this realm that was not your natural home."

Verek's voice softened as he turned to Carin in the gloom. "My intended treachery ate into my soul until I thought I would go mad. How could I choose? The safety of this world, or the life of the innocent trespasser whose fiery spirit had melted my heart—a heart that had been crusted with ice for twenty years." Verek reached his hand toward Carin, but he did not touch her. "With every fiber of my being, I fought against falling in love with you. I knew if I showed you the least tenderness, if I admitted my feelings for you, I would not then find the will to do my duty to destroy you the instant the necromancer was dead."

As Verek turned away from Carin to gaze at the path ahead, his eyes caught the glimmer of the witchlight. They looked moist. "My desperate attempts to harden my heart led me to behave abominably toward you. Oh yes, *fileen*. I very much wished to bespell you to forgetfulness. I wanted you to forget, for I feared you could never forgive my treatment of you, the cruelty I showed you in our early days together."

Carin listened, fascinated. Verek had never said all of this to her before. She had never needed him to say it—she'd understood, no explanation required. But his almost frantic worry for her, earlier tonight, when Carin hadn't come back to him at the expected hour … evidently his day of missing her had him in a confessional mood. She was glad enough to listen, for it seemed Verek needed to unburden himself of old worries and past uncertainties, much as she had needed to voice her newfound understanding of all that she had lost, as well as gained, as a servant of the Powers.

She reached across the space between their horses and took Verek's hand. Carin leaned to kiss the back of it, then let him go as she straightened.

"From the moment we met," she said, looking at him, "I could see you were a man at war with himself. You seemed split in two—half of you a healer with a touch so gentle, you took my breath away … but the other half, a brute with a violent temper. Exactly when I figured it out, I don't know, but somewhere along the way I came to realize that at least part of what you were wrestling with, deep in your heart, had to do with me." Carin laughed lightly again. "I got a strong hint of it, that night in Welwyn's cabin when Ladra bewitched me into kissing you—and you most definitely kissed me back."

"Ladra!" Verek exclaimed, sounding half amused now, but still a little solemn. "By Drisha, it took every particle of self-restraint I could summon that night, to keep myself safely on Welwyn's couch, with a closed door separating you from me."

"'Safely' is right," Carin said, still grinning. "If you'd tried anything, you might have found more than a door blocking your way. Master Welwyn would have put your lights out."

"And had my guts for garters." Verek made a sound like a growl. "Before we left the mountain glen where sits his lonesome cabin, Welwyn told me he would have kept you for himself if I had not already asserted my claim on you."

"Was I to have no say in the matter?" Carin exclaimed with mock indignation. "Perhaps I would not have wanted either of you. Ever think of that?"

Verek heaved a troubled sigh. His reply relapsed into his deep seriousness of moments ago. "The distinct possibility that you would reject any advance I might offer was constantly before me. I thought you must despise me—and rightly so, after the way I treated you. *Fileen*, I have no word for the intensity of the feeling that swept me up, that day you appeared out of nothingness to take my hand and bring me through the void, out of your world and back to my own." Verek reached again, blindly, for Carin's hand. "Hope flared in me like a sunburst through storm-clouds, to think you might care for me—enough, at least, to deliver me from a lonely exile."

Carin gripped his hand. "Rescuing you was the least I could do, after sending you through the wrong door to the wrong planet." She leaned from her saddle toward him. "But I trust that any lingering doubts you might have harbored, regarding my feelings for you, were dispelled shortly after we splashed together into the millpond outside Granger, back again on Ladrehdin. Of that night under the willow trees, my memory has always been *perfectly* clear. I couldn't get your wet clothes off of you fast enough."

Verek threw back his head and laughed, all the seriousness leaving him. "Drisha's bones, how they clung! Soaked through, and heavy as armor. But indeed, my lady, by the time the next day's sun had climbed above those grasslands and slanted in through the willows where we lay together, you had relieved me of every shred of uncertainty—as well as every stitch of clothing. I fell in love with you all over again, that night."

"And I, with you," Carin whispered, leaning toward him until she risked unseating herself. But then a thought darted in, and jerked her upright.

"Oh!" she exclaimed. "Now I know why you seemed hesitant, early this summer, when I asked you to help me repair my broken memories. Even a little ago this evening, you didn't sound thrilled when I told you I'd got my recollections back together and in order." Carin grinned. "You really were hoping, weren't you, that I'd forgotten what a beast you were, our first months together. Not a chance, my lord! I remember it *all*."

"Then why have you never reproached me?" Verek demanded.

"Oh, for the love of Drisha!" Carin swore. "Reproach you?" Again she reached for Verek across the slight gap between their horses—they'd ridden knee to knee for miles. "While you were working so hard at keeping your distance from me, desperate not to fall in love, I was just as determined to make myself hate you. As you may recall, I came within a hairsbreadth of stabbing a knife through your heart. I'd say we fought that battle to a draw, wouldn't you?"

"Quite so, my lady," Verek murmured.

"I'm tired of talking," Carin declared. "But maybe you do need to hear one last thing from me tonight: There is nowhere in all of existence, in any realm, domain, or otherworldly vastness, that I would rather be than in your arms, you infuriating man!"

Verek reined up; Carin did likewise. He threw one arm around her and hauled her bodily out of her saddle. While pinning her to him—Drisha love the man, his strength was iron—Verek kissed her fiercely as Carin melted against him, one of her knees finding a little purchase on his stirrup leathers, her other leg braced against his.

When they had to break off to breathe, Verek lowered her to the ground, smoothly without jolting her. As he swung off his horse to stand with her, a snap of his fingers summoned the largest and brightest witchlight orb she'd ever seen him conjure.

Its light showed her a lush, open woodland. She and Verek were no longer hemmed in by oaks. The trees had thinned to reveal glades, thickly carpeted in grass and dotted with the blooms of late-summer flowers. So bright was the oversized witchlight that Carin could make out the colors: reds, yellows, purples.

Not far off the lane they had traveled into these small hours of the night, a sheltered spot cut the base of a hill among moss-covered stones. Tree boughs roofed the spot, and a latticework of flowering vines wrapped it on two sides, forming a natural bower.

Without another word spoken between them, Verek took Carin's hand and led her to the bower. Just as they reached it, he lobbed the witchlight high into the branches above their heads. The orb shattered, sending up sparks even higher into the tree's crown.

What a magical thing it is to be loved by a wizard, Carin thought as she gazed upward at the seeming infinity of flickering sparks, like a celestial dome of stars hanging in the tree. Some of the sparks drifted downward, far more slowly than snowflakes falling on a windless night. It would be hours—all the hours between now and dawn, Carin suspected—before the last of those twinkling sparks would fall into the grass.

Then Verek was laying her down in that grass, on a carpet of ferns and sweet clover. He buried his hands in the hair she had loosed from her discarded cap, and after that they had little need of talking, or even of thinking. Nothing remained but sensation, the touch of his hands and lips, and desire in Carin's veins like fire, as power crackled between them. Their bodies joined in shared urgency, ever-rising to exquisite release. Then all of it again, a fiery flood cresting under the stars, with his heart so close to hers, she felt its thudding beat.

Somewhere in those hours, with brilliant sparks drifting down to cool her naked skin and his, as Carin inhaled the fragrances of the flowers and Verek's own musky, earthy odor, she had but a single truly coherent thought:

Thank the Powers and all the gods of all the worlds, that I didn't stab a knife through his heart that night in the cave of magic.

Chapter 10

Master Magicians

Summer drew to a close. On an evening cool and fresh, with autumn in the air, all the household strayed outside to enjoy the sunset, even Myra and the bevy of maids and kitchen helpers who now answered to her.

During the warm months, the men of the house had built a table and set it in the garden, under myrtle trees amid violets. Sitting now at that table, Carin and Verek sipped *dhera* and watched Welwyn lead the children off to bed. Or to a story, more likely. The monk often kept his charges awake, reading them tales of adventure or instilling a knowledge of Ladrehdinian history, the latter couched in the language of legend, to which Nina and Galen would listen spellbound.

As Welwyn disappeared into the house, Carin turned to Verek. "A while back," she commented, trying to sound casual, "Master Welwyn said something that has bothered me."

Verek looked at her in the fading daylight. "Concerning the children?" he asked, sharply.

She laid her hand on his. "It's no cause for worry, at the present. But I have wondered what it might mean for the future."

Briefly, Carin described Welwyn's reaction when he learned of Carin's marriage to Verek having been officiated by the chief magistrate of Fintan.

"Welwyn wanted to know whether we had both signed the marriage record," Carin said, studying Verek's face. "He was pleased when I told him everything had been properly and lawfully witnessed. He seemed to think it was important, that it would establish Nina and Galen as your 'entitled heirs' — that's the phrase he used. Welwyn also said something about their birthright being challenged in the future."

Carin frowned. "I didn't like the sound of any of it. When Welwyn saw he'd upset me, he tried to brush it off as just an old man's ramblings. But I've been wondering: Was he saying that Nina and Galen might someday be driven out of Ruain, because of me? Because their mother is a foreigner?"

Witchlight flared in Verek's hand. He set the orb on the table between them, where it lit both his face and hers. His motions deliberate, he took Carin's hands in his own and pulled her around to face him squarely, his gaze locked on hers.

"No," Verek said, his voice firm. "Welwyn was saying nothing of the kind. My lady, do you not remember the eagerness and joy with which the people of this province welcomed you, when we rode to the coast and back? Have you forgotten the delight the people took in Nina and Galen?" He dropped his chin to peer at her. "You need not fear. None will dispute their right to inherit. My people know that your children will assure for their own descendants a secure future."

Verek smiled, and added, "As for you being a foreigner … that is all to the good. No other would suit the folk of Ruain so well. You have inspired every bard in the land." He released Carin's hands and lifted his to run his fingers through her soft, thick hair. "No week goes by without a new song sung or a poem written about the goddess from afar with the copper mane and emerald eyes."

Carin laughed to cover her self-consciousness. The attention she attracted every time she journeyed through Ruain at Verek's side was flattering, to be sure. But having spent her formative years attempting to escape all notice, she still found it disconcerting to be a figure of public interest.

Gently, she tugged Verek's fingers out of her hair. Though she liked the way he played with it, Carin wanted him focused on her questions, for at least a while longer.

"But I do wonder," she said, insistent, "why Welwyn spoke as he did, that evening when you were out of the room. What danger did the man foresee?"

Verek reached for his goblet of *dhera*, and heaved a slightly impatient-sounding sigh.

"Our Master Welwyn has a long memory," he muttered. "Too long, I sometimes think. Regarding Nina and Galen, I suspect Welwyn was not 'foreseeing' danger so much as remembering a time when our two could indeed have been challenged. The fellow lets his thoughts stray back, and recalls the warring of *wysards* in an age that might fairly be called antiquity." Verek sipped his drink, then lowered his glass and asked, "Have you any idea, my lady, how old our good monk truly is?"

Carin eyed her husband, then slowly shook her head. "Perhaps I don't. You're saying he was *there*, in Ladrehdin's distant past?"

"He was. He has walked this world — in one form or another — nearly since the age of Archamon. Welwyn remembers the long-ago strife among *wysards*, when powerful houses sought to dominate the lesser families." Scowling, Verek glanced toward the house, then back at Carin. "His words to you were ill-spoken. Those days are long past. Only a comparative handful of *wysards* now live in this world, relics of a time when magic almost died. And most of them exist in solitude and near poverty, little more than hermits in hovels."

"Or monks in mountain cabins?" Carin ventured.

Verek laughed. "I would not advise you to let Master Welwyn hear you say so. But yes, you have the right of it. Except for his time in the monastery, for many a long year Welwyn lived a hermit's life, alone with no apprentice to teach."

"Which explains why he showed up on our doorstep, to take our two in hand," Carin remarked, "as soon as he reckoned they were old enough and we were exhausted enough."

"I thank the Powers that he did," Verek replied. "Our children could have no greater teacher. When he's done with them, they will be amply prepared to contend with whatever befalls them in life, whether mundane or magian."

Darkness had closed in as Verek spoke, and all the household—except the two at the table—had retired for the night. The garden was silent but for crickets chirping and leaves rustling in a cool breeze. Carin reached for her glass of *dhera* and sipped the warming liquor as she listened to the night sounds.

Presently she turned back to Verek and asked, "Won't there be many new apprentices to train—enough, maybe, for all the old wizards of this world to take several in hand—now that the bleeding has stopped and the Power is replenishing itself?"

By the witchlight, Carin saw Verek nod. "It is happening now, more each day. Gifted young adepts—and some, in truth, who are not young—are finding their ways to the masters of magic, to be schooled in the craft. Years must pass, however, before any of those apprentices may achieve even a tenth of the supremacy required to challenge the strength of Ruain.

"And by then, my lady," Verek added, reaching above his head and arching his back in a stretch, "our children will themselves be masters of the craft, teaching apprentices of their own."

"While handing their own hellions over to Welwyn, I hope," Carin murmured. "May he live for a thousand years yet."

She studied Verek in the steady glow of the conjured witchlight, trying to imagine her hot-blooded *wysard* as a grandfather—and finding it impossible, since Verek looked younger now than when Carin first knew him, that angry swordsman who'd nearly handed her her head.

As he ended his stretch, Verek caught Carin gazing at him. He looked at her with an expression that began as a smile, but then edged into a thoughtful frown.

"This talk of master magicians brings to my mind the words you spoke to me, that night of our long ride through the hills,"

149

Verek said. "You accused me—and Welwyn with me—of regarding you as something of a disappointment, for failing to exhibit in recent years the terrifying strength that you showed while conjuring magian fire against invading predators, or traveling the void to break perilous bridges." Verek rubbed his ear, his frown deepening. "It troubles me, my lady, that you should harbor such doubts—either about your own gifts, or concerning the value I place upon them."

Carin reached for his hand. "I'm not doubting myself or you, Theil. I'm merely accepting the facts as they stand. You can't pretend that my 'gifts' these days rise anywhere near the heights they occupied when I conjured a dragon or called lightning to my hand. Now I look at the rows of spellbooks in the library, and I'm overwhelmed by how little I know, and what a vastness I must learn." She smiled. "I hope Welwyn is right about me living as long as you will. I'll need centuries to get through all those instruction manuals."

"If you peruse them all, *fileen*," Verek muttered, "then you will accomplish a feat that no *wysard* in the history of Ladrehdin has undertaken. Those books are better sampled than swallowed whole. Already in your study of them, you have surpassed many a magician who bears the title 'master'."

Verek laid his other hand atop Carin's; his grip was strong and warm. "By turning now to a serious study of the craft," he said, gazing at her, "you have put yourself on a path that will bring you into the first ranks of Ladrehdin's *wysards* of legend. Few magicians are equal to the effort you expend among the books. The vast run of adepts content themselves with the wizardry they can work even as children. What comes to them as instinct is all they desire to know or to use.

"That will be the case with our young ones, I'll wager," Verek added. "Nina will work water-magic. Galen will make fire. Those elements, they have in their natures. But you, *fileen* …"

Verek paused, and the witchlight seemed to dance in the darkness of his eyes as he looked at Carin. "You, my lady, will achieve true greatness. You have the gift, the desire, and the patience to master the craft as few have." He raised one hand to stroke his close-cropped beard. "I wonder: Amongst the memories which you have stubbornly retained of my early misdeeds toward you, do you find those words I spoke, a foretelling I offered you? Even then, I saw the potential within you. I said this, and today I believe it more strongly than when I first uttered the words: 'The time shall come when all wizardry, from the simple to the consummate—'"

"'Will be present to my senses with perfect clarity,'" Carin finished for him. She nodded. "I remember. Your prediction terrified me at the time." She glanced toward the house, and saw no light burning in any window of the suite of rooms where Welwyn lodged with his apprentices. Story-time was over, it seemed, and all slept.

"Well, my lord," Carin said as she turned back to Verek. "In light of what you tell me, I may deprive our children of hours they would otherwise spend to their advantage with their tutor. From Welwyn, I may demand instruction in spellcraft more challenging than arrowpoint-sharpening." She grinned. "That is, if you're sure Welwyn doesn't regard me as his failed novice and your unsuitable wife. I *am* foreign-born, after all."

"Feh! I'd have the old fellow's head if he expressed any such sentiment about my lady of Ruain."

Verek eyed Carin in the witchlight, as though to assure himself that she spoke in jest, to tease him, and was not in fact leveling a charge against the monk that would compel Verek to actually decapitate his old friend. But then a flash like a spark of revelation came into the *wysard*'s gaze. Verek threw back his head and exclaimed, "Ah!"

"What?" Carin demanded, alarmed lest her flippancy provoke real bloodshed.

Verek fixed her with a look that seemed to glimpse her inmost being. "I now understand the reason for that extraordinary question you asked me, on the night we brought the children home from the seacoast. That question came off Welwyn's tongue. He not only distressed you with ancient tales of rivalry among wizards, he put it into your head that I was no faithful husband, but had fathered a legion of bastards who would rise against the children of your flesh." Verek shot up from the table. "Whether I find our good monk nodding over a storybook or dead to the world in his bed, I will kick the old fellow awake again."

Carin grabbed Verek's hand, restraining him as she exclaimed, "Wait! It wasn't Welwyn. Not that part, anyway. He only mentioned the possibility of somebody, someday, challenging Nina or Galen. I sort of …"

She paused to silently admit: *No 'sort of' about it. I invented it.*

Aloud, Carin hurried on: "It was me, not Welwyn. I put one thing with another, the way I do, and convinced myself Welwyn was being sly, dropping hints that you might have other children." She looked up at Verek. "He never suggested such a thing. I just … imagined it. Because I want you all to myself, Theil."

For a moment, he was silent. Then he reached down, drew Carin to her feet, and held her close. He swept her hair aside and kissed her on the neck. Into her ear, he whispered, "I would grumble at you, about your habit of 'putting one thing with another' and reaching—at times—the most preposterous conclusions. But more than once, I have owed my life to your imaginings. I think, therefore, that you should go on building intrigues from chance remarks."

Carin heard the smile in Verek's voice as he added, "The results are sometimes wildly astray, but never dull. You, my lady, have made my life extraordinarily interesting."

Chapter 11

Plans

Carin prepared carefully. She hid her sling, bow and quiver, and a good throwing knife in the darkest corner of the least-visited section of the library. On these unlit shelves, Carin suspected as she brushed past them, rested the most dangerous books in Verek's collection: treatises on blood sacrifice, demonic sorcery, and death cults. Here was where he would keep those volumes Carin had insisted on perusing, though they sickened her and left her feeling soiled. Verek had assured her the books were firmly secured against accidental discovery by curious children who might go poking into such dark corners as she'd chosen for her secret weapons stash.

Also figuring in Carin's preparations was another dose of Megella's memory tea. Coaxing a cupful from the wisewoman had taken effort. Megella had disbelieved Carin's assurances that the concoction gave her only a slight headache, while producing results so beneficial that she was more than willing to endure the minor discomfort the drug induced. At last, however, the wisewoman had yielded and handed over the tea, accompanying the dose with a measure of complaining about the difficulty Megella would have, replenishing her uncommon inventory of ingredients from herbs that barely grew this far north.

Carin had thanked the woman, then ridden back home—by the direct road—to sit in the cavern of *wysards*, sip the tea, and try to remember. Exactly what memories Carin sought this time, she wasn't certain. Her first experience with the potent brew had reconstructed her broken recollections and realigned them almost perfectly. To the best of her knowledge, she now had only two gaps in the story of her life. This second dose of tea did not resurrect her earliest childhood memories, of her time on Earth before Morann snatched her across the void. Neither did it reveal what had befallen Carin in the harbor of a forgotten seaside town called Easthaven. Even so, once her headache subsided, the drug left her attentive and alert, her wits knife-edged.

There was much to be said for the role a good memory played in mental acuity, Carin thought as she climbed the stairs from the cavern to the library. At its desk, she set aside the spellbooks she'd been studying: those archives that were consulted by scholarly *wysards* — Carin among them — who wished to better understand the deep fundamentals of their craft. Unlike the forbidden volumes she wished she'd never seen, these books adhered to the creed of Archamon, that ancient philosopher-*wysard* from whom the House of Verek descended. Every spell described and illustrated in the manuals of wizardry had Archamon's stamp of approval. In learning his magic, Carin would not risk straying into demon lore.

This afternoon, though, she had no interest in mastering new spellcraft. She sought memories. She wanted every scrap of her past that might aid her future plans.

Rising from the desk, where she'd cleared a space amid the thick books of enchantment, Carin walked to the cabinet in the bookshelves that held *dhera* and goblets. She removed these to a nearby shelf, then reached in and tugged loose the slat that closed the cabinet's back. Exploring deeper in the wall cavity behind the shelves, Carin brought out a letter.

The missive was addressed to her, but in the name she'd borne on Earth: *Karen* with an English *K*. That the message had come into her hands, across time and space, was something of a miracle. If Carin hadn't mistakenly sent Verek to her childhood home across the void, the letter might have remained forever lost, wedged between the frame and glass of a mirror in the bedroom Carin had occupied in her Earthly girlhood. Upon discovering the letter, Verek had been tempted to destroy it, fearing to let Carin see it lest she choose to return to Earth and seek the message's author. But conscience had smote him, and at last Theil had pulled a crumpled envelope from his trousers pocket and handed it to Carin.

As she studied the envelope now, Carin was again struck by the oddness of its clear protective cover. To keep the letter clean and dry, its writer had enclosed it in an envelope of plain paper, and then slipped the envelope inside a thin bag made of a material unknown on Ladrehdin. Yet, some distant corner of memory supplied Carin with a name for the material: *plastic*. The stuff had been everywhere in Carin's Earthly home. She herself, on her subsequent return to that secluded house on the bay, had written a note of her own, addressed it to her parents, and sealed the message inside a plastic water bottle. She had tossed the bottle into the sea, setting it adrift on a vast ocean with little hope that any Earthly survivor of the bleeding disease would ever find or read her note.

Now, Carin slipped the plastic bag off the letter from the cabinet and stood fingering the strange material, reminded of another exotic substance which had once come into this house. That material, however, had proved far less persistent than the plastic of Earth. Carin had handled that other substance only once, and briefly. In her hands it had been nearly as light as plastic and as translucent, pliant like a sheet of polished horn split paper-thin. The object's long teardrop shape had made Carin think of a giant dragonfly wing. Later, however, she would learn the artifact's true nature: It was the wing of an otherworldly whirligig, a creature that twirled in swarms above the sands of an alien desert, flying from the voracious predators of that world.

The stray wing Carin had held and examined had ceased to exist before sunrise of the day she discovered it. She'd handed the object to Verek and gone off to her bed, to catch a few hours' sleep after a night of braving magical storms and watching alien predators wash up on the shores of Ladrehdin. The wing had disintegrated in Verek's hands, he'd eventually told her:

"Brief was the thing's existence in this world where it had no business to be. The relic crumbled, and sifted like dust through my fingers ... but no dust fell upon the floor of the *wysards'* cavern. Even the residue of its dissolution ceased to be, so alien was the object."

Just as well, Carin thought. *If it had held together, I would have ended up carting it with me through the void, searching for the thing's natural home.* She'd had enough to do without it, returning to their proper worlds a book, a honey-colored "wand" that was in fact a kind of stick insect, and then all of the amulets with which Morann had built unnatural bridges to potentially deadly worlds.

Shaking off these distractions, Carin laid the plastic aside and opened the plain white envelope that the bag protected. The only world that interested her at this moment was Earth, where Carin evidently still had family living ... and where the demoness Morann had found refuge, if Theil read aright the clue diffused within the vivid red of that world's bottle-glass.

Carin took the letter to the desk and spread its pages flat in the space she'd cleared for it. She pored over the missive, in silence, then read it aloud, stumbling a little over the words of its language, English. Only seldom in the last fourteen or fifteen years had Carin needed to speak that language, her native tongue. It had never left her, though, and when Verek first asked her to read him a book written strangely in that language, she'd had no great difficulty translating from English into the common speech of Ladrehdin. Also, in the summer just past, Carin had easily read the more recent letter from her parents, that message being conveyed through the void by some method known only to the woodsprite, instigator of that world-bridging communication.

The recent letter was fresh in Carin's mind. But the older missive, the one Verek had found, hadn't been out of the cabinet since before Nina's birth. Carin wanted it now to jog her recollection of its contents, and also because her mother had addressed her in that earlier letter as the child Carin had been when she'd disappeared from her girlhood home. Perhaps something in the woman's phrasing would reawaken in Carin a child's affection for its mother.

It pained her, in a vague and distant way, to know that this woman of Earth still remembered her, loved her, and welcomed the woodsprite's stories about her. If Carin meant to journey back to that world, and there destroy the necromancer who refused to leave Theil Verek in peace, then she might possibly encounter her parents in that place. It would be well, Carin thought, to have the words of her native tongue clear in her mouth once again.

Moreover, she would like to recognize her parents if she saw them.

Carin studied the photograph her mother had tucked inside the envelope with the folded pages of the letter. The image showed a little girl—Karenina, as Carin had been affectionately nicknamed—standing between two adults, holding a hand of each. The woman had auburn hair and green eyes. In another ten years or so, Carin would look exactly like her. The man was sandy-haired, and he wore an expression of fatherly pride that reminded Carin of the look in Verek's eyes when he watched Nina and Galen at their hell-raising.

Examining the background in the image, Carin could make out a corner of the cottage on the coral-sand beach where she had lived with those people, her parents. Behind the cottage grew an orchard and banana groves. Edging into the image was a horse barn and the gate of a paddock.

The setting was familiar. Carin had seen it twice since this photograph was made: once when she leaped through the void to rescue Verek from exile there, and again when she splashed into the teal-blue waters of its bay after removing from Ladrehdin the alien crystals that stole power from the vast wellsprings of this world.

But though the scene was known to her, Carin could not summon memories of the man or the woman who locked gazes with her as she studied the old photo. Only vague impressions came into her heart—not memory, more a sense of disconnection, a feeling that even if she were to encounter these people again, they might have little to say to each other, so great was the gulf of time, space, and experience that lay between them now.

With a sigh, Carin propped the photograph against the stacked spellbooks. She set her mouth and tongue to shape the sounds of her native language. Addressing the people who looked out at her from the image, Carin began again to read aloud the letter from Earth, the letter that opened with her mother's plaintive questions:

My child of the sea — where are you? Where did you go? Will you ever read this?

* * *

Carin had all in readiness, her language practice done, the letter and photograph slipped back into their envelope, rewrapped in plastic, and returned to the hidden space behind the liquor cabinet. Her weapons were assembled in the darkest corner of the library, with them a belt pouch holding stones for her sling. Now, Carin had only to wait.

For what, she wasn't sure. Possibly for another disturbance of the *wysards'* waters, which might provide a link by which she could determine Morann's precise location. Or perhaps Carin waited for nothing more substantial than a feeling that her time had come and she must act. She would trust the voice of the wizards' well to call her, as it had called to her before.

* * *

Young Nina, however, made more definite plans. And when the child felt her time arriving, Nina executed her plans perfectly.

Chapter 12

Fire and Water

As the days grew short and the leaves began to turn, all the family gathered in Myra's kitchen to drink mulled wine or, for the children, sweet cider. Nina and Galen stickied their hands and mouths with the berry-filled tarts they wheedled from the housekeeper. The children left juicy kisses on the faces of both their parents as they said their good-nights and headed upstairs, supposedly to bed.

On any other evening, Welwyn would have been on the children's heels, shooing them along the upper corridor, giving them no opportunity for mischief on their way to their quarters. This night, however, Welwyn delayed to answer a question Verek posed about a recipe for a burn poultice that he'd found in his grandmother Merriam's book of herbal lore.

When the alarm sounded, therefore, the men had their heads together over the book, while Carin listened to Myra lament her purchase of a disappointingly ill-dyed length of indigo fabric: "I'd meant to make Nina a new tunic from it," the housekeeper complained, "but the child would turn blue as a berry, so badly does this color run."

All conversation in the room ceased as if a sword blade had sliced through the words, when down the length of the kitchen passageway came a great blast reverberating from the landing at the top of the foyer stairs.

Carin, who stood nearest the passageway, was the first to race along it to the foyer, but Verek's boots pounded the wooden stairs right behind her as Carin leapt up those steps. Heat rolled down the staircase to toast her face, her first hint of what awaited as she reached the landing that fronted the door of the once securely locked blue bedchamber.

The door was in flames. Or had been in flames. The fire dwindled, in the space of seconds, to only a few red tongues burning at its edges. The tongues licked the door's jamb and casing. The door itself was all but gone, burned so completely that not even wood-ash remained to show where its mortised timbers had hung.

Galen sat cross-legged on the landing immediately before the threshold. He giggled in high delight, applauding the fire he had made—a fire so hot, Carin noted as she hurdled the boy and felt the scorching, that it had melted the iron of the lock which Verek had placed on the door to physically reinforce his magical seals. The molten metal lay in a glowing lump where it had clumped to the floor in the heat of Galen's fire-summoning.

Carin also saw, as she landed her leap in the bedchamber beyond the boy, that the child's hair was singed, and his face reddened as with sunburn. Had the young firedrake been touching the door when he made the inferno that opened the way for his sister the water-nymph to work her own enchantments?

For clearly, Nina had put Galen up to it. Carin burst through the narrow connecting doorway into the bathing room barely in time to see the girl leap from the rim of the springwater pool. Nina vaulted her nimble little body high into the air above the potent waters of that previously untouched wellspring of magic. As the girl soared upward, she made a two-handed beckoning motion—a gesture directed not at Carin, but at the pool beneath the child, as if Nina commanded those warm and gently flowing waters to rise to meet her.

The waters obeyed. From the near side of the pool a wave billowed, swelling with supernatural rapidity to tower above Carin's head.

Carin cried out as the wave surged toward Nina like a wall of water that must break the child in half if it struck her.

But an instant before the wave reached its maker, it broke and flowed smoothly under the child's still airborne body. Nina came down upon it, landing on the wave as if it were a soft, fat pillow. The water rippled only slightly as it rolled beneath the child and buoyed her up, the great wave continuing its surge toward the pool's far side.

The noise of the magical upwelling was deafening in the chamber of stone that enclosed the pool. Even so, two things came plain to Carin's ears: Nina's laughter, and her single shouted word. The girl's high, gleeful voice cut through the rumble of rushing water to name Nina's destination and her determined purpose:

"Beach!"

And then Nina was gone, carried away by the magic the girl had made. The cresting wave still swelled high above the pool. But no young *wysard* rode upon it now. The waters were empty.

No—not empty. Carin's mad dash had brought her to the pool's rim, where she now gathered herself ready to spring into or upon that surging water, to follow her daughter as best she could. But a light blazed searingly in the pool's depths, arresting Carin's leap and whipping her gaze downward.

She saw it barely in time. A bolt of lightning streaked up, hurtling at Carin's head. She jerked aside and felt its blistering heat full in her face as the lightning erupted from the pool's roiling surface. With a thunderous crack and a blinding flash, the bolt struck the chamber's roof. Chunks of stone shattered down into the pool and around its rim.

Carin, stumbling backward, had scarcely regained her footing when a woman's hand thrust upward from the pool. Its twisted fingers flung droplets aside as they cleared the water's churning surface.

In the palm of that gnarled and liver-spotted hand, a flame flickered: a sorcerous fire as dark as burnt ocher.

Her reflexes quick as a finger-snap, Carin struck.

"Stop, witch!" she screamed as she cast her own distinctive spellcraft with such force that the hand stabbing up from the

water not only disintegrated, but the power of Carin's spell also blasted the grainy residue all the way across the bathing room. Gritty sand hit the chamber's opposite wall with a noise like a rockslide, audible above the boom of the conjured wave that still rippled over the pool.

Morann emerged from the water screaming. The momentum of the witch's journey through the void carried her upward and out of the pool, and flung her onto its rim.

At once, another force struck the witch, cutting off Morann's shrieks as it knocked her backward and slammed her against the far wall. There the necromancer lay: soaked and gaunt, and in apparently excruciating pain. Whimpering now, emitting low moans, Morann curled her skeletal body around the stump of the hand that Carin had sandblasted off.

"Where is Nina?" Verek bellowed from behind Carin.

She had no need to look over her shoulder: the angle of the attack that had thrown Morann into the wall said Verek was standing in the narrow doorway between the blue bedroom and this chamber—this now-defiled repository of magic that Carin had long called a bathing room. Verek had hurled his own powerful spell at the witch as soon as Morann cleared the pool.

Before Carin could answer him, Galen piped up from the hallway landing.

"Who's that old lady, Papa? What's wrong with her?"

The boy's voice reached Carin clearly, for Nina's magical wave had subsided. As quickly as it had risen in answer to the girl's summons, the wave now collapsed back into the spring-water pool.

In its wake, silence pervaded the bathing room, disturbed only by Morann's panting breaths and pain-filled groans.

So, Carin thought, staring at the broken demoness. *I didn't have to hunt you down. You came to me. That's the worst move you ever made, witch.*

Chapter 13

Wellsprings

"Who *is* that, Papa?" Galen asked again from the floor where the boy sat poking at the lump of molten metal which was all that remained of the massive iron lock Verek had fashioned.

"No one," Verek answered the child brusquely. "Do not trouble yourself about *her*, son. She will not be here long." He called over his shoulder: "Welwyn! Take the boy to his room and make *certain* he stays there. Put him well under, if you must. Then return here at once."

"I understand, Theil," the monk called back, sounding breathless from his hurried climb up the stairs from the kitchen. "The lad will enjoy the best sleep of his young life tonight."

Galen complained, "I'm not sleepy!" and made further noises of protest as Welwyn hauled him down the second-story corridor. But soon both were gone, master and apprentice, safely away to the larger wing of the house, leaving Carin and Verek alone with a glowering witch whose hatred for them contorted the woman's face.

Carin looked Morann over, seeing almost no resemblance — beyond the still-black hair and piercing dark eyes — to that falsely elegant enchantress who had risen from a throne of acid in the west of Ladrehdin. This creature was hideous, shrunken, emaciated. Her gown appeared to be a faded, tattered remnant of the midnight purple and shimmering green robe the woman had been wearing when the dragon attacked and she fled … *leaving her wellspring and thus most of her power far behind her,* Carin realized.

Evidently, the witch had found the pickings poor in the world to which her ruby-glass amulet had taken her. Morann looked well along the path to bodily starvation.

As Carin's gaze raked the hag who huddled on the floor, she glimpsed it: a gleam of red in the clear light of the bathing-room's glowing walls.

"Theil!" Carin called. "The bottle—it's tied at her waist."

"I see. Catch it."

With a snap of his fingers, Verek magicked the bottle away from Morann and sent it arcing over the pool to Carin. She snatched it neatly from the air, left-handed, her guard never wavering as she held her other arm out before her, ready with the spellcraft that would reduce the demon to dust.

"*You!*" Morann spat, cradling the stump of her disintegrated hand.

"Yes, witch," Carin growled. "We meet again. I promised myself that I would kill you the next time I saw you. For the present, though, I will only impress upon you how *perfectly* capable I am of destroying you."

With precise control, Carin cast her spell at Morann's head. The woman's right ear crumbled to sand.

"Ahhh!" the witch screamed, her intact hand flying up to cup the new injury.

Carin smiled. "I can take you apart piecemeal, Morann. When first we met, I was a frightened girl who didn't know my own strength. But then I summoned the dragon against you, and I traveled the void, and broke the bridges you had made that endangered this world and others.

"In the course of that bridge-breaking," Carin continued, her hard stare meeting the terrified and astonished gaze of the sorceress, "I removed the parasites that, for ages, had drained this world of its strength." She nodded. "Yes, witch. Where you failed in your schemes to take power from others, I succeeded in restoring the potency of magic in this world by ending the slow depletion of Ladrehdin's elemental forces. You fled a world that was half dead from an alien race's leechcraft. But you have returned to a realm that is well healed and stronger than you can possibly know."

Carin laughed at the look on the witch's face.

"Do you understand me, Morann? Do you know that you have made a fatal miscalculation? I remember what you said about taking the seat of House Verek for yourself. That's why you've come, isn't it? You saw your chance when the portal opened, and you thought you would catch Theil unawares. Perhaps you imagined he would be forever weakened by the injuries you dealt him that day on your altar of evil. You came to destroy him, as you tried to do before, and then you thought you'd claim this place of power as your own."

Carin pointed at Verek. "But in him, you behold a master *wysard* who has no superior in this world. His powers now equal those of the ancients. For he draws his strength from a world that is stronger than it has been in five thousand years. And it is a pure strength, unsullied by the filthy sorceries of pain and death that *you* practice, you monstrosity."

Slowly, Carin swung her arm back to point again at Morann, enjoying as she did so the sight of the witch groveling before her on the bathing-room floor.

"No, I won't kill you," Carin said, snapping off her words. "His is the right of vengeance against you, for he has suffered far more from your malice than I ever have. Though I ache to reduce you to dust, you abomination, I will content myself with taking revenge for only a small part of the harm that you did to Theil when he was a boy."

With this, Carin bespelled the little finger of Morann's left hand, which the cowering woman still held at her ear. As the witch screamed and writhed in renewed pain, Carin watched with grim satisfaction as the finger crumbled, becoming mere grains of sand that fell and bounced and mingled with the other particles which Carin's spellwork had scattered on the floor.

"It concentrates the mind wonderfully, does it not, you fiend," she growled.

Turning away from the wretched spectacle, Carin joined Verek at the narrow door into the blue bedchamber.

"Nicely done, my lady," he muttered as she stood beside him.

"Megella and I will have a job of it," Carin murmured back, "cleaning up all that sand. I don't think we should let Myra or the housemaids touch it. I want to be absolutely certain that not a grain of it remains in this house."

Verek arched an eyebrow. "I agree. And I thank you, my love, for leaving that demon's final destruction to me."

"What will you do?"

"Only lock her in the dungeon for now, until I can craft a fitting conclusion to that *daēva's* story."

To let Carin slip past him, Verek turned slightly in the doorway, never taking his gaze from Morann nor lowering his outstretched hand. "But now, wife, will you go find our wayward daughter? Do you know where she is?"

Carin rubbed her forehead. "I believe so. The only question in my mind is which beach she's gone to: Ruain's coast, or across the void to the sandy shores of my old home. I think it's quite likely, when Nina leapt onto that wave she made —

"Were you close enough behind me to see it?" Carin interrupted herself. "That little hellion rode the water as if it were a flying carpet. You must be *so* proud to have fathered such a child."

"I am," Verek murmured, and smiled.

Carin grinned, too.

"Anyway," she continued, "when the water billowed up and Nina rode her wave out, I saw Morann rise from deep in the pool. Nina was entirely out of sight before the witch broke the surface. I doubt they caught even a glimpse of each other, in the whitecaps and froth. But if Nina's conjured wave pulled so strongly on the magic of this realm that it created a current potent enough to lift Morann into this world, then it's likely the backwash took our girl in a great cosmic circle, through the void to that very place where Morann has been all this time."

Verek nodded. "I follow your reasoning, and I bow to your experience in these matters. You know the ways of the void far better than I." He glanced at Carin and briefly regarded the ruby-glass bottle she held, then returned his gaze to his prisoner. "Shall I lock up this demon forthwith, then accompany you in the search?"

Carin considered, then shook her head. "I don't believe you should leave that monster guarded by Welwyn alone, even as crippled as she is. Morann is cunning. Now she's backed into a corner, she'll be even more dangerous in her desperation. Be careful, my husband."

"And you, my wife. I cannot live if I lose you, Carin. You must come back to me." He hesitated a moment, then added: "Do not forget me in the void. I've seen what that oblivion does to you."

"I could never forget you, Theil!" she cried. "You are my world."

Verek dropped his chin, and Carin gave him a quick kiss as she squeezed past into the blue room. "Don't worry about me. I'll find Nina and get us both home … while you deal out justice to that witch in the fullest measure which she deserves."

From the landing outside the bedroom, Carin leapt down the stairs to the foyer. At a run, she took the hallway to the library. Banging open its heavy oak door, she darted into the dark corner where her weapons waited. Quickly Carin strapped on belt pouch and throwing knife, draped her sling around her neck under her shirt, and shouldered her bow and quiver of arrows.

Hurried steps took her across the room to the cabinet among the shelves. Heedless of crystal broken in her haste, Carin reached in and yanked out the slat that closed the cabinet's back. Deeper still, her searching fingers found and removed the wood-wrapped red bottle that held the latest message from her mother.

Carrying a bottle in each hand — Morann's bejeweled amulet in her right, and the vessel bound with wood from her home-world in her left — Carin spiraled down the library stairs to the cavern of wizardry. Behind the bench of the crescent moon, she skidded to a brief halt to nod obeisance to the pool before rushing to stand on its rim.

"I beg forgiveness for this intrusion," she said to the unseen but always felt Power of that place, "but my daughter is missing once more, and I must find her. Please tell me: Is Nina anywhere on Ladrehdin?"

The upwelling in the pool's center bubbled with increased vigor, forming a fountain of white water, and a small wave rose opposite Carin. It rolled toward her. When it broke at her feet, the pool's silvery, seashell voice spoke a clear, "No."

Carin bowed her head. "Thank you. I suspected that was the way of things."

Standing with her booted toes hanging over the pool's rim, Carin tucked the wood-veneered bottle inside her pouch. She held her right hand in front of her and locked her gaze onto the jewel-encrusted amulet.

"Take me back along the circle," she said.

A mist rose from the *wysards'* well, enveloping Carin in warm fog as she stepped from its rim.

At once, the vapor grew chill. Then it thinned, wafting away on a light but cracklingly cold breeze to reveal a night of moonlit clarity. Under the moon Carin emerged at the edge of another pool of magic. Above the sparkling waters of this open-air pool, trees towered, their sleek limbs gleaming in a frosty, cloudless night. Around the pool stretched a wide pavilion that was paved with flagstones of some semi-translucent mineral which caught and reflected the moon. The paving stones seemed to glow in their depths, touched with yellow like gemstones of topaz. At the pool's far end stood a tiered structure, a dais with four levels, all of them empty except for the witchlight orbs that glimmered from each level.

It was a testament to Carin's willpower and to the wizardly training she had completed since her last visit to this place, that she neither cried out nor took a step back from the rim of Morann's former vat of acid. She only shifted the ruby amulet to her left hand, freeing her stronger spell-working hand to point at the knot of strangers who stood clustered around the dais.

An odd-looking group it was. Half of the strangers appeared ancient, their faces wrinkled, their bodies stooped, several leaning on canes. The other half of the crowd was young, both male and female, strapping youths and slender maidens. The young people gawked at Carin, openmouthed, seemingly too startled to react to her sudden materialization in Morann's old stronghold. A number of their elders, however, answered Carin's outstretched hand with similarly threatening gestures of their own.

"Who are you?" demanded one old fellow who wore a pointed hat several sizes too large for him. It fell down over his ears.

Carin gave the man no more than a glance. He looked feeble, holding onto a staff with both his hands and barely propping himself up. He also appeared to be wearing Carin's old green cloak, the garment she had abandoned in Morann's boneyard. She barely noticed it, though, for her attention was on those among the ancients who were poised to cast spells in her direction. Projecting her voice, firm and clear, she declared to the group at large, "I am Carin, Lady of Ruain. Who are you?"

At first, the moonlit silence that followed her question was broken only by the hooting of an owl. Not one of the strangers responded by naming themselves. Names have power, as Verek had long ago taught her, and all in this crowd would guard theirs. But after a beat or two of shocked stillness, there came from the group audible intakes of breath, startled outcries, and one clipped yelp from a young man as he fainted and fell against his neighbor.

The rest of the young people threw themselves flat on the paving stones, prostrate, some of them whimpering.

Carin, watching bemused, found the reactions of their elders more interesting. Charming, in fact. Several of the ancient men bowed to her, bracing on their sticks and struggling to re-straighten their backs. The women mostly had sense enough to know that any attempt at curtseying, at their ages, would end badly. A few, however, tried it, and needed the arms of the others to keep from toppling over.

"Honored Elders," Carin called across the pool. "Please be at peace. I thank you for your greeting."

They'd dropped their hands now, but they shifted uneasily when Carin lowered her own hand only slightly. She held her arm relaxed, elbow bent, but kept her fingers in position to meet any show of hostility that might yet arise from this convocation of obviously old *wysards* and their young apprentices. She bobbed a perfect curtsy to the elders, keeping her back straight, her fingers locked, and her focus on one sketchy fellow who had retreated to the back of the crowd. He seemed livelier than many of the others who were still on their feet, and his furtive glances around other people's heads spoke volumes. He did not want to be noticed—which ensured, of course, that Carin noticed him above all others.

Her courtesy in addressing the elders, though somewhat at odds with her battle-ready stance, stirred certain of the ancients to speak.

"The Lady of Ruain is come among us!" cried one beldame who wore layers of shawls, even more of them than Megella favored, though the witchlight showed these to be of more somber hue than the wisewoman's colorful wraps.

"She who summoned a dragon against the blood sorceress!" croaked another voice from out of the crowd.

"More than that: This is the enchantress from a far country who broke Lord Legary's spell of concealment upon the *Book of Archamon*," exclaimed a man in the group, as though that was the be-all and end-all of Carin's accomplishments.

Another in the crowd emphatically disagreed. "Beggar Legary's spell," a woman swore, startling Carin with her use of an expletive that she'd heard from no one in Ladrehdin except herself and the wheelwright of Granger. "Many can break spells. This adept, however, is the breaker of otherworldly chains and yokes, our saviour of magic ... the Chosen One of the Powers. Lady Carin, you honor us with your presence."

The speaker was silver-haired and rather better dressed than most in the group. They all wore clothing that had seen better days, and their garments were mismatched collections of trousers and coats, skirts and tunics. The diviner, however — she who knew Carin's favorite swearword — was cloaked much like a magistrate of Ruain in a dark, flowing garment with a high neck. Unlike a magistrate's robe, however, this woman's cloak was spangled with silver stars and white crescent moons. In the cold witchlight she seemed to throw off sparks, a commanding figure standing straight and tall amid her mostly stooped companions.

She made her authority clear, moreover, when one of the prostrated apprentices offered to get to his feet. The magisterial woman planted her boot in the middle of the young man's back and flattened him again.

Carin smiled. She liked this woman, and under other circumstances she would have welcomed a chance to know her better. The sketchy fellow, however, was edging ever farther away from the crowd. He would soon leave the circle illuminated by the witchlight orbs on the dais, around which this convocation centered. Carin wished to be gone from this place before the fellow left her sight. His untrustworthiness was palpable.

"Honored Diviner," Carin ventured, and was pleased to see the woman smile and give a small nod acknowledging the respect Carin conveyed with the title. "I regret that I cannot remain here to speak with you all, the Wise Ones of these mountains … and your gifted apprentices."

At this, startled noises escaped from the face-down forms, as though the young people were shocked that Carin even noticed their existence. *These apprentices are kept firmly in their places,* she mused. *I doubt that Nina or Galen would fit well with this crowd.*

Aloud, Carin said her good-byes. "I have urgent business elsewhere tonight, as it chances, and I may not tarry longer. Good evening to you all."

The untrustworthy man was passing from her sight as Carin started to bob another curtsy. Aiming to surprise him, and all the rest of them as well — in case any others in the group were ill-disposed toward her — she turned the curtsy into a leap that propelled her above Morann's pool of magic.

Carin had never slackened her hold on the ruby bottle which had "closed the circle" by bringing her to the place it had occupied before Morann fled through the void. Now she jerked the amulet up and reissued her command — choosing her words more precisely this time.

"Take me across to where my daughter has journeyed," she ordered.

As a cold mist rose from the glittering pool beneath her, Carin detected no corruption in the vapor, no poisons or acids. She smelled no decay and saw nothing suggesting disembodied eyes. Nothing seemed to remain of the evil which had once permeated this place of power. Did the Elders of the western mountains gather in this high eyrie to refresh their strength after their long years in exile? Carin would have asked their purpose in convening here tonight, if she hadn't been so pressed for time.

But now she was entering the void, where time went its own way and estranged her from its flow. Witchlights winked out below her, the giant trees that spread their branches above the pool passed beneath her, the moon disappeared, and nothingness enfolded her.

Through that blankness cut the murmur of the ocean, surf upon a shore, waves breaking on the sand. Carin's native waters waited to welcome her.

Chapter 14

The Beach

She landed her leap through the void still knowing who she was and why she'd come. The nothingness had not taken those memories from her.

Her feet met land, not water. She did not stand on a pool's rim, nor on a seashore. But the ocean was near. She smelled its briny tang. And from only a little way behind Carin came the noise of the surf chafing against rocks.

The sound seemed to fade, though, fading almost to silence, replaced by a buzzing in her ears as she looked upon the vision of horror that stretched in front of her.

Bodies lay everywhere—blood on their clothing, their necks, their faces—some grotesquely mutilated and very obviously dead. But other bodies had a spark of life still in them. From these came moans of agony.

A few of the living possessed strength enough to raise their arms in supplication, begging for help from the little girl who worked calmly and purposefully among them. Other people were there, too, uninjured women and men who appeared almost slack-jawed as they cut bloodstained clothes away from grievous wounds, or washed the gore from victims' faces. One brief, appraising glance told Carin that the elder attendants posed no threat: every face wore the same expression of shocked incomprehension.

Only the child seemed fully possessed of her wits. Moving amidst the carnage, Nina worked methodically, covering each victim's wounds with what appeared to be dark and glistening bandages. Carin stood watching, half hidden under trees at the edge of the body-strewn clearing, blinking at the bright sun that flooded the space. It hurt her eyes after the darkness of the mountain night she had just left, and the deep blackness of the void she had crossed to get here.

Though feeling much like the other adults looked—stunned—Carin prodded herself into motion as her eyes adjusted and the buzz in her ears subsided. She pocketed the ruby amulet that had brought her here in roundabout fashion. She unshouldered her bow and quiver and leaned them against a tree. Quietly and unobtrusively then, she slipped into the clearing and wended her way through the bodies to Nina.

The child greeted her matter-of-factly, without surprise, as if Carin were expected. "Mama, these people got hurt. I'm helping."

Carin squatted, both to look Nina in the eye and to see more clearly what "bandages" the child was applying. "You're doing a wonderful job, Nina. What's that you're putting on the wounds? Are those leaves?"

"Kind of," Nina said. "It's seaweed leaves. I need more."

The child turned from the unconscious man whose gashed and bloody torso she was covering in seaweed fronds. Nina gazed in the direction from which Carin again heard the surf slapping the shore. The child waved, a beckoning or summoning motion.

Carin straightened and whirled. Catching sight of a woman approaching, she grabbed for the throwing knife at her belt. But then Carin froze and stood staring. The woman who walked toward them, lugging a bucket that overflowed with glistening brown and dark-green seaweed, was an older version of Carin: copper hair, emerald eyes, slender body.

The woman halted a few feet away. Her eyes were wide, and her mouth trembled. For a moment she swayed, as if on the verge of fainting. But Nina beckoned again, impatient, and the woman obediently stepped forward, picking up an empty pail as she set her full bucket down in its place beside Nina's patient. The girl chirped, "Thank you," and turned back to the unconscious man.

With complete confidence, her little hands quick and certain, Nina resumed her ministrations …

… While Carin and the woman stood gaping at each other. Then Carin reached out, tentative. The woman, without hesitation, dropped the empty pail and folded her into an embrace. Carin found she was crying, and realized they both were.

After a bit, they held each other at arm's length, each studying the other's face, seeing themselves reflected in the other's eyes. The woman's mouth worked, as though she couldn't form the words she wanted. But then she managed to whisper, "Where have you been, Karenina?"

Carin heard the words like an echo from her language practice in the library. Even this woman's voice was like her own. Carin knew the words, knew their meaning, and called up more from inside herself, holding this language—English—foremost in her mind, shaping her lips and tongue to form the sounds of that speech.

"Hello, Mother," she murmured, her mouth dry and her tongue stumbling a little, despite her practice. "I've been … a long way from here."

Carin's mother nodded. "I knew you couldn't be anywhere in these islands. Your father and I would have found you. We never stopped looking."

Tears welled up again in Carin's eyes. She dashed them away, for now was not the time.

"What happened here?" she asked, indicating the bodies that lay all around them. Though she knew the answer, Carin had to ask. "Did an animal do this?"

The woman shook her head. "No. This is the work of a demon."

Carin looked at the blood, the ghastly wounds, the stomachs that lay open, entrails spilling out of mutilated bodies …

Damn her to farsinchia for all eternity, Carin silently swore, flinging the curse across the void to lay it on the witch she had

177

left to Theil's justice. The sorceress had ripped these people open in a final, desperate bid to gain power from their pain. This world, where so many of the inhabitants were long dead from the plague that entered it when Morann pulled Carin out of it: this world had not been kind to the witch. Morann had arrived here to find only scattered pockets of survivors. She could not work her grisly sorcery on corpses. What was there in death to draw upon? Death was cold. Morann fed on hot-blooded agony, and from these victims—Carin's one-time countrymen—the witch had extracted all the life-force she could, racking these bodies with pain in her futile effort to strengthen herself for her assault on House Verek.

All in vain. Morann had done this unspeakable horror for nothing. It had gained her only enough power, Carin suspected, to blast that lightning bolt at Carin's head as the witch hurtled from the void. Morann had arrived in the springwater pool on the strength of Nina's fortuitously timed magic, not the demon's own. And she'd returned to House Verek much too weak from her years of starvation in this world to have any chance of besting the master of that House—or of escaping Carin's wrath.

Carin's mother was staring at her. Bringing her thoughts back to the moment, she put away her forgotten knife and reached for the woman's hand. "I know the demon of whom you speak. You need have no more fear of that monster. She is gone, never to return to this world ... or any other."

The expression with which Carin's mother met this statement was a little quizzical. *She's unsure what I mean by 'other worlds,'* Carin thought. But in a moment the woman seemed to accept Carin's words as no more bewildering than the idea that demons did, in fact, exist.

She gripped Carin's hand, picked up the dropped pail, and turned back toward the sound of the surf, leading the way through scattered dead bodies and down a short path to the shore. There, a few other women and two men were harvesting seaweed and filling buckets with the heavy, wet fronds.

As Carin joined the work, soon sweating under the brilliant sun that warmed the shoreline, she questioned her mother about Nina's role in all of this. Clearly these people trusted the child to treat the wounds of their comrades, but why should that be so?

The story the woman told almost rocked Carin back on her heels.

Agonized screams and shouts of terror had brought the would-be rescuers running to the scene, but Carin's mother and the others had reached the clearing to find Nina already rendering aid. The child had lugged an armful of seaweed up from the beach, and was busily applying it to gaping wounds and ripped throats.

The girl had so much blood on her, the rescuers thought, at first, that she was herself injured. One well-meaning woman attempted to scoop the child up and carry her to safety. Nina put a stop to that with a wall of water that knocked the woman flat. The wave came from nowhere, and after rolling a short way past the woman it had struck, the wave collapsed and splashed to the ground, wetting a large patch at the edge of the clearing.

"That's when I knew we were dealing with no ordinary child," Carin's mother added. "I've met your friend the woodsprite, and I've heard its tales of magicians and enchantments. So I was willing to believe the evidence of my eyes, especially when that raven-haired girl flicked her wrist, and fresh water gushed from a stone in the middle of the clearing."

Overcome by astonishment—and more than slightly in thrall to the wizardly powers of Nina, Carin suspected—the rescuers did not argue or resist, but did as the child bid them. With definite and well-understood gestures, the girl directed some of the women to wash the victims' torn flesh with the warm, clear water she'd conjured from the stone. Nina sent the men and the strongest women to gather seaweed. She showed a few others how to apply it to the wounds.

"We couldn't understand a word the child said, but we knew exactly what she meant for us to do," Carin's mother added. "Those eyes! I've never seen eyes so deep and dark, or so piercing. She looks at a person, and you almost fall over yourself doing what she wants."

Carin smiled. "Nina has her father's eyes. He can raise blisters with a look when he's angry."

"Does the girl also get that air of authority from him?" Carin's mother asked. "She's not four feet high, but she has the commanding presence of a five-star general."

Carin wasn't entirely sure what a "five-star general" was, but she got the gist of the comment. "Yes, Nina is like her father that way, too. When he speaks, people tend to do what they're told and not talk back."

"He sounds … alarming." Carin's mother picked up the filled bucket and headed for the path to the clearing. "You must tell me more, but later. Right now, I'd like to know where a six-year-old child gets medical training. How does she know to use seaweed as a wound dressing? She's up there surrounded by blood and some of the worst wounds anyone could imagine, and it doesn't seem to faze her. Where did she get *that* from?"

Carin fell into step beside the woman. "I'm not certain," she admitted. "I've never seen Nina do this before. Her father is a skilled healer—she may have learned from him. Nina also has a tutor who knows a lot about herbs and medicinal plants."

Carin paused as Megella's words came to her: *"I advise you to spend more time with your children,"* the wisewoman had said.

After this, I will, Carin silently promised. *I've obviously missed some things.*

Aloud, she addressed the woman at her side. "When I get Nina home, I'll be asking some questions myself."

The woman stumbled. As Carin reached to steady her and to take the heavy bucket from her, inwardly she reproached herself:

This lady — my mother — has been looking for me for years. She's finally found me, and I'm already talking about taking her granddaughter and myself away again. Drisha! I need to learn to be quiet.

They came again to the blood-soaked clearing, to find that Nina remained in charge. With Carin there to translate for her, the child gave her troops their new orders: Those with the gentlest touch were directed to change the seaweed dressings on the most grievous wounds, replacing older fronds with fresh weed from the refilled buckets. Other workers, whom Nina judged to be too ham-handed to treat patients, or who simply could not stomach the sight of mutilated flesh, were sent to the far side of the clearing to dig graves.

In short order, the girl had the survivors ready to be carried to a place of shelter. The nearest community proved to be the hamlet where Carin's parents had only recently taken up residence. Before that, her mother said, they had lived on their boat and kept mostly away from other people.

"When the plague was at its worst," the woman said, "no one went near a stranger. Everyone was terrified of catching the disease and dying a horrible death. But now it seems likely that those of us who lived through the plague are safely immune. Slowly, people are coming together again. We have neighbors now for the first time since the world ended."

As the still-living among Morann's victims were borne away on litters or carried in strong arms to beds and couches in the hamlet, Carin walked to the tree where she had left her bow and quiver. Her mother made no comment as Carin shouldered the weapons, but a look of something like loss came over the woman's face.

She has no idea who I am now, Carin thought. *She remembers a little girl who liked storybooks and stuffed animals and wooden beads strung on necklaces.*

Nina came skipping up and took Carin's hand. "Let's go to the beach now, Mama!"

"Of course, child," Carin replied in the common speech of Ladrehdin. Looking down into the large dark eyes with their piercingly direct gaze, she added, "We couldn't come all this way and not go to the beach, could we?"

Nina shook her head vigorously, then raced down the path to the sea. The child was again only a child, not a bred-in-the-bone healer who must remedy wounds of the flesh.

"It's like an impulse with them," Carin murmured. And whether she spoke in the tongue of Ladrehdin or in the language of her mother, she did not know.

"Sorry?" said the woman who walked beside her. "I didn't catch that."

Carin looked at her and smiled. "I was just remembering something Nina's father did, the day I met him. About healing wounds, I mean. He had other things on his mind altogether. But the instant he saw blood streaming from a cut knee, he was digging out his medicine pouch and tending the wound. At the time, I thought it was demented. It seemed so ... different ... from the side of him I'd seen up 'til then."

She pointed at Nina, who had reached the shore ahead of them and was splashing into the shallows. "It's much like what Nina did today, though. She came here to play on the beach and swim in the ocean. But the minute the child saw wounds, she had to tend them." Carin rubbed her lower lip. "I think that's something else Nina has inherited from her father: an impulse to heal. That will make three of them."

"Three?" asked the woman beside her. "Do you mean you have three children?"

Carin grinned. "Not yet. I'm sure I *will* have three—at least—before I'm done. I meant there will be three healers in my family, if Nina proves to be as skilled in the art as her father is. We also have Theil's great-aunt. She, too, can heal wounds and cure sickness."

"Theil? That's your husband?"

Carin glanced at the woman, and nodded. "He'll be worried about us. I'll need to take Nina home soon."

Her mother reached again for Carin's hand. "I know you can't stay, Karenina," she murmured. "It's clear your life is in … that other place." The woman gave Carin a pleading look. "But please, come to the cottage with me and speak to your father. *He's* been worried about you for years. Let him meet his amazing granddaughter, too."

Carin's emotions floundered as she looked at this woman, her mother. The woman appeared older than Carin thought she must be: Fighting for survival while a plague killed most of the people of her world had aged her, she guessed. Even so, looking at her was like gazing into a mirror that showed the future. Carin would have exactly this woman's face, with the still-slender body and thick auburn hair that proclaimed them mother and daughter.

How do I tell her I don't know her? Carin wondered silently. *She and the man she calls my father are a nearly blank page in the book of my life.*

But to say it aloud would be cruel, after all the years the pair had spent searching for her, never giving her up for dead. So Carin made no reply other than a quick nod of assent.

She beckoned to Nina, who was bobbing in the low breakers like a seal with only her sleek head poking up. The child came out of the water with her black hair streaming and her clothes sodden, but much cleaner than when she'd gone in. The ocean had washed away the gore from Morann's bloodletting and also the slimy stains from Nina's liberal application of seaweed to demon-inflicted wounds.

"Nina, child," Carin called. "This lady has asked us to visit her and her husband in their home. Would you like that?"

Nina clapped her hands, delighted. The girl came running up the beach, pausing on the way to collect her slippers from where she'd dropped them on the white sand. She'd removed only those, not her blouse or short britches. As she reached the women, the child thrust her shoes into Carin's free hand. Then Nina gathered herself with an air of concentration, adopted a look as nearly angelic as the little hellion could manage, and dropped a curtsy to the woman who stood at Carin's side.

"I am honored, my lady, by your kind invitation," Nina said in her most formal and serious voice—surprising Carin yet again. Evidently Master Welwyn had managed to instill something of the social graces. Then: "My name is Nina," the girl chirped. "Who are you?" she demanded, dispensing with further formalities.

The woman looked a little unsettled as she released Carin's hand and attempted to return Nina's curtsy. Clearly, she had no idea how to position her body to perform the dip. To help her cover her awkwardness, Carin provided a quick translation:

"Nina says she's happy to go to your cottage. She also asks what she should call you."

The lady shot Carin a startled look. But then she seemed to understand that it was too soon, perhaps, to tell this strangely powerful child that she was meeting her only living grandmother.

"My name is Kate," the woman replied. She smiled at Nina. "My husband is Edward but everyone calls him Eddie."

Relieved, herself, to have been given the names she'd forgotten, Carin relayed this information to Nina. Both she and Kate responded with praise when the child made a creditable effort to mimic the unfamiliar sounds. Though accented with the inflections of Ladrehdinian speech, both names came out recognizably close as Nina repeated them, the girl seeming to savor the shapes they made on her tongue.

The walk to Kate's cottage was not long. With Nina frisking ahead of them, splashing into the shallows wherever the irregular shore permitted it, the three followed the curve of the beach until it brought them to a deeply incised bay. There they took a path leading up to a tree-shaded overlook, from which a set of weatherworn and rickety-looking steps descended to the rocky shore below.

Kate stepped to the overlook's edge, where it was bounded by a newer-looking wooden guardrail. Leaning far over the rail, the woman scanned the shoreline beneath, then gestured with both arms to catch the attention of someone below.

"Ed!" she cried. "Eddie! Come up here right now. You won't *believe* who's here."

For a moment more, Kate stayed at the rail, beckoning with both hands. Evidently satisfied that Eddie was on his way, the woman turned back to Carin and Nina.

"That's a stroke of luck," she said. "Eddie just tied up, down at the dock. He took our boat out this morning, and I'm never sure how long he'll be. Sometimes the fish are biting and he catches all we need in thirty minutes. Other days, he's out till nightfall." Kate took another look over the railing. "Get up here, Ed! You won't believe your eyes."

Carin was still translating the gist of this for Nina's benefit when a man like a storybook sea captain came hurrying up from below. Launching himself from the top of the shaky stairs, the man took two steps onto the firmer footing of the overlook, then stopped dead.

No one spoke as Eddie stared at his long-lost daughter, and Carin stared back.

She immediately liked the man's face, weather-burned as it was from his years of sailing island-to-island, keeping himself and Kate safely offshore as the plague burned through this world. From what she had read in her mother's letters, Carin surmised that her parents had survived the collapse of society — and the ensuing violent struggle to stay alive in a shattered, lawless world — by coming to land only when they must to make repairs or obtain what supplies they could not procure from the sea itself.

Carin's tongue was tied. A simple "hello" seemed inadequate, and to call him "Eddie" would sound disrespectful; but neither could she bring herself to greet this man as "Father," though Carin knew he must be. His was the face that had looked out at her from the old family photo, his pride in his daughter evident.

The man named Eddie sank to his knees. He cried out, a cry that expressed both joy and soul-deep pain. Then Eddie was weeping, great racking sobs that shook his body.

Nina sprang from beside Carin and darted to embrace the man. Wrapping her arms around him as far as she could reach, the girl hugged Eddie with all the strength in her small, wiry body — a strength that was beyond an ordinary child's, for Nina had been trained in the use of weapons since she was old enough to hold a bow or grasp the hilt of a rapier.

Eddie hugged her back, responding more by reflex than with conscious intent, Carin thought. For then the man looked shocked when he raised his tear-streaked face and met Nina's obsidian-black eyes locked onto his own. The child regarded him with that piercing — very nearly scorching — gaze that Nina had inherited from her otherworldly *wysard* father.

Eddie's startlement restored Carin's voice. "It's all right," she hastened to reassure him. "Nina is only worried that you're hurt. Show her you're not injured, and she'll stop staring at you quite so … intently."

The man glanced up at Carin. His throat moved as he swallowed with evident difficulty. Slowly then, as though fearing to make any sudden motion, Eddie held his arms out straight.

Nina turned her attention from Eddie's face to his arms. She felt along them, then fingered his neck and torso—looking, Carin thought, for wounds of the sort she had recently dressed. Finding no injuries there, the girl stepped back and imperiously motioned for Eddie to stand.

He did so, quickly.

When he was on his feet, Nina checked his legs and ankles for wounds. Stepping back farther, to gain a better vantage point—he towered over her—the girl looked him up and down. Then she whirled and spoke to Carin.

"I don't know why he was crying, Mama," Nina said with exasperation. "There's no blood. Can we see their house now?"

Carin grinned at her strange, precocious hellion. "I expect we'll be there soon. But, child, aren't you forgetting your manners? Give Master Edward your best curtsy, the same as you did for Lady Kate."

"Oh." Nina whirled back to face him, and Carin saw Eddie's muscles tighten as he forced himself to stand his ground. He was almost twice the girl's height but obviously intimidated by her.

I know how you feel, Carin thought, sending Eddie her silent sympathy as she flashed him a reassuring smile. *I've faced the mature, masculine version of that searing gaze. It's no shame to you, master mariner, if you find it terrifying.*

The man relaxed a little, however, when Nina bobbed a demure little curtsy to him, then turned to reclaim her slippers from Carin. Nina put her shoes on and skipped over to take Kate by the hand. The woman had stood watching without speaking as her husband met his otherworldly granddaughter. Now Kate heaved a sigh of what sounded like relief as she walked on up the path, swinging Nina's hand in her own.

Carin and Eddie were left staring at each other once again. The man no longer cried—Nina had stunned his tears away. Now Eddie looked dazed, struggling to take in the events of the last few moments.

As terns and other seabirds wheeled overhead, filling the air with raspy cries, Carin stepped to the man, took his hands in her own, and kissed him lightly on his leathery cheek.

"Thank you for looking for me," she whispered, meeting his sad brown eyes. "I'm sorry I caused you such pain. I never meant to, but there was nothing I could do except try to stay alive." Carin squeezed Eddie's hands, and added, "Thank you, also, for keeping yourself and my mother alive. I think it couldn't have been easy."

"It wasn't," Eddie murmured, the first words Carin had heard him speak. His voice was hoarse, but whether from emotion or from years of salt air and stormy seas, Carin couldn't say.

"It was worth it, though," Eddie added, looking at her with wonder and something close to awe. "Worth everything we went through, to see you again … to see you *here*, alive, and a grown woman. You're as beautiful as your mother."

Carin smiled at him. "I think she and I startled each other, we look so much alike."

Eddie scraped a finger along his jaw. "You were exactly like her even as a child. Same eyes, same hair. But," he added, grinning, "you took after me where water is concerned. I had you swimming before you were walking. You were such a natural, the dolphins practically adopted you. You'd swim with them like you were one of their own."

"Nina's at home in the water, too," Carin said as they turned together to walk up the trail a few steps behind Kate and the child. "She was going on six the first time she ever saw an ocean, but she dived in and swam so easily, anyone would think she was born a sea creature."

"Or a sea goddess," Eddie murmured. "Criminy! That child is … well, she's unearthly. There's something about your Nina that is older than six years. And far larger than this world. I look into that girl's eyes, and I see the universe."

Carin inclined her head, considering, then nodded. "That's a good way to put it. Nina is much like her father. They're both sort of … uncontainable … and ageless, in the sense that counting up birthdays is not helpful in knowing who they are. Nina is older than her years, as you say. Her father is younger than his." *And getting younger all the time,* Carin thought, remembering how the silver at Verek's temples had disappeared, darkening to crow-black as the potency of Ladrehdin renewed itself.

"But what was all that," Eddie asked, "about Nina worrying I'd been hurt, and her checking me over before she'd stop looking daggers at me? I'm happy to think the child was concerned for my health … but her bedside manner needs some work."

Carin laughed. "Your strange little granddaughter is not only a natural swimmer, she was born to heal wounds. It's in her blood. If she sees any living thing that might be injured, she's compelled to do everything she can to heal it."

Like a thunderclap inside her head, Carin heard the truth of her own words. The dead jellyfish on Ruain's shore … the dead bird under the trees at Megella's cottage: Nina was drawn to them, not because they were dead, but because she had felt in her inmost being the urge to heal their broken bodies, if any such healing were remotely possible. The child was the categorical opposite of Morann. Nina's power was not death: Nina's power was life — the restoring and rebuilding of life, if even a faint spark of it remained.

They had reached the house where Kate and Eddie had paused their seafaring ways, for the present at least. Studying the wind-burned profile of the man beside her, Carin suspected Eddie might not long be content to stay ashore. She also supposed it was a mariner's penchant for having all things ship-shape that she saw in the cottage before them. The house was small but neat, with a covered porch that wrapped all four sides and large windows standing open to the tropical sea breezes. Both the house and its porch railings were freshly painted in dark coral trimmed with green.

Freshly painted.

Carin stopped in her tracks as an image flashed before her mind's eye: this man, Eddie, sitting on the beach with a paint-brush in his hand. Not a wide brush for house-painting, but a fine brush — an artist's brush. Carin saw the canvas Eddie had propped on an easel; she saw him painting the landscape before him, a landscape flecked with flowers, a soaring wall of rock in the background. Whether Megella's memory tea had summoned the image, or it was Eddie's voice and presence that acted on Carin, she was re-experiencing a moment in time that her past travels through the void had stolen from her.

"You painted," Carin said as Eddie halted beside her. "I remember. Oil paintings. You would sit on the beach in front of our house and paint flowers and the ocean and that huge rock-cliff across the bay."

Eddie looked at her with an expression both pleased and sad. "That seems so long ago. I'm surprised you remember … I barely do. That was another life, when I had time to mess with oil paints." He sighed. "All that got left behind when your mother and I moved onto the boat. We took just the bare necessities."

He gestured toward the cottage, where Kate awaited them. "Come sit on the porch and talk to me, Karen. I've got questions."

Chapter 15

Fragments

Nina had bounded up the porch steps ahead of Carin and made a beeline for a map that hung framed on the house's exterior wall, protected by the overhanging roof. The large and strikingly colored map created a focal point between two wickerwork chairs that faced each other on the porch's seaward exposure.

"Mama!" Nina called, gesturing for Carin to join her at the map. "So much blue! Is that an *ocean?*"

"Yes, child. This map is tinted just like ours at home. The green and brown show the land, and the water is blue. Here are lakes." Carin pointed out a cluster of blue, like paint splattered near the top of one landmass. "Here's a river," she added, indicating a mighty watercourse that cleaved a continent. "But all this is ocean." She traced the outline of the enormous blue expanse, which on the map bore the name *Pacific*.

"Sweet mercy!" Nina breathed, staring at the blue immensity as though it were a mystical vision.

Carin started to chide the girl for swearing, but decided to let it go. At times in life, she silently conceded as she unshouldered her bow and leaned it against the porch railing, swearing was the only thing to do.

"We found that map in a closet," Kate said as the woman emerged from the cottage's open front door. She carried a tray bearing a pitcher and four glasses. "Here in this house, I mean, when we happened across this place. It had been abandoned, like so many other houses in the islands … like we abandoned our old home when things got too lonesome under that wall of rock." Kate set the tray on a glass-topped table between the wicker chairs. "Eddie insisted on hanging that map out here. He can hardly stand to be inside, so most evenings we sit here on the porch and watch the sunset."

"I study that map and wonder who's still alive, out there in the world," Eddie commented. He had followed his wife into the cottage and now reemerged carrying a light molded chair in each hand. These he arranged for his guests within reach of the refreshments on the table. "I've thought about going to look. But that's a big ocean to cross in a small boat."

"Do travelers ever come here, bringing news?" Carin asked as she took the offered seat and accepted from Kate a glass of some unfamiliar, citrusy drink.

"Not often," Kate said. "Those poor people we saw today were the first strangers I've come across in months."

"You didn't know the ones who died?" Carin glanced at Eddie and wondered how much Kate could have hurriedly told him of the bloodbath under the trees. The couple had been alone together, out of Carin's hearing, for only brief moments while she examined the map with Nina and they stepped into their cottage to fetch drinks and chairs.

Kate was shaking her head. "No, thank goodness. I'd never seen them before. But our neighbors" — Kate gave a one-handed wave in a direction vaguely up the shoreline — "our neighbors have talked about people straggling in from time to time. Pathetic little groups of survivors are slowly coming together again ... now that the few of us who are still on our feet feel pretty safe in assuming we're immune to the plague."

Carin sipped her drink, hiding behind her glass so they couldn't see her face. It would serve no good purpose to tell these people that Carin not only knew what pestilence had burned through this world, she knew where it came from. She also knew the precise moment it arrived. The alien disease had entered here when Morann raised the magical vortex that had snatched Carin from her childhood bedroom.

192

You're not responsible, Carin told herself with silent ferocity. *You couldn't have stopped any of this from happening. Done is done.*

"That's the last time I leave you here alone, Kate," Eddie interjected, grim-voiced, as he reached for his wife's hand. "From now on when I take the boat out, you're coming with me. What if you'd been with those people when … all that happened. You could have been killed."

Again Carin wondered how much Kate had managed to say of the gruesome events. Had the woman mentioned a "demon," or given her husband Carin's assurances that the witch would never trouble these shores again?

They seem almost too calm, too accepting of what they must surely see as a monstrous attack by some barely glimpsed devil, Carin thought.

But then again, maybe the couple had witnessed other horrific attacks by other devils—if not Morann herself, in her frenzies of pain and blood, then perhaps they had seen the work of other killers, once-normal people driven to brutality by a desperate need to survive in a world where untold numbers lay dead. Maybe Kate and Eddie had seen too much to feel anything more than mild pity for those strangers who had died in the clearing.

"Pony!" Nina cried so suddenly that Carin jumped, her hand going reflexively to the knife at her belt.

As she looked past Eddie to where the child still stood under the map, Carin saw an expression of approval lighten the man's face. He had seen her go for the blade, and was pleased by Carin's evident competence with weapons. She'd also noticed him looking appreciatively at the bow and quiver she'd left against the porch railing.

All three adults were brought to their feet, reacting to Nina's exclamation. They turned to see the child dash to the far end of the porch and then leap down narrow side steps to a grassy plot that stretched away beyond the cottage. Nina flew across the grass, calling excitedly. Then the child dug in her heels, brought to a sudden stop when the four-legged object of her delight showed signs of bolting away.

"It's all right," Eddie said to Carin. "That's just Bill. He's friendly when he gets to know you, though a little leery of strangers. Which makes him a smart horse in my book." As they stood together watching Nina slowly approach the pony, reaching to stroke the animal's dappled chestnut neck, Eddie added: "Bill wanders by here most evenings, and sometimes we give him sugarcane. No idea where the fellow comes from. Whoever owned him is probably dead. But he seems to be making out fine on his own. There's plenty of grass, and fresh water in a lake back of those trees." Eddie pointed to a grove of candlenut trees behind the house.

"Nina loves horses," Carin said. "Her horse at home is a giant, especially compared to that little pony. But she'll be riding 'Bill,' next thing we know." Carin looked at Eddie and asked, "Will you watch her for me, and keep her from straying off? I'd like to speak to … my mother … for a moment."

Eddie glanced at her. He'd noticed Carin's pause before the words, "my mother."

Does he suspect? Carin wondered. *Does he realize that I don't really remember either of them? That I recall only the tiniest fragments of my childhood with them?*

But the man only murmured, "Be glad to." He descended the steps and walked out to where the child stood combing her fingers through the pony's rough mane.

Carin reseated herself next to Kate. "Did you tell him everything you saw today?" she asked, unable to contain her curiosity about what the woman had — or had not — revealed about a scene of butchery that lay hardly more than a mile from this cottage.

Kate shook her head. "No, I didn't. If I told Eddie how bad it really was, he'd have us on the boat and out to sea before nightfall. I'm tired of living on the water." She tapped one open-toed shoe on the porch's weathered deck. "I need to feel solid ground

under my feet again. And it's so *good* to have neighbors to talk
to." Again Kate waved in the general direction of people who
must live relatively nearby, Carin surmised, though no other
house was visible under the trees shading the shoreline.

"For years," Kate added, "your father and I had only each
other for company. I love him dearly. But sometimes I need to
talk to another woman."

Carin smiled. "I don't know what I'd do without Theil's aunt
Megella. She's the only one I can speak to, about some things."

"About him? About your man, you mean?"

Carin laughed. "Occasionally. At times he'll do something
so infuriating that I have to go fuming to Meg about it, to keep
from killing him. But mostly, I talk to her about the children.
You've met Nina, so you can guess how … challenging it's been,
raising that child. Nina's little brother, Galen, is a handful, too."

Briefly Carin considered telling Kate about the boy's supernatural talent with fire, but decided that was more than the
woman needed to know about a grandson she would almost
certainly never meet.

"Does Galen look like his father, too?" Kate asked.

Carin shook her head. "No, you'd see yourself in that one.
He's red-haired, and his eyes are green, exactly like yours and
mine."

This pleased the woman, Carin could tell from the soft smile
that touched Kate's lips.

Be careful, she warned herself. *Don't build this woman's hopes.
Remember where you are, and how vastly distant this place is from
Ruain.*

But Carin had already said too much, as became evident
when Kate spoke again.

"Can you bring him to meet us?" the woman asked. "Is that
possible?"

Carin sighed. She reached for Kate's hand; the woman took
hers and gripped it.

"Coming here is … a little dangerous for me," Carin replied, gently. "It affects my mind. I've only recently remembered … certain events that are so important in my life, it's incredible to me that I could have forgotten them, *ever*. But I did forget, and it's because I've made so many journeys through—"

The void, Carin almost said. But would this woman grasp even a trace of the enormity signified by that simple word?

"Through a kind of nothingness where time behaves strangely," Carin amended, struggling to put the inexpressible into plain language. "Some of my journeys have aged me. I returned to Theil older—and wiser—than when I left him. But at least once, it was like time stood still. For me, not him. I don't know exactly how it affects my body, what it does to me physically. I only know it leaves me feeling … unstuck in time. What's most clear is that it damages my memory."

Carin looked at the woman, searching for a sign that Kate understood her. *Does she realize what I'm saying?* Carin wondered silently. *Is she comprehending that I remember almost nothing about her and Eddie? That I have no life in this world? This is not where I belong.*

Kate met Carin's gaze. "'This be such a time as the world's reckoning of moments will not measure,'" she said softly.

Carin's question must have shown in her face, for the woman smiled and added, "I read that in a book somewhere. Liked it, but never knew what it meant. Now, I think I may understand."

Slowly, the woman closed her eyes, squeezing the lids shut as though to ward off tears.

"I won't see you again, will I?" she whispered, opening her eyes and searching Carin's face as though to impress upon her memory every feature, every contour, every scar. Life on the world called Ladrehdin had not left Carin unmarked. Her face still bore the faint lines of the lacerations inflicted by a miscarriage of her powerful sand-spell.

Carin squeezed the woman's hand. "I can't risk it …
Mother," she said almost shyly, her lips having a moment's difficulty forming the seldom-spoken word.

Then, more firmly, Carin added: "I *won't* risk forgetting any
part of the life I've made with the man I love. He's waiting for
me, and he might need my help. When I came after Nina, I left
Theil facing a demon. I must go home. Now."

Carin stood, drawing Kate up to stand with her. They embraced, each knowing it was for the last time.

"Thank you, Karenina," the woman whispered. "Thank you
for letting us see the strong woman you've become, and for
bringing your astonishing daughter to meet us, and for telling
me about your husband. Of course you must go back to him."
Kate smiled. "I can let you go now, with a light heart. After all
these years of being afraid for you, I can stop worrying. You
obviously can take care of yourself."

Carin thought her mother was alluding to her weaponry, the
quiver and bow she retrieved from the railing and slung over her
shoulder. But Kate's next comment made clear what the woman
meant.

"If you're longing to return to a man who confronts demons,
and who is capable of fathering a child like *that* one," Kate said,
pointing at the raven-haired girl who was riding the pony on the
grass beside the cottage, "then you must be the bravest woman
I've had the privilege to know. When I picture a grown man with
those eyes and a frankly terrifying gaze, I get a little shiver up my
spine."

Carin inclined her head, and smiled. She'd journey across
the universe to look again into Theil Verek's eyes and feel that
delicious shiver race up her spine.

"Nina!" Carin called to the child. "We must be going. Say
good-bye to Master Eddie and Lady Kate."

Carin deliberately pronounced the syllables *good-bye* in the
language of this place, to test the girl's ear. Nina had heard the

language spoken all around her while she tended the wounded in the clearing. The girl had heard Carin translate her instructions to the rescuers who brought seaweed and afterward carried away the survivors. Nina had listened as Carin conversed in that tongue with Kate and Eddie. How much of the language had the child already absorbed?

Enough, it turned out, to bid her Earthly grandparents a clear and unaccented farewell.

"Good-bye, Master Eddie," Nina said as she slid from the pony's back and stood before the man. The child bobbed another curtsy, less studied than the one she had accorded him before.

Eddie crouched, bringing his eyes to Nina's level. "Good-bye, little goddess," he murmured, and held out his arms to the child. Without hesitation, Nina rushed to hug him. She lifted her face to be kissed, and to kiss him in turn.

"Good-bye, Bill!" the child said when Eddie released her and she skipped back to the pony. She gave the beast a pat and lightly kissed its muzzle.

Lastly, Nina bounded up onto the porch and threw herself into Kate's outstretched arms. "Good-bye, Lady Kate," the girl whispered, her voice barely audible, wrapped as she was in the woman's embrace and with her face pressed against Kate's neck.

Eddie had walked to the porch but he stayed down in the grass, leaving the pony standing alone a short distance from the house. Bill looked dejected. The pony's eyes and small, alert ears remained trained on Nina as if the animal was sorry to see the girl leave.

Eddie's face wore a similarly forlorn expression as Carin descended the narrow side steps to take her leave of the man. Neither of them spoke. Words seemed inadequate once more. They might have questioned each other for hours and still failed to bridge the gap that time and experience had forged between them. They only embraced. Eddie held her close for a moment, then pressed a kiss like a benediction on her brow and released her.

With tears filling her eyes, Carin turned from him. "Come, Nina," she called, thickly. "We must go."

The child extricated herself from Kate's arms. Nina repeated "Good-bye!" quite loudly, as if to impress the shape of those newly learned syllables into her tongue. And before the girl jumped down from the porch to join Carin on the grass, Nina paused for a last study of the map that stretched across the wall—the clearly readable map that proclaimed how much of this world was covered in blue ocean waters.

She's committing it to memory, Carin thought, watching Nina. *I may never return here, but there's no force in the cosmos that could keep that girl away forever. This is a world profoundly in need of healing ... and it's got endless beaches. It's made for her.*

When Nina at last broke away from the map and came to take Carin's hand, only the child looked back as they hurried down the path to the overlook, then descended further to the beach. When they stood on the sand, a quick glance along the shore in both directions confirmed Carin's instinct to head away from the scene of Morann's atrocities. In the distance on that bearing, people were visible. A few moved along the rocky edge where the surf foamed and seaweed grew. Others walked under the trees that screened the blood-soaked clearing, coming and going as if searching.

Maybe the people were attempting to understand what had happened in that clearing, Carin thought, watching them. They would still be burying mutilated bodies, and perhaps they were asking themselves: "What did this?" ... unsatisfied, many might be, with Kate's inference of a demon.

Carin had no interest in enlightening the searchers. The fiend who had ripped bellies open in this world would threaten no one here, ever again.

Turning in the opposite direction, Carin hurried Nina along the shore of the deeply notched inlet where Eddie had dropped anchor. She paused only to scoop the child up and carry her when Nina complained that Carin was walking too fast. The girl seemed to catch the urgency which vibrated now in every fiber of Carin's being. Nina made no effort to wriggle out of her grasp until they were deep along the inlet and had gained the cover of a thick stand of trees.

The grove shaded a low promontory that jutted into the sheltered cove where Eddie moored his boat. Carin couldn't see the vessel from where she stood on the point of land. He would secure his boat well out of sight, she thought, given how vital that craft had been in saving his and Kate's lives, and how Eddie valued it even now as a means of ready escape to the open sea, if such became necessary once more.

"Nina," Carin murmured, setting the child down. "There's something I must do, and you must help me."

"Yes, Mama," the girl whispered, still impressed into obedience by the tension that showed in Carin's words and movements.

"I must leave you for a moment," Carin said. "I won't go far—only under the bank there, where the trees grow thickest. You won't see me in their shadows, but I'll hear if you call. Summon me only if you must, however. I need you to stay right here, and be as quiet as you can until I return. Do you understand?"

"Yes, Mama," Nina repeated, a bit sullenly this time. The girl looked disappointed that the "help" Carin wanted from her was only that she stay out of the way. But with an air of resignation, Nina crouched and began rearranging the dead leaves and twigs that littered the floor of the grove.

"Thank you, child," Carin whispered as she turned away and hurried into the dimness under the tree-shadowed bank. Shielded there from all eyes, she dug into her pocket for the small bejeweled bottle that had been in Morann's possession for count-less years.

That it had its origins in this world, Carin was now certain. The ruby of the bottle's crystal exactly matched the red of a drinking glass which Kate had brought to the porch on a tray to serve her guests. The red glass would have been Nina's, if the child had dragged herself away from her map and her pony, even long enough to sample the refreshment that Kate poured for her. But as it was, no one except Kate had touched that glass. Carin, however, had eyed it closely, impressing upon her memory the tumbler's precise shade.

Its red was the ruby of the amulet that Carin now held in her hand. No glassmaker of Ladrehdin had ever achieved such a rich, deep tint as this.

Carin set the amulet on a ledge of rock and snapped her spell of sand upon it, obliterating the glass and its decorative gem-stones. Twice she recast her spell, pulverizing the grit until nothing remained of the bejeweled bottle except a minutely fine powder. Even its color was annihilated. The bottle's dusty resi-due appeared indistinguishable from the thin coating of soil that lay on the rock.

That's done for her amulet, Carin thought with silent satisfac-tion as she scraped the dust off the ledge and watched it drift away, disappearing into shadows and air. *It's back in its own world. Now to see what's become of the demon in mine.*

Carin turned from the shelf of rock, but had taken only two steps back toward Nina's location when a reedy voice addressed her, seemingly from thin air:

"My friend!" the voice cried. "I am more pleased to see you than I can say."

Chapter 16

The Restless Sea

"Woodsprite!" Carin exclaimed, startled into a near shout before collecting herself and lowering her voice. "Where are you?"

"I'm here before you, in this tree," the sprite replied. "Can you make me out?"

Carin whirled, running her gaze over the trunks of the unfamiliar trees that grew in this grove. *There*—she saw it: a familiar sparking in a gnarled, exotic specimen.

She rushed to wrap her arms around the trunk, hugging it so tightly that its rough bark cut her face.

"My friend!" the sprite shrilled in her ear. "I feared I would never see you again. Each passing day deepens my regret that I was cold toward you at our last parting."

"Cold?" Carin echoed, puzzled. "I don't remember you being distant with me. You made music, and the limbs of your tree bent down to tickle my ribs." She laughed at the memory. "You weren't at all standoffish."

"Ah," said the sprite. "I confess I might have been showing off for you. I wished you to know how far I had progressed in my mastery of timber." The creature sparked near Carin's face as it whispered, "In truth, I was rather angry with you."

"You had every right to be furious with me." Carin peeled herself off the tree's bark but stood leaning both hands against its trunk. "What I did was unforgivable—deserting you on that world of weeds."

"But then I contrived to make my own way back to the magician's world, did I not? And there, you rescued me again when the trees of his realm refused me admittance. I would have died, if not for you."

Carin patted the jagged bark, noticing as she did a smear of blood from where she'd cut herself on it. "I've lost count of how many times we each saved the other, woodsprite. Tell me now, though, how you fare in this world where I was born. Are you content here?"

"Perfectly, my friend. The trees here have voices of their own, and I have learned their languages. I move freely among them and speak with them daily. I also visit the man and woman who gave you life. They feared me a little, when first I approached them." The sprite flickered, as if recalling the consternation with which Kate and Eddie must have received its early overtures. "But when I learned enough of their tongue to make myself understood, and they discovered that I was *your* friend, they welcomed me and asked endless questions about our adventures together."

"I'm sure you've bent their ears for hours," Carin said, laughing. "How much of what you've told them is true, I wonder, and how much of it have you invented?"

"I've scarcely needed to resort to invention," the sprite protested. "When I think back on our times together, I marvel at the journeys we made and the things we saw."

For a moment Carin was silent, remembering. Then she leaned close to the tree.

"Woodsprite," she whispered, "I can't stay. I've lingered in this world too long already. I must be going. And when I take my leave of you this day, I think it will be for the last time." Carin hugged the tree again, and felt its bark slice her other cheek. It seemed fitting, that she should bleed for this creature whom she had so badly wronged.

Resolutely pushing herself away, Carin dug into her belt pouch for the other bottle she had brought on this final journey to her homeworld. As she lifted the wood-wrapped vessel into view, she heard the sprite's sharply indrawn breath.

"Carin!" the creature exclaimed. "I succeeded! You found it."

"More like it found me. A dolphin brought me your message, off the coast of Ruain." Carin gave a wondering shake of her head. "I don't see how you could have managed it, sprite, and I can't stay to find out. But knowing—as you now do—that you can get a message to me, I want you to ask my parents to write down your words from time to time. They can put your messages in a bottle with their own, for you to send as this one was sent." She twiddled the wood-encased glass, then paused as a thought struck her. "You *can* do it again, and this *wasn't* the last bottle with a good stopper? It must float, or it'll never reach me."

"Bottles and stoppers number near to infinity in these islands," the sprite assured her, sounding breathless with its excitement. "And I most certainly can repeat the methods that succeeded with *that* one.

"But," the creature added, now with a note of worry in its voice, "by what means could you answer me?"

Carin shrugged. "It may be that I can't reply, for a while at least." She glanced in the direction where Nina had been told to await her. *Slim chance that girl is still there,* Carin thought, *after all this time.*

She patted the tree, then squared her shoulders and stepped away. "I must go, woodsprite. Nothing more can I say except that I will seek for a means to answer your messages. If I fail, and if you never hear from me again, then I want you to know this, above all: I am your friend, sprite, now and always. Good-bye."

Carin whirled and ran. She couldn't bear to hear the woodsprite's farewell. It was too painful. This leave-taking hurt worse than parting from Kate and Eddie. Carin barely knew them. But she remembered the sprite in every particular, and she would never forget how she'd betrayed the creature's trust, in her misguided determination to return every lost thing to its own domain and break every bridge between the worlds.

Some lost creatures—herself among them—did not belong to the place of their birth. Moreover, some bridges could not—and should not—be broken.

Nina, of course, was not waiting where the girl had been told to wait. Only the child's careful arrangement of twigs and leaves marked the now-abandoned spot.

Carin was opening her mouth and filling her lungs to shout the girl's name, but then she saw movement through the trees in the direction of the blue-water inlet. Not far from the edge of the low promontory but still under the cover of its concealing grove, Nina had sprung to her feet and was racing toward the water.

"No!" Carin cried as she launched herself into a sprint to catch the girl before Nina dived in—for clearly it was the child's intent to enter the water. And who could blame her, when irresistible temptation had presented itself in the form of a dolphin pod?

From the deep water beyond a rocky outcrop, the creatures leapt and spun, clicked and whistled. Carin couldn't tell if they were calling deliberately to Nina. But as the child ran toward them, the dolphins seemed to swim nearer the edge of the headland from which Nina would momentarily throw herself.

Not now! Carin screamed inwardly. They'd already stayed here too long. If Nina jumped into the water and swam away with those dolphins, only Drisha knew how many hours—or days—might pass before Carin could collect the child and drag her, probably unwilling, back through the void.

The margin was whisker-thin, but Carin's longer legs and the anxiety in her heart impelled her to victory. Just as Nina reached the promontory's edge, Carin also gained it. The speed of her sprint carried her off the brink, and for an instant she flailed in midair, grabbing for the child's hand.

In that moment, suspended between sea and sky, the pounding of the surf came to her, the crash of waves against rock. She felt two powers touch—the Power which bore the name Amangêda, and the vast force of the ocean that surrounded Carin in this world called Earth. In the core of her being, those two potencies combined, and in the grip of their strength she achieved understanding. She'd received no answer when she'd sought Amangêda's help against the necromancer, for the voice of Power knew what Carin was only now realizing. *The restless sea casts forth the greatest gift.* She, Carin of Ruain and of Earth, could draw at will upon the strength of both worlds: Ladrehdin, and these her native waters. She was master and servant to them both.

They served her now as Carin seized Nina's fluttering hand and locked her gaze onto the wood-wrapped bottle she held before her. Ignoring the startled cries of the child who sailed through the air alongside her, Carin focused her inner eye on her destination: the springwater pool that adjoined the blue bed-chamber.

The great wellspring of power in its cavern below the library might have been a safer place in which to land. Many times wider and deeper than the pool upstairs, the well of the *wysards* would offer a greater margin for any error that might creep into this void-crossing magic. In any case, the currents which moved unseen in the nothingness might tend to carry her back to that wellspring despite her conscious wishes, for Carin had begun her pursuit of her daughter from the rim of that pool, with Amangêda knowing what she was about.

Carin was unwilling, however, to transport the child to that mysterious pool or into the cavern of enchantment where magical forces thrummed with daunting potency. Verek had chosen to conceal the place from his children thus far, deeming them too young and too inexperienced to encounter the powers which were concentrated in that cave. Indeed, Carin had come to appreciate that, in all the extended household, she alone felt truly at ease in the presence of that Power. Megella freely admitted the

place terrified her, and even Welwyn approached it rarely, pre-
ferring to stay abovestairs and leave the wellspring of Ruain to
the *wysards* of House Verek.

Theil himself was more relaxed in the vault of magic, these
days, than he had been when he first led Carin to that cavern.
Now that his world was recovering its equilibrium and the
waters of the wellspring had regained their natural warmth, no
longer threatening glacial death to anyone who entered them,
Verek's demeanor when nearing the pool was a little less
hushed, a little less suggestive of an acolyte in a temple. Even so,
Theil's relationship with the wellspring was less intimate than
Carin's. For in the throes of its great need, as pestilence swept
the land and potency drained from the world, the Power had
chosen Carin, not Verek, as its conduit for healing.

Nina, however, had forged a bond with the previously un-
tapped waters of the upstairs pool. When the child roused those
waters to bear her away to "the beach," so powerful was Nina's
wizardry that the backwash had swept Morann into the void and
into the pool, through a kind of cosmic interchange. The demon
reentered Ladrehdin as Nina left it.

And so, Carin set her sights on that smaller, more youthful
wellspring, for it must welcome Nina as the one who had commanded it to rise and serve her.

Too, the necromancer Morann had sprawled, injured but
alive, on the floor just outside that pool, when Carin last laid eyes
on the witch. If time in Ruain had advanced with little or no haste
during her absence beyond the void, Carin might discover the
creature just as she'd left her, and have the satisfaction of sand-
blasting another finger or ear from the demon.

The bathing room, however, was empty when Carin and
Nina hit the pool together, dead center, with a splash that set the
stone walls echoing. The child came up spluttering. But Carin,
braced for the impact, emerged from the water flinging her hair

out of her eyes, alert to the possibility of danger. She took in every significant detail with one glance around the room.

Where Morann had slumped against the wall, nothing now marred the space except faint sprays of blood and the gritty residue of Carin's sand-spelling. On living flesh, the spellwork produced an effect similar to a cautery knife: only a little blood had sprayed from the instantly coagulated stump when Carin pulverized Morann's hand. Enough time had passed that the misted blood was dried and dark.

Opposite the barely visible stains, the chamber's narrow doorway was empty. But where Verek had stood, his right hand stretched toward the witch to deliver a deathblow if Morann invited it, a fresh gouge scored the stone beside the opening. The gouge suggested that the viper had struck at least one last time. Evidently, however, Morann had missed her target: no blood was splattered there.

Carin had not loosened her grip on Nina's hand. Tugging the still-spluttering child to her, she hauled Nina up the pool's steps and plopped the girl down on its rim, between the chunks of stone that Morann's first thunderbolt had ripped from the chamber's ceiling.

Carin sat on the rim facing the child and gripped Nina's arms. Now—in this fleeting moment, when the girl was bewildered and stunned by the speed with which Carin had snatched her home: *now* was Carin's best and perhaps only chance to make a lasting impression on the headstrong child. Returning to Verek and the unfinished business with Morann had stoked only a part of her urgency in fleeing the world of the demon's depredations. In this moment of rare receptivity on Nina's part, Carin needed to make the girl understand the peril of that place.

"Nina, child, listen to me," she began in a voice of commanding intensity. "I know you're going back to that world—someday. I saw how it calls to you. It's in your blood just as Ladrehdin is. But you *must* wait. To return now is too dangerous."

Carin caught and held the child's wide-eyed stare as Nina sat dripping wet but no longer gasping with surprise. The girl's look of close attention deepened as Carin continued speaking.

"Those people you helped, those poor souls with their torn throats and ripped bellies? A woman of Ladrehdin did that to them. I think their friends were shocked almost beyond words by what they saw. Certainly they were astonished to see in their midst a child as young as you, ordering them about while you calmly treated such horrible wounds. In their shock and surprise, the people of that island asked few questions … at the time. But now they've had chances to speak among themselves, and to question the survivors. From those survivors, they will learn of the woman who attacked them."

Carin held Nina motionless, her gaze remaining locked with the child's. "I have seen that woman, Nina. I know that woman's face, her hair, her eyes. You look like her … or as she did when she was young. You have the same hair as she … and the same remarkable, memorable eyes.

"People will speak of the resemblance. I've no doubt that some of the victims you helped were awake enough, aware enough, to have seen you standing over them. Some of them will also remember Mor—" Carin broke off before she named the witch. "They will remember the woman who hurt them. They won't understand, but they will talk. Stories will spread, and people will search for a black-haired girl with a piercing gaze.

"That is why you *must* wait, child," Carin said, and she knew from Nina's focused look that the girl absorbed every word. "You must *not* return to that place until such time as you have completed your training with Master Welwyn. I, too, have much to teach you, beginning with the language of those people. From me, you will learn to speak it, read it, write it—

"So that, when you *do* go back, you will be able to explain all that happened on the day a witch of Ladrehdin ripped the living hearts from innocent victims. By your words and deeds, they will know that you had no part in the evil which was done. You came to them as a healer, in the hour of their great need. And when you return to them, you will bring new healing to a world that sorely needs it.

"Give me your promise, Karenina," Carin demanded, gripping the girl's arms hard enough to bruise her and holding her with a searching gaze. "Give me your most solemn promise, on the *Book of Archamon* and by the oath of your House, that you will not return to that ocean world until Welwyn releases you from apprenticeship and I have taught you all I know of that distant realm. Swear it, now."

"I swear," Nina whispered, awestruck by the intensity of Carin's words and looks. "I swear by Archamon and by the oath of my House, the House of Verek, that I will do as you bid me, Mother. I will not go visit Lady Kate or Master Eddie—or Bill—until you tell me that I may."

Carin struggled to hide a smile at the inclusion of the humble, earthly pony in this high oath of Ruain. *Ghost has a rival for the child's heart,* she thought, but answered aloud: "I accept your solemn promise, Nina, and I will hold you to it.

"Now tell me something," Carin added. "Did you bespell those people to make them obey you?"

"A little bit," Nina said.

"I thought so. They would not have been so biddable otherwise. Especially since they did not know the words you spoke to them."

And particularly in light of what must be a deep reluctance, among all those people, to touch the blood of strangers, after enduring the horrors of the bleeding disease, Carin thought as she studied her daughter and silently wondered: Just how powerful *was* the enchantment the child had cast over those people, to overcome what had to be an extreme aversion to blood?

Nina looked like she couldn't tell whether she was being praised or reprimanded. To leave the child in no doubt, Carin smiled and added, "You did well, Karenina. You used your gifts to save people's lives.

"And now," she concluded, "you may go to your quarters and change into dry clothes. If Master Welwyn is not there, I bid you seek him out and tell him all that you have done and promised today. I will leave it to him, your master and governor, to administer such punishments as he may see fit, for the damage you and Galen did to the bedroom door—and for your unsanctioned magic-making with these waters." Carin pointed at the pool they sat beside.

"Yes, Mama," Nina murmured, as abashed as Carin supposed was possible for such an obstinate child.

The girl scrambled up from the pool's rim and dashed into the adjoining bedchamber—straight into her father's embrace. Verek had that moment entered the doorless room from the stair landing.

"Welcome home, child," Verek said after a long moment of cradling her close. He held Nina off and pinned her with his gaze. "If you ever do anything like that again, I will boil you in oil. Do you understand me?"

"Yes, Papa," Nina chirped. "I missed you, too."

Then the child was gone, skipping—or squelching—down the corridor toward her bedroom in the house's main wing. Before Nina passed out of earshot, Carin heard her practicing those syllables of a foreign tongue that the child had learned today. "Good-bye," Nina called, loudly enough to echo down the corridor. "Bye, Bill. Bye, Kate."

Verek, as he entered the bathing room through its narrow, slightly damaged doorway, looked at Carin with one eyebrow raised.

Carin shrugged. "Among other things," she said as she got to her feet, dripping as much water as Nina had, "your daughter is a parrot. Four hours on a distant world, and the girl's already speaking the language."

"Four hours?" Verek growled. "You've been gone a night and a day. I was growing frantic."

Carin blinked at him, then heaved a sigh of mixed dismay and resignation.

"It's the void," she said, a little helplessly. "You know I lose track of time in there."

"No matter." Verek's voice was tight with suppressed emotion. "You're here now. Come to me." He held out his arms to her.

"I'm soaked. I'll get you wet," Carin murmured as she did as he bid her and entered the strong, reassuring circle of his arms.

"That wouldn't be for the first time," Verek muttered, burying his face in Carin's damp hair. "I deserve no less for having married a water-sylph with a foreign sea in her blood."

"Alas for you, my love," Carin whispered into his ear, "your daughter is even more of a far-swimming fish than I am."

Chapter 17

The Fate of Wysards

What to do with a broken demon?

As the bloodless gouge in the bathing-room's doorway testified, Morann had attempted to fight, once Carin was off to find Nina, and the witch was alone with Verek. The emaciated creature had expended the final dregs of her strength on a single sorcerous bolt, aimed at Verek's head where he'd stood in the door. He'd dodged easily. With his vastly more potent spellwork, Verek had flung Morann back so hard against the wall behind her, the witch lost consciousness. It had been a simple matter then, for him to carry Morann's limp body down the stairs to the foyer and thence to the cellar-dungeon.

Which is where the creature now lay, behind rusty iron bars, on a thin pallet that kept her skeletal body off the damp, deathly cold floor. She'd even been given a blanket, Carin saw by the light of the five witchlight orbs that illuminated the cell the witch occupied. And she'd been fed. A tray of bread, cheese, and ale sat on the floor beside the pallet.

'The murder of one's mother is a hard thing to contemplate, even for a son born of a demoness.' Verek had said it on the night of his soul-baring, when he'd met Carin on her long ride home through oak-covered hills. Would he now find it impossible to deal out the justice this fiend deserved?

If he can't do it, I will, Carin silently vowed as she stood in the cellar between Theil and Welwyn, the three of them staring at the sleeping, bone-thin figure. *Though, I would like the witch to be awake when I reduce her to sand,* Carin thought. *I want my power to be the last thing she ever feels in this world.*

As though to grant Carin's wish, Morann stirred from her uneasy sleep. A groan escaped the witch's dry, cracked lips. Her mangled left hand crooked around the stump of her right hand, all that remained to her after Carin's sand-spelling. Then the witch opened her eyes, and her dark, glittering gaze fell upon the three *wysards* who stood at the bars of her prison, contemplating her in her final hour.

She glowered at each of them in turn, but the look she fixed upon Verek was a glare of deepest hatred. Had she possessed the strength to do so, the demoness would have ripped out her son's heart in that moment.

Morann snarled, showing broken, yellow teeth. Carin looked from her to Verek, and saw revulsion in Theil's face. Any last hesitation, any final compunction he might have felt about killing his own mother: Morann herself had put to flight all such qualms. Verek's right hand came up, his fingers straight and stiff, aiming a deathblow at the witch's head …

A blow that never landed. In that moment, the ground shook. There came a great cracking noise, like the rending of the world itself, and alongside Morann's pallet the rock split open. A chasm gaped. For an instant that could not be measured in comprehendible time, Morann balanced on the shattered edge of that chasm.

And as she hung suspended, a stern, commanding voice issued from deep in the stone. "Give the murderess to me," the voice demanded. "I will have vengeance on the demon for us both, Theil."

"Legary!" cried Morann, wild-eyed now, and struggling to push herself back from the brink of the lightless pit that yawned below her. *"How – ?"*

Her question was never fully voiced. Any other words she might have shaped gave way to screams of raw terror as another powerful tremor shook the ground and sent her tumbling, pitching down into the gulf that had opened to receive her. Her pallet and blanket followed her into darkness, and even the tray of bread and cheese clattered down into the depths, leaving nothing behind that the witch had touched.

Carin, fighting to keep on her feet between an also wobbly Welwyn and Verek, heard the woman's screams grow ever fainter as she plummeted into the abyss—

—Until the crack in the rock slammed shut behind her, with such finality, cutting off the sounds of terror so completely, that Carin wondered if she herself had been struck deaf in that instant.

"Theil!" she shouted, mostly to test the health of her hearing. "Sweet mercy! *What just happened?*"

When the shock wore off a little, with the ground no longer trembling and the three of them again feeling their legs firmly under them—and when they could stop gaping at the now-vacant cell in the dungeon—they climbed the steep, worn steps which led up from that freezing space underground. Seeking the warmth of Myra's kitchen, they gathered at the trestle table. Despite the far-advanced hour of the evening, the housekeeper was there to serve them a hot supper.

Even if Myra had earlier retired for the night, Carin reflected, she had to have felt or heard the quaking of the very foundations of the house, deep below this wing of it. Indeed, the housekeeper looked flustered, and she remained uncommonly silent as she set a meal on the table for the equally untalkative diners. As of yet, no one had answered Carin's question.

Welwyn was the first of the witnesses to recover his voice. When he'd washed down a few spoonfuls of stew with a generous measure of ale, the monk turned to Verek. He gave the tongue-tied and visibly unsettled wizard a sympathetic but knowing smile.

"I had long suspected hidden talents in that secretive grandsire of yours, don't you know," Welwyn said. "When you told me how Legary's voice echoed from the mountainsides when you and Carin confronted the demoness in her lair, I regarded my suspicions as proved, even then. Now I am doubly certain: Your grandfather died in body, but not in spirit. Legary remained in this world ... in the rock of Ruain, in the stones of its streams, in the roots of Ladrehdin's mountains, near and distant. He lingered ... waiting, watching always for the moment when he could have his singular revenge on the deceiver who murdered his son, and yours, Theil."

"You believe my grandsire is now wholly gone from this world?" Verek asked, soft-voiced. His brief reunion with Lord Legary had left him dazed, too overcome by wonderment to do more than whisper.

Welwyn inclined his head. "Legary dragged that blackheart straight to *farsinchia,* where she will suffer the torments of the truly damned, for all time. How pleased I was to see Morann fully awake and aware when that rock cracked and Legary spoke, in his old familiar voice. In that moment, she knew her fate." The monk smiled again. "It was music to me, hearing that witch scream as she took up her eternal residence in the abyss."

"I'm not sure I understand," Carin interjected, glancing from one to the other of the men. "You're saying the demon's corpse isn't, at this very moment, buried in the cellar of this house? That's kind of what it looked like, to me."

Welwyn looked faintly amused. "In a manner of speaking, Lady Carin, you could regard those foul remains as having been entombed here, just as you say. I invite you, however, to recall the ground-shaking thunder which resounded through the deepest bones of this world when Legary slammed shut that crack in the cellar floor. I believe you can rest easy, knowing—as I do—that *nothing* remains of Morann in this world, not an atom of her being. In body and essence, the witch is now captive in *farsinchia,* and there she will remain."

"With my grandfather attending her?" Verek asked, his voice still low. "Legary, too, committed crimes for which he owes payment."

Welwyn shrugged—a gesture Carin suspected he had picked up from her.

"In the monastery," the old monk said, "I was taught that payment is exacted in proportion to the crime. We cannot doubt that Morann has damned herself for eternity. But Legary? No. I believe the time will come when Lord Legary has discharged his debt. Then he will be free to go where dead *wysards* go."

"And where is that?" Carin asked with more than academic interest.

"I've no idea, my dear." Welwyn grinned as he reached for the hot bread Myra had just placed on the table. "That's one of life's great mysteries."

* * *

After surveying the damage to the blue bedroom and the chamber of the springwater pool, Carin and Verek cleaned it up themselves, unaided by Myra or any of the housemaids. Neither did they call for Megella's assistance, deeming the sorcerous residue too potentially dangerous for any hands but their own. While Carin worked with a fine brush and dustpan to remove every grain of the sand which had once been Morann's hand, ear, and little finger, Verek shoveled up the chunks of stone that Morann's thunderbolts had blasted from the chamber's ceiling and entryway.

The *wysard* used magic only for raising and removing the fragments of rubble that had fallen into the pool itself. For cleaning the bathing-room's floor, he relied strictly on physical labor, even deigning to wield a broom to sweep up the coarse stone-dust that escaped his shovel and bucket.

Carin regarded this astonishing sight without comment. She'd occasionally seen Verek magicking dust off the books in the library—which explained how that room stayed so clean when Myra seldom entered it, and her maids were strictly forbidden to cross its threshold. Never before, however, had Carin witnessed her warlock with a broom in his hand. She engraved the sight into her memory, predicting—correctly—that she'd never see such a thing again.

As she stood watching, she couldn't help musing on how the final business with Morann had worked out. Both she and Verek had vowed to kill the witch, but in the end, neither had done so. Only Flynn's death could now be laid to Carin's account. More importantly, Theil had not been forced to destroy his own mother. Legary had taken that cup from him, while delivering justice for the murder of Verek's first, young family.

What an unpredictable thing life is, in a wizards' world, Carin thought.

When the bathing room was pristine, they removed the charred fragments of wood that hung in the bedchamber's outer doorway—those blackened fragments being all that remained of the substantial timber door which had once closed off the room from the stair landing and upper corridor. They made no provision for replacing the door.

"Let's leave it open as an invitation to both our hellions," Carin said as she stood in the hallway beside Verek. With the broom she'd taken from his hand, she reached for the last of the burnt wood-chips that lay scattered on the floor. "Welwyn's been hammering into them the indispensable wizardly virtue of self-discipline. Let's see if any of it has stuck."

Verek bent to pick up the bucket holding broken stone. "And if, perchance, the lesson is not yet driven fully home," he said, straightening, "you and I may more readily intervene if no obstacle but our own bedroom door stands between us and the springwater pool. It is well that we sleep so near the blue room, the better to keep our ears open for mischief-makers in the night."

* * *

It seemed, however, that Welwyn had succeeded in impressing upon the children the need for restraint. Galen — having discovered the delightful properties of molten metal — spent his free time begging scrap-iron from the gardener and the groom, then casting his ferociously hot fire-spell to melt those odd bits of garden tools and stable gear. Verek showed the boy how to make molds from sand and clay, and soon Galen was melting and refashioning rusty iron remnants into serviceable hammer heads and hinge straps.

Nina, too, stayed too busy for mischief. Not only did Welwyn pile on extra lessons in spellcraft and herb-lore, Carin spent hours with the girl every day, teaching Nina the language the child had heard on that ocean world which had so enthralled her.

When Carin set out to tell Nina the story of "Alice Through the Looking-Glass," she realized she remembered the tale almost word for word, so closely had she studied the book with a captivated Verek. Carin wrote out the story in its native tongue, hewing as near as she could to the original — omitting only the poem that called the Jabberwock dragon. The manuscript became the text by which Carin taught Nina to read, write, and speak its language.

To these lessons, Carin added everything she could remember from her four return journeys to the world of her birth. She began these recollections with the "errand" Verek had sent her on, to return the looking-glass book to her childhood bedroom and "retrieve" the dolphin-shaped crystal that Verek had mistakenly believed was a talisman belonging to the world of Ladrehdin. Carin did not tell Nina a great deal about the crystal or its mates, or how she had eventually rid both this world and her homeworld of the parasitic devices. The crystals were gone — forever, Carin believed — and they would not figure in whatever life Nina was preparing herself to lead.

Carin did, however, describe her childhood home in detail. Her deepest instincts said the girl would find that house, soon or late, after Nina returned to those islands in the great ocean called the Pacific. The girl might, in fact, be drawn to live in that house. Certainly Nina seemed charmed by Carin's descriptions of its airy rooms, fruitful orchard, and secluded setting on the teal-blue bay where dolphins swam. She pored over a sketch Carin made of the house's floor plan and the surrounding landscape, including the steep wall of rock that rose across the bay from the house's tree-ringed, parklike setting.

Nina's obsession with the distant ocean-world did not, however, supplant the girl's fixation on Ruain's own beaches. In her eleventh year, Nina rode forth on Ghost, eastbound, openly challenging anyone to stop her.

"Let her go," Verek said, waving his hand in casual dismissal. "I'll wager she's back in two days. The girl hasn't so much as a blanket in her packs, nor any waybread or waterskin. Hard experience teaches valuable lessons."

On the second night of Nina's journey, the skies opened, and for hours the rain fell. Within a day of the storm's passing, the girl straggled home, looking half drowned. Ghost's legs were muddy; his normally flowing tail drooped, and his face wore an expression of disgust. Nina stabled the horse, waved off the groom's offer of help, and set about cleaning the animal from his nose to his tail. She sponged off every splatter of mud, combed out Ghost's mane and switch, brushed his coat until it shone, then fed him an extra ration of oats. Only then did Nina wordlessly creep up to her room and bathe away the mud she herself had collected.

Months passed, with none in her family ever mentioning Nina's aborted journey to Ruain's seashore. The girl threw herself into her studies, learning everything Welwyn, Verek, and Megella could teach her of herbs, remedies, and the healing arts. She practiced with bow, sling, and blade until Verek declared her ready for her final test.

He arranged for Cian Ronnat's three strapping sons to ambush Nina one afternoon as she rode Ghost through the woods, returning from an herb-gathering excursion that Welwyn had assigned her. The young men sprang from hiding, yelling blood-curdling threats and brandishing weapons—real swords, not practice blades. For if his daughter truly meant to leave Ruain and his protection, Verek meant to satisfy himself that Nina could stand against a coordinated attack by three men. He watched from horseback, unseen by the combatants but prepared to turn them all to stone to keep them from actually killing each other.

Verek need not have worried. Nina raised a wall of water and crashed it down on the men with such force, their weapons were knocked from their hands, and they themselves were laid out cold on the woodland floor. Calmly the girl rode over to look down on the three from the back of her long-legged mount, the imperturbable Ghost.

From where he watched, Verek saw Nina stiffen and throw up one hand in a gesture of surprise. The girl had just recognized her attackers. Both she and Galen had visited the Ronnat home many times, and the three young men had often been to Weyrrock on their father's business of horse breeding and trading.

Nina dropped her reins and raised both her hands high over her head. Verek correctly interpreted the signal not as surrender—for clearly the girl had won this brief battle. It was, rather, a sign that she understood the nature of the attack: she knew she was being tested.

Like lightning then, Nina dropped one hand, grabbed her knife from the sheath at her belt, and sent it slicing through the hood of the oldest boy's cloak, pinning the splayed-out garment to the damp earth less than the width of two fingers from the fellow's gristly ear. An instant after the knife left her fingers, Nina had her bow in her hand. She buried an arrow in the ground between the spread legs of the second brother, so close to the lad's manhood that Verek, spurring up to see more clearly, could not help but gasp at the near miss.

The girl, however, was not yet finished demonstrating her competence with weapons. Moving so quickly that Verek could not follow her actions, Nina whirled her sling and released a stone that slammed into Verek's left shoulder with such force, she unhorsed him. Verek tumbled backward, and found himself sprawled on the ground, spared serious injury by the carpet of fallen leaves but feeling the blow to his shoulder — and his pride — as if he'd been struck down by a young giant.

Hearing Nina's giggle, Verek opened his eyes to see the girl standing over him, digging in her herb-collecting sack. Nina pulled out fresh leaves of the plant with the nearly unpronounce-able name, which Verek himself used to make poultices for blunt-force wounds and deep bruises.

"Here, Papa," the girl said, grinning as she thrust the leaves at him. "This will make it feel better."

Verek sat up. With a muttered oath, he accepted the green-ery from her, crushed the leaves, and reached inside his shirt to press the cool pulp to the bruise, unable to stifle a sharp intake of breath at the extreme soreness.

"Did I pass?" Nina asked, smirking at Verek like the devil-kin she was.

"You did."

"May I ride to the coast now? Just me and Ghost?"

"You may."

Nina paused, then surprised Verek with an unexpectedly sensible suggestion. "Do you have messages you would like me to take to your sheriffs and such, my lord father? I could deliver them on my way east."

Verek rubbed his chin, regarding her, then nodded. "I do, and I thank you for your offer. Help me to my feet, you imp, then go catch my horse for me, and I'll ride home to write my dispatches."

Nina took Verek's outstretched hand, planted her feet, and pulled. He, however, stayed firmly on the ground, determined that the child would know defeat at least once this day. The harder Nina pulled, the more steadfastly Verek resisted, until at last he jerked the girl off her feet. As Nina tumbled into Verek's arms, laughing at this game they hadn't played since she was a child of six, he planted a kiss on the top of her head. Then Verek stood—needing no assistance, now or ever—and swung Nina to her feet.

He caught up his own horse. As Nina walked off to collect her arrow and knife as well as her faithful Ghost, Verek called to her. "You may follow me home at your leisure, Karenina, or go where you please. I am now quite certain that you can take care of yourself. Which does not mean I will cease to concern myself with your well-being, you must understand. Wherever you go in all of existence, near or far, you will be the eldest daughter of my House, and the pride of my heart."

Three days later, Nina kissed her parents good-bye, hugged her brother, and dropped a perfectly correct curtsy to Master Welwyn. Mounting her horse, she rode away east, the picture of confidence. The girl's saddle-roll held tent canvas and blankets; her bags were packed with jerked meat, dried fruit, cheese and waybread. Verek had gifted her his well-used, much-traveled waterskin. From him also, Nina carried messages addressed to various magistrates and stewards along her route.

"This is practice," Carin muttered as she stood with Verek, watching the girl ride away. "This is all part of Nina preparing herself to return to the ocean world where her grandparents live on the sea, and the dolphins call to her. We'll lose her before she's thirteen."

A grated "Drisha's knuckles" was Verek's only response for a long moment.

He turned from the manor's gate to watch Galen amble back to the smithy the boy had built against the stone wall that enclosed the grounds. Moments after Galen reentered his workshop, roaring blue and dazzling white flames spouted from its doorway. The boy had returned to his favorite pastime: bespelling scrap iron into molten metal, which Galen poured into molds of his own design to create everything from saddle stirrups for the Ronnat clan to unbendable pot-hangers for every kitchen in the precinct.

Speaking then to Carin at his side but still watching the flames that erupted through the smithy's door, Verek said, "Welwyn tells me the boy is interested in nothing except metalworking. Galen is competent in his other studies, he's mostly read the *Book of Archamon* ... and as his weapons master, I can attest to his ability with bow and blade."

Verek paused, then added, "But Galen's only real passion is smithcraft. Welwyn knows of a *wysard* far to the southwest of here, where the desert hills are shot through with veins of ore and every second inhabitant is an expert metalsmith. The *wysard* of Welwyn's acquaintance is an acknowledged master of the craft, an artisan in gold and silver as well as copper and iron. Welwyn suggests apprenticing Galen to him on the boy's fourteenth birthday."

Carin looked at her husband. "Will you agree to that? To lose them both?"

Slowly, Verek nodded. "Yes. Our children have every right to find and follow their own paths. I would not see either of them made miserable by my insistence that they must prepare to someday take my place as sovereign of this realm."

Carin let an eloquently silent moment pass. Then she stepped around to face Verek directly. Casually resting her fingers on the wide belt at his waist, she looked up into his face. "Then it would seem, my lord, that you are in need of a new heir. Do you not think you should apply yourself, without delay, to the business of begetting one?"

Verek's gaze dropped to Carin's with the speed of a falcon stooping to the attack.

"Never in my life," he murmured, looking at her with something near to fire in his eyes, "have I received a more beguiling proposal. My lady, would you care to adjourn to our bedchamber, and … join ourselves to the purpose, this very hour?"

Carin grinned, and tightened her grip on Verek's waist. "*Joining* with you in that endeavor, sir, will give me great pleasure."

The way he was looking at her, Carin wasn't sure they'd make it all the way up the stairs to their bedroom. But they did, and no member of their household saw them again for many magical hours.

Chapter 18

Future's Hope

"First we made a creature of water, then a crafter of fire," Carin said when her womb quickened for the third time. "What's next? Air, or stone?" She smiled. "I wonder what Welwyn will do if we give him an apprentice who conjures the four winds, or a child who can move mountains."

Verek laughed. "The old *wysard* will welcome the challenge. He'll not admit it, but he's had the best time of his life, these years in Ruain, attempting to stay half a step ahead of Nina and Galen. Outwitting those hellions—or striving to do so—has sharpened his wits and made him young."

Carin's question proved prophetic, for the third child she bore to Theil Verek demonstrated an affinity for wind and weather while still in the crib. They named the boy Dalton and gave him into Welwyn's teaching as soon as the child could toddle outdoors, first with a parental hand aiding the tot downstairs, but soon needing no support beyond his own sturdy legs.

Like his older sister and brother, Dalton preferred learning in the open air. The child could indeed summon the winds to do his bidding, and rainclouds as well. He doted on the gardener, an attachment which delighted the fellow. Whatever conditions of weather would best serve the garden, Dalton could conjure: spring rains, gentle summer warmth, crisp autumn nights, winter cold snaps of precisely the length that certain seeds required to break their dormancy and germinate in the new year.

The boy never interfered with natural cycles or imposed his will arbitrarily on the passing seasons. But deftly and subtly he enhanced the gifts bestowed by the natural elements so that the manor's orchard produced fruit beyond any harvest ever seen within those walls. By the age of eight, Dalton had his father's blessing to extend his weather-working beyond the manor's grounds and into the surrounding countryside. So fruitful were the fields and farms of their immediate neighbors, Lord Verek felt no hesitation—but rather, an obligation—to allow this second son to work weather-magic across the whole of Ruain.

What followed was a time of prosperity exceeding any era in the province's long history. The people grew more food than they could eat, and more flax, hemp, and jute than they could weave into clothing and tapestries, hook into rugs, braid as ropes, or stretch as tent canvas.

As Dalton grew to manhood, his merits established him as Verek's heir apparent, recognized as such by all who witnessed his deeds—parents, siblings, and liegemen. Verek named the young *wysard* chief steward of the realm, and in that role Dalton set the canvas-weavers of eastern Ruain to making sails. Under his direction, shipwrights built large oceangoing vessels that greatly expanded the province's fishing fleets.

Gradually these new ships sailed southward along the coast, venturing beyond the borders of Ruain itself—a passage unattempted since ancient days. Along the eastern seacoast as far as the grasslands, Ruainian captains and traders shipped the province's surplus grain and cloth. Sailing always with favorable winds, summoned at need by the weather-mage at their head, the captains returned to their own, still-secret shores laden with foodstuffs unknown in the north, and with their ships' holds carrying fabrics of southern making—light, silky materials that delighted the whole of the province, from dairy maid to Carin herself.

* * *

In extending Ruain's interests to the lands beyond its borders, Dalton followed the example of his elder brother. Galen had indeed been apprenticed at fourteen to the metalsmith of the southwestern hills. That desert region lay so distant from other settled places of Ladrehdin that its people had never succumbed to the fear of wizardry which had led to strife and bloodshed elsewhere—those "Wizards Wars" that had driven the adept into hiding, generations earlier. Galen's new master, Orton the Smith, was known throughout the hills for working magic, both in his metalcraft and in the assistance he gave those who needed aid, whether that be remedies for sickness or training in the arts of which he was a master.

Galen, therefore, had no need to hide his own gifts. The boy openly practiced the spellcraft that made fire hot enough to melt ores and extract metals. From Orton he learned to work those metals into narrow iron staves and flat-bottomed cooking pots, then delicate necklaces and golden rings, and eventually the finest cutting edges any bladesmith ever made.

The quality of Galen's knives, daggers, and even scythes earned him a reputation that extended far beyond the desert. As his work began to be bought and resold throughout the region, even those who might once have feared to touch a blade wrought by "witchery" were brought around by Galen's skill—and the boy's ready laugh. The giggling red-headed hellion had grown into an amiable man who passionately did the work he was born to do.

Never given to wasting breath on speech, Galen proved equally sparing with the written word. Carin received only one missive from her eldest son after he left for the desert. A small packet came by messenger one spring morning. She unwrapped it to find an exquisite bracelet fashioned of gold, silver, and copper, its delicate strands braided in a complex pattern unlike any seen before in that land.

With the bracelet was a cloak pin, a copy of the device Verek had worn for years, its design retaining the golden-rayed sun of the original badge. Galen, however, had transformed the crescent moon of the badge's other half, replacing the crescent's horns of silver with ocean waves that curled and locked around the sun, waves crafted in a metallic blue so highly polished that sunlight flashed from their rippling surfaces as from a mirror.

Accompanying the jewelry was a four-line letter written in Galen's most formal, scholar's hand:

I send this wristlet of my Making to my Beloved Mother as a mark of my high esteem for the Lady of Ruain, Blessed Reviver of Magic. I beg that She will present to my Honored Father this other device of my Making and say to Him that I bend my knee to his Lordship daily in deepest respect and gratitude for His gift of my Apprenticeship to Orton the Smith. Please give my greetings to my Sister and Brother. Master Orton also sends his respects.

As beautiful as the cloak pin was, Carin hesitated to give Verek Galen's gift, for clearly it was intended to replace the crescent-moon token of Verek's first wife with Carin's own oceanic emblem. She carefully rewrapped the pin with Galen's note affixed, and first showed Verek the bracelet their son had made for her. Only after sharing in his praise of that fine piece of workmanship did Carin present Galen's gift to him, handing the small packet to Verek almost shyly and stepping back a pace as he read his son's note, then unwrapped the pin.

Verek caught his breath audibly. He let the wrapping fall to the floor as he stood for a moment unmoving, holding the pin as if it were a fragile confection of spun sugar rather than a device worked in silver and steel. Abruptly then, he raised the badge to the morning sun and uttered an exclamation as its mirrored ripples reflected the light in multicolored streaks all around the room.

"The waves! They move, or seem to move as do the billows and swells of a mighty ocean. This is magical craftwork indeed." Verek reached with his other hand to draw Carin to him. He gave her a lingering kiss, then stroked his fingertips along her cheekbone and across her lips. "You have my thanks," he whispered, "for giving me a son who can draw the power of the depths into *such* an amulet as this. It will never leave me."

He held Carin a little longer, smiling at her in a way that expressed pride and perhaps a little awe at the talent of their metalworking son. Verek pocketed the badge then, and when the weather turned cold he affixed it to his cloak, the pin's rayed sun and shining waves becoming the only device with which he would fasten his cloaks through all the centuries of his life.

What he did with the older pin, with its crescent horns of silver, Carin never discovered. Perhaps, she thought, he was moved to visit the tomb of Alesia just that once, to place the token of their brief but devoted union upon the crypt which held her remains and those of their murdered son.

The note with the jewelry was all his parents had from Galen for years ... until the young *wysard* appeared one evening at the gates of Weyrrock, having ridden alone from the distant desert to make a formal and personal presentation to Verek of a breathtakingly beautiful — and razor-sharp — sword. Galen had crafted the weapon as the final trial-piece of the boy's long apprenticeship.

Lifting her gaze from the magnificent blade of watered steel to study her adult son's much-changed face, Carin feared that Galen had poured too much of himself into the making of that sword. He was thin to the point of bones protruding. Galen's frame appeared too reedy to anchor the muscles that bulged in his powerful smith's arms.

It transpired, however, that Galen had been so preoccupied on his ride from southwest to northeast, exploring ore-bearing deposits along the way, the boy had seldom remembered to eat. Myra soon restored the meat to his frame.

Besides bringing the sword to Verek, Galen carried another gift for Carin. This object, however, was nothing of Galen's making. As the young man was skirting the foothills of the desert mountains in the early weeks of his journey, Galen had encountered a delegation of mostly old *wysards* who had come down from the far-northern mountains, seeking the boy. Word had reached the Elders that the son of Carin of Ruain was plying his craft in the hills due south of them, and those old worthies had ventured from their hideouts — some of them for the first time in centuries — to ask the young adept to bear their greetings to the Lady of Ruain.

The Elders handed Galen a scroll of parchment, wrapped and tied by leather thongs from which dangled tiny bells, the knots in the thongs sealed with wax. The scroll, they directed, was to be presented to Lady Carin with all the solemnity and dignity Galen could bring to the occasion.

And so the rawboned young *wysard* drew the object from his saddlebags, knelt before his mother in the courtyard of Weyrrock, and offered it up to Carin as a Drishannic priest would present a parchment of Holy Writ.

With Verek and Welwyn looking on, all of them a bit bemused, Carin took the scroll and started to thank her son. But then she flung the object to the ground and snapped a spell of confinement upon it.

"Sweet mercy!" Carin exclaimed. "What *is* that thing? It's shot through with power, but not the Power of Ruain. I've never felt anything like it … except maybe the emanation that comes off my least-favorite book of ancient languages. You know the one, Theil? That book I was showing you in the library, where it's shelved with the language studies but has a secretive feel to it, like a warning, like it doesn't want to be studied too closely."

Verek frowned. "The language of that book went extinct — deservedly so — far back in the night of time. Or so I thought. If this scroll is written in that script, then the tongue remains known to at least one *wysard* who still lives in the far west of Ladrehdin." He looked at Welwyn. "What say you — the only one among us who hails from the West? Shall we destroy this thing unread? Or satisfy our curiosity while keeping its power closely fettered?"

"The latter, I suggest," Welwyn replied. "Much effort has been expended to bring this object into Lady Carin's hands. I would see what it is. However," the monk added, "let us remove it beyond the manor's walls before we unroll it. If the thing holds danger, we'd best examine it in the clear, where we three — we four, that is," Welwyn amended with a nod to Galen, "may bespell it into oblivion if need be, without imperiling hearth and home, don't you know."

So saying, Welwyn levitated the scroll off the ground, and keeping the object within Carin's spell of confinement, the monk floated it through the gates and out away from the manor's walls. The other three followed him into the surrounding oakwoods, where Welwyn dropped the scroll, its bells jingling, on a bed of dry leaves.

"Now," the monk said. "Lady Carin, will you do the honors?"

By this point in her studies, Carin had absorbed enough from reading and practice, mastering the difficult finger positions required for advanced wizardry, to be confident of her ability to open the scroll. With delicate spellwork, never touching the thing physically, she broke the wax seals and twitched away the embellished leather ties and wrappings. Still keeping her hand well clear of the object, she directed the subtle flow of Power through herself and into the parchment, to unroll and stretch it flat on the ground.

All but Galen bent then, to study the scroll, puzzling over its script. Their combined language skills were required to extract meaning from the writing. No literal translation proved possible, so tangled was the phrasing, but in essence the document's antique language commended Lady Carin for restoring the fullness of magical power to Ladrehdin. The parchment bore numerous scribbles that Welwyn said were signatures. To Carin's eye, all were illegible, but the monk recognized the marks made by certain *wysards* of his acquaintance.

"I believe this tribute to our Lady of Ruain was prepared and delivered with honest sincerity," Welwyn said. "The elders of the craft are keenly aware of Carin's service to us all in halting the decline of this world's potency. I, however, would not have this thing in the house, if I were you."

"We will not take it indoors," Verek said, and reached for Carin's hand. Lifting his gaze from the parchment, he regarded her thoughtfully. "Well deserving you are of this honor, my lady. But I could wish that it had been offered in words less … contorted. However well-meant the sentiment that lies upon the surface of this thing, within its coiled script other intentions, less generous, may be hidden."

Carin frowned. "Something is definitely 'off' about it. I don't like the way it feels." She turned to Welwyn. "Among the elders who put their marks on this scroll, are there any you know of, who might be ill-disposed toward Ruain? Or toward me?"

"Possibly," the monk replied. "Morann had admirers amidst the *wysards* who hid farthest west, in mountains beyond her lair. Some of those ancient and mostly forgotten magicians even applauded the witch's efforts to rejuvenate the magic of this world. They chose to shut their eyes to her methods, desperate to regain power, though it be unsustainable … built on death as it was, while the true Power of wizardry arises from resurgent life and endless renewal."

"As Archamon teaches us," Carin commented.

Welwyn grinned. "As you demonstrated, my lady, in a manner so far-reaching that every true-hearted *wysard* of this world now worships you. Evidenced, don't you know, by the proclamation at your feet."

"I don't need worship," Carin retorted. "I'd settle for a simple 'thank you' and no nefarious schemes. You think one of Morann's 'admirers' hid something evil in this scroll?"

"I believe it's likely. I suggest you bask for only a moment in the warmly meant sentiments expressed by the great majority of those who signed this document. Their goodwill, you have in abundance. But at least one of the signers wishes you harm. It's time — now — that you destroyed this thing."

"Allow me, I beg you," interjected Galen, breaking his silence as he stepped forward and touched Carin's wrist, where she wore the bracelet he'd made for her. The young man had listened quietly to all that was said. Now his face wore a stricken expression as he kneeled at Carin's side.

"Honored Mother," the boy mumbled, "I beg your forgiveness. Never would I have laid a thing of evil into your hands, had I known its nature. Those who entrusted it to me, deceived me."

"I believe most of those old *wysards* were themselves deceived," Carin said, reaching to draw Galen to his feet. "You're not to blame, son. And no harm's been done. I've read and humbly received the words of the Elders. Now you, Galen, may cast your fire-spell upon the parchment. Please burn every particle of it — but have a care for the oaks. Don't set fire to our forest."

Galen did as he was bid. Summoning a pure white flame, so hot it could have melted a mountain, the *wysard* blasted the scroll into nothingness, leaving no ash, no trace, not even a drop of molten bronze from the tiny bells of the wrap-ties. The dead leaves upon which the parchment had rested were untouched.

Verek took the youth aside for a low-voiced discussion about trust: "It's a fine thing to give and to have, my son. But take care in future where you bestow your trust."

"I'll not be a tool in any man's hands," Galen growled, his green eyes flashing and his shame building to fury at having been used as a messenger for evil intent. "If ever I see those old magicians again, they'll regret the day they came looking for me."

Later, over evening *dhera* in the library, Welwyn reported that Galen had carried yet another missive from the wizardly delegation, but this was a personal message that could be trusted: The monk was friends with the *wysard* who'd scrawled the note for Galen to deliver.

"My correspondent sends us news," Welwyn said as he sat before the fire with Carin and Verek. "If such a message can, indeed, be called 'new' this many years on, don't you know. Nevertheless, my friend relates that the coats and cloaks the pair of you discarded in Morann's bewitched burial ground were long ago retrieved. Those garments being of excellent make, they were given to the more impoverished among our brethren in the society of *wysards*. Such a gift has my blessing. You may recall that I myself supplied the two of you with much of that winter gear as you departed my cabin on your westward journey." Welwyn chuckled. "You fortunate ones who are possessed of wealth may leave your apparel scattered in your wake and never miss it. But humbler folk are glad to get a good cloak ... even one third-hand that has warmed a grave for a time."

"I'd almost forgot!" Carin exclaimed. "We went from freezing in the mountain snow to sweating in that witch's graveyard." She shuddered. "I saw only flowers in a grassy meadow. I even took off my boots and walked barefoot through the 'grass,' and bruised my feet on what I thought were tree nuts." A groan escaped Carin as memories flooded in. "Those weren't nuts. They were bones. Knobs of old bone. Drisha have mercy."

Welwyn pulled at his lower lip, studying Carin. "How it must have delighted the old ghoul, to deceive you into trampling unshod upon the bones of untold numbers of her victims. That's why Morann made the illusion, I'm sure. Raising flowers fed by the rotting remains of her sacrificial vassals ... summoning warmth from the coldness of death. She took a macabre pleasure in tricking you both."

"Who in their right mind would enter those grounds," Verek grumbled, "even if tempted by the good clothes we shed there?"

"My correspondent does not name names," Welwyn replied. "But his note suggests that the deed was done in the spring of the year after you expelled the necromancer from her eyrie. Morann's absence may have allowed Nature to work its will upon those grounds. Whoever ventured into that graveyard might have found a more softly weathered, somewhat less ghastly collection of old bones."

"Ugh," Carin muttered as she stood and headed for the desk. "I'm making myself a note right now, to remind us to send a bundle of clean wool cloaks westward with the next *wysard* who goes that way. Our brethren in the mountains oughtn't to wear clothes that should have been burned years ago."

The next *wysard* to head west from Ruain was, in fact, Galen himself. But the young smith would not soon return to his desert hills after delivering a magnificent sword to Verek and a cursed parchment to Carin. As soon as Dalton learned that his big brother was home, the weather-mage came from the farthest reaches of Ruain to call both Galen and Verek on an expedition into the province's own mountain peaks. On Ruain's steep and thickly forested north slopes, gold had been found.

There followed a time of new labor and even greater prosperity, as the province added finely worked treasures of gold to the other sought-after goods that Ruain shipped southward. Galen stayed on the north slopes for years, overseeing the mine, smelting the ore, and training his own young apprentices in the goldsmith's craft.

Eventually, however, the artisan-*wysard* returned to his beloved desert. Galen married the daughter of a local wise-woman, and their children were gifted in both the *wysard's* art and the metalsmith's.

* * *

The fourth child born to Carin and Verek was also a son, and also destined to leave home. They named the lad Legary for the great-grandsire he so closely resembled. Indeed, Myra caught her breath every time she laid eyes on the boy, he looked so much like the Lord Legary who had taken her on as housekeeper many years before. Some who were old enough to remember the elder Legary said this new son of House Verek must be the old lord re-embodied.

Carin didn't know whether she believed that. But watching her youngest son at his play and pastimes, she was frequently reminded of what Myra had said about the old lord, when the housekeeper first told Carin of the powerful *wysard* who was Verek's grandfather and teacher.

The elder Legary "was a wizard beyond compare," Myra had said. The old lord "could enchant the stones so they became a host and routed his enemies." His namesake, too, showed an immediate inclination for bespelling rocks in perilous ways. The boy could send boulders flying without the aid of a catapult: he needed only a flick of his wrist. Merely by lifting a finger or two, he could raise enormous slabs of rock and upend them as walls, or crash them to the ground as flat as any mason-built foundation.

Welwyn had had easy work tutoring the naturally re-strained and high-minded weather-mage, Dalton. But this new pupil—the child who loved stone—challenged the monk as rigorously as the first two hellions Carin and Verek had produced. Young Legary was not given to willful destruction: the boy did not hurl rocks to shatter windows or splinter doors. He was, by nature, a builder. But his instinct was to build on a grand scale. He would raise house-sized blocks of stone from deep underground, leaving pits behind like quarries.

When the boy had uplifted all the walls, flattened all the foundations, and gouged all the craters the surrounding countryside could comfortably hold, Verek sent him to Dalton on the coast. There, young Legary was usefully employed in building breakwaters and wharfs to accommodate Ruain's expanding sea-trade.

When he came of age, Legary sailed with the traders and found employment in the southland. He stayed there, building walls, piers, arenas and amphitheaters, first in coastal towns, then farther inland. The young man even reached Granger, the farming village where Carin's life in Ladrehdin had begun. There he met and married the daughter of Brin, the quick-witted young herbalist who had taken Megella's place as the village wisewoman.

From time to time, rumors would reach Carin of her youngest son's exploits. Legary's friends among Ruain's sailors brought the stories home from their southern voyages, and Dalton passed along the tales that he deemed fit for their mother to hear. One of the rumors, which some thought farfetched, struck Carin as entirely credible. Young Legary was said to have raised a multitude of boulders and sent them like soldiers against an upstart would-be tyrant who oppressed a territory between Granger and the southern seas. Legary's boulders routed the tyrant's forces, and the oppressor ended his days crushed to a bloody pulp beneath a wall of Legary's attacking stones.

Carin was sitting at the kitchen table talking with Myra when this story reached their ears. The women locked gazes, and Carin could only tilt her head in a half nod when Myra exclaimed, "That young man *is* the old lord reborn, as sure as I'm sitting here!"

* * *

After producing four children who were dedicated to the Elementals—water and fire, air and stone—Carin hoped for a child with a less obsessive, more well-rounded nature. In daughter Vivienne, Carin got her wish. This fifth offspring had her father's manifold gifts. Like Verek, she could summon fire with a snap of her fingers, send objects flying with little more than a thought, and mend broken bones with a grain of white lightning.

As Welwyn's student, Vivienne proved endlessly curious, eager to learn all that she could do and know. She read the *Book of Archamon* with such close attention, she well-nigh memorized the volume, thick as it was. Verek joined the monk in suggesting further books for the girl's study. Theil also involved himself more directly in her wizardly training than he had tended to do with his older children. Welwyn did not object, for the monk recognized that Vivienne was to Verek as Theil had been to old Lord Legary: not only progeny, but the richly gifted apprentice every *wysard* dreamed of teaching.

Though the girl had her father's multifaceted talents, in appearance brown-haired Vivienne most closely resembled her great-grandmother Merriam—not such a twin as to have people believing in rebirth, but similar enough to intrigue Megella. The wisewoman brought Vivienne to spend a year with her in her cottage outside Fintan, and took the girl on herb-gathering and curative visitations around the neighborhood. Vivienne learned herb-lore and the arts of healing as quickly and naturally as the girl absorbed all other crafts, whether mundane or magian. In her tenth year, her teachers declared the girl wholly qualified to treat maladies ranging from simple burns to shattered bones.

This youngest daughter also had her father's natural grace and physical vitality. On horseback, the child was one with the animal, like a centaur of legend. Under Verek's tutelage, Vivienne became expert with weapons, mastering the bow and rapier. Carin also taught the girl knife-throwing and stone-slinging.

Perhaps none of her gifts pleased Carin more, however, than Vivienne's talent for drawing. Alone among Verek's children, this girl proved to be his equal as a painter. Over time, as her older siblings either returned home for occasional visits, as was the case with Galen and Dalton, or Vivienne came to know their faces through Verek's own sketches of the absent Nina and south-dwelling Legary, the girl painted a series of strikingly realistic portraits.

These, Carin hung in the sitting room of the apartments she shared with Verek. The first time Carin had entered that private suite, the paintings on either side of the fireplace had been Verek's own skillfully rendered portraits of his first wife, Alesia, and their son, Aidan. With those portraits, Verek had hung a landscape of the lake where the pair died … and inexplicably, in Carin's view, he'd also depicted snow-capped "craggy heights," recalling those mountains which hid Morann's altar of evil. Those paintings had come down, of course, before Carin returned to Verek's house and moved into his bedroom with him. Over time, other paintings the *wysard* produced in his downstairs workroom had hung in their places, flanking the mantel.

Vivienne's portraits, however, of her brothers and sister took pride of place as each was finished. So lifelike were they, Carin almost started each time she walked into the room, thinking her four eldest had all come home.

This youngest daughter was sixteen when Welwyn released her from apprenticeship, declaring her a fully trained and qualified *wysard* of Ladrehdin. The monk then made a startling proposal: that Vivienne accompany him westward, to seek out and train the promising young adepts who had come to his notice over the intervening distance, Welwyn learning of these prospects by his mysterious methods of communication that Carin had never quite worked out.

Verek exploded. *"You?"* he bellowed. "You old reprobate. You think to take my unmarried daughter vagabonding with you? Breath and blood! I'll have your head, sir."

With difficulty, Carin and Vivienne calmed him enough to sit him down in the library for a long, private—and weapon-less—talk with the monk. Mother and daughter adjourned to the garden, to the table under the trees, and there Carin sought many of the same answers that Verek was undoubtedly demanding of Welwyn.

"Have you thought this through, Vivie?" she asked the young woman. "If you're simply tired of studying—or you're bored with life in this out-of-the-way corner—then why not go east to the coast? Ruain's port cities are bustling. They even have theaters and arenas for games, since your brother Legary passed through and couldn't help but build the biggest and grandest edifices ever seen in the land."

Carin reached to take Vivienne's hand. "I'm sure your father will gladly give you a house of your own, anywhere you'd prefer to live within his borders. You'd have all the kitchen help and gardeners and grooms you could want or need. In a city, you'd make new friends and have much more of a social life than you've ever known out this way."

"That's not what I want, Mother," Vivienne replied, smiling. "I wish to see the world beyond Ruain's boundaries. I want to meet other *wysards*—those old ones who are known to Welwyn, but more so their students who are newly trained as I am … and who are not my blood relations. I might find a husband among those adepts," Vivienne added, her brown eyes sparkling.

"But more than anything, I want to teach, as you and my father and Master Welwyn have taught me." Vivienne gripped Carin's hand. "This world is pulsing with magic—because of your courage, Honored Mother—and I want to be a part of it, too."

"But," Carin began, then hesitated as she sought the words that would convey her doubts without insulting her daughter or maligning the monk.

"Welwyn is truly a gifted teacher," Carin started again, carefully. "But when I first met him, the man had a bit of a reputation for—" *Lechery,* she started to say, but that was too harsh, and not accurate. Had it been true, the old monk would never have been allowed to tutor Nina or Vivienne past the age of nine.

Amending her words yet again, Carin continued: "Let's just say that Welwyn was known for enjoying a smutty song and a well-turned ankle. If you go off alone with him, and you're seen at his side, riding back to his old haunts near Cardan, you'll likely be the subject of petty gossip—and freshly minted rude songs—from the borders of Ruain clear to the mountains."

Vivienne laughed, a light, utterly unembarrassed sound. "Let them gossip, Mother, and let them sing. The man's old enough to be my twenty-times great-grandfather. He's my teacher, my friend, my favorite old uncle. I'd no more regard him romantically than I would my brothers.

"And besides," the girl added, still laughing, "if Welwyn ever propositioned me, I'd turn him into a toad. You know I can do it—and so does he."

Carin chewed her bottom lip, considering. Then she smiled. "That does ease my worries, child. You're as capable of taking care of yourself as your brothers or your father. Or your mother either, I'll add," Carin muttered, thinking of the unfortunate Flynn. "After I came of age and realized my own strength, only one man ever dared offer me an insult. He paid for it with his life."

Vivienne looked at her with interest but no surprise. "You've never told me that story, Mother."

Carin shook her head. "It's not a story I like to remember, and you need not know the particulars. Only take from it the lesson I would teach you. It's a lesson I know your father has also instilled: never kill casually. But neither stay your hand if your life or your body is threatened. Strike fear in the gut of any man who would forget for even an instant that you are a daughter of House Verek—and a formidable *wysard* in your own right."

Vivienne leaned to give Carin a kiss.

"I won't forget it, Honored Mother," the young woman said, straightening. "Permit me to tell you a little secret, also. Welwyn wants my protection when we approach the vicinity of his old monastery. When last he was in the area, he … engaged in a small indiscretion. The woman's husband has vowed revenge. Master Welwyn believes I will lend him an air of harmlessness, and thus turn aside the man's anger. What my old guv'ner does not know is that I will turn both himself and the angry husband into brown rabbits and let them pull out each other's fur while I speak with the woman involved. I'll decide what to do, then, when I learn which of the two *she* prefers."

Carin blinked at Vivienne. Slowly, a laugh formed deep in her belly, making her entire body shake as it traveled up her windpipe and burst from her lips with a choking, spluttering sound.

Both women were bent double, laughing so hard their tears flowed, when Verek came to the garden with Welwyn to reluctantly give his youngest daughter leave to depart. Neither man ever knew what had sent Vivienne and Carin into those gales of laughter.

Before Vivienne left, her parents took the young woman to the cavern of the *wysards'* waters and presented her to the Power of that place. Only Dalton had been similarly introduced to the deep mystery of that wellspring. After Vivienne made her obeisance to the pool, and Verek gave her a brief and hushed history that touched on its great antiquity, he and Carin retreated and left the young *wysard* to make of the place what she could.

Or more likely, Carin thought, *the Power will judge the girl's fitness to be in its presence.* On that score, neither parent had concerns. A more worthy young adept had not stood gazing into those waters since Theil Verek himself first entered the cave in the company of his grandfather. No *wysard* of Ruain had ever brought to that cavern a deeper understanding of Archamon's folly in attempting to obtain and use more of Nature's power than was his right. Vivienne embraced with her whole self the ancient philosopher-*wysard*'s Creed, which had sprung from his own realization of his error, and which recognized that the Power belonged to the Elementals, and must never be abused, squandered, or taken for granted.

After an hour or so, Vivienne climbed the winding stairs and joined her parents in the library. For a time she stood silent beside the fireplace, looking into the flames. Then she turned, and with a slightly dazed smile Vivienne murmured, "Was there ever a voice more beautiful?"

What the voice of Power might have said to its new acolyte, none but Vivienne ever knew. In two days' time, she strapped her bags on her horse and rode west with Welwyn—leading a packhorse loaded with winter cloaks for impoverished mountain magicians and new apprentices.

Diligent about sending regular assurances of her safety and happiness, Vivie wrote her parents long, joyful letters in which she described the accomplishments of her wizardly pupils. She and Welwyn established a school of sorts, and within a few years they had drawn to their open-air classrooms a great many aspiring young magicians, some immensely gifted, others at least respectably capable. The wizardly arts had never died out completely in the northwest of Ladrehdin, as had been their fate in most southern climes. Welwyn and Vivienne played central roles in revitalizing the magic arts throughout the western mountains, even past the borders of that haunted, now-abandoned realm which had been Morann's stronghold.

In a desolate valley a little beyond that crumbling necropolis, searchers discovered the despoiler of what had been a sincerely meant tribute to Carin. When the Elders of the craft learned from Welwyn how their parchment had been corrupted—how its elaborate ancient tongue had been twisted in a failed attempt to lay a curse upon the Lady of Ruain—the old *wysards* sent their apprentices looking for the maker of that curse. The evil magician was easily found out: He'd been the one who'd suggested penning the accolade in a nearly extinct language that few living *wysards* could read.

The searchers came upon the sorcerer living amid sulphur and decay on the fringes of Morann's old haunts. The magician had held off the ravages of time and prolonged his life well beyond his appointed span of years by practicing his own brand of 'necromancy': He slaughtered animals by brutal methods that inflicted all the agony possible until death released the creatures. Before the apprentices dispatched the blackheart to go wherever dishonored dead wizards go, the villain confessed to taking his inspiration from Morann, his former mentor.

And so ends the untrustworthy fellow who didn't want me to notice him, that time I dropped in on a convocation of wysards, Carin thought, reading Vivienne's account of the matter. Welwyn had sought out the magisterial leader of that gathering, and from her he'd learned that the group's purpose that night had been to ritually purify the waters of Morann's pool of power, consecrating them to the service of true wizardry. When the magisterial Diviner learned that a blood sorcerer had been present that hallowed night, she spat a curse of destruction upon him. Her apprentices—who still thrilled at the memory of the Lady of Ruain deigning to notice them—had led the effort to end the blackheart's existence.

To the best of anyone's knowledge after that, no magician remained in the mountains—or anywhere in the world of Ladrehdin—who had fallen into the wicked ways practiced by

Morann or her late admirers. Only the Creed of Archamon was taught now. Apprentices walked "the bright path" and shunned the perversion of power that Morann had learned from her fore-bears — and which the demoness had meant to pass down to her son. Theil Verek, however, had proved impervious to the necro-mancer's blood-soaked bewitchments.

* * *

From the mountainous northwest, *wysards* newly trained by Verek's gifted daughter Vivienne and his old friend Welwyn began making their slow ways southward. One or two drifted into the desert where Galen had made his home, and brought him welcome news: not only of the justice that was dealt to his mother's would-be accurser, but also favorable word of the baby sister Galen had not seen since Vivienne was a girl.

Others from the northern school of spellcraft eventually reached the southern seas. From there, they wandered east to Granger and beyond, even to the coast.

Throughout that region the gifted ones found a populace which had grown more accepting of them and more open to the arts of wizardry. The younger Legary had won admiration and gained a wide following after his army of enchanted stones crushed the southland's would-be tyrant. The people acclaimed Legary as their headman, and for the rest of his astonishingly long life he served as their leader, never with any formal title or badge of office, but as an arbiter, captain, chief builder, or what-ever they required of him. With his wife, who was a skilled healer and wisewoman, Legary trained uncounted apprentices, some in the arts of healing and spellcraft, others as master stone-masons.

His sister Vivienne stayed in the West for years. When at last Vivie returned home to Ruain, she brought a husband, Xavier, a pupil who had grown to become a master *wysard* like herself.

Though not Vivienne's equal in the range of his talents, Xavier nonetheless had a multilayered complexity to his nature that charmed Carin and won Verek's respect. Both welcomed him as they would a son of their flesh, and delighted in the grand-children the young couple gave them.

As all who knew him had anticipated he would, Welwyn closed his school at the foot of the mountains and followed his former pupils back to Ruain. Seemingly unchanged by the pas-sage of years, his salt-and-pepper ponytail still showing as much dark hair as gray strands, the monk moved himself back into his former apartments and took up his post as tutor and governor to a new generation of House Verek hellions.

Verek's chief steward and heir-apparent, Dalton the weather-mage, was almost never seen at the manor house, but spent his days riding the length and breadth of Ruain, summon-ing to each field and farm the weather each needed to produce bumper crops. Dalton oversaw the harvests, and ensured the dis-tribution of food and goods throughout the province so that all his people prospered in an endless season of plenty. The surplus, of which Dalton's weather-working created vast quantities, he saw shipped to the eastern ports and thence to southern markets, continuing his work of expanding Ruainian trade beyond the borders of a land that was becoming slightly less of a secret with each passing year.

Amid the responsibilities of stewardship and commerce, Dalton never found time to marry. When it became clear that he would not father an heir, he declared himself Vivienne's liege-man for life and recognized his baby sister as his successor.

It would be in the time of Lady Vivienne that the "spell of omission" finally dissipated altogether, and Ruain rejoined its world. By that time, the people of Ladrehdin would fully accept the gifted ones, for all the *wysards* who walked the land followed faithfully in the footsteps of Archamon, vowing fealty to his ways, the now-forgotten blood sorcery renounced forever.

Copyists would be employed to create replicas of the *Book of Archamon* that had resided for millennia in the library at Weyrrock. In the copies they made for the world's growing society of *wysards* and scholars, the scribes were instructed to omit nothing except the two final entries that had been penned by old Lord Legary. Those were the concern and the business of House Verek alone.

Lady Vivienne sliced those pages out of the original *Book,* and with a spell of permanent suppression she ensured that the leaves would not grow back, as the one page had restored itself when Carin tore it out long ago. Vivienne locked away the removed pages, revealing their hiding place to Verek and Carin only.

Both were content to leave Legary's narratives to whatever the passage of time might ordain. Thus, after Vivienne, Lord Legary's final writings were never read again. Over the course of ages, the words faded to invisibility, and the magical paper on which the lays were penned crumbled to dust. With the pages went the name, *Morann,* which by that time was written nowhere in the cosmos except in the two lays penned by the witch's repentant father-in-law. When Morann's name became dust, all knowledge of the necromancer passed from existence.

As for the six antique volumes of forbidden sorcery that had horrified Carin, the Lady of Ruain would get her wish. None of Carin's children ever laid eyes on those books except for the well-prepared Vivienne. As was her right, and perhaps her obligation, Vivienne would lug the moldy volumes down to the cavern of wizardry, and with permission from the voice of Power, she would dump the lot into the wellspring of magic. In a blink, the books dissolved into nothingness, and all knowledge of sinister arts and the cults of degradation passed from the world forever.

* * *

In all these ways and more, the children of Carin and Verek reshaped the world of Ladrehdin and reintroduced the land's magical vitality and potency, so that the people prospered in ages of peace and plenty. But Ladrehdin was not the only world so favored. Their eldest child — the daughter who was even more of a sea creature than was Carin, in whose veins flowed the salt-water of Earth — that child would remake the ocean world that Nina adopted as her own.

On Earth, Nina would grow from a water-nymph into a being of legend.

Chapter 19

A World Apart

As Carin had predicted, Nina was not quite thirteen when the girl conjured a wave from the springwater pool and rode it to the distant shore where her earthly grandparents lived. With her, Nina took Carin's handwritten copy of the *Looking-Glass* story from which Carin had taught the girl its language. The young *wysard* also carried her own neatly lettered duplicate of the book of herbal remedies created by Verek's grandmother Merriam. Verek had wanted Nina to take the original, but the girl shared Carin's opinion that the heirloom belonged in Ruain and must stay in the library of the manor house.

So valuable was the extensive herb-lore contained within it, however, Nina had meticulously copied the book, letter for letter in its native tongue, duplicating the original with but one change: Nina moved Merriam's recipe for strangleweed sauce to the front of the book. There had been no indication of alien strangleweed crossing the void to infest Earth, but such an invader would find prime habitat in that ocean world if ever it made the leap. Carin wanted Nina watching for the stuff and ready to boil it down to make a medicinal sauce for combating any recurrence of the bleeding disease, if the girl found herself confronting either of those pestilences.

After preparing her Ladrehdinian copy of the herbalist's handbook, Nina wrote it out again, this time translating its contents as far as possible into the common language of the islands where the girl was bound. In that translated copy, Nina wrote the names she knew for each listed herb, but she also inserted blank spaces, intending to fill those blanks with the names and descriptions of possibly equivalent plants as she came to understand and use the healing aromatics of the ocean world.

In this endeavor, Verek could lend a surprising amount of assistance, for the lord of Ruain—while awaiting his rescue—had tarried long enough on the island of Carin's birth to learn something of its plants and their properties. From memory, Verek sketched the island herbs that he had ventured to sample, either ingested as brewed teas or applied as skin treatments. A significant number of them were almost identical to plants depicted in Merriam's recipes.

In her preparations for life on Earth, Nina received help from yet another unexpected quarter: New messages arrived from that world, flung through the void in another bottle of colored glass—dark green this time, but wrapped, as before, in a veneer of wood.

Verek had sent instructions to every town and fishing village on Ruain's coast, ordering that any bottle found anywhere along the shore be brought to him. When Nina, at twelve, had ridden seaward with Verek's blessing, after convincing him of her fitness to journey by knocking him from his saddle, the girl had scoured Ruain's coastline and swum with every *dolphyn* she saw. On her beach expedition, however, Nina's hopes of receiving another dolphin-delivered message were dashed. There was no repetition of the episode that had brought a ruby-red bottle into Carin's hands when Nina, then a child not yet six years old, had first swum in an ocean.

All were surprised, therefore, when a messenger, bearing a wood-wrapped bottle, appeared at the manor's gates not long after Nina returned from her solitary ride. The green bottle thus delivered from the coastlands of Ruain proved to hold a recent letter from Kate and Eddie, as well as a missive from the wood-sprite, the creature having dictated its message for Kate to transcribe.

The notes relayed nothing of major significance, only assurances that Nina's grandparents still lived in the cottage above the overlook, and they were healthy, content, even reasonably happy, given the brokenness of the world they inhabited. Eddie regularly took their boat out fishing, and "Bill" the pony just as often stopped by the cottage for his treat of sugar. The community continued to grow, slowly, as ragged bands of survivors drifted in and found shelter in previously abandoned houses. Not all of those who had lived through Morann's depredations had chosen to remain in the vicinity. In some of the demon's victims, psychological scarring went deeper than the physical mutilation they'd endured. Their nightmares forced them to move on. Carin shuddered at this reminder that Nina was set on returning to the scene of that bloodbath.

But the girl would not go unprepared. The chief value of the newly received messages lay in the additional practice they gave Nina in reading, speaking, and writing the language that she needed to master before traveling to the world of her grandparents. Repeatedly, Nina read the letter aloud while Carin helped with pronunciation. For writing practice, Nina copied the message until she could clearly form the letters of her grandparents' script. Then she rendered the message into the common tongue of Ladrehdin, and back again, learning the pitfalls of attempting literal translations of idiomatic speech. *"It's raining cats and dogs,"* or, *"Snagging the fishhook really threw a spanner in the works,"* made little sense in the Ladrehdinian tongue when transcribed word-for-word.

All of these efforts, Nina repeated with the woodsprite's message. The sprite's missive held the most interest for Carin. It opened with extravagant praise of the trees in which the creature dwelt—"So noble! So majestic!"—and continued with a sort of travelogue. The sprite told of exploring every corner of the island where Kate and Eddie now lived, and hinted that the creature wasn't above stowing away in the wooden hulls or planks of passing boats, relying on unsuspecting mariners to take it across from one island to the next. In the years since Carin had borne the sprite beyond the void to her native world, the creature had grown intimately familiar with the land, its trees, and its inhabitants, two-legged and otherwise.

Pointing this out to Nina, Carin suggested that the girl would want to make the creature's acquaintance first thing.

"Remember, the sprite speaks your native tongue, and it's learned the language of your grandparents, too. It can translate, if you get stuck." Carin paused, then added, "For all I know, the sprite can teach you to talk to trees. It claims the trees have languages of their own. I don't doubt it. You and I both know a *wysard* who's rather secretive about his own talent for convincing oak trees to carry messages for him. You can learn from the woodsprite, Nina. I trust the creature to be as great a friend to you as it has been to me."

As the day neared for Nina's departure—when the water-nymph's raising of her magical wave would bear her to a world apart—Carin insisted that the girl submit to one last act of preparation: Nina's hair must be cut.

"But why, Mama?" the girl wailed. "I like my hair."

"So do I, Nina," Carin replied, grimly. "But I want you looking much different from the witch of Ladrehdin who killed those people that horrible day. Enough time has passed—here, at least, though Drisha knows how long it's been in that other place. But I am hopeful that the passage of time has dulled the memory of any person who witnessed the demon's atrocities. Even so, we must do everything in our power to reassure the survivors that you have come to their world to help them, not hurt them."

Nina so passionately resisted the hair-cutting, however, that Verek was obliged to take charcoal in hand and sketch the demoness Morann. That it cost him a savage effort was clear in the set of his jaw and his tightly clenched teeth. Verek penciled a strong likeness of Morann in the guise of the enchantress he and Carin had seen in her mountain lair. On the same sheet of paper, he dashed off another sketch depicting the witch as the gaunt hag that Morann had been when she burst from the springwater pool. In both sketches, Verek emphasized Morann's darkly brilliant eyes, penetrating gaze, and long, raven-black hair.

Carin gasped when she beheld the finished sketches. Verek and Nina had those same eyes, same gaze, same hair. Yet never had Carin seen the witch in either her husband or her daughter when she looked upon their beloved faces. Blazing forth from both of them were inner qualities — decency, compassion, an innate uprightness — which transformed their faces so fundamentally that any superficial physical resemblance to the necromancer disappeared entirely.

The sketches, however, had their intended effect on Nina. The girl also caught her breath when Verek sat her down, put the drawings in front of her, and tersely explained that *this* was the woman of Ladrehdin who had mutilated and tormented those people to whom Nina had ministered that day.

Carin watched, silent, aching for them both as Nina looked up from the sketches, studied her father's anguished gaze and grim expression, and then raised a slightly unsteady hand to touch her own face and hair. The girl was too sharp-witted to miss the obvious implication: that her father and, thus, herself were blood relations of the witch he had sketched. Nina never asked, but Carin harbored the conviction that the child had worked it out for herself. Indeed, presented with such clear pictorial evidence, Nina could hardly fail to do so.

In any event, after viewing the sketches — which Verek burned the moment she'd turned away from them — Nina submitted to the hair-cutting. Carin chopped off the girl's locks just below her ears, and cut her bangs straight across slightly above her eyebrows. Then she wrapped a satiny blue ribbon around the girl's brow and tied it in a bow to one side. The effect precisely mirrored a bobbed hairstyle that had once been wildly popular in parts of the ocean world. In the islands to which Nina was bound, many women had readopted that cropped style as a practical means of managing their hair in a world where basic survival took precedence over vanity.

Thus, Carin unwittingly but providentially sent her daughter back to Lady Kate and Master Eddie looking very much like the girl belonged in that place.

* * *

Much sooner than anticipated, a mere three days after Nina's departure, Carin and Verek received a message from the wayfarer. It arrived in the evening, by way of the springwater pool, a long letter written on sheets of lined notepaper that were sealed in a tightly stoppered, cobalt-blue bottle.

Verek snapped the bottle's neck in his haste to get at the message inside. He cut his hand on the broken glass, and was forced to leave the retrieving of the letter to Carin while he threw a spell of mending upon his profusely bleeding hand. So much colorful swearing did he mix with the words of magical healing, Carin wasn't sure the spellcraft would succeed.

But by the time she had pincered the message out through the bottle's shattered neck, Verek had stopped the bleeding and knit together the edges of the gash. That the laceration was painful, however, was clear from the steady stream of profanity which continued to pass his lips. Only when Carin had flattened the rolled paper and thrust the letter into Verek's uninjured hand did the *wysard* fall silent, giving his full attention to the report his eldest daughter offered of her journey and arrival. Carin, reading the missive over Verek's shoulder, experienced a dizzying range of emotions, from pride to longing to loss, as she scanned the lines Nina had penned in the girl's neat, familiar hand.

Nina's passage through the void had been quick and uneventful. She'd landed where she'd intended: on the beach at the foot of the path which led up to her grandparents' cottage. Given

255

that the most recent letter from Kate and Eddie was several months old—as reckoned by Ladrehdinian time—neither Nina nor Carin had been certain that the couple would still be there. Eddie's inclination to feel safer aboard their boat might have uprooted them again.

It seemed, however, that life ashore had grown secure enough, and the surrounding community stable enough, to anchor the couple in their small and pleasant home. They welcomed Nina with astonished delight when the girl presented herself on their front porch.

She came to them outfitted with only the clothes she wore, and carrying on her shoulder a sack holding the few personal treasures the traveler had chosen to bring: Carin's longhand, intentionally incomplete version of the *Looking-Glass* book, along with Nina's faithful copies of Merriam's herbal in both the tongue of Ladrehdin and the language most used in these islands. Perhaps the most striking aspect of Nina's appearance—the element most likely to raise an eyebrow, apart from the girl's remarkably dark, arresting gaze—was that Nina arrived on their doorstep armed in the same ways Carin had been: with bow and quiver, sling and knife.

The girl's weapons, however, were not what made Kate and Eddie view Nina with openmouthed amazement. She'd been a child of six when they'd said good-bye. Now Nina was an adolescent, just shy of thirteen, and nearly as tall already as she would ever grow to be. Adding to the wonder with which her grandparents regarded her, Nina now spoke their language fluently. The girl had progressed—overnight, in their reckoning—from a nestling who giggled over the odd-sounding words "Good, bye" to a young lady who conversed with ease in a language she could not possibly have had time to master.

Carin's meticulous tutoring in that language, which Nina had so avidly absorbed, served the girl well as she unshouldered her possessions, sat her dumbfounded grandparents down in their wicker chairs, and worked out the reason for their shocked looks. It seemed that time did indeed pass differently in this world, or perhaps it was only those who journeyed through the void who experienced time in peculiar ways. Whatever the explanation, it appeared that not more than two years had passed on the ocean world while Nina was home in Ruain for seven years, preparing herself in body, mind, and skills for her return to this place that demanded her presence.

Kate understood and accepted this state of affairs straight-away, for the woman recalled what Carin had said about time's convolutions in the void and how her travels had affected her body. Eddie, however, had not been present when Carin spoke of time's strange behavior in the nothingness between the worlds. He took longer with the idea, wrestling with it. But in the end he had to accept at face value what both Nina and his wife were telling him. For he could not otherwise explain Nina's presence before him — this startling granddaughter of his, grown in too little time from child to young woman, now articulate in his language and able to sensibly answer him.

There followed a long session of questions and answers, on both their parts — Eddie eagerly returning to the questions that Carin had given him no time to pose, when she'd hurried away, tears in her eyes, after their brief reunion. Now, there was time.

From Nina, the couple learned of Carin's deep contentment with her husband and the life the pair led in the peace and seclusion of Ruain. Kate ventured only an oblique question about the fate of the demoness who had torn open the bellies of innocent victims two years previous. Nina surmised, from her grandmother's careful phrasing, that Kate had never told Eddie everything she'd witnessed that day. The girl found it simple to answer Kate's indirect question with equal vagueness of her own, for Nina knew none of the particulars, only that the witch had been destroyed and would never again threaten any living soul.

In their turn, Kate and Eddie told the girl what little news there was of life for the survivors on this island and its near neighbors. Small groups continued to wander in, seeking to join this now-established community and benefit from the work and talents that were contributed by various newcomers. Some were expert sailors, fishers, or farmers; a few knew weaving and cloth-making; several had carpentry or stonemasonry skills which were valuable in restoring the many formerly empty houses. Across the island, cottages that had stood abandoned were now occupied as survivors filtered in, some by land, most by water, and settled down to rebuild their lives, as Eddie and Kate had done.

The community's most urgent need was for healers, for it seemed that few of the world's trained physicians had survived the bleeding disease. Eddie speculated that most doctors had stayed at their posts too long, fighting a hopeless battle against an intractable plague, and had themselves succumbed to it. Locally there were competent midwives, a few nurses, and one or two who bore the title medic, but Nina saw that her skills could be put to immediate use.

Indeed, Eddie was keen to take his newly returned, much matured granddaughter to look in on an unwell neighbor that very day when Nina stepped up on his porch. But as the girl related in her next message—a bottled note which appeared in the springwater pool three days after the first—Kate was more cautious about making Nina known in the community.

The woman insisted on first finding the girl some clothes that would attract less attention than those Nina was wearing when she came to them. Nina understood that it wasn't her leggings and tunic themselves that seemed out of place, for in the aftermath of plague and societal collapse, people wore a hodge-podge of whatever clothes they could find or fashion. Rather, it was the quality of the fabric that would be remarked on, Kate explained. Nina's clothes were of vibrantly dyed Ruainian linen in a close, fine weave that gave it a lustrous sheen. The richness of the cloth, and of the embroidery that adorned it, would draw every eye, Kate said.

Reading this in Nina's second letter, Carin realized how far she herself had traveled from the tattered vagabond who'd strayed into Verek's realm. When Myra gave her a crisp linen shift and soft woolen kirtle to replace her filthy, threadbare servant's garb, Carin had nearly cried in gratitude. Now the Lady of Ruain was so accustomed to having garments made for herself and her children from the finest cloth produced by master spinners and weavers, Carin hadn't spared a thought for the effect such fabrics might have on a beaten-down, ragtag people who were barely scraping by.

Nina's letters came regularly, timed so predictably that Carin and Verek could stand watching on the rim of the spring-water pool, and the instant they caught the glint of colored glass in its depths they'd slip their own sealed bottle into the pool at the water's edge. As the arriving message welled up in the pool's center, the currents created by both the flowing hot-spring and Nina's perfectly controlled water-magic would catch the outbound message and fling it back through the void, straight to Nina's hand where she stood on the beach at the foot of the cottage path.

As expected, Nina's skills as a healer were soon acknowledged and employed throughout the island. The girl apprenticed herself to island elders who knew the plants and herbs that grew wild on the land and seashore. With their guidance, she began to collect, catalog, and understand the properties of the plants. Many were so similar to the herbs she knew from Ruain and had read of in Merriam's book, Nina could use them with confidence for ailments such as skin rashes, stomach complaints, and insect bites.

Though deeply curious, the girl never asked about the victims of Morann's blood sorcery whom she had helped that day, barely twenty-four months in the past by local reckoning. Her parents' cautions and anxieties over the matter had sunk in: Nina deemed it wisest to avoid associating herself with that horror in any way. She did, however, encounter one survivor of Morann's attack who had been conscious enough, while a six-year-old child packed seaweed into his gaping chest wound, to have remembered scattered fragments. The man studied Nina's face, then asked if she had a baby sister who looked a lot like her.

No, she did not, Nina answered, smiling as she spoke the perfect truth.

Besides that survivor, a few of the locals who had joined the rescue that day also looked at her now, a little too closely for her comfort. But every individual whom the younger Nina had ordered to wash wounds and haul seaweed, and who now seemed to find the thirteen-year-old somehow familiar, passed off the impression as a trick of the mind that Kate called *"déjà vu"* — which Nina described in her letter home as an odd, mistaken feeling that one has seen something before.

Indeed, the older wayfarer was so different in appearance and manner from the seemingly speech-impaired child who had taken charge that day, imperiously issuing orders in no kind of understandable language, that no serious credence could be given to the idea that they were the same person. Six-year-old Nina's long hair had tumbled around her face, strands of it trailing in the gore as she pressed wet seaweed into horrific wounds. The child's clothes had been sodden and filthy, weed-stained and soaked with the victims' blood.

Now as a teenager dressed in worn denims and a faded but clean T-shirt, with her black hair neatly bobbed and usually covered by a straw hat for protection from the island's bright sun, Nina's only real resemblance to her younger self — or to the demon who had ripped people open — lay in her piercing gaze.

To subdue the effect of that notable attribute, Kate provided the girl with dark eyeglasses. Almost everyone on the island wore similar spectacles to keep the sun out of their eyes.

And so Nina was accepted by all, as both the much-loved granddaughter of Kate and Eddie, and also in her own right as a skilled healer with a remarkable understanding of the uses and properties of wild plants and herbs. She worked almost daily in the village infirmary. Once when Nina had occasion to bring in a bucket of the same seaweed with which she had countered Morann's savagery, the sight and smell of the weed prompted her workmates—a young nurse and an older medic—to remember the time they'd seen weed packed into the wounds of badly injured people.

"Every one of those poor beggars would have bled out, if someone hadn't known to cram that stuff into all the rips and tears before the survivors even got to us," the medic said, somewhat absently as his attention was on refilling his medical bag.

The young nurse nodded. "Kept down the infection, too. We've so few antibiotics left, I thought sepsis would kill anybody who survived the initial shock and blood loss. But all of them that reached us pulled through, except that one hopeless case with his intestines hanging out." She shuddered. "Did they ever figure out what did it? I thought it had to be some kind of wild animal, but there's nothing in these islands could do that to a person."

"Nothing native, maybe," the medic replied. "But who knows what could have floated in here on some big piece of driftwood or maybe a ghost ship. Plenty of derelict boats drifting wherever the waves and currents take 'em." He shrugged. "Could've been a tiger escaped from some zoo."

"Well," said the nurse, "whatever it was, it's long gone, they say. I just think it's amazing that we didn't lose more of those folks who were torn up so bad. I heard there was a little girl in the middle of it all. They say it was her who did the thing with the seaweed."

The medic scoffed. "Might a'been a midget down there, ordering people around. But I never bought the story about the weird little girl who couldn't speak a word of English but had everybody dancing to her tune." The medic uttered a swear-word, and Nina—listening in with a knowing smile—mentally added the word to her growing collection of local profanities. She was, after all, her father's daughter.

"Ain't no six-year-old kid who'll be knowing to use seaweed for wound packing," the medic added. "I only learned it myself as a Navy corpsman, back before the world ended."

That evening, back at her grandparents' cottage, Nina included this instructive conversation in the letter she wrote home. Carin received the news gratefully, thankful that so many of Morann's final victims had survived, but more than anything, proud of her daughter's inborn impulse to save those strangers.

So detailed and descriptive were Nina's regular reports, Carin felt she was at the girl's side, seeing the ocean world through her daughter's eyes—and learning much about her own early history in that world. Kate and Eddie told Nina stories of Carin's childhood, how she loved the water, what a natural swimming talent she had, and how precocious and avid a reader the child was. By age ten or eleven, Carin had filled her bedroom shelves with books, among them the Lewis Carroll classics, *Alice's Adventures in Wonderland* and *Through the Looking-Glass*. Carin also had a good ear for languages, Kate told Nina. The child was just beginning to study the native language of her island home when she vanished.

"Nothing about Karen's disappearance made sense to us then," Kate said. "The authorities concluded she had either drowned or been kidnapped. Drowning seemed out of the question, she was such a good swimmer—unless maybe a shark had killed her. But we also wondered how she could have been kidnapped, given that where we were living was almost impossible to reach by land. A kidnapper would have had to bring a boat into the bay. And by night, that cove by our old house was tricky to navigate, even for Eddie, who knew it like the back of his hand."

Kate shook her head. "What made the whole business even more baffling was that the *Looking-Glass* book was the only thing missing from Karen's room. She'd been reading it at bedtime. Why was it gone, if she'd drowned? She wouldn't have taken a book to the water with her if she'd gone swimming that night. And if somebody snatched her, it didn't seem likely that Karen could have held on to her book all the way down to the dock. She would have dropped it—whether she was knocked out, or fighting like a wildcat—she would have dropped the book and we would have found it somewhere between her bedroom window and the water."

"All of which," Eddie put in, "is why I never gave up looking for Karen. Deep in my gut, I knew that girl was still alive ... somewhere."

"But then the plague came," Kate added with a sigh. "When people all around us were dying, we hunkered down in our private little corner of the island to try to wait it out. But we knew we'd run low on supplies, so Eddie took us in the boat to see what we could find up the coast a ways."

What followed for the couple were years of wandering from island to island, living on their boat, eating mostly fish and restocking their provisions whenever and however they safely could ... Until finally Eddie found another secluded inlet where he felt secure enough to drop anchor, and they climbed the rickety stairs to the overlook ... and venturing up a badly overgrown path they discovered an abandoned cottage that needed only a little work to be habitable.

"That's when we met that fantastic creature which calls itself a woodsprite," Kate said. "The stories it told about itself and our Karenina seemed beyond belief. But we never doubted that the creature really did know our girl, because everything it said about her rang so true."

"We knew from the sprite's tales that it had been at our old house," Eddie put in, "so of course we took the boat back around there." He clicked his tongue. "That was a hard day, to see how the old place had run down. And then to find that scrap of a letter on the floor ... Between getting rained on through a half-rotted roof, and chewed up by insects, there wasn't much left of that note."

"All we could read was something about the bleeding disease and surviving it," Kate said. "I convinced myself our Karen had left that note for us. But the writing was nearly illegible, so really it could have been any survivor who'd passed through. That house had been stripped of everything even remotely useful, even Karen's books, and every old T-shirt that Eddie and I had left behind when we took off."

Nina's accounts of the couple's recollections reached Carin along with notes dictated by the woodsprite, which Nina enclosed with her regular void-crossing communications. The sprite had immediately sought out the new arrival, anxious for news of Carin and eager to repeat all its old stories to a new listener.

From the sprite's narratives, Nina learned a great deal about her mother that Carin had never told the girl — not so much from any unwillingness to share the tales, as from the recurring difficulty of sorting her time-addled memories into a coherent history. Though Megella's memory tea had restored most of Carin's recollections, her knowledge of her past continued to slip maddeningly in time and space. Her final journey through the void — that quick trip to meet her parents and retrieve her then six-year-old daughter—had again exposed Carin to the void's time-twist-ing, challenging her to extract her story from its distortions.

As the messages went back and forth, however, in their col-orful glass bottles, what Nina repeated of the sprite's tales aided Carin in fixing her memories into place. The reordering that she'd achieved on the night she rode the long way home, after drinking with Megella, finally found permanence as weeks be-came months, then years, and Nina's correspondence with her parents continued.

Carin and Verek shared a suspicion that in her letters home, Nina sideslipped a great many matters that would have horrified them if they'd known the details. Her casual mentions of hauling scoundrels in front of the local magistrate had them imagining the perils of life in a loose-knit community barely pulling itself together after a time of chaos and pillage. Their worries grew when the girl breezily glossed over her raising of a wall of water against pirates when Eddie took her in his boat one day to see the couple's old home in its secluded bay.

That steep-sided cove, as Nina described it, was not terribly distant from the cliffside cottage where Kate and Eddie now dwelled. Indeed, the girl deemed it near enough to swim the dis-tance on her own, whenever Nina the water-nymph felt the call of the dolphins who came regularly to that cove. Those dolphins seemed to speak to her, Nina said. She'd swim with them for hours in the rolling surf, and they treated her as one of their own.

It was in that bay that the dolphins finally delivered the mes-sage Carin had slipped into an empty water bottle and flung into the ocean, years before. The dolphin who brought the bottle to Nina played with it for a bit, knocking it around and agilely retrieving it before tossing it like a beach ball to Nina.

She carried it out of the water and sat on the coral-sand beach to twist off the bottle's cap and get at the paper inside. Reading her mother's awkwardly scribbled note to Kate and

Eddie, Nina laughed in delight at finding this unexpected scrap of her own history. For when this note was written, Nina had already been seeded in her mother's womb, and would be born quite soon after Carin recrossed the void and made her way home to Ruain.

"Thank you," Nina called to the dolphins who frolicked in the bay. She voiced her gratitude in every language she knew, including the common tongue of Ladrehdin, the language of the *Looking-Glass* book, and the way of speaking that Nina had begun to learn from the elders of these islands, those indigenous people who knew the wild plants and still remembered a fluid, musical, native tongue. *"Mahalo nui."*

In her letters home, Nina often asked about her younger siblings, though all but Galen were strangers to her, or nearly so. She'd left Ruain when Dalton was a baby. Even so, the girl seemed eager for news of the four, but Carin could tell her only of Dalton's work as a weather-mage and his father's chief steward, and of Vivienne's dedication to training a new generation of *wysards*. Carin seldom had news to share of either Galen or young Legary, for both men had sunk their roots deep into their adopted southern provinces and sent messages to their parents only infrequently, generally announcing the birth of a new child.

Even after Vivienne left her work in the west of Ladrehdin and came home to Ruain, Vivie stayed so busy with her own young family that her presence at Weyrrock seemed less constant than Nina's visits, at least in Carin's perception. Though she loved all her children, Carin couldn't deny that her eldest had a special place in her heart. For Nina the water-nymph was the most like her, and had been the child conceived behind the wagon when Carin and Verek finally stopped denying the obvious.

As she read Nina's lively messages from the ocean world, Carin often wondered how the girl might have been affected by her travels through the void—in particular, that journey Carin had made to Earth, then back to Ladrehdin, when pregnant with the imp. In her womb, Verek's seed had seemed not to grow during the—weeks? or months?—when Carin had hurtled through nothingness, then splashed into ocean waters, swum ashore, and found herself once again in her parents' abandoned house on the bay … where she swam with dolphins and wrestled with the potential lethality of her seemingly uncontrollable sand-spell.

But what had that time on the water-world called Earth done to the dormant seed within Carin? Had Nina's future been written before Carin gained mastery of her own magic and set her own course for the life *she* wanted? —a life in Ruain with Verek.

Now it came to Carin, as she read Nina's letters, that each of them had gone where their hearts led, and as a result their worlds were again in balance. One water-sylph had taken the place of the other, and each had brought healing to their adopted realms. By removing the power-draining crystals, Carin had restored magical potency to Ladrehdin. Now Nina was revitalizing her chosen world.

At eighteen, the girl married a young man of the islands. The boy, Makani, was the foster son of the survivor whose life Nina had saved after a sadistic witch laid open the man's chest. Makani was a skilled builder and carpenter, as well as an expert sailor and fisher. Together, he and Nina restored the old home of Kate and Eddie and made it their own. Under Nina's care, the orchards and herb gardens yielded bountiful harvests; and in the waters off the island, Makani caught all the fish they needed.

Only gradually did Nina reveal to her young husband who she was, where she came from, and all that she could do. But she need not have been overly concerned about shocking him: A native youth of the islands, Makani had a mystical streak of his own. He accepted Nina's otherworldliness as the perfect explanation for why he was so besotted with her: she was a gimlet-eyed goddess whom no man could resist.

Laughing a little at this, Nina wrote to Carin that Makani often boasted to his friends that he'd married a sea goddess. He talked of her water magic—how Nina raised walls of water, whether ashore or at sea, to crash down like divine wrath upon any marauders who offered a threat.

When Makani's matter-of-fact accounts of her wizardry caused no great stir among any who knew the young couple, Nina began, little by little, to openly display her abilities: not only her water-spells, but also her mastery of weapons including the fine bow she had brought from Ruain—the bow her father had crafted for her.

Already prepared to think Nina was extraordinary because of her preternatural talents as a healer, the people of the islands accepted the proofs they witnessed just as gradually and naturally as Nina offered those proofs. Over time, the people began to speak of her as their guardian angel, or to regard Nina as a reborn goddess of water and the sea, straight out of traditional island mythology.

Her mystique deepened as the years passed, and others aged while Nina did not. She bore many children, and as they grew to maturity Nina seemed hardly older than her offspring. Each of her children was uniquely gifted, exhibiting some definite talent that surpassed the ordinary, whether as healer, herbalist, sailor, fisher, farmer, builder, or any of a dozen other aptitudes.

Her children married the islanders' sons and daughters, and in their turn begat offspring as hardy, vigorous, and capable as themselves. Going forth across the islands, the gifted ones brought a hope for the future that some who remembered the plague years had not thought to ever feel again.

During all this time, messages in bottles continued arriving in the springwater pool abovestairs, though not as frequently as they once had. Carin could ride with Theil to the ends of Ruain without worrying that they might miss a letter from Nina. Verek continued to keep a sharp eye on the well-being of his people. He often stayed on the road inspecting the harvest, dispensing justice in matters beyond the authority of his local magistrates, or consulting with Dalton regarding Ruain's ever-expanding sea-trade. When Carin accompanied Verek on his journeys across the province, he frequently asked her opinion and followed her advice in matters great and minor.

"I'm not the traveler your mother is," Verek told his son and steward. "Lady Carin has seen worlds you and I can barely imagine, endured trials beyond any undertaken by any native-born *wysard* of Ladrehdin, and made magic far beyond my own powers. This province is blessed to have her, as am I. And you must count yourself a fortunate son to have such a mother. If ever you seek my counsel on any subject, and I for whatever reason do not answer your call, then appeal to your mother. She is better-read than you. Indeed, she's mastered books that few *wysards* of this world have opened, and her spellcraft rises to that of the most gifted among the ancients. My lady possesses a deep knowledge of the wizardly foundations and strengths of this land — and she knows the magical ways of strange other-worlds besides. Give heed to all that your mother says to you, son, for she has been where you will never walk."

Later, when they were alone, and Carin was running her fingers through Verek's glossy, crow-black hair, she asked him: "What was all that, about you not answering if Dalton needs you? When have you ever failed him on any question? Or for that matter, neglected any appeal from any corner of this land?"

Verek had his eyes closed as Carin combed her fingers through his hair, both of them relaxed and easy on the veranda of the local sheriff's house in the town they were visiting. Without lifting his lids, Verek muttered, "Mishaps can befall even *wysards*. I might tumble off my horse and break my neck."

Carin snorted. "Not likely! When was the last time you fell off a horse!"

"When Nina knocked me off."

A moment passed in silence as Carin considered this. Then she burst out laughing.

"Your pride still hurts from *that?* Love of my life, it's been *years!* Rather than nurse your wounded vanity, be proud that you fathered a girl who could unhorse you, when no man ever has."

Verek opened his eyes and looked up at Carin. He smiled. "I am proud. Vastly proud of our Nina. Will she ever come home, do you think?"

Carin tipped her head, then nodded. "I think she may. When her grandparents are dead, her children's children are scattered to the four corners of that world, and even her beloved Makani has gone the way of all mortal flesh … I think we might persuade our water-nymph to come home."

Wysards live long. So much longer than mortals. The day came when Nina had the painful task of helping Lady Kate bury Master Eddie. Ed died in his sleep, in his ninety-first year. They brought his body to the old home he had shared with Kate, and buried him in the orchard.

Kate stayed there afterward, living with Nina and Makani, lovingly cared for as she descended into her twilight years. Though her mind was grown too clouded to know them for her own descendants, still Kate delighted in the noisy children who came and went from that house and its cove, as the generations stretched across the years, and even Makani had trouble keeping track of which were his grandchildren and which his great-grandchildren or their offspring. For Makani lived long enough to know five generations of the family he made with Nina.

But though time might cease within the nothingness that both Carin and Nina had crossed as young women, time moved constantly forward on the ocean world called Earth. Kate died and was buried beside Eddie. Then Nina lost her Makani.

His body, she wrapped in the fine linen tunic she'd worn from Ruain. Though life in the islands was far easier these days than it had been when Nina first arrived, and many people had now mastered the skills of spinning and weaving, still there was no cloth made in the islands—or any place where island sailors now traded—that could match the fineness of the Ruainian fabric.

Nina gave it as a shroud to the man she had loved, and committed Makani's body to the ocean that had strengthened them both, the sea which sustained the life of the world.

Not long after Nina sent word of Makani's death, Carin also heard from her that the woodsprite had disappeared. By this time, the sprite was rooted deep in island folklore. Many people had seen and spoken with the creature, and all of Nina's extended family were on friendly terms with the sprite. When Nina learned that no one had seen the creature for nearly a year, she went looking for it.

No trace of it did she find. Speculation ran rife: Had the sprite attempted too long a leap from one tree to the next, missed its mark, and tumbled into the sea? Had it perhaps drifted away on a floating mat of fallen tree branches, hoping the ocean currents would sweep it to a new landmass, with a new forest to explore? Or had the creature pressed itself into the hull of some ship outbound from the islands, curious to see more of the world to which Carin had brought it, so long ago. Perhaps, Nina thought, the woodsprite had simply reached the end of its long life and died in its sleep, its bright flicker going dark as it rested in the heart of a favorite tree.

All Nina could say with certainty, in the long letter she wrote to Carin about her search for knowledge of the creature's fate, was that the woodsprite's legacy lived on in the islands' trees. That they had voices of their own, no one now living in the archipelago could doubt. On windless nights, low murmurs were heard from groves, orchards, and forested mountainsides throughout the islands. Those with a good ear for languages—a hallmark of many in Nina's large family—could catch intelligible words and phrases.

Certain trees were even known to snap a clear command— "Stop!"—at anyone who approached them with axe or felling-saw in hand. Some enforced the prohibition with a limb thrust out threateningly. These trees gained a reputation as dangerous, or haunted—or in the view of many, as sacred—and they were left undisturbed. As time passed, more trees learned to speak at least that one word in a tongue understandable to all islanders. Trees would thunder an imperious "Stop!" and fling out a re-straining branch at children who ventured too near a cliff's edge … or at builders who cleared too much land for houses or farms, or reapers who gathered more nuts and fruits than the trees con-sented to give.

"They've awakened," Nina wrote. "The trees are awake, and I cannot doubt that it's the woodsprite's doing. I do not believe the people of this world will ever again abuse the gifts of Nature, as they were wont to do in the long years before the bleeding disease killed billions of them. The trees will not allow it, nor will the sea. The ocean now knows its own strength. I speak with the dolphins—I know their language now—and they tell me: If ever humankind attempts to take more from the sea than is seemly and fit, then the ocean will withhold its gifts. Schools of fish will flee and hide themselves far from any fisher's net. No sea turtles will nest on these beaches. Even the crabs will refuse the fisher's bait."

Reading Nina's words—and hearing her eldest daughter's voice in her head, as she always did when she read a letter from Nina—Carin was powerfully reminded of what Morann had divulged on the day Carin summoned an otherworldly dragon against her. When the witch had opened the void to snatch a book-loving child through it, Morann had sensed in Carin's homeworld an age-old magic, an ancient power that had fallen into slumber. Morann had wanted to exploit that power for her own gain. But the witch could not draw strength from it or command it—neither then, nor later when Morann was trapped in that world and withering to impotence. For the magic would not answer to a blackheart who corrupted the power with her victims' blood.

Perhaps a few in that world called Earth had known the old power was there, deep, pristine, neglected and drowsing. Certainly one scribe of that world had tapped its potency: the Master Carroll who wrote the *"Jabberwocky"* incantation had weaved such wizardry into his words that they had the power to call forth a dragon from wellsprings of magic far distant from his own.

Idly, Carin wondered how and where copies of that strange rhyme might still exist. She herself had been careful to omit the incantation from the version of the *Looking-Glass* story she'd written out for Nina. The original book, Carin had long ago returned to the world from which it had come. Kate had said that book was stolen, with others, from the old house on the lonely bay, during those years when the house had stood empty and vulnerable to looting after she and Eddie left it and before Nina and Makani reclaimed it.

Perhaps the thief had ripped out the book's pages to use for fire-starting, for papering walls—for wiping his buttocks, possibly. But surely the book that had belonged to Carin was not the only copy which remained in all the lands of the ocean world. Now that Nina had awakened that world's sea of sleeping magic, could an unsuspecting lover of stories unintentionally summon a dragon from the waters of Earth by reading those strange words aloud?

"If they do it, I hope they find a way to undo it," Carin muttered over the letter she was writing.

The vast ocean she'd seen depicted on the map at Kate and Eddie's cottage had touched the shores of many lands. A magical dragon raised anywhere in that Pacific ocean might wreak bloody havoc on seaside communities from pole to pole. Carin had seen her conjured Jabberwock claw the walls of Ruain's enchanted cavern with such violence that it gouged out chunks of solid bedrock. She'd seen it break an alien *mantikhora* in two and swallow the body, head first. Before that, the dragon had killed three chickens, passing Verek's first test of its deadliness. It would have killed Morann, too, if the witch hadn't been clutching an otherworldly amulet, and thus made her escape through the void, by the narrowest of margins.

Biting the inside of her mouth, Carin put these thoughts aside and returned to the letter she was crafting, choosing her words with care to tell Nina only enough, and not too much. Carin had never revealed to Nina the dragon's existence or how it might be summoned. If she even hinted of such a possible peril still looming over the people of the ocean world, Nina would never come home.

Nor would Carin write openly of what Morann had said about "the promising world" which was, in many ways, very like Ladrehdin. That demon's name must never be written or spoken again in the cosmos, nor should Morann's words be repeated exactly as she'd uttered them.

But Carin got the gist across, distilling her roving thoughts to their essentials: That with its own peculiar magic, the woodsprite had awakened the islands' trees and set them as guardians of the land. And Nina herself, wielding the powers she possessed as a worker of water-magic, had brought an even vaster awakening to the oceans of Earth. No longer did the magic of that place lie dormant. Nina had roused and invigorated it.

You have given that world all it needs from you, Carin wrote. *As you say yourself, the trees and the ocean will now care for the people, protecting humankind as they protect themselves from misuse and injury. Your children and theirs, for generations to come, will see to whatever else the people may need as they leave the plague years behind and build for themselves a new future. You have done well, Karenina, my daughter, my eldest, the child of my heart. Will you not come home now, home to Ruain?*

As Carin penned these words, she was again struck by the parallels between her life and her daughter's. Nina had restored magic to the ocean world, albeit in a very different manner from the way in which Carin had reclaimed Ladrehdin's wizardly potency from the parasitic crystals. The result, however, was the same: two worlds healing, two worlds again finding balance with the Elementals.

Carin tapped her pen on the paper, wondering how much of this to include in her appeal to Nina. In the end, she decided she'd written all she should, she'd made her case for Nina to take her Ruainian bow in her hand and use it like a beacon to guide her return through the void.

But … wait. Perhaps Carin might strengthen her appeal just a little, she realized with a smile, thinking quickly of the only time Theil Verek had been unhorsed. It was a downfall the *wysard* would never forget.

Did Nina also remember it? Did the girl have any idea what an impression her skill with a sling had made on the Lord of Ruain?

Again putting pen to paper, Carin ended her letter, just below the line *Will you not come home now?* with a postscript that would surely set Nina to wondering, and might bring the water-nymph splashing into the springwater pool to learn what umbrage she had provoked:

Your father wants a word with you, child. Right now.

Chapter 20

The Book of the Two Kareninas

Nina came home, her journey across the void an easy step from the shore of her earthly home to the rim of the upstairs pool. However far distant the two worlds might be in time or space, in their natures Ladrehdin and Earth were close kindred.

Nearly the first order of business when Nina returned was to face her father in a fencing match. Verek issued the challenge; Nina accepted. Verek won handily; Nina conceded graciously.

No great marvel, Carin thought, looking on, amused, as the match was speedily concluded in Verek's favor. *Has it not occurred to you, love of my life, that your daughter cannot have touched a sword in a hundred years or more?*

Quite possibly, that fact *had* escaped Verek's notice. For his eldest daughter seemed only lightly altered by the passage of time.

Thirteen when she left home, Nina now appeared no older than twenty-five. Even as an adolescent, the girl had had the graceful poise and presence of a woman who was a natural athlete. Then as now, her skin was smooth, her muscles toned, her raven hair sleek and shining. Perhaps Verek could be excused for imagining that his daughter had been away for only a little while … and was not, in fact, a great-grandmother many times over on that world where Nina's descendants would carry her legacy to every shore.

Such was the paradox of a powerful *wysard* who had traveled to a stricken world like a sea goddess bestowing the gift of healing, and then through time and space had returned to her ancestral home, there to become again only the beloved eldest daughter in what was now a very large family.

With honor satisfied as far as her father was concerned, Nina set out to know all her kin, starting with the baby sister, Vivienne, whom she'd never met. The two had hardly broken their embrace before Vivie had her artist's brush in her hand, painting Nina seated with Verek, marveling at the resemblance between them. Verek grumbled at being made to sit for a portrait, but Carin knew from the barely restrained smile on his lips that he delighted in the company of both his gifted daughters. He assented without complaint when Vivienne asked him to send for Dalton, the middle child who had been only a babe in Carin's arms when Nina left home.

As soon as Dalton arrived and stood before his elder sister — a little in awe of her, it seemed to those watching — all understood why Vivienne, the artist, had wanted to see the siblings together. Dalton's hair, pale blond at his birth, had lightened in his years of riding horseback, under the sun from one edge of Ruain to the other. Now the weather-mage's hair appeared almost white. Like a cloud or a blizzard it was, Carin thought, studying her second son as though she'd never seen him before, so great was the contrast presented by Dalton's snowy mane against Nina's raven tresses.

Vivienne sat the two down and ordered them not to move while she captured on canvas the juxtaposition of the siblings in their remarkably contrary coloring.

There followed a time of family gatherings across the breadth of the province, as Nina worked her way eastward from the manor house, meeting those among Vivienne's descendants who still made their homes in Ruain. Many of Vivie's line had moved beyond Ruain's boundaries, both south and west, continuing the work of gradually reintroducing magic to the common folk of Ladrehdin, and discovering among them a growing number of candidates for wizardly apprenticeship. Here and there, a country girl was found using a forked stick to dowse for water. Or a weather-savvy farmhand came to light, displaying a crude but effective ability to call the rain and sun. These and others who displayed traces of the gift were offered training in spell-craft, and the most promising became full apprentices.

To all the homes of Vivienne's far-flung descendants, Nina would eventually travel on her grand tour of family places. Early in her homecoming, however, the prodigal was bent on meandering eastward across Ruain, accompanied by Carin and Vivienne. The trio stopped to see kindred and toured the towns Nina had ridden through on her long-ago test-journey to Ruain's seacoast, when the girl had satisfied herself and her parents that she was ready to follow her heart to Earth.

Verek and Dalton joined the ladies at points along their seaward route, as the men's duties allowed. Eventually all five met up in a bustling port on the seaboard, and there Nina declared her intention to sail south on the next outbound trade-ship.

"I'm going to see my brother Legary in Granger. I've never laid eyes on the fellow, and I'm curious. From there, I'll head west and look up Galen in his desert." Nina grinned like a devil-kin. "Anyone care to wager on the odds of him and me getting into mischief?"

Verek laughed. "No surer bet was ever placed."

"Here," he added, digging into the coin purse at his belt. "Dalton will secure your passage on his fastest ship, and your fair-haired brother will escort you as far south as he chooses. But once you disembark, my girl, you're on your own. Take some money, for you'll need a horse and something to eat along the way."

Vivienne stepped forward then, and also pressed gold into Nina's hands.

"I beg you, Honored Sister," Vivie said, pushing back a strand of Nina's shoulder-sweeping hair — her tresses long grown out from the cropped style the water-nymph had worn when she'd crossed to Earth. "When you see our brother Legary," Vivienne said, "compel him to sit for a portrait with you. Employ the most renowned painter in all the southland. Pay that artist any price for a faithful likeness of you and Legary together. For I despair of our stonemason brother ever returning to Ruain, and I wish to know how he now appears."

"Gladly will I do as you ask, baby sister," Nina replied, smiling. "I will be disinclined, however, to pack along a painting when I leave Legary's home and ride to the desert to find our Galen. If a dependable messenger can be engaged to carry the portrait to the coast, perhaps Dalton could see to its stowage on a ship bound for Ruain."

Vivienne nodded, pleased. Transport by sea would bring the portrait into her hands much sooner than she could expect it if Nina were to lug the painting with her, far southwestward as the wanderer continued her grand scheme of family reunions.

As Vivienne turned to Dalton and Verek to settle the details of the shipping arrangement, Carin drew Nina aside. Into her firstborn's ear, she whispered suggestions of her own, concerning the hoped-for portrait of the two siblings who had long been absent from their ancestral lands.

With much embracing then, and tears, mostly of happiness, the family group broke up. Nina took ship, escorted southward by Dalton. Vivienne made her way to the home of her youngest daughter, an accomplished sculptress whose large house in this port city was filled with art.

Carin and Verek turned for home, setting their route through the Penfield maple groves to buy arrows from the town's fletchers. Heading back to Weyrrock then, the pair did not rush, but neither did they tarry as Carin and her daughters had while satisfying Nina's craving for family reconnection. Carin had a small but significant task awaiting her, which she anticipated completing as soon as she got home. With the finishing of it, she wanted Verek's help.

The task was simple: to make a book from all the letters that had been exchanged between two worlds, most of them flung through the void by Nina's water magic, others delivered by the woodsprite's never-explained bottle-wrapping method, and at least one carried secretly by hand: the letter to Carin that Verek had stuffed in his trousers pocket and almost kept from her. Carin, of course, had saved every letter Nina had sent home during the decades the water-nymph wore the mantle of sea goddess. It transpired that Nina had also kept the letters her parents wrote to her. When Nina stepped away from Earth and returned to her homeworld, the wayfaring *wysard* brought all those letters with her.

Carin arranged them in order, interleaving each with the letter sent or received in reply. The missives were numerous and made a thick chronicle, with the woodsprite's dictated notes inserted in their proper places, and the early letters from Carin's parents retrieved from behind the liquor cabinet and given pride of place at the front of the collection. With those letters, Carin included the note she'd slipped into a water bottle, to toss into the wide Pacific while entreating its dolphins to deliver her message.

The dolphins had not done exactly as Carin had asked. But in time, the perpetually smiling creatures had put the message into the hand of their friend and mistress, the goddess of the seas. Nina had saved that note with all the others, and when the water-nymph recrossed the void, she brought the letter back to its author.

Carin prefaced the compilation with an introduction, intended for the benefit of future readers, in which she described all those named in the letters, telling of their birthplaces and tracing their travels. She gave the finished pages to Verek to bind into a book.

The artful *wysard* created a beautiful volume, making its covers from close-grained birch wrapped in goatskin leather. Verek ornamented the cover with his own drawing of a *dolphyn,* which he embossed in gold, together with the volume's title: *The Book of the Two Kareninas – A Chronicle of Both Their Worlds.*

The finished work was shelved in the library alongside the *Book of Archamon*, both volumes to be read and treasured and passed down in House Verek for generations to come.

Chapter 21

Old Griefs

The portrait commissioned by Vivienne, of Nina and her brother Legary, arrived in due course, brought up from the south on a ship captained by Dalton himself. That Nina had found a masterful artist for the work was evident the moment the painting's wrappings came off: the sea goddess and her stonecrafter brother practically stepped off the canvas, so lifelike were they.

A second painting, however, accompanied the first … and it was this variation on the family theme, commissioned by Carin, that provoked the strongest reaction from Verek. His intake of breath, upon viewing the portrait, came markedly near to a gasp.

Carin was well pleased that Nina had relayed her instructions precisely, and the painter in the south had followed her directions perfectly. In the second portrait, raven-haired Nina was depicted as a young man whose crow-black hair framed a lean, strong face from which darkly brilliant eyes looked out in a fierce gaze. Indeed, so close was the resemblance between Nina and her father that the artist had done little more than give their shared features more angular lines. The painter had squared the jaw, edged it with a close-cropped beard, drawn a thin moustache curving down to join the beard, and then introduced a frown-line or two, roughening the visage into rugged, hot-tempered masculinity. With the hair swept back from the forehead, the face that looked out was Verek's.

Even less effort had been needed to transform young Legary into the old lord for whom he was named. The artist had slightly aged the face, depicted the hair as roguishly windblown, and altered Legary's garments to suggest a style of cloak from an earlier era.

The result, for all anyone viewing it could tell, was a portrait of Theil Verek and his grandsire, Lord Legary, seemingly drawn from life. Drawn, without question, from that circle of life which had produced each generation of House Verek, past, present, and future.

When all had admired both portraits, and Verek had recovered from the shock of seeing himself apprenticed again to his grandfather, the pictures were taken upstairs to be hung. Vivienne insisted that the masterful likeness of Nina and young Legary should replace the paintings she herself had made, years earlier, of her absent siblings. The recent portrait captured brother and sister so exactly, none could doubt that the painting belonged over the mantelpiece in the sitting room of Carin and Verek's private apartments.

Verek, however, seemed in two minds about the eerily accurate portrayal of his younger self with his grandfather. Though the *wysard* heaped praise on the artist's skill, and on Carin's imagination for envisioning how their children could open a window into the past, Verek couldn't settle on where to display the painting. For a time it stayed in their sitting room, not hung but resting on the floor near the room's recessed window, leaned up against the wall and half hidden behind the table of marble that stood beside the sofa.

Then Verek moved the painting into his workroom, but still he did not hang it. He set the portrait against a wall, where he could see it from his herbalist's workbench … and where the depiction of his grandfather could seem to watch Verek in his practice of the healing arts, the foundations of which the *wysard* had learned in his boyhood as the old lord's apprentice.

Carin could not help but notice, however, that the painting began gradually to disappear amidst Verek's endless projects: the bowstaves he was shaping, the metalcrafts he was fashioning, his newly stretched painter's canvases, and various items of clutter. In exasperation, she rescued the portrait from his busy workroom and took it into the library. Climbing the same ladder she had used in her long-ago efforts to bring order to the collection, Carin heaved the painting onto a high shelf, lowered herself again to the floor, and stepped to the windows to see how visible — or not — the portrait would be to someone reading at the desk beneath those windows.

Good. The portrait came into view only if the desk-worker leaned back in the chair and looked deliberately up toward the library's high ceiling.

Carin returned to Verek's workroom, got a hammer and two hooks from his metalworking bench, and reentered the library through the connecting stair-landing that also opened upon the spiraling steps to the vault of magic. Again climbing the ladder, she pounded the hooks into the section of shelving where she'd propped the painting. Balancing precariously, Carin tipped the portrait off the shelf and onto the hooks, resting most of her weight on the picture's frame to be sure of the hooks' ability to hold the heavy painting.

Satisfied, Carin climbed down, and waited.

Verek took three weeks to notice the painting's new location. One morning while working at the desk, as the rising sun turned the world outside the windows a soft red and gold, Verek leaned back and looked up. He focused at first on the middle distance as he pondered affairs of the realm laid before him by some steward or sheriff. Carin was also in the library that morning, finishing the book of woods' lore that Verek had given her many years previous, and wishing she'd read it sooner. The book contained much that would have served her well on their long-ago quest into the snow-choked western mountains.

"Ah!" Verek exclaimed, breaking Carin's concentration.

She glanced up from her reading, and had no need to follow Verek's gaze to know what he was looking at. The angle of his head and the surprise in his face told her.

"Is it all right?" Carin asked. "I like the painting, even if you don't."

Verek dropped his gaze from the ceiling and trained it on Carin.

"If you doubt for an instant how highly I value your gift of that remarkable piece of portraiture," he said, "then I have been remiss in failing to convey my gratitude. I treasure the painting."

Carin narrowed her eyes at him. "You could have fooled me, the way you left it lying around, buried under this and that. I'd decided you hated it. But I wanted the picture where I could see it without shifting a mountain of clutter."

Verek rose from the desk and came to sit with Carin on the bench before the hearth. A pleasant fire crackled there, warming the room against the chill of an early winter morning.

"*Fileen*," the wizard murmured, his fingertips sliding over Carin's temples, down her cheeks, across her lips. "I value the painting, but more so the care of me that you showed in having it made." Verek looked into her eyes, drawing Carin into the depths of his gaze. "If I have seemed indifferent to the portrait, it is perhaps because the picture takes me into the past—to old griefs and a heart that lay broken in my chest, as cold as pond ice in winter and shattered under the weight of my sorrows."

"Oh, Theil!" Carin whispered. "I am sorry. I didn't think. I only meant the picture as a tribute to your grandfather, and a reminder of how great was Lord Legary's love for you." She dashed away a tear. "I'll take the painting down, this minute."

Carin tried to rise, but Verek pinned her in place, pressing her down to the cushions of the bench they occupied.

"You'll do no such thing, my lady," he growled. "I marvel that you did not break your neck in the course of raising that picture to the rafters. It was Providence alone that saved you, I'll be bound, and not your own good sense—of which you sometimes betray precious little." As Verek traced Carin's curves with one hand while running the fingers of his other through her hair, he added less gruffly, "The painting will stay where it is. My lord Legary was much at home in this library, and I welcome his gaze upon me as I endeavor to fulfill his expectations of me."

"I'm not sure what Legary may be expecting, but I think he's about to see plenty," Carin whispered, meeting the increasingly fiery gaze of her husband and lover. "I'll just lock the door ... in case anyone else is around."

Carin reached around Verek, and with an expert flick of her wrist, a perfectly cast spell of securing, she barred the library door without so much as glancing its way.

All her attention was on the magician whose touch filled her with liquid fire and ignited desire in every nerve of her body. The power crackled between them and the heat spread, wave upon wave of it, building to an intensity that made black spots dance in front of her eyes, though her lids were now closed. She swam deep in a sea of sensations that ran together and overflowed, raising within her an urgency that Verek matched and brought to exquisite release ... but not too quickly ... not before time.

The sun had climbed high in the morning sky before Carin unlocked the library door.

* * *

* * *

* * *

The spacefaring strangers drew energy from many worlds. When Carin broke their hold on Ladrehdin, severed their link to Earth, and left them connected only to the world of slime and plague, the strangers noticed a barely significant power drop. Before she left the void, however, Carin flung the combined trio of crystals back along the ribbon of power to the pestilential planet. When it landed there, the device built for siphoning power created such an enormous drain on the energies of that planet, it triggered a global volcanic explosion … the force of which traveled on the ribbon of transmission back to the strangers' world, where it wreaked massive destruction, planetwide.

Never again would the strangers steal the life-force of another world.

Chapter 22

In the Fullness of Time

When Myra retired as housekeeper at Weyrrock and Megella closed up shop as the wisewoman of Fintan, the two Weird Sisters moved in together and launched a new endeavor. Myra baked cakes and breads that Megella infused with invigorating herbs, many having the properties of love potions and aphrodisiacs. Their venture was a rousing success.

Master Welwyn took the circlet of braided "witches" hair that Carin forgot she'd left in the cavern of wizardry. Verek never knew that Carin had made the seer's circlet with hairs from his head, her own, and Welwyn's. No one knows what Welwyn did with the amulet, whether he destroyed it, kept it as a memento of his time with the couple, or perhaps used it for his own purposes of seeing.

After departing the House of Verek for a final time, the monk went where the apprentices were. For years Welwyn taught gifted adepts from the borders of Ruain to the shores of Ladrehdin's southern seas, then westward through Galen's desert and up the spine of the mountains, until the old monk returned again to his cabin in the glen above Cardan. Where he went from there, none could say. Perhaps Master Welwyn walks the world even now, in another guise but ready with wise advice for young *wysards* who aren't quite sure they're ready to embrace their gifts … or even admit they're in love.

Lanse never fully recovered from the woodsprite spearing a tree branch through his gut. But Carin's would-be executioner regained enough of his wits to take vows and join the monastery at Cardan. Lanse was there for life, and upon his death his monastic brethren buried him with suitable rituals in the abbey grounds.

The woodsprite was not heard of again. Nina, however, sparked a lively discussion at Weyrrock when the wayfaring *wysard* returned home after completing her grand design of meeting all her far-flung Ladrehdinian kindred. One evening at supper in Myra's former kitchen, Nina mentioned a tree, strange in its appearance, bearing no fruit or flower, growing solitary in a lonely spot some distance from the house on the bay that had been Nina's family residence during the century or more of the prodigal's sojourn on Earth.

Verek, looking at his eldest daughter through narrowed eyes, sharply questioned Nina until he established that the lonely spot she'd named was the exact place in which he had burned and buried the untested magical amulets that he'd packed to that world from the necromancer's eyrie. The tree that had sprung up from those buried remains was not native to the islands, Nina attested. Or, if it had indeed sprouted from the seed of a tree that belonged there, it had matured in ways so at odds with the natural life of the islands as to make it appear altogether alien to that place.

Carin and Verek stared at each other.

"If that tree grew out of an artifact from another world, and if it makes a bridge to that world," Carin said, her voice low, "then maybe the woodsprite jumped over that bridge and found itself a new home, across the void."

"Good riddance to the creature, if that's the way of things," Verek muttered. "But you and I, my lady, have seen that other-worldly bridges commonly permit comings as well as goings."

"By the Powers!" Nina swore, looking from one of her parents to the other. "Are you suggesting that the strange tree up behind my old house could let another plague into my beautiful ocean world? Beggar it all!" Nina exclaimed, taking one of Carin's expressions. "I'll have to go back."

Carin started to object, but held her tongue as she studied her firstborn child. Nina's life was hers to live. The onetime water-nymph had grown into a great *wysard*—remembered in the lore of the Pacific islands as a deity, in fact. Besides, Nina had family in that world.

They're your family, too, remember, Carin reminded herself, struggling a bit to regard those faraway offshoots of House Verek as her own blood relatives. But such they were, and of course Nina would go back to keep them safe from alien invaders.

"Karenina, child," Carin said, turning her gaze full upon her daughter. "While you're on the island chopping down that tree, there's something else I want you to look out for. You may need to ask around. More than likely it's gone for good. But just in case somebody found a certain old book and read a poem from it when they shouldn't have, at the wrong place under just the right circumstances, they might have brought an ocean of trouble down upon their heads and others. There's a dragon, you see, and there's an incantation that calls it ..."

Carin got up from the supper table. "I'll tell you about it while we're finding you some properly elegant clothes for the trip. You can't go saving Earth—or visiting our relatives across the void—looking anything less than the goddess you are, my girl."

Epilogue

Carin studied, and practiced, and achieved mastery of the *art magick*. As Verek had foreseen, she joined the ranks of Ladrehdin's great *wysards* of history and legend. Her name was spoken evermore with the same veneration accorded Archamon.

When Carin had reached the pinnacle of her craft, Amangêda permitted her to remember all that had happened in the Easthaven harbor, every detail of her face-to-face meeting with the primordial spirit of the world, the embodiment of Ladrehdin's natural elements. Carin wept in awe as she recalled her encounter with the sublime, that moment beyond time and existence which transcended all boundaries of the flesh.

Centuries passed, and the number of Carin's gifted descendants, near and far, proved nearly uncountable, when at last she and her hot-blooded warlock joined themselves to the purpose and went together into the mystical waters of Ruain ... and journeyed on from there, to wherever it is that *wysards* go when they pass from the world of water and fire, stone and air, and reenter the circle of life ... in realms far beyond the void.

END of BOOK FOUR of WATERSPELL

Author's Note

Dear Readers: Thank you for sticking with me. I feel I know you all, and I consider you friends. In your company, I am safe in opening up about my writerly journey and its unwanted detours.

When the Waterspell trilogy came out in 2011–2012, it was the culmination of a decade-long dream. The books were published to favorable reviews, and I was connecting with bloggers and Goodreads reviewers and people of all sorts in the book world and across social media.

But suddenly, quite unexpectedly, my husband died, two months after Book 3 came out. He was diagnosed with esophageal cancer on a Monday; six days later, on a Sunday morning, he died. Neither of us had time to absorb what was happening. Or to in any way come to terms with it.

For a long time afterward, I was nonfunctional. I couldn't write, I had no urge or capacity to write. And of course, all of my book outreach ended as abruptly as my husband's life had ended. Even after I began to heal, years passed before I regained the emotional capacity that writing fiction requires. A numb writer cannot give convincing emotional life to characters.

At last, however, I began to feel again, and to feel deeply. I could experience the joys and sorrows and fears of my other-worldly people, and at least hope to capture a glimmer of their passions with mere words on paper.

During the 2020 Pandemic Year, in my isolation I wrote and revised this fourth book of Waterspell. In 2021, I revised it again, while simultaneously working with a narrator to produce audio-books of the complete series. As 2022 got under way, I sought to answer the question of whether it was possible to relaunch a series after all of us—writer and readers alike—had spent a decade away from it.

On that question, the jury's still out: I don't know if it is possible to regain this major part of what *Life* with a capital *L* took from me. But I'm working hard to reintroduce Waterspell to fantasy fans, and I could really use your help. Reviews mean the world to a writer. They don't need to be long or detailed: a simple "I liked it" (if you did like it) is wonderful.

Word-of-mouth and personal recommendations are also valuable beyond imagining. Could you perhaps tell your friends about Waterspell? And send other reviewers my way?

I keep a cache of review copies on hand, both print (paperback) and ebook (any format). If you know an avid fantasy reviewer, please put them in touch via waterspell.net or email deborah@waterspell.net. I can mail print books within the United States, or send ebooks domestically and internationally.

Thank you for reading this far. Reviews from you and your circle would mean so much. May your days be filled with magic.

♥

With my gratitude, Gentle Reader.
I hope you have enjoyed this history of a Far Country.

Deborah J. Lightfoot
(Deborah Lightfoot Sizemore)
(Mrs. Gene Sizemore)

January 2022
A fish out of water in
Texas, USA

www.waterspell.net

~~~~~

www.ingramcontent.com/pod-product-compliance
Lightning Source LLC
Chambersburg PA
CBHW020342180626
46812CB00001B/308